Also by the author:

CATCH-22
SOMETHING HAPPENED
GOD KNOWS

GOOD
AS
GOLD

Joseph Heller

A DELL BOOK

Published by
Dell Publishing Co., Inc.
1 Dag Hammarskjold Plaza
New York, New York 10017

Portions of this book originally appeared in *The New York Times* in 1976 and in *Playboy* magazine in 1979.

Dell® TM 681510, Dell Publishing Co., Inc.

ISBN: 0-440-13186-3

Printed in the United States of America
First Dell printing—October 1985

I dedicate this book
to
The several gallant families
and
Numerous unwitting friends
whose
Help, conversations, and experiences
play
so large a part.

I've got his pecker in my pocket.
—LYNDON B. JOHNSON
as U.S. Senate Majority Leader

If you ever forget you're a Jew,
a gentile will remind you.
—from a story by BERNARD MALAMUD

I

The Jewish Experience

GOLD had been asked many times to write about the Jewish experience in America. This was not strictly true. He'd been asked only twice, most recently by a woman in Wilmington, Delaware, where he had gone to read, for a fee, from his essays and books, and, when requested, from his poems and short stories.

"How can I write about the Jewish experience," he asked himself on the Metroliner returning to New York, "when I don't even know what it is? I haven't the faintest idea what to write. What in the world for me was the Jewish experience? I don't think I've ever run into an effective anti-Semite. When I grew up in Coney Island, everyone I knew was Jewish. I never even realized I was Jewish until I was practically grown up. Or rather, I used to feel that everybody in the world was Jewish, which amounts to the same thing. Just about the only exceptions were the Italian families living at the other end of Coney Island and the two or three living close enough to us to send their children to the same school. We had an Irish family on our block with a German surname and there were always a couple of Italians or Scandinavians in my class who had to come to school on Jewish holidays and looked persecuted. I used to feel sorry for them because *they* were the minority. The Irish family had a dog—no Jews had dogs then—and raised chickens in their back yard. Even in high school just about all the boys and girls I hung around with were Jewish, and virtually all of the teachers were. And the same was true at college. It was not until I went to Wisconsin for a summer session that I found myself among gentiles for the first time. But that was merely different, not unpleasant. And then I came back to Columbia for my degree and doctorate and felt right at home again. My closest friends there were also Jewish: Lieberman, Pomoroy, Rosenblatt. Ralph Newsome was the only exception, but I felt no different with him than with anyone else, and he seemed perfectly at ease with me. I wouldn't know where to begin.''

He began by going to Lieberman.

"*Whose* Jewish experience?" Lieberman, a hulking, balding redhead, asked with blunt distrust when Gold presented the idea.

"Mine."

"Why not mine?" Lieberman's narrow eyes blazed. His desk was littered with typewritten manuscripts and dark correcting pencils as thick and grubby as his fingers. All through college Lieberman's dearest wish for the future had been to manage a small, intellectual magazine. Now he had his magazine, and it wasn't enough. Envy, ambition, and dejection were still ravaging what few invisible good qualities he might have been born with. Lieberman had never been generous.

"You'd like me," Gold recapitulated with amusement, "to write a piece about you, for publication in your magazine?"

Lieberman saw the light moodily. "It wouldn't work."

"You would have to write it."

"I can't write. You and Pomoroy convinced me of that."

"You rely too much on rhetorical questions."

"I can't seem to help it. What did you have in mind?"

"I haven't worked it out yet," Gold began. He avoided Lieberman's eyes. "But I would do a sober, responsible, intelligent piece about what it has been like for people like you and me to be born and grow up here. Certainly I'll go at least a little bit into the cross-cultural conflicts between the traditions of our European-born parents and those in the prevailing American environment."

"I'll tell you what," Lieberman responded. He broke one of his thick pencils between his hands and paced. "We've got a very sober and responsible magazine for highly intelligent readers. I want something racier from you on that subject, spicier. Frankly, we're usually very dull. Sometimes we're so dull, I don't believe

I'll be able to continue. What was it like the first time you saw an uncircumcised cock? How does it feel to be screwing gentile girls?"

"What makes you think I screw gentile girls?" asked Gold.

"Fake that part if you have to," Lieberman answered. "We want viewpoints, not facts."

"How many words will you take and what will you pay me?"

Lieberman deliberated. "How about fifteen or twenty thousand words? Maybe I can build the whole issue around it and cut my other editorial costs."

"I'll want six thousand dollars for that."

"I'll give you three hundred."

"I won't do it for less than twenty-five."

"I won't pay you more than seven. I'll feature you big on the cover."

"Let's settle for fifteen."

"We'll call it a thousand. That's high for us."

"I'll want six hundred today. And I want the three hundred that's still coming to me for 'Nothing.' "

"We haven't published that yet."

"The deal was on acceptance," Gold argued with some feeling. Months earlier, Lieberman had purchased an article commissioned from Gold by a popular sex magazine, which then had rejected it as inferior to the minimum standards of intelligence of its readership—an item of information Gold discreetly elected not to submit with the manuscript. The full title of the piece was "Nothing Succeeds as Planned," and Gold still waited for the money owed him. "Why don't you publish it already? It might cause some comment."

"I'm waiting until I have enough to pay you." Lieberman uttered a staccato laugh and eased himself into his chair. Lieberman was invariably pleased with himself whenever he made a joke. "I read your review," he began at a slower, disapproving pace, "of the President's book."

Gold was guarded. "And I read yours."

"I found it interesting."

"Yours was not."

"I thought you equivocated unnecessarily," Lieberman pushed on. "It seemed to me you lacked the courage to come right out on the side of the Administration."

"You didn't hesitate at all." Gold waited until Lieberman nodded as though accepting praise. "But I got a call from the White House. They all enjoyed my review, it seems. I assume that includes the President."

Humanely, Gold did not mention that there had also been suggestion of a government appointment. Torturing Lieberman was fun; crushing him to death might be going just one step too far.

Lieberman studied him with porcine malevolence. "You're making that up," he decided at last.

"Remember Ralph Newsome?"

"He's in the Department of Commerce."

"He's on the White House staff now. He telephoned."

"Why didn't they telephone to compliment me on mine?"

"Maybe they didn't see it."

"The President is on my complimentary list."

"Maybe they didn't like it."

"Newsome never liked me," Lieberman recalled, brooding. "You and he were always close. You got that foundation grant together."

"Not together. At the same time. You didn't like him."

"He's anti-Semitic."

"I doubt that."

"Ask him," Lieberman challenged. "He doesn't have brains enough to lie." Lieberman shook from his mind like dust whatever disagreeable feelings had gathered. "I've got another good idea for your piece," he offered, with calculating enthusiasm. "Profitable. Give me thirty or forty thousand words for the same money and I'll feature it in two issues. Make it sexy and light and you'll have most of what you'll need for a popular book that could turn out to be a big best seller. Throw in blacks, drugs, abortions, and lots of interracial screwing. I bet Pomoroy will snap a book like that right up."

Pomoroy, on the contrary, looked grave, and Pomoroy grave was as ominous and distressing as an upright cadaver in rumpled shirt, green corduroy, and large eyeglasses. He was a tranquil and unhappy man of forty-eight, Gold's age. Pomoroy had worked his way up to the position of executive editor in a thriving, faintly disreputable, commercial book-publishing house. The more successful he grew, the bleaker became his outlook. Pomoroy thought he knew why. This was not what he'd had in mind. And he could think of nothing else.

"The trouble with people like us who start so fast," he had once observed in his most funereal tones, "is that we soon have no place left to go." And Lieberman, naturally, had disagreed.

Pomoroy seldom laughed or raised his voice; when he did laugh, it was usually in a vain effort to reassure some troubled author that things were not going to turn out as awful as they threatened. He had no tolerance for deception and never found need to practice any.

"What exactly are you talking about?" he inquired when Gold paused.

Gold was fidgeting beneath Pomoroy's inexpressive gaze. "A book. One just right for you. I've been asked to do this extended study."

"By whom?"

"By several magazines. Lieberman will definitely publish it if we can't get someone better. A study of the contemporary Jewish experience in America," Gold persisted with increasing heaviness of heart. "What it's been like for people like you and me, our parents, wives, and children, to grow up and live here now. I don't think it's ever been done."

"It's been done hundreds of times," Pomoroy corrected him. "But I'm not sure it's been done by someone like you."

"Exactly. I can make it racy and light enough to appeal to the mass market. There'd be a strong tilt toward sexuality."

"I'll want a scholarly, accurate work that will be useful to colleges and libraries. With the strong tilt toward the psychological and sociological."

Gold was deflated. "There's no money in that."

"I'll give you a guarantee of twenty thousand dollars. We'll charge five of that to research as a publishing expense instead of against your royalty account, and you can have that this week."

"Make it six thousand. When can I have more?"

"Five. When you show me two hundred pages."

"Two hundred pages?" Gold echoed with pain. "That can take forever."

"Forever goes quick," Pomoroy observed.

Leaving Pomoroy's office, Gold was exuberant.

Early each autumn Gold considered how much money he would need to continue through to the following summer and pay still one more year's tuition and related expenses for a son at Yale, a son at Choate, both on partial scholarships, and a dissident twelve-year-old daughter at home who attended private day school and was perpetually in danger of being expelled. Beyond his salary as a college professor, Gold would need twenty-eight thousand dollars. Eight he could count on from royalties and speaking fees, which left twenty. He had just made one thousand from Lieberman and twenty from Pomoroy. But he owed Pomoroy a book. He could toss that one off swiftly once he had his material. Jews were a cinch. It was good as gold.

II

My Year in the White House

FOR Friday evening, there had come an invitation to a dinner for his father and stepmother at his sister Ida's apartment in Brooklyn that his wife, Belle, had accepted in his absence. Gold would have given an excuse.

"All of them?" he asked with foreboding. "Muriel and Ida made up?"

"Apparently."

Gold longed unreasonably for a blast of arctic air to come howling down before the weekend and induce the abrupt departure for Florida of his father and stepmother to the furnished apartment they rented each year, with clandestine financial help, Gold suspected, from Sid, his older brother. A muted effort was afoot to persuade them to buy a condominium, in the hope they would stay later in spring and return there sooner each fall. This year they were especially evasive about their plans for departing. The annual autumnal heat wave known among Jews as the High Holidays, and elsewhere as Indian summer, had already come and gone. His father found other Jewish holidays. Gold hoped Sid might be absent, but guessed he was destined for disappointment on that score as well. Faced by his father and older brother, he had no way to avoid those dreaded moments of acute misery in store. His father would insult and belittle; Sid would bait subtly in skillful ways Gold found impossible to combat. Gold's helplessness had engendered in him over the years a rueful admiration for Sid's guile and crafty capabilities. Sid was sixty-two now, fourteen years older than Gold. His father was eighty-two. Among Gold's childhood memories was the lucid recollection that Sid had lost him deliberately in Coney Island one summer day on Surf Avenue near Steeplechase in order to go running after girls, and that one of his older sisters, Rose, or perhaps Esther or Ida, had come to the police station to bring him back home. Gold's intelligence of that occurrence had never ceased to pain him.

Gold's last class of the week ended after lunch on Friday. Education was one of the several fields of knowledge in which he was considered an expert by people who did not know better. Gold had learned from experience that he himself took no pleasure in going away weekends and that most college students did, and he always scheduled at least one class for Friday afternoon in order to keep enrollment low. Normally it was not until the latter half of a course that Gold lost interest in his subject matter and starting disliking his students. This term it was happening at the outset.

He went by subway from his Brooklyn campus to the small apartment in midtown Manhattan that he called a studio to see if any messages had come from old girl friends or potential new ones. There was a letter from his earliest girl friend saying she might come into the city again for a day next month and hoped to see him for lunch, which was okay with Gold, who would arrange for sandwiches and coffee to be sent up. Whiskey was already there. From the doorman he picked up a manila envelope addressed to Dr. Bruce Gold and knew it was a late written assignment from an apprehensive student. The weight saddened him; the manuscript was thick, and he would have to read it. He telephoned Belle to see what time they were leaving.

They rode by taxi to Brooklyn from their apartment on the West Side of Manhattan in the tail end of the evening rush hour, Belle quiet, Gold bored. A foggy darkness was falling over the river. Belle carried in her lap in a paper shopping bag the heavy potato kugel she had cooked that morning.

"Try not to look like you wish you were somewhere else," she advised without turning her head. "Try not to start any fights with Sid. Try to talk at least a little bit to Victor, Irv, Milt, and Max. Remember to kiss Harriet."

"I always say hello. Sid starts fights with me."

"All he does is talk. He doesn't even talk to you."

"He talks to steam me up."

"I'll try to interrupt."

Gold slid his tongue up into a front portion of his cheek and tried to concentrate all his ill feelings upon the book about Henry Kissinger he had been planning for almost a year. The subject was not sufficiently magnetic, and as the taxi emerged from the tunnel into Brooklyn, his thoughts returned to the dismal tumult that lay ahead.

He felt ghastly.

Everyone else would enjoy it. Family parties had turned for him into grueling and monotonous tests of fealty to which he submitted with sorrow and anxiety whenever he was left with no civilized alternative. There would be nobody there he wanted to see. Conversation, for him, would be impossible. He no longer liked his father or brother, if indeed he ever had. He did occasionally feel some gratitude and pity toward his four older sisters, but the locus and depth of these affections varied with his different memories of which had been kindest to him after the death of their mother and in the years before. All knew he had some fame as a writer and could not figure out why.

Gold's distaste for family dinners, his aversion, in fact, toward all forms of domestic sentiment, stretched back distantly at least until the time of his graduation from high school and his moving into Manhattan to attend Columbia College. He was pleased to be entering so prestigious a university and vastly relieved at escaping a large family of five sisters and one brother in which all his life he had felt both suffocated and unappreciated.

"I was going to quit college and fight in Israel," he had bragged to Belle at the time they were falling in love, "but I had this scholarship to Columbia."

Gold had not once thought of quitting college or fighting in Israel. And he did not go to Columbia on a scholarship but on money provided by his father, most of which, he understood now, must have been channeled through the old man's irresponsible hands from Sid and three of his older sisters. Muriel, the fourth, had never been known to part happily with a dollar for anyone but herself or her two daughters.

Another sister, Joannie, lived in California. Mercifully, she was younger. Joannie had charged away from home in delinquency a long time before in hopes of succeeding as a model or movie actress and was married now to an overbearing Los Angeles businessman who disliked coming East and disdained everybody in the family but Gold. Several times a year she flew to New York alone to see just the ones she wanted to.

Gold had found himself the center of family attention ever since bringing home his first faultless report card, or a composition with an A plus. Muriel, who was closest to him in age and aimed her bad temper these days mostly at Ida, was nasty to him also even then. Ida, officious, was the sister who would impress upon Gold his need to do better in school, although what he did was always perfect. There were times now Gold thought he might go mad from the drenching reverence and affection that still poured over him from Rose and Esther, his two eldest sisters. Whatever expectations he had aroused, he had apparently fulfilled. They shimmered with love whenever they looked at him, and he wished they would stop.

While he was in college, Rose would frequently mail or give him a twenty-dollar bill, he remembered, and so would Esther. Like Sid, both had gone to work after high school as soon as they could find jobs. Ida was able to go to college and become a schoolteacher. Ida handed him fives, always with strict instructions about how the money was to be spent. Rose and Ida still worked, Rose as a legal secretary with the firm that had hired her during the Depression, Ida in the public-school system. Ida was assistant principal now in an elementary school, and she was fighting for her sanity against militant blacks and Hispanics who wanted all Jews gone, and said so in just those words. Esther had been widowed two years before. Much of her hair fell out almost overnight, and the rest turned white. She talked vaguely at times of finding employment again as a bookkeeper. But she was fifty-seven, and too timid to try. Muriel, whose husband, Victor, did well in wholesale beef and veal, was a distinct contrast to the others. She dyed her hair black to camouflage the gray and played poker with friends who also enjoyed outings to the racetrack. A chain smoker with a hoarse voice and a tough manner, Muriel was constantly spilling cigarette ashes that Ida, with her zeal for order, would brush away with scolding, high-minded comments of disparagement, even in Muriel's own house.

Between Sid, the firstborn, therefore, and Gold, the only other male child, stood these four older sisters who often seemed like four hundred and fifty when they flocked around him with their questions, censures, solicitudes, and advice. Ida cautioned him to chew his food slowly. Rose telephoned to warn that it was icy outside. He thought of them all as outdated, naive, and virtually oblivious to the very real proximity of sinfulness and evil. Except for Sid, Gold recalled, and therefore Harriet, his wife. Sid in nimbler years had been discovered one time in San Francisco when he was supposed to be in San Diego on business, in Acapulco one time when he was supposed to be in San Francisco, and on a houseboat in Miami when he was registered at a hotel in Puerto Rico. Once possessed of the means, Sid had learned how to ease his way effortlessly through hotels.

Now he went out of town only with Harriet on brief vacations or to visit his father in Florida in the winter. Sid was a large, genial, heavyset man with soft flesh and parted gray hair; he had a pronounced facial likeness to their father, although the latter was short and chubby, with bushy white hair that stood almost straight up like the hair of a figure in a comic strip receiving a powerful charge of electricity. Gold was lean, tense, and dark, with vivid shadows around his eyes in a crabby, nervous face women found dynamic and sexy. Sid was easing compliantly into an antiquated generation, wearing plain gray or blue suits with white shirts and wide blue or maroon suspenders, whereas their demanding, autocratic old four-flusher of a father, the retired tailor Julius Gold, was dressing more and more each year like a debonair Hollywood mogul, favoring cashmere polo shirts and suave blazers. Inexplicably, Sid seemed to be growing more fond of their father. Far back, Gold remembered, Sid had run away from home and stayed away a whole summer to escape the old man's domineering eccentricities and cantankerous boasting.

Gold and Belle were nearly the last to arrive at Ida's apartment on Ocean Parkway; Muriel and Victor entered a minute afterward. Irv, Ida's husband, was convivial in his role as host. He was a dentist with offices above a paint store on Kings Highway. Already, Gold was having difficulty distinguishing one person from the next. It was a way of coping. He shook hands quickly with Irv, Victor, Sid, Milt, Max, and his father, differentiating between them only in the accumulating letdown he felt with each.

Max, Rose's husband, who was slightly diabetic, sipped at a glass of club soda squeamishly. The other men, along with Muriel, drank whiskey, the rest of the women, soft drinks. Belle had vanished into the kitchen to oversee the unpacking of her potato kugel and be of assistance to Ida, who probably was simultaneously shooing her away and giving her things to do, and reprehending her in the same breath for failing to do them swiftly enough. Everybody there, including his father, had at least one child who was a source of heartache.

Gold took bourbon from Irv and began kissing the cheeks of the women. Harriet accepted this greeting without pleasure. His stepmother authorized his approach by bobbing her head above her knitting and inclining her face. Gold bent to her with both forearms at the ready, fearing she might run him through the neck with one of her knitting needles.

Gold's stepmother, who was from an old Southern Jewish family with branches in Richmond and Charleston, habitually made things difficult for him in a variety of peculiar ways. Frequently when he spoke to her she did not answer at all. Other times she said, "Don't talk to me." When he didn't talk to her, his father moved up beside him with a hard nudge and directed, "Go talk to her. You too good?" She was always knitting thick white wool. When he complimented her once on her knitting, she informed him with a flounce that she was crocheting. When he inquired next time how her crocheting was going she answered, "I don't crochet. I knit." Often she called him to her side just to tell him to move away. Sometimes she came up to him and said, "Cackle, cackle."

He had no idea what to reply.

Gold's stepmother was knitting an endless strip of something bulky that was too narrow to be a shawl and too wide and uni-

formly straight to be anything else. It was around six inches broad
and conceivably thousands of miles long, for she had been working
on that same strip of knitting even before her marriage to his father
many years before. Gold had a swimming vision of that loosely
woven strip of material flowing out the bottom of her straw bag to
the residence Sid found for his father and her each summer in
Brooklyn in Manhattan Beach and from there all the way down the
coastline to Florida and into unmeasured regions beyond. She
never wanted for wool or for depth inside her straw bag into which
the finished product could fall. The yarn came twitching up through
one end of the opening in her bag, and the manufactured product,
whatever it was, descended, perhaps for eternity, into the other.

"What are you making?" he'd asked her one time out of curiosity that could no longer be borne in silence.

"You'll see," she replied mysteriously.

He consulted his father. "Pa, what's she making?"

"Mind your own business."

"I was only asking."

"Don't ask personal questions."

"Rose, what's she knitting?" he asked his sister.

"Wool," Belle answered.

"Belle, I know that. But what's she doing with it?"

"Knitting," said Esther.

Gold's stepmother was knitting knitting, and she was knitting it
endlessly. Now she asked, "Do you like my wool?"

"Pardon?"

"Do you like my wool?"

"Of course," he replied.

"You never say so," she pouted.

"I like your wool," said Gold, retreating in confusion to a
leather armchair near the doorway.

"He told me he likes my wool," he heard her relating to his
brothers-in-law Irv and Max. "But I think he's trying to pull it over
my eyes."

"How was your trip?" his sister Esther asked dotingly.

"Fine."

"Where were you?" said Rose.

"Wilmington."

"Where?" asked Ida, passing with a serving tray.

"Washington," said Rose.

"Wilmington?"

"Wilmington."

"Washington."

"Washington?"

"Wilmington," he corrected them all. "In Delaware."

"Oh," said Rose, and looked crestfallen.

"How was your trip?" asked Ida, passing back.

Gold was going mad.

"He said it was fine," answered Esther before Rose could reply, and drifted toward a coffee table on which were platters holding loaves of chopped liver and chopped eggs and onions under attack by small knives spreading each or both onto round crackers or small sections of rye bread or very black pumpernickel.

"Meet any pretty girls there?" Muriel asked. The youngest of the sisters present, Muriel was ever under obligation to be up-to-date.

"Not this time," Gold answered, with the required grin.

Muriel glowed. Irv chuckled and Victor, Muriel's husband, looked embarrassed. Rose stared from face to face intently. Gold suspected that she had grown hard of hearing, and perhaps did not know. Her husband, Max, a postal worker, was slurring his words of late, and Gold wondered if anyone but himself had noticed.

Esther returned with a plate prepared for him, and a saltshaker aloft in her other hand. "I brought these all for you," she announced in her trembling voice. "And your own saltshaker."

Gold cringed.

"Don't spoil him," Muriel joked gruffly, spilling ashes onto her bosom from a cigarette hanging from her mouth.

The women in Gold's family believed he liked his food excessively salted.

"Don't salt it until you taste it," Ida yelled from across the room. "I already seasoned it."

Gold ignored her and continued salting the cracker he was holding. Other people's fingers plucked the remaining pieces from his plate. Esther and Rose each brought him more. Sid watched with amusement. So many fucking faces, Gold thought. So many people. And all of them strange. Even Belle, these days. And especially his stepmother.

He would never forget his first encounter with his stepmother. Sid had flown to Florida for the wedding and returned with her and his father for a reception at his home in Great Neck. There was an uncomfortable silence after the introductions when no one seemed sure what to say next. Gold stepped forward with a gallant try at putting everyone at ease.

"And what," he said in his most courtly manner, "would you like us to call you?"

"I would like you to treat me as my own children do," Gussie Gold replied with graciousness equal to his own. "I would like to think of you all as my very own children. Please call me Mother."

"Very well, Mother," Gold agreed. "Welcome to the family."

"I'm not your mother," she snapped.

Gold was the only one who laughed. Perhaps the others had perceived immediately what he had missed. She was insane.

GOLD'S stepmother had been brought up never to be seen eating in public, and she entered the dining room as always with her knitting needles and her straw tote bag. Fourteen adults were grouped elbow to elbow at a table designed for ten. Gold knew that his was not the only leg blocked by supporting braces underneath. I have been to more meals like this than I can bear to remember, Gold lamented secretly. Ida's daughter was out for the evening, her son was away at college.

"I can see on the table," Sid announced with such generalized amiability that Gold's muscles all bunched reflexively in anticipation of some barbed danger nearby, "Belle's potato kugel, Esther's noodle pudding, Muriel's potato salad, and Rose's . . ." He faltered.

"I made the matzoh balls," Rose said, blushing.

"Rose's matzoh balls."

"And my wool," said Gold's stepmother.

"And your wool."

"Do you like my wool?" She seemed coquettishly dependent on Sid's good opinion.

"It's the tastiest wool in the whole world, I bet."

"*He* doesn't like it," she said with a glance at Gold.

"I like it," Gold apologized weakly.

"He never tells me he likes it."

"I like your wool."

"I was not talking to you," she said.

28

Victor laughed more loudly than the others. Victor was convinced that Gold and Irv both looked down upon him. This was true, but Gold bore him no unkind feelings. Victor, red of face and sturdy as a bull, was sweet to Muriel and liked Belle, and could always be relied on to send one of his meat trucks and some laborers when anything heavy was to be transported. His posture was so nearly perfect both sitting and standing that he seemed to be holding himself erect at enormous physical cost. Gold was positive he would be the first among them to be felled by a heart attack.

"I made a honey cake," Harriet put in poutingly. "I'm sure I ruined it. I was going to make a Jell-O mold but I know you all must be sick of it."

"And Harriet's honey cake."

"Much starch," said Max, who, in addition to having diabetes, was susceptible to certain circulatory imbalances. Wearing a worried frown, Max declined everything but some chicken wings, a slice of pot roast, from which he separated the fat, and string beans.

Esther was served by Milt, a suitor courting her in almost wordless patience. She waited stiffly without looking at him. Milt, the older brother of her deceased husband's business partner, was a careful, respectful man who talked little in the presence of the family. Milt was past sixty-five, older than Sid, and had never been married. With a movement that approached vivacity, he flicked a second spoonful of Esther's noodle pudding onto her plate, and then a spoonful onto his own. Esther thanked him with a nervous smile.

There were platters of meatballs and stuffed derma on the table, too, and a deep, wide bowl of potatoes mashed with chicken fat and fried onions that Gold could have eaten up all by himself.

Ida asked Gold, "What's new?"

"Nothing."

"He's writing a book," said Belle.

"Really?" said Rose.

"Another book?" scoffed his father.

"That's nice," said Esther.

"Yes," said Belle.

"What's it about?" Muriel asked Gold.

"It's about the Jewish experience," said Belle.

"That's nice," said Ida.

"About what?" demanded his father.

"About the Jewish experience," answered Sid, and then called across the table to Gold. "Whose?"

"Whose what?" said Gold warily.

"Whose Jewish experience?"

"I haven't decided yet."

"He's writing some articles too," said Belle.

"Most of it is going to be very general," Gold added with perceptible reluctance.

"What's it mean?" Gold's father wanted to be told right then.

"It's a book about being Jewish," said Belle.

Gold's father snorted. "What does *he* know about being Jewish?" he roared. "He wasn't even born in Europe."

"It's about being Jewish in America," said Belle.

Gold's father was fazed only a second. "He don't know so much about that either. I been Jewish in America longer than him too."

"They're paying him money," Belle argued persistently. Gold wished she would stop.

"How much you getting?" demanded Gold's father.

"A lot," said Belle.

"How much? A lot to him maybe ain't so much to others. Right, Sid?"

"You said it, Pop."

"How much you getting?"

"Twenty thousand dollars," said Belle.

The amount, Gold could see, made a stunning impact, especially on his father, who looked unaffectedly disappointed. Gold himself would have deferred naming a figure. It must seem a fortune to Max and Rose and Esther, and even, perhaps, to Victor and Irv. They would see only a windfall, and forget the work.

"That *is* nice," said Rose.

"That ain't so much," Gold's father grumbled dejectedly. "I made more than that in my time."

And lost more too, Gold thought.

"Some people write books for the movies and make much more," Harriet observed in a disheartened way, while Sid chuckled softly.

Gold opened his mouth to retaliate when Belle said, "Well, that's only a start. And five thousand of that is for research. It isn't even charged against the guarantee."

"That's nice," said Esther quickly, eager to come to Gold's support. "I bet that's very nice."

"What does that mean?" asked Sid seriously.

"It's hard to explain," said Belle.

"No, it isn't."

"That's what you told me."

"You wouldn't listen when I tried."

"Don't fight," Harriet flittered in quickly with malice.

"It means," Gold said, addressing himself mainly to Sid and Irv, "that five thousand is charged off as a publishing expense instead of to me, even if I don't spend it. I can make that much more in royalties from book sales."

"Isn't that what I said?" said Belle.

"That sounds like a very good provision," Esther's elderly beau, Milt, observed ever so diffidently, and Gold remembered he was an accountant and would understand too.

"Bruce," Irv ventured, putting a thumb and forefinger to his chin. Since his dental practice had ceased growing, Irv had developed a tic in his right cheek that often gave him the appearance of smiling inexplicably. "You aren't going to write about any of us, are you?"

"No, of course not," Gold responded. "Why would I do anything like that?"

A wave of relief went around the table. Then all faces fell.

"Why not?" demanded his father. "Ain't we good enough?"

Gold's voice still tended to weaken in argument with the old man. "It's not that kind of book."

"No?" bellowed his father, rearing up an inch or so and stabbing at Gold an index finger that curved like a talon. "Well, I've got news for you, smart guy. You ain't gonna do it so hot without me. It's what I told you then, and what I told you now. It's what I told you from the beginning. You ain't the man for the job." He changed in a second from choleric belligerence to serene self-confidence and sat back with his head cocked to the side. "Good, Sid?" he asked, turning and looking up.

"You said it, Pop."

Julius Gold allowed his eyelids to lower in a look of narcissistic contentment.

Those two bastards, Gold told himself, reaching with misplaced hostility for the bowl of mashed potatoes and onions to ladle himself out another large helping. And they never even liked each other.

"Did you ever hear from the White House again?" asked his sister Rose, beaming.

"No," said Belle, before Gold could reply, and Harriet looked pleased.

"But he heard from them twice," said Esther. "He got two phone calls."

"It wasn't really the White House," Gold corrected. "It was from a friend I went through graduate school with who works in the White House."

"That's the same thing," said Ida. "He's in the White House, isn't he?"

"I don't know where he was when he made the phone call." Gold's tone was faintly sarcastic.

"In the White House," said Belle, with no change of expression. "Ralph Newsome."

"Thanks," said Gold. "There was some chance I might forget his name."

"I never heard of him," said Harriet.

"Well, he's on the President's staff," said Muriel, and turned to Gold. "Isn't he?"

Gold plunged his face into his plate and was silent.

"I went past the White House once when I was a sweet and very pretty little girl up from Richmond," Gold's stepmother recalled. "It looked dirty."

"But he said he liked your book, didn't he?" Esther recalled.

"Not my book," Gold explained uncomfortably.

"His review of the President's book," said Belle.

"I'll bet the President liked it too," said Rose.

"He did," said Belle. "They offered him a job."

"The President?" asked Ida.

"They did not," said Gold irately. "Not the President. I was only asked if I'd ever given any thought to working in Washington. That's all."

"That sounds like a job to me," said Irv.

"You see?" said Belle.

"What'd you say?" asked Max eagerly.

"He said he would think about it," said Belle.

"I told you not to tell them."

"I don't care," Belle answered. "They're your family. You said you'd probably take it if the job was a good one."

"You said you wouldn't go," said Gold.

"I won't," said Belle.

"Twenty thousand?" Gold's father suddenly exclaimed with a gargantuan guffaw. "*Me* they would give a million!"

Ashes, Gold grieved wildly, chewing away at his mouthful of mashed potatoes and bread more vigorously than he realized. The food! In my mouth to ashes the food is turning! It has been this way with my father almost all my life.

From the beginning, Gold ruminated now. When I said I was thinking of going into business, he told me to stay in school. When I decided to stay in school, he told me to go into business. "Dope. Why waste time? It's not what you know. It's who you know." Some father! If I said wet, he'd say dry. When I said dry, he said wet. If I said black, he said white. If I said white, he said . . . niggers, they're ruining the neighborhood, one and all, and that's it. *Fartig*. That was when he was in real estate. Far back, that peremptory cry of *Fartig* would instantly create an obedient silence that everybody in the family would be in horror of breaking, including Gold's mother.

It was no secret to anyone that his father considered Gold a *schmuck*. It would be unfair to say his father was disappointed in him, for he had always considered Gold a *schmuck*.

"From the beginning," his father showed off again with inverted familial pride, as though Gold were elsewhere, "I knew he would never amount to much. And was I right? It's a good thing his mother never lived to see the day he was born."

"Pop," Sid corrected him tactfully. "Bruce was already in high school when Mom died."

"And a finer woman never lived," responded Gold's father, nodding for a moment in bewitched recollection, then glaring at Gold vindictively as though her death at forty-nine had been his fault. "Or died," he added faintly.

Once when Gold was visiting in Florida, his father drew him across a street just to meet some friends and introduced him by saying, "This is my son's brother. The one that never amounted to much."

His father's lasting appraisal of Gold—as of almost every other human in the world, including Sid—was that he lacked business sense. Despite his father's unbroken record of failure in more occupations and business ventures than Gold knew about, he judged himself a model of splendid achievements and rare acumen, and he never shrank from presenting himself as a shrewd observer of everyone else's affairs, including those of Sid and General Motors. One of his more penetrating entrepreneurial judgments this year about American Telephone and Telegraph was that "they got no talent in the front office."

"They're big, all right," said Julius Gold, "but they don't know what to do. If I owned all those telephones, oh boy—no business would run without me."

His visit to New York this year, ostensibly for dental work, had commenced in May. A staunchly irreligious man, he now seemed oddly determined to remain through all the Jewish holidays, and he kept disclosing new ones of which the others had not heard.

"He must be reading the fucking Talmud," Gold had grumbled to Belle when his father cited Shmini Atzereth. Belle pretended not to hear. "Or else he's making them up."

In Harriet, Gold found a kindred antipathy that surpassed his own. "What's the matter?" she had muttered snidely the week of her father-in-law's arrival. "They have no dentists in Miami?"

It was a fragile and temporary alliance, Gold knew, for Harriet had been methodically putting distance between herself and the family for some time, as though in thrifty preparation for some clear and farsighted eventuality. Harriet had a widowed mother and an older unmarried sister to help support.

Gold's father was five feet two and subject to unexpected attacks of wisdom. "Make money!" he might shout suddenly, apropos of nothing, and his stepmother would add liturgically, "You should all listen to your father."

"Make money!" he shouted suddenly now, as though sprung from a trance with a burning revelation. "That's the only good thing I ever learned from the Christians," he continued with the same volatile fervor. "Roast beef is better than boiled beef, that's another good thing. And sirloin steak is better than shoulder steak. Lobsters are dirty. They ain't got scales and crawl. They can't even swim. And that's it. *Fartig*."

"You should listen to your father more." It was on Gold that the reprimanding gaze of his stepmother rested last, longest, and most severely.

"And what does he want me to do?"

"Whatever he does," answered his father, "is wrong. One thing," he said, "one thing I always taught my children," he went on, as though addressing somebody else's, "was not the value of a dollar, but the value of a *thousand* dollars, *ten* thousand. And all of them—except one"—in fantastic disregard of the facts and to the visible embarrassment of the others, he paused to look with murderous disgust at Gold—"have learned that lesson and now got plenty, especially Sid here, and little Joannie." His eyes misted over at mention of his youngest daughter, who had bolted from the fold so early. "I always knew how to advise. The upshot is, that when I get old"—Gold could no longer believe his ears as he heard this preposterous braggart of eighty-two declaiming—"when I get old, nobody will ever have to support me but you children."

Gold, his temper rising, felt no compunction about lashing back. "Well, I don't like to boast," he replied roughly, "but when I was with the Foundation seven years ago—"

"You ain't with them any more!" his father cut him short.

Gold surrendered with a shudder and pretended to search his

plate as Rose, Muriel, and all the brothers-in-law clapped in delight
and Esther and Ida rocked with laughter. Gold had the terrible
presentiment that some might leap onto their chairs and hurl hats
into the air. His father again sat back slowly with that smile of
self-enchantment and let his eyes fall closed. Gold was constrained
to smile. He would not want anyone to guess how truly crushed he
felt. And then, Sid spoke.

"Behold a child," Sid intoned rabbinically without warning, as
though musing aloud upon a slice of Esther's stuffed intestine held
on a fork halfway between his plate and his mouth, and Gold felt
his spirits sink further, "by nature's kindly law, pleased by a rattle,
tickled by a straw."

Gold saw in a flash that he was totally ruined. It was check,
mate, match, and defeat from the opening move. He was caught,
whether he took the bait or declined, and he could only marvel in
dejection as the rest of the stratagem unfolded around him as sym-
metrically and harmoniously as ripples in water.

The others were struck with wonder by Sid's eloquence and
pantheistic wisdom.

"That sounds okay to me," Victor murmured.

"Me too," said Max.

"It's nice," said Esther. "Isn't it?"

"Yes," Rose agreed. "Beautiful."

"See how smart my first son is?" said Gold's father.

"You should listen to your older brother more," said Gold's
stepmother, and aimed the point of her knitting needle at Gold's
eyes.

"It really is beautiful," Ida assented reverently. Ida, the shrew-
ish schoolteacher, was considered the intelligent one; Gold, the
college professor, was a novelty. Ida looked Gold fully in the face.
"Isn't it, Bruce?"

There was no escape.

"Yes," said Belle.

Gold was trapped two, three, four, maybe five or six ways. If he
mentioned Alexander Pope, he would be parading his knowledge.
If he didn't, Sid would, unmasking him as an ignoramus. If he
corrected the prepositional errors, he would appear pedantic, quar-

relsome, jealous. If he gave no answer at all, he would be insulting to Ida, who, with the others, was awaiting some reply. It was no fair way, he sulked, to treat a middle-aged, Phi Beta Kappa, cum laude graduate of Columbia who was a doctor of philosophy and had recently been honored with praise from the White House and the promise of consideration for a high-level position. Oh, Sid, you fucking cocksucker, lamented the doctor of philosophy and prospective governmental appointee. You nailed me again.

"Pope," he decided at length to mumble unwillingly, keeping his face steadfastly down toward his portion of Ida's meatballs.

"What?" snapped his father.

"He said 'Pope,' " Sid informed him congenially.

"What's it mean?"

"It's by Alexander Pope," Gold asserted loudly. "Not by Sid."

"See how smart our kid brother is?" Sid announced, chewing contentedly.

"He didn't say it was by him," Harriet pointed out nicely in defense of her husband. "Did he?"

"Isn't it just as beautiful anyway?" Ida reasoned with him pedagogically.

"Yes," said Belle.

"Is it any less beautiful because it's by Alexander Pope and not by Sid?" asked Irv.

Belle shook her head firmly, as did Victor, Milt, and Max.

Gold found them all abhorrent. "The implication was there," he exclaimed sullenly. "And the prepositions are wrong."

"Brucie, Brucie, Brucie," entreated Sid generously, the essence of tolerance and reasonableness. "Are you going to be sore at me just because of a couple of prepositions?" There was a murmurous shaking of heads. "We'll make them right if you're going to be so finicky."

"Sid, you're fucking me over again!" Gold shouted. "Aren't you?"

The next few moments were exciting. The women averted their eyes, and Victor, who did not like bad language ever in front of women, reddened further, as though keeping his temper in check, and straightened menacingly. Then Gold's father jumped to his feet

with an incredulous shriek. "He said fuck?" His voice ascended
to such shrillness that he sounded like a chicken in a frenzy.
"Fuck, he said? I'll kill him! I'll break his bones! Someone walk
me over to him."

"All of you leave Bruce alone," Ida ordered sternly, restoring
order. "This is my house, and I won't permit any fighting."

"That's right," entreated Rose, a large, kindly woman with a
saddle of freckles across her nose. "Bruce is probably still very
tired."

"From his trip to Washington," said Esther.

"Wilmington," said Belle.

Sid, licking his lips with a look of triumph, reached with his
fingers for a second piece of Harriet's honey cake.

In the cab going home, Gold had heartburn and a headache. He
could remember meals far back when his father reigned like the
absolute tyrant he was, pointing the lethal scepter of his finger at
whatever he wanted passed to him, and everyone else would has-
ten to ferry everything in that area to him. "Not that! *That!*" he
would roar. He would not lower himself to specify, and the challenge was further complicated by the fact that he was mildly
cross-eyed. Gold's father would toss cups, saucers, plates, and
serving bowls, empty or full, from the table to the floor if he spied
a chip or a hairline crack in any of the porcelain. "I don't eat from
broken china," he would proclaim like an affronted monarch. Gold
could remember his mother and sisters inspecting all the dishes
beforehand to segregate those defective ones that must never come
before his scrutiny.

"The thing is," Gold recalled in a manner quietly morose, "they
used to hate each other. Sid ran away from home once because he
couldn't take him any more. He was still in high school and stayed
away a whole summer."

"I can't believe Sid hated him."

"I'll have to ask Rose. Now Sid coddles him like they've always
been pals. You interrupt me a lot, don't you?" Gold accused,
slouching in a corner of the taxi with his face drooping on his hand.

"I don't interrupt you at all." There was stubbornness in Belle's
manner, never defiance, but a stolid, homespun refusal to give

more ground, regardless of cost. "You told me you don't like to be interrupted, so I never interrupt you."

"Then you disagree with me."

"How can I disagree with you," Belle wondered evenly, "if I'm the one who says it first?"

"You answer questions for me."

"What's the difference who gives the answer?"

"Sometimes your answers contradict mine."

"Can't I contradict you?" Belle asked.

"No."

"Never?"

"No." Gold spoke austerely, leaving no room for misunderstanding.

Belle responded with a shrug.

"And I'm not going to see them all at dinner again, maybe forever."

"For three weeks," said Belle. "They're coming to our house. I invited them. You said you'd be home."

"Call it off," he directed.

"Don't come," she answered. "It's Rose's birthday. And I'm making her a surprise party."

"At sixty?" His stress of surprise was edged with ridicule.

If Belle answered he didn't hear. There was distance between them now that neither made attempt to deny. He was thankful she did not force him to talk about it. Belle was a pudgy woman nearly his own age, and she seemed smaller and rounder as she sat hugging on her lap the paper shopping bag with the empty Pyrex kugel pan inside, her head up straight in a matter-of-fact way that seemed to be saying, "I know also that I'm getting old and never was a beauty, and that I don't know how to make you happy any more. I don't like it either. Do what you want."

Gold stared across the river at the house lights in New Jersey and was glad he had never had to live there. Soon, he reflected peacefully, he might be free of Belle, for he had learned something more from Ralph that could improve his own situation: it was not mandatory that a husband wait until the youngest child moved off to college before he left his wife.

Buoyed by the encouraging prospect of an early separation from

Belle, he allowed his imagination to float in joyous expectance to the secret project he had no intention of mentioning this early to Pomoroy or Lieberman. Another book. Now that he had finally abandoned his novel, he would be that much quicker to start.

Kissinger.

How he loved and resented that hissing name.

Even apart from his jealousy, which was formidable, Gold had hated Henry Kissinger from the moment of his emergence as a public figure and hated him still, a mental and emotional judgment not so original as to guarantee in itself a Nobel Prize for peace or a Pulitzer Prize for investigative disclosure. However, Gold had an angle for a book on Kissinger he believed might do both. Gold had file drawers filled with all Kissinger's writings and public statements and with newspaper and magazine clippings of everything said about him. He collected clippings also of the writings and public statements of David Eisenhower.

Sometimes he thought of mixing the two collections up. Sometimes he found it difficult to keep them apart.

IT was a cause of prolonged vexation to Gold that almost no one he knew read any of the publications in which his work was likely to appear. Let Gold's name surface for a single mention in *Playboy* or *Ladies' Home Journal*, however, and the whole world took cognizance at the same moment. Even Lieberman. Even Pomoroy. Even his father and stepmother, who read only the *Times* and *Daily News* in New York and nothing at all in Florida. They preferred watching news broadcasts and old movies on television, taking bizarre delight in identifying dead actors and actresses and recounting the circumstances of their demise.

"Hey, bigshot," his father would bellow on the telephone, and Gold would wilt at once. "I see you got your name in *Playboy* again. That guy didn't think so much of you, did he?"

"Why?" Gold was rankled. "He paid me a very nice compliment."

"Sure, that's what he wrote," said his father. "But I could read between the lines."

Encouraged and accompanied by Gussie, Gold's father would move after dinner to the television set in whatever home he had decided to be driven to that evening and begin watching old movies with the energetic vigilance of a custodian of dead souls. The movies themselves made no difference. The responsibility for keeping score was only his.

"That one's gone," he would shout elatedly like the grim reaper himself, as though collaring another trophy for his collection. "A hundred years ago. Old age did him in. Remember that lawyer for the defense? *Geshtorben*. Heart attack. Gone in an instant. Look at that big guy there pushing everyone around. You know where he is today?''

"Dead?" inquired Gold's stepmother delicately, glancing up from her wool. In such moments, she recalled to Gold's mind the image of Madame Defarge knitting at the foot of the guillotine.

"You bet, baby," answered Gold's father. "In *d'rerd*. Now he ain't pushing around people. He's pushing up daisies. A suicide. They tried to hush it up, but they couldn't fool me."

"I do believe," said Gold's stepmother, "that old governess has passed away too."

"Sure, she did," Gold's father agreed. "Cancer. It ate her up. See that taxi driver, the funny one? *Toyt*. Like a doornail. A stroke. Maybe twenty years ago. Lingered a few weeks, then good-bye Charlie. That crooked cop? *Bagruben*. In *d'rerd* also. In a fire, I think. Whiskey had something to do with it too. That one was a *faygeleh!*''

It was their favorite recreation, even in Gold's apartment. Gold would sit with gritted teeth for as long as he could and then excuse himself with the explanation he had work to prepare. Belle, to her credit, remained, with the same hospitable consideration she showed to her own widowed mother.

"He ain't no Jew!" Gold's father had decided in Gold's living room one evening as he watched another newscast of Secretary of State Henry Kissinger smiling still one more time into the press cameras as he descended from still one more airplane. Gold's father turned to Gold as though daring opposition. "No, siree. He said he was a cowboy, didn't he? A lonesome cowboy riding into town to get the bad guys, didn't he? All by himself. Well, no cowboy was ever a Jew."

"Not," said Gold's stepmother, "on your life."

"Show me one," challenged Gold's father. "Shepherds, maybe. No cowboys."

And Gold wondered if the Creator, in the giving of His laws to Moses on that cloud-covered mountain, had not also in His wisdom and mercy imparted a time limit on at least one of His Commandments that had somehow been lost in translation after the tired old Patriarch made his way back down on a day that had been for him more than usually distracting. How was it possible to honor a father who was so abrasive and married now to such a fucking wack?

Yet it was shortly after this visit from his father that Gold opened his dossier on Henry Kissinger and began outlining his strategy in closest secrecy. His file thickened rapidly. He began collecting clippings on David Eisenhower because he could not resist. From David Eisenhower he read:

> One improvement in the Nixon adminis-
> tration, due to Watergate, is that Mr.
> Nixon is no longer considered an un-
> qualified goody-goody. I never liked that
> idea. The image of the Nixon administra-
> tion is part of my heritage as well, and I
> don't think I'm a goody-goody either. I
> am a contentious person in a lot of ways.
> I'm glad that to a certain extent this min-
> isterial cloak can be lifted from my
> shoulders. I'm not just a goody-goody.

For the first time in his life, possibly, Gold's mind boggled. David Eisenhower, after all, was probably the outstanding Amherst alumnus of his generation. Gold was thankful he'd clipped that interview. Someday, in respite from work that he knew was largely undistinguished and, in every nuance of the adverb, abominably intellectual, he might want to write comedy.

Often since, Gold was amazed by things he found in newspapers and magazines.

> Many such groups of heckling, young
> hoodlums roamed at will among the
> crowd of 125,000 gathered at the Wash-
> ington Monument for Human Kindness
> Day, robbing or beating 600 people.

He clipped them all. They boggled his mind.

GOLD WAS the author of six nonfiction books, one of which, his first, was genuine, and that one an expansion of his doctoral dissertation. Four collections of his shorter work had been published. Two of these collections each contained four or five fairly perceptive pieces in which he had been able to say something original effectively; and a third included a long essay on the symbiotic relationship between cultural advance and social decay that had been reprinted widely and was still made reference to by commentators on both sides of the matter—those in favor of social decay and those opposed. The remaining collection, his latest, was worthless. Gold thought much less of his work than even his fussiest detractors, for he knew far better than they the diverse sources of most of his information and even of much of his language. Gold's current scheme for a new collection was a volume of pieces from his previous collections.

His short stories were mannered and trite, and he was content that they were published in far-flung quarterly magazines of very small circulation. His poems, he sensed, were atrocious, and these he submitted to obscure literary magazines in Pretoria and the Isle of Wight and to English-language university publications in Beirut, Spain, and Teheran. He felt safer talking about his poetry with people who had never read any. A problem with his stories and poems, Gold knew, was that they tended to be derivative, and mainly derivative, unfortunately, of works of his own. His novel, a work he had wrestled with, on and off, for almost three years, he had finally abandoned after one page. The novel was derivative of a poem Gold had written seven years before that was itself derived from a brilliant exegesis by a young Englishman of the works of Samuel Beckett that Gold wished he'd written himself.

ALTHOUGH IT was taken for granted by now that no one in Gold's family was obliged to read anything he wrote, he nevertheless was held in some kind of baffled awe by everyone but his stepmother, who was fond of remarking that she thought he had a screw loose.

Collections of his books and the periodicals in which reviews and articles by him had appeared were maintained in each of the households. Esther and Rose kept scrapbooks. Ida, the practical schoolteacher, combined literature with painting by hanging copies of his book jackets in art frames in her foyer and living room. Belle's mother pasted his titles on each piece of her luggage. Even Harriet and Sid showed his work off prominently in their large home in Great Neck on a polished sideboard facing the entrance to the house almost dead-on. But that was it. Beyond the title and opening sentences, he could have written *fuck-all* anywhere and the words would not have come to their attention. None of them, not even Belle or his two older sons or his unambitious twelve-year-old daughter, were caught up irresistibly by his speculations on the fallacies of truth, his concepts for an ideal university, or his theories of cultural phylogeny and ultimate universal doom. It was usually after the publication of something new by Gold that his stepmother was prone to mention that his brains, in her opinion, were twisted, or that he had a screw loose.

Gold, for his part, believed that she, in pace with his father, was losing her marbles, and that neither had many left.

Only Joannie in California and her husband, Jerry, seemed to understand who he really was and appreciate the high regard in which he was generally held by people who had never met him. Jerry gave parties whenever Gold came to California and relayed invitations for Gold to speak at temples and churches and before various adult civic and professional groups in Los Angeles and Beverly Hills, invitations Gold always declined. Jerry, the boorish overachiever, was too wealthy the community figure to suggest that Gold be paid a fee, and Gold was too successful the scholar to convey that he never spoke without one.

If anything, his relatives had long ceased struggling to figure out what he was writing about or why. Their beliefs were simple. They liked education, the larger the amount, the better the effects. Gold could have demolished this simple faith in a pulverizing thunder-clap had he wished. They voted piously in every election, even Julius, his father, as though their doing so made a difference, but had no interest in government. Gold had no interest in government either, but pretended he did, for politics and governmental operations were among his most rewarding areas of discussion. Gold no longer even voted; he could not, in fact, find any beneficial role for popular elections in the democratic process, but that was something else he could not disclose publicly without bringing blemish to the image he had constructed for himself as a radical moderate.

Gold was a moderate now in just about everything, advocating, in Pomoroy's description, fiery caution and crusading inertia. Inwardly he simmered often with envy, frustration, indignation, and confusion. Gold was opposed to segregation and equally opposed to integration. Certainly he did not believe that women, or homosexuals, should suffer persecution or discrimination. On the other hand, he was privately opposed to all equal rights amendments, for he certainly did not want members of either group associating with him on levels of equality or familiarity. And for the soundest reasons: his reasons were emotional, and emotions, he was concluding, particularly his own, could constitute the highest form of rationality. Problems were increasing in all areas to which he could no longer find uncomplicated solutions, but he kept these embarrassing dilemmas to himself and continued to manifest in public an aspect of cordial poise and balanced judgment that made him acceptable to almost everyone.

Gold could speak with aplomb now on politics, diplomacy, economics, education, war, sociology, ecology, social psychology, pop culture, fiction, and drama—and on any combinations of these in infinite permutations, for he had an inventive ability to relate anything to anything else.

Gold was flexible and unopinionated now and able—with just a few minor adjustments in emphasis—to deliver essentially the same speech to an elderly reactionary religious group that he had given the day before with equal success to a congress of teen-aged Maoists. Gold could produce newspaper evidence that a former governor of Texas had not been brought to trial on all the counts for which he had been indicted, and he had used this information one evening to confirm the suspicions of an audience of millionaires that the federal government had it in for all rich Texans and to insinuate convincingly the next afternoon to an assembly of college students just thirty miles away that justice, in the presence of rich politicians, was not blind but merely looking the other way. The college students paid him seven hundred dollars for this talk. The millionaires gave him shit.

He preferred the millionaires.

In the last Presidential election, Gold had allowed his name to be listed among the sponsors of separate full-page newspaper advertisements supporting the candidates of both political parties. For the advertisement supporting the candidates of the Democratic Party, Gold was asked to pay twenty-five dollars. For the other, the Republican Party met the whole cost in secrecy. From this Gold concluded that the Republican Party was the more humane and philanthropic, and he eased himself one stage farther toward the political right, and called it the center. Although he did not go so far as Lieberman, who was all for a totalitarian plutocracy, backed by repressive police actions when necessary—as long as the men on top were good to Jews like himself and let him have a little—and called it neoconservatism. Lieberman, whose name had appeared fraudulently as a contributing sponsor only in the ad deceitfully paid for by the Republican Party, was incensed that Gold, for only twenty-five dollars more, had his name in the newspaper twice.

Gold, like Lieberman, loved getting his name in the papers, and his strongest surviving political sentiment lay in his wish for the good government position Ralph hinted might be found for him. Gold had neither illusions nor misgivings about the burdens of public office: the only great weight of public office he could see was staying in, and he was in a quandary only a moment when the opportunity came to review the President's book.

There had been no advance word that such a manuscript even was in preparation. He was surprised, of course, by the oddity of a President who had chosen to write about his experiences in office after being there so short a time. But Gold had managed to cast even this unusual circumstance in a favorable light in the thoughtful appraisal he wrote of *My Year in the White House,* paying respectful tribute to a chief executive willing to open communications from the start with what Gold luckily described as his "contemporary universal constituency." The term proved more felicitous than Gold could have imagined. The President himself repeated it twice daily on a whirlwind goodwill tour he made to parts of the world in which he was despised. Journalists felt conscience bound to credit Gold with the phrase whenever they reported it. Gold had no idea what it meant.

Even more surprising had been the telephone call from Ralph Newsome to thank him on behalf of the White House.

"Where do you shine in?" Gold inquired. Ralph still sounded truthful. They had lost touch with each other since their fellowships at the Senator Russell B. Long Foundation seven years back.

"I'm at the White House now," Ralph answered. "I'm on the staff."

Gold was impressed. "How come I haven't read about you?"

"You probably have but didn't realize it," said Ralph. "I do a lot of work as a source. An unnamed source."

"Seriously?"

"Yes. You see, Bruce, I'm in the inner circle and very little of what I do gets outside. It really boosted my stock here when they found out I knew you," Ralph continued. "The President was very pleased with what you had to say."

"Tell him," said Gold, "I'm glad. Tell him I tried very hard to be fair."

"You were," said Ralph, "and he knows that. Very fair. We got lots of gushy reviews, like Lieberman's, but most of those were from people who wanted something. I can't think of any that was more pertinent and balanced than yours."

"I hope," said Gold, "that I wasn't too unsparing."

"You were just unsparing enough," Ralph reassured him. "This President welcomes criticism, Bruce, and he found your suggestions helpful. Particularly those about his sentence structure and paragraph organization. You seemed to understand him better than anyone else."

"Well, Ralph, there were a few things that did puzzle me."

"What were they, Bruce?"

"Well, frankly, Ralph—"

"Be frank, Bruce."

"Most Presidents wait until their terms are over before they write their memoirs. This one seems to have started right in the day he took office."

Ralph assented with a modest laugh. "That was my idea," he admitted. "This way he has a crack at more than just one best seller. He might do one every year. That boosted my stock way up with him too."

"There was one more thing. But I decided not to go into it."

"What was that, Bruce?"

"Well, Ralph, he must have spent an awful lot of time his first year in office writing this book about his first year. Yet, nowhere in the book does he say anything about being busy writing the book."

Ralph cleared his throat softly. "That's a point I think we overlooked. I'm glad you didn't go into it."

"Where did he find the time?"

"We all pitched in and helped," Ralph replied. "Not with the writing, you understand, but with most of the other junk a President has to attend to. Every word was his own."

Gold said he understood.

"This President really knows how to delegate responsibility, Bruce. Otherwise, he never would have gotten it done. It would be a lot like Tristram Shandy trying to write down the story of his life. Bruce, remember *Tristram Shandy* and that paper I copied from you?"

"I certainly do," said Gold with a touch of pique. "You got a better grade than I did and even had the paper published."

"I got a better grade on all the papers I copied from you, didn't I?" Ralph reminded him. "Bruce, this President is a very busy man. He has to keep doing so many things a lot faster than he's able to write about them, even when he's doing nothing more than writing about all the things he's supposed to be doing. That's why he needs all the help he can get. Bruce, have you ever thought of working in government?"

Gold learned in that instant what a heart felt like when it skipped a beat. "No," he answered steadily. "Should I?"

"It's fun, Bruce. There are lots of parties and you get lots of girls. Even actresses."

"What kind of job would I have?"

"That's difficult to say now. I'll have to ask around. But you've got the right educational background and a gift for punchy phrases I think we can use. I can't promise anything this second. But I'm sure it would be something very, very big, if you'll say you'd consider it."

"I would consider it," Gold disclosed, after a breathless pause.

"Then I'll sound out sentiment diplomatically. I'm sure it will be favorable. I keep running into Andrea Biddle Conover down here. Remember her?"

"Of course," Gold replied.

"I thought you would. She had a crush on you that year at the Foundation."

"She didn't."

"Sure, she did. Still does. I always felt there might be something between you."

"There wasn't," Gold insisted, with regret. "She never said anything."

"She was too shy."

"I always liked her."

"She always asks about you."

"How is she?"

"As nice as ever. Tall, pretty, cheerful, smart. And very, very rich, with those fine, strong, beautiful teeth."

Gold pursed his lips and whistled silently. "Give her," he said, "my best. Tell her I asked about her."

"I will," said Ralph. "Are you still married to Belle?"

"Of course."

"In that case, give her my love."

"I will. And you say hello to Sally."

Ralph said, "Sally who?"

"Your wife," said Gold. "Aren't you married to Sally?"

"Oh, heavens, no," Ralph replied. "I've been married to Ellie ever since my divorce from Kelly. There was that legal problem over my annulment from Norah, but Nellie, thank the Lord—"

"Ralph, wait, for Chrissakes!" It was in self-defense that Gold protested. "You're boggling my mind."

"What was that?" Ralph asked in surprise.

"You're boggling my mind."

"Bruce, that's a good phrase," Ralph cried crisply. "Damned good. I don't think I've ever heard boggle used with an animate subject before. I'll bet all of us down here can start getting mileage out of that one right away. That is, of course, if you don't mind letting us have it."

"Ralph—"

"Excuse me a minute, Bruce. I want to get it down exactly the way you said it. How did it go?"

"You're boggling my mind."

"I preferred it the first way."

"That *was* the first way."

"I guess it's good enough." Ralph sounded disappointed. "Now what was it you wanted to say to me?"

"Ralph, you're boggling my mind."

"That's the way!" Ralph exclaimed.

"It's the same way!" Gold retorted.

"You're right, Bruce. I'm glad we didn't lose it. How, Bruce? How am I boggling your mind?"

"With your Nellies and your Kellys and your Norahs and your Ellies. I thought you and Sally were so right for each other."

"We were," Ralph answered, sounding puzzled.

"Wasn't the marriage working?"

"Oh, yes." Ralph was emphatic. "We had a perfect marriage."

"Then why did you get a divorce?"

"Well, Bruce, to put it plainly, I couldn't see much point in tying myself down to a middle-aged woman with four children, even though the woman was my wife and the children were my own. Can you?"

Seldom had Gold come to a conclusion so swiftly.

"Be sure to tell Andrea Conover I was thrilled to hear about her," he said. "And that I hope we'll bump into each other soon."

"I'll get back to you quickly."

"Please."

Gold's pulse raced with excitement. He had visions. He knew he was ten times more intelligent than Ralph and could go one thousand times farther in government if ever he got a foot in. And if Ralph could get married to Ellie after his divorce from Kelly after that trouble over the annulment from Norah or Nellie, there was no reason in the world he must stay married to Belle.

Gold had just captured this point in his deliberations when his telephone rang again.

"It looks good, Bruce," Ralph declared happily. Not more than five minutes had passed, and Gold could picture Ralph sounding out sentiment diplomatically with a shout down a corridor. Except that Ralph was too well-bred to shout. "You're really boggling my mind the way you're boggling everyone's mind with those phrases of yours. First 'contemporary universal constituency' and now this 'you're boggling my mind.' I tried it out on a couple of people and it boggled their minds. We all feel it would be a good idea to start using you here as quickly as possible if we decide we want to use you at all."

"What kind of job would I have?"

"Any one you want," Ralph replied, "depending on what's open at the time we take you on. We have lots of turnover."

"Oh, come on, Ralph," Gold disagreed pleasantly. "You can't mean that."

Ralph seemed faintly puzzled again. "Why not?"

"A Senator?"

"That's elective."

"An ambassador?"

"Not right away. At the start, we'll want you in Washington. You see, Bruce, we have a very big need for college professors, and we can't go back to Harvard after all *they've* done. The country wouldn't stand for it."

"How's Columbia?"

"Still clean. I don't think anyone here associates Columbia with anything intellectual. And Brooklyn, of course, is perfect."

"What would I have to do?"

"Anything you want, as long as it's everything we tell you to say and do in support of our policies, whether you agree with them or not. You'll have complete freedom."

Gold was confused. He said delicately, "I can't be bought, Ralph."

"We wouldn't want you if you could be, Bruce," Ralph responded. "This President doesn't want yes-men. What we want are independent men of integrity who will agree with all our decisions after we make them. You'll be entirely on your own."

"I think I might fit in," Gold decided.

"I'm glad. Gosh, it will be good being together again, Bruce, won't it? Remember all those great times we used to have?" Gold could remember no great times with Ralph. "We'll want to move ahead with this as speedily as possible, although we'll have to go slowly. At the moment, there's nothing to be done."

"I'll need some time anyway," Gold volunteered obligingly. "I'll have to prepare for a leave of absence."

"Of course. But don't say anything about it yet. We'll want to build this up into an important public announcement, although we'll have to be completely secret." Gold listened for some signal of jocularity in Ralph's voice. He listened in vain. "If the appointment we give you is unpopular," Ralph went on in the same informative way, "we'll start getting criticism about it even before we announce it. If the appointment is popular, we'll run right into tremendous opposition from the other party and from our own left, right, and center. That's why it's good you're a Jew."

That word *Jew* fell with a crash upon Gold's senses. "Why, Ralph?" he managed to say. "Why is it good to have someone . . . who is Jewish?"

"That will make it easier at both ends, Bruce," Ralph explained with no change of tone. "Jews are popular now and people don't like to object to them. And a Jew is always good to get rid of whenever the right wing wants us to."

Gold said nonchalantly, "You're being rather blunt about that, Ralph, aren't you?"

"Well, Bruce, it's better than adopting their policies, isn't it?" Ralph breezed on innocently, missing the point of Gold's objection. "And that's the time we can make you an ambassador, if there's a good European country open that needs one. Or we can make you head of NATO if you'd like."

"Ralph, are you serious? Could I really be head of NATO?"

"I don't see why not."

"I have no military experience."

"I really don't think that matters, Bruce. Don't forget, there are other countries in NATO. I'm sure they have people who know about things like that."

Gold saw no profit in disagreement. "I think I'd rather be an ambassador," he decided.

"Whatever you choose. But that's looking far ahead. I'll get back to you immediately, Bruce, although it might take time. Just try not to think about it. Don't phone me here. They don't like personal calls."

Five days passed during which Gold found it impossible to think of anything else. At the start of the second week, an evil thought entered Gold's mind and refused to depart, a perversive blot of caustic wisdom first obtained by him as a sullen insult from a student to whom he had given a failing grade the semester before.

"Don't trust Whitey."

THE MORE Gold speculated on his conversation with Ralph, the more he inclined toward the ambassadorship in preference to command of NATO. Military life did not appeal to him: he was not comfortable near explosives. And military prestige was of little weight outside the camping grounds. Neither position, he was forced to remind himself, was a probability. Ralph had guaranteed nothing. Belle had declared stoutly that she would not move to Washington with him if he took a job there, and he was relying on her to keep her word.

An ambassadorship, though, would be lovely, he fancied in periods of luxurious reverie that reappeared between his longer spells of uneventful disappointment. He could easily imagine himself in extravagant quarters in Kensington, Mayfair, or Belgravia, married now not to Belle but to some languorous, exquisite, young blond Englishwoman of noblest birth. She was a floating seraph of ageless and ethereal beauty who brought him tea with sugar cubes on a tray. She was tall and gracefully round-shouldered, had thin limbs, pale, pearly skin, and narrow violet-blue eyes of fascinating depth and brightness, and she adored him. He, for his part, could take her or leave her alone. She never spoke. She wasn't Jewish. They had separate bedrooms with many sitting rooms and dressing rooms in between. He wore elegant silk dressing gowns all day long. His breakfast was brought to him in bed.

When a second week went by without word from Ralph, Gold got to work on the book he owed Pomoroy and the digest of that book he owed Lieberman. He wondered which to do first.

His mother was dead and he could write about her: a young woman, a girl, really, with Sid, who was just a child, and Rose, who was even younger, emigrating from an inhospitable Russian countryside with that young cockalorum of a husband—good God, was he that way even then?—to live in this alien land and die before she was fifty. He had forgotten that Rose was born in Europe too. His mother had never learned English well enough to read it or to understand much when the children were talking to each other. He recalled that long period when her neck was swaddled in odorous bandages—was it goiter? He would have to ask. And he was ashamed to be seen with her in the street. Now, people were emigrating north from Puerto Rico, Haiti, and Jamaica. Blacks had moved down from Harlem and were overflowing into groups interloping from the South and West, and Gold felt besieged and invaded, his safety eroding, his position marginal and impermanent.

His marriage to Belle was just about dead, and he could abstract from that—if he ever learned what those words meant. He did not know what was intended when people complained their marriage was dead or that it was no longer a real marriage. Were marriages ever different? Or was it that people and their surroundings had changed, and that every change had been for the worse? Gold had a thought for another article. On a slip of paper he printed:

EVERY CHANGE IS FOR THE WORSE
by
BRUCE GOLD

He pinned the slip to the bulletin board above the desk in his studio and began making notes for that work too while he waited to hear from Ralph.

Every Change Is for the Worse

THEY had all come together some thirty years earlier at Columbia University in New York, Ralph arriving late with an undergraduate degree from Princeton, Pomoroy departing early without his doctorate after completing his course work and passing his oral examinations. Appraising his talents and wants realistically, Pomoroy had wisely terminated all thought of producing a dissertation on a subject of no authentic appeal, and gone off to find the best job he could. He began as an editorial assistant with a small textbook firm. Now he was executive editor with a larger, general publishing company, where he would likely prosper and remain.

Pomoroy was the editor Lieberman sped to whenever he had still another soiled clump of hastily written pages he felt certain would make an important book, and Pomoroy was the editor who always spurned him first. Lieberman had started one novel, three autobiographies, and several searching studies of current problems he believed indispensable to people charged with solving them. Gold went to Pomoroy only when his chances were better than elsewhere. Pomoroy was no fool.

Harris Rosenblatt, another Jewish acquaintance of the period, was a plodding, unimaginative dumbbell who had come to college from a private school in Manhattan that required students to wear blazers and to have their hair cut and combed trimly and their necks and ears washed. By steadfast drudgery, Harris Rosenblatt had made it through Columbia College with honors and then had fled from graduate work in less than a year before the lengthening threat of unavoidable failure. He married shortly afterward and went to work in some arcane department of an investment house controlled by his wife's family—he himself was incapable of describing what that department did. There he excelled, at work he did not understand and whose meaning he could not apprehend, and he was now a respected adviser to Presidents on national fiscal matters, to whom he always impartially made the same terse recommendation: "Balance the budget." And for these few words, Harris Rosenblatt was regarded in elite business and social circles with something approaching veneration.

Harris Rosenblatt had found, in Pomoroy's acerbic depiction, his ideal habitat, the only one, in Darwinian terms, in which he was fit to survive: three pounds of human brain mass dumped immovably on an area of financial specialization too minute to be defined, in a cranny too obscure to admit any irritating rays of light. It was Harris Rosenblatt, Gold suspected, who had arranged for Lieberman's invitation to the White House at the time of the Vietnam war. Not many people other than the President allowed Lieberman into their homes for dinner. If the White House was going to be so unparticular, Lieberman was not the person to dismiss the opportunity.

"Listen," he had boasted once to Pomoroy and Gold with his crude and exultant laugh, "I got invited to the White House for dinner once, just for supporting a war. I would support a war every day in the week if I knew I could eat at the White House again." And then was thrown into confusion as both Pomoroy and Gold shrank from him with looks of undisguised abhorrence. Gold had known Lieberman since childhood and had never liked him. It was an unfading source of pleasure now to be able to say, "You know, truthfully, Maxwell, I never really liked you."

In high school, Lieberman had demanded of everyone that he be called Maxwell. Now that the name had grown unbearable to him, Gold took relish in using it, especially in the company of other people who knew him only by his auctorial identity, M. G. Lieberman, and to whom the name Maxwell came as a source of delight. Not till college had Lieberman adopted the affectation of using just the initials of his given names on everything he wrote, even homework. In conversation and on radio talk shows to which he was occasionally invited he asked to be addressed by his middle name, Gordon, or by the happy-go-lucky sobriquet with which he had festooned himself when he was already past forty-five, the nickname Skip.

"Skip," Pomoroy repeated sourly, as though discovering a wedge of lemon between his teeth. "Why not Curly?"

"My hair isn't really curly."

"And your name isn't Skip," Pomoroy had replied.

"It's my nickname."

"No, it isn't. People don't *give* themselves nicknames, Lieberman. They inspire them in others. Whatever you are now, Lieberman, or ever hope to be—please don't interrupt me, you baldy, fatheaded buffoon, I have spied your name often at testimonial banquets at which fascists and anti-Semites were among the featured speakers—you are not now and never will be a Skip."

"It's what my friends used to call me," Lieberman pouted.

"No, it isn't." Gold did not look up from the turkey sandwich he was eating. "You never had a nickname. I did, but you didn't. They called me Four-Eyes for a while. They called you Fatso, but that was a description. And you didn't have any friends. I didn't have any either. But I had more than you."

"I was your friend."

"I didn't want you. I only used you when nobody better would play with me."

Lieberman and Gold had lived in Coney Island across the street from each other in walk-up apartment houses near Surf Avenue, and Gold had never cared any more for Lieberman than others had cared for Gold.

Gold spent much of his childhood on the fringe of exile. When sides were chosen for any kind of game, Gold would not know until the captains came down to the dregs if he would be picked at all; when he was, he was so grateful he could have wept. On Saturday afternoons when everyone went to the movies in groups, he was never confident he would be asked by any. At no single time in the first fifteen years of his life would he have hesitated even one second if given the chance to exchange his precocious intelligence for friendships with such local ne'er-do-wells or social leaders as Spotty Weinrock or Fishy Siegel. Fishy's older brother Sheiky, an illegal beach peddler of ice cream in summer and street vendor of costume jewelry in the winter, was now the owner of millions of dollars in computer and reinsurance stocks and the controller of perhaps many millions more in real-estate syndicates and mutual funds.

Go figure *him*.

It was mainly because of Rose's or Esther's scrupulous devotion that Gold's myopic astigmatism was discovered early, and Gold was probably the first his age in the neighborhood to wear eyeglasses. Even Sid and Muriel called him Four-Eyes. Perhaps Gold was able to get top grades in elementary school because he was the only one who could see.

Lieberman was more ambitious from the start. By the time he was eight, he was already given to chesty boasting.

"When I grow up," he announced to Gold in the third or fourth grade, "I'm gonna be fat. I'll be the fattest guy in the whole world."

That was one of the earliest of Lieberman's goals, to be fat. In every class, he seized command of all positions open, from blackboard and wastebasket monitor to class messenger, and, ultimately, the capstone of this phase of his career, chief of the safety patrol. Lieberman, rolling with a cockier swagger whenever he wore his metal badge, set records for reporting students for jaywalking until Fishy Siegel threatened to break his head if he didn't stop. Spotty Weinrock said he would do the same. Lieberman cried. That afternoon he resigned from the safety patrol.

Lieberman ate and talked unceasingly. By the time he was nine, he never hesitated to dispute socialism, fascism, and the labor movement with old European Jews on the Coney Island boardwalk. His characteristic argument was that they did not know what they were talking about.

It probably was not true, as Pomoroy had remarked, that given the option, Lieberman would have elected to be born prematurely just to get a headstart. But it was probably not entirely false. Lieberman still could not keep his hands off food, his own or others', even though he no longer wanted to be fat. He had never held any elective office in school because he could not find anyone to nominate him, second him, or vote for him.

"I don't care," Lieberman proclaimed to Gold in the fifth or sixth grade, holding back tears. "When I grow up, I'll be a fat cabinet officer. I'll be the first Jewish Secretary of State. I bet I'll even get to meet the President."

Then he moved away from Coney Island to the bordering, more elegant neighborhood of Brighton Beach. By the time Gold entered Abraham Lincoln High School, Lieberman was already there as a sophomore, having vaulted ahead one school year somehow, and was making a name for himself as an outstanding student and a *putz*. He was on the staff of the literary magazine and the school newspaper. By his junior year, Lieberman took uncontested control of both. He was active in political matters and co-captain of the debating team, which always lost.

Gold avoided him. Shunning the literary magazine in high school because of Lieberman, Gold mailed ten of his short poems to *The Saturday Review of Literature*. Six came back with rejection slips and four were accepted, at a price of ten dollars each. Lieberman turned blue. He swore he would never forgive Gold for acting alone instead of sharing his initiative. To teach Gold his place, Lieberman mailed twenty-five of *his* poems to *The Saturday Review of Literature*. Thirty-nine came back.

"What do I care?" Lieberman sneered. "When I grow up I'm gonna be rich. I'll be more famous than anyone. I'm gonna marry a rich and famous heiress. I'll never lose my hair. I'll wear lots of rings. I'll go into politics and win. I'll be a mayor, a senator, and the governor of all New York. I'll be a big millionaire. When I grow up," he vowed, "I'm gonna fuck a girl."

Instead, he went to college.

He was still fat. His hair was no longer thick. Everything he ate he still ate with both fists. He gorged himself from other people's plates.

Pomoroy was there from a college-educated family in Massachusetts, and Harris Rosenblatt from his private school in Manhattan and a strict, proud German-Jewish family on Riverside Drive. In graduate school Ralph Newsome, from a wealthy family in Michigan, joined the group by way of Princeton University.

It was inevitable that Lieberman would make a shambles of each class. He interrupted with contrary views and overblown objections and shouted answers to every question asked. Students and faculty learned to yield him a wide berth rather than contend with him. Experienced professors blanched when he signed up for their courses, and mature students, including tough marines from Iwo Jima and army veterans of the Battle of the Bulge, calmly rearranged their programs when they found him in class on the first day of term. Many switched to other fields of study. For many of the most illustrious scholars and teachers on the faculty, Lieberman was precisely the factor needed to bring them to decisions perhaps long in the balance—divorce, murder, mental breakdown, early retirement, or changes to different occupations or new teaching positions at other universities. And finally, when Lieberman, with Gold and Ralph Newsome, had completed all the requirements for his doctorate, he surveyed with disgruntlement the campus from the steps of Low Library and complained, "You know, this isn't such a first-rate university any more, is it? We should have gone to Yale."

He chose to forget that all had been rejected by Yale. All but Ralph, who had been accepted everywhere. Ralph had chosen Columbia because he wanted to live in New York for a while, and because he had guessed that he would be able to find someone like Gold who would make his work there easier.

"The truth is," Pomoroy had observed in customary melancholy the last time the three had lunch together, "that none of us have really accomplished very much."

And Lieberman, vowing he would never forgive him for saying that, began another autobiography.

THE PITY lay, Gold reflected on the indoor track at the Y after completing the first of his nine sets of eight laps without dropping dead, in their having wanted to achieve some kind of glorious success almost from the moment of birth. Goals, he muttered as he pounded along steadily on the short oval course while the pain

departed from his chest and settled and throbbed in his dangling
kidneys, we ain't got any real ones. Still, it's better to have shit to
shoot at than nothing. Gold held to the superstitious belief that if
he could survive the first eight laps without some fatal bursting of
the blood, he would make it to the end with the Angel of Death still
behind, a loser again. The track was almost empty, which pleased
him. It was there on the track while running his grueling three
miles several days a week that many of Gold's best thoughts came
to him, and there also that he discharged, for a time, the stewing
hostility and mordant self-pity that pooled like poison almost daily
in his soul. Envy would dissolve with exertion into euphoria by the
time he had showered and dressed and was limping away. There is
no disappointment so numbing, he brooded as he entered the last
lap of his first mile and felt the muscles of his calves cramp, as
someone no better than you achieving more. Forty-eight laps to
go. There would be no heartburn today. Soon the muscles of his
calves would feel fine, as his kidneys now did, and the tendons of
both ankles would whine with each footfall. He could look forward
next to a strain in his left groin and then to a vertical shaft of pain
on his right side that was rooted in his appendix and rose through
his liver, chest, and shoulder blade to his collarbone and neck.
Each wound in the sequence could register only singly. Another
thought that returned often when he jogged was that it was a fucking boring way to spend time. Gold had discovered, since starting
to exercise strenuously several years before, that he was able to
make love with greater vitality, stamina, and self-control than formerly, and with much less pleasure. He also found he had less time
for it and was often in too much physical torture and debilitation
afterward to want to. He lusted more desirously for a nap. Gold no
longer suffered from early-morning lower backache. Now he had it
all day long.

For Gold, Lieberman, and Pomoroy, there had been sound reason for their expectations. But the real stars had sprung from other
quarters, and before they knew it, they had been left behind. All
had gotten what they wanted, and felt dissatisfied. Lieberman had
wanted to edit a small intellectual publication, and he did. Gold
hoped to obtain a decent teaching post in New York and gain some

stature as a writer, and he had. Pomoroy wanted to be a book editor, and he was. All were successful, and felt like failures.

Gold no longer pretended to understand the nature of success. Instead, he pretended not to. He knew the components that were necessary:

None.

Or maybe one:

Dumb luck.

Harris Rosenblatt, with his inanimate powers of concentration and no ability at thought, was now a name to be reckoned with; he was a member of Protestant clubs that admitted no Jews, and a trustee of Jewish clubs that admitted only Germans. "Balance the budget," appeared to be the longest, and perhaps only, recommendation he could put together. While Sheiky from Neptune Avenue, truant, high-school dropout, and raffish summer ice-cream peddler, had millions and had jousted with Nelson Rockefeller at a formal dinner for fat cats when the latter was campaigning for governor of New York.

"Hiya, fella," said Nelson Rockefeller to Sheiky from Neptune Avenue. "I will be grateful for your support."

"What's in it for me?" asked Sheiky. He kept his hands in the pockets of his pants. Never in his life would Sheiky from Neptune Avenue offer an unguarded greeting to anyone or shake the hand of a person who might want something from him.

Rockefeller drew back in bewilderment.

"Good government," an eager aide with a florid face interjected quickly.

"Who needs it?" Sheiky said, grinning amiably. "I'm doing just fine with the kind we've got."

Sid, who related that episode often, was another anomaly in the freakish catalogue of success. Silent and complicated in the home when young, low-keyed in ambition, and of only average attainments in school, Sid had somehow managed to acquire and improve certain patents for commercial laundry equipment after returning from the army in 1945. Ideas for other machines followed, then a company for processing fabrics. Now he had plenty of money and dispensed it more liberally than Harriet liked.

Earlier he had worked harder, half days after school and full time in summer as a laborer at the Brighton Laundry when the red vans were still drawn by horses. Sid was afraid of the horses. After graduating from high school he stayed as an assistant to a supervisor of some kind, preferring anything to working in the tailor shop his father owned off and on in those hazardous years following 1929. Mixed in somewhere in his history was the summer he had run away from home. Sundays, when he could, and even Saturday nights, he worked in the checkroom at catered affairs at a banquet hall. He did not like these weekend jobs or the rented tuxedo he had to wear, but this was the Great Depression. His father's income was uncertain, his occupations erratic. Rose and Esther sought work in Woolworth's after school as soon as each was old enough, and at the hot-dog and custard stands on the boardwalk in summer. All were pressed into duty to deliver the suits and dresses and obtain payment in cash. No one's credit was good.

Julius Gold was always selling and returning to the same tailor shop, on the sidewalk level of the apartment house in which they lived. They had an Atwater-Kent radio in the living room, and they were one of the first families on the block with a telephone—in the store. They were also the only family with as many as seven children. With unerring intuition, he always sold to incompetents or invalids, and the shop was always available to him for just the rent whenever his newest escapade into the fashionable world of trade and manufacturing had again gone bust. Gold's mother was a good dressmaker and seamstress and would work downstairs in the store when she was not shopping for meals or tending the house. The tailor shop was a bustling extension of the apartment upstairs; sandwiches would be devoured with milk by Rose, Esther, Ida, and Muriel during the lunch recess at school or with giant bottles of flavored soda pop from the candy store across the street. Gold could remember whole mornings and afternoons idled away on the bathroom-tiled floor, with his sister Joannie just outside the plate-glass window in a baby carriage for as long as the sunlight fell there, his mother whizzing away at the Singer sewing machine or stitching by hand with a thimbled finger, while his father hummed or sang bouncy dance tunes as he darted about in disorder or

shouted horrible imprecations at the presser. Gold had hazy re-
membrances of a catastrophic spell long before World War II when
his father abruptly divined himself a singer of extraordinary talents
and sought to enter singing contests and perform on radio amateur
hours. The older members of the family seemed in panic and
shock. They were stunned and mortified again by another family
disgrace after the war, this time Gold too, when they discovered
that Joannie, with a friend, was working in a sleazy purple night-
gown at one of the stalls in the amusement area near the train stop,
lying in bed doing nothing while patrons threw baseballs at a
bull's-eye that would tumble her out. There was sickly silence in
the house for weeks. She was just eighteen. And then she was gone
with the friend, to enter beauty pageants, work for entertainment
directors at resort hotels, and then to Florida, California, and even
Cuba, in search of a Hollywood career as an actress, or as a dancer
or model. By then, his mother too was gone. By the time of the
war, in 1942, she had been ailing for several years, and the tailor
shop was closed. His father, with partners, was doing subcon-
tracted defense work in a small loft on Canal Street, drilling holes
through templets for small parts of Bendix airplane turrets that Sid,
an enlisted man in the Army Air Force, was helping maintain in
North Africa. His father wanted to expand rapidly, build the whole
turrets—"What do we need *them* for?"—and was quarreling fe-
rociously with his partners. Rose was married to Max, and she and
Esther had real jobs, Rose the job she never would change. Ida
was in college and Muriel and Gold in high school. Gold's father,
Gold judged sourly later, was probably the only person in the country doing defense work and losing money.

Sid made sergeant as an armorer, loading bombs and belted ammunition into planes, servicing weapons. He was fascinated with
this first contact with cams, springs, sears, solenoid switches, and
hydraulics. He was inspired by the technology of the .50-caliber
machine gun. From the machine gun had come his reposeful laundry machines.

"What minds!" Sid mused now on the patio of his house in
Great Neck. "To invent machines. A piece of metal doing one
thing that can make another piece of metal do something else. I

swear to God if not for those machine guns I never would have thought of that laundry equipment.''

"Who helped you, Sid?'' reminded Gold's father, in a bid for praise.

"You, Pop. But Sheiky from Neptune Avenue put in the money. And Kopotkin with the ice skates did most of the work. He had his own machine shop after the war.''

"You trusted them, you dope?'' said Julius Gold. "How'd you know they wouldn't steal from you?''

Sid handled the question with benevolence. "I just didn't think about that. Maybe friends didn't steal from each other then. Pop,'' Sid finally found nerve enough to suggest in a voice that was delicate and kind, "I think you ought to buy a condominium.''

The old man tensed. "I don't stay in Florida that much.''

"You could rent it out when you're here, and probably get back all your costs.''

The old man took a long puff on his cigar. "You'll explain to me next weekend, when you come to us for lunch. You come too,'' he said to Gold.

"It will all work out fine,'' Sid murmured with a smile, crossing his hands over his middle with a deep sigh and sinking back further in his recliner.

But Gold wasn't fooled by Sid's air of contentment, and was positive there abided in Sid still, like a hole, the retrospective regret that he had missed out on college. But thoughts of a college education were simply not in the cards for high-school graduates of Sid's time in that place. The most one might reach toward, like Rose's Max, was an excellent score on a Civil Service examination. Max had been second best in the state on a test for the Post Office Department. His picture was in the Brooklyn section of the *Sunday News*. He had worked in a post office ever since.

The sole exception in the neighborhood was crazy Murshie Weinrock, who plodded away in night classes in college for four, five, six years, until World War II. Then the army moved him to Swarthmore College into one of those opulent training programs for college students for the remainder of his senior year and then to the Harvard Medical School. Again, dumb luck. If not for Adolf

Hitler he might still be sweeping trimmings in his uncle's gritty millinery factory. Today he was an internist in Manhattan with a practice growing almost faster than his ability to handle it. Dr. Murray Weinrock always made room for old friends.

Gold had been to him in the middle of the week. Skinny Murshie Weinrock was now an overweight, haggard chain smoker with the troubled look of somebody endlessly overworked. With Gold, he exercised a fitful sense of humor that Gold could only describe as weird, and perhaps depraved.

"You sure look lousy."

Gold, always in low spirits at his yearly checkup, said, "Thanks, Mursh. So do you."

"How do you feel?" asked Mursh Weinrock urgently, in the middle of the examination. "Right now?"

"Awful. You've got that thing up my ass."

"How long have you had that cough?"

"Since you stabbed that tongue depressor down on my tongue."

In the room with the electrocardiograph, Lucille, the large, handsome, dignified, unsmiling black nurse Gold had known for years, bent toward him with a baleful glare and said, "I know you been fucking the doctor's wife. Lie still, please. How you expect that motherfucking machine to do what it's s'posed to?" Gold felt all strength drain from him. Lucille was an educated technician with enunciation superior to his own. "Next time I X-ray your chest," she warned, "I'm gonna aim that machine right at your balls. Didn't I ask you to please lie still? Next time you pee in a bottle I'm gonna put poison in without telling anybody and the doctor going to cut both your kidneys out."

"Uh-oh, this might be serious," Mursh Weinrock said in his office with an ominous start when he studied the waves on the electrocardiogram. "It looks to me like you've been fucking my wife."

"How *is* Mildred?" Gold asked wryly. "You saw my father last week."

"He told me I was doing everything wrong."

"How's his lungs?"

"Clear as a whistle and as good as gold. He's got the descending bowel of a healthy adolescent. You could eat your food off it."

"I could throw you out the window for a remark like that," said Gold. "Shouldn't he be in a warmer climate?"

"Only when he's cold. The old man is fine. He's got arthritis of the hip and foot and a definite hardening of the arteries, and that will keep him feeling miserable much of the time."

"Why don't you fucks find a cure for that already?" Gold grumbled.

"Biology doesn't want us to. Nature abhors old age."

"He still starts off the day with a herring and baked potato. And some Greek olives."

"So?"

"Is that good for him?"

"When it isn't, he'll know it before we do. Look, Bruce, your father's past eighty. How much difference will it make if we feed him baby food? Let's get back to you. Venereal disease . . . yet?"

"You're the last one I'd tell."

"Patient denies venereal disease."

"You rig this for me, don't you?" Gold charged.

"Rig what?"

"You know fucking well what I mean. You and Lucille certainly don't handle all those other people out there this way, do you?"

"Which way?"

"You're the perfect anodyne for somebody with tension."

"Tension?"

"I may be changing jobs soon, for a big one in government. That has to remain secret."

"Who cares?"

"Don't coddle me."

"See my lazy kid brother much?" Gold shook his head in reply to this question about Spotty Weinrock. "I don't think Spotty's done one minute's hard work in his whole life."

"Nah, Mursh," Gold reminded. "Remember how he got his nickname, working for my loony father—for just about a day and a half, now that you mention it—taking stains out of clothes in the old man's tailor shop."

"His nickname was Speed at home, and he got it from my mother as a sarcasm. It was the first word of English she learned. 'Spit' is what she used to call him. Goddamn it. Even when he was sixteen he still pretended he didn't know how to put his socks on. One or the other of us would have to rush in and finish dressing him so he could go to high school. Then—'' Dr. Murray Weinrock waved a forefinger in the air with the apocalyptic vengeance of a Biblical prophet—''then I knew how Cain must have felt about Abel, and my sympathies shifted. If I had the thighbone of a bullock handy, I would have walloped him dead a hundred times. I hate sloth. Let's get serious now. Your weight is good and your heart and blood pressure are fine. Sid could lose some weight and use some exercise, but so could I.''

''What about my fatigue?''

''Too much sex life. I want you to stop fucking my wife.''

''There are nights I can't resist.''

''Get yourself a cute young girl instead.''

Gold's differing view was that most women did not even learn to begin enjoying sex until they were almost thirty, but this was another valuable finding he could not publish while he was still teaching, while he was still married, and while his twelve-year-old daughter was still under thirty.

Even without a business education, Sid understood *merger* better than Gold ever would. With hardly a pause for breath, Sid had taken the old man's final business enterprise, a wobbling leather-products factory on the brink of collapse, submerged it forever in an overlapping mist of other business entities, and conjured up magically an asset sufficiently grand to enable their father to retire with a fixed yearly income and a blazing self-respect that was inflated and inimitable. He displayed like an aura the lordly demeanor of a man who not only had dined on success throughout his lifetime but also had been born into it. Sid fed extra money to him, as did most of the others. Gold had chipped in for the good used car in which Gussie drove them about in Florida. To Sid, Julius gave all credit.

''Sid fixed it so I would first get my unemployment insurance, then my Social Security.''

''If he'd worked a little bit harder,'' Gold quipped meanly, ''he could have had you on welfare.''

When Gold was a child, Sid was already working summers,

weekends, and weekday afternoons. When Gold was in high school, Sid was overseas in the army. And the year Gold entered college, Sid was discharged from the service, eligible for higher education under the G.I. Bill of Rights, but already thirty-one. Conceivably they might have begun as freshmen together, and Gold could have cut him to ribbons in the hectic rivalry of classroom exhibitionism. Gold was alert to incongruities: Sid, who had sacrificed, was exempt from complaints, while Gold, the beneficiary, teemed with them. Gold was not sure of many things, but he was definite about one: for every successful person he knew, he could name at least two others of greater ability, better character, and higher intelligence who, by comparison, had failed.

And Gold knew something else: he was in a predicament, confronted, so to speak, with a crisis of conscience that could not much longer be concealed. All his words had a starkly humanitarian cast; yet he no longer liked people.

He was losing his taste for mankind. There was not much he did like. He liked goods, money, honors. He missed capital punishment, but did not feel he could say so. Gold had a growing list of principles, causes, methods, and ideals in which he no longer believed; and near the top it contained a swelling subdivision of freedoms that included such sacrosanct issues as academic freedom, sexual freedom, and even political freedom. Alternatives were hellish. By no stretch of the imagination could he feel that *this* was what the Founding Fathers had in mind. Either Gold had grown more conservative or civilization had grown progressively worse.

Or both.

Certainly, nothing proceeded according to desire. In the long run, failure was the only thing that worked predictably. All else was accidental. Good intentions had miscarried, and bad ones had not improved.

The American economic system was barbarous, resulting, naturally, in barbarianism and entrenched imbecility on all levels of the culture. Technology and finance mass-produced poverty at increasing speed, the sole manufactured item in the whole industrial inventory that had not once suffered a slackening in rate of growth in the last fifty-five years, not in acreage or in populations. Communism was a drab, gray, wintry prison at the end of a cul-de-sac from which no turning back was imaginable. And this was with a revolution that had succeeded. What else was there? Imperialism, that faithful ogre? The receding of colonial imperialism had not brought peace, riches, or liberty to the emancipated peoples; instead, there were oppressions, corruption, and warfare, and a truculent majority in the United Nations that was now not only anti-American, but anti-Americans like Gold. *Vus nuch?*

Medicaid?

Gold had another list.

A symbiotic system of new criminal classes; and medical science had created something infinitely worse, a long life span, with a larger and larger number of old people who were unneeded by society, had nothing to do, and were not revered. How much longer would grown children hope their parents going into surgery would come out alive? What would Gold himself really feel the next time his father had an operation? He knew about Sid and Rose and Esther, but he would not bet on himself or vouch for Muriel, or even Ida. Or Joannie, an alien mystery to him now, a distant cipher whom he understood best and knew least.

The labor movement had come to its end in garbage strikes and gigantic pension funds invested by banks for profit. There seemed no plausible connection between cause and effect, or ends and means. History was a trash bag of random coincidences torn open in a wind. Surely, Watt with his steam engine, Faraday with his electric motor, and Edison with his incandescent light bulb did not have it as their goal to contribute to a fuel shortage someday that would place their countries at the mercy of Arab oil.

Results attained were unrelated to objectives envisioned.

Once, ten or fifteen years earlier, Gold had given testimony in defense of novels by Henry Miller and William Burroughs against charges of obscenity; now there were massage parlors and pornographic movies everywhere and newspapers and magazines on display that *were* obscene. The health club in the basement of the apartment house in which he had his studio had converted gradually into an elegant massage parlor; and his annual membership had been rudely terminated.

And when he'd marched in Selma, Alabama, with Martin Luther King and campaigned so loyally against all forms of racial segregation, the thought never once crossed his mind that a day might come when his own neighborhood would alter for the worse and his own children be sent to costly private schools to evade the physical dangers of busing and integration and the decay in the quality of education offered by the public ones. They were not accustomed to being a white minority.

Gold never doubted that racial discrimination was atrocious, unjust, and despicably cruel and degrading. But he knew in his heart that he much preferred it the old way, when he was safer. Things were much better for him when they had been much worse. It was a fact, one that did not touch on the virtue of the situation, but a fact nonetheless, that many people like himself who had worked and argued for the annihiliation of Jim Crow were those who would be least inconvenienced when they succeeded. Gold himself lived in a building with a doorman, and Negroes were not numerous in places he went to for the summer. Had they been, he would have sought new ones. When he came to realize this, he realized also that he was not just a liar but a hypocrite. A liar he knew he had been.

Ida's sixteen-year-old daughter was threatened with busing to a high school in a dangerous neighborhood in which she would be hated, where she could form no friendships, and in which she would be foolish to linger or wander, and only Ida's sneaking influence within the Board of Education might save her: but only by the substitution of somebody else's child. Gold was helpless to advise; but he did feel that no law should force this upon anyone. To the clear-cut issue of equality had been added the discordant elements of violence, crime, enmity, insurgence, and negation. With so much to be said on all sides of the question, he was sorry there was such a question. Solutions did not appear so readily as before, and things were not so clear as they once seemed. Things were just not working out as planned. Nothing ran smoothly. Nothing was succeeding as planned.

"Nothing Succeeds as Planned" was the title of Gold's article, and he was not surprised that Lieberman published it immediately after Gold had extracted the rest of the payment from him.

Ralph called him at home the day after Gold mailed him four copies.

"What did he say?" Gold demanded hungrily.

"Dina took the call," said Belle, just returned from her afternoon job as psychological counselor at a public elementary school.

"He was calling from the White House," Dina said.

"What did he say?"

"And he sounded so nice. I wanted to keep talking with him but he said he had something to do."

"Must I break your head? What did Ralph Newsome say?"

"He'll call back tonight. You can take it in my room if you like."

Gold took the call in his study with the door closed.

"God, Bruce," Ralph began, "I can't tell you how you're boggling our minds. If nothing succeeds as planned—and you really present such a strong argument—then the President has just the excuse he needs for not doing anything."

Gold, though surprised, was nonetheless pleased. "I hadn't looked at it in just that light," he confessed.

"We're having photocopies made. We want everyone in government to read it, although we've stamped it secret so nobody can. It would have been better, I suppose—" here Ralph's voice dropped in gentle reproach—"if you had shown it to us first and the President could have introduced the proposition as his own. But it might prove even more convincing now that he can cite you as an authority. Don't be surprised, Bruce, if he makes reference to it tomorrow. That should boggle minds."

"Has the President read it?" Gold, with boggling mind, could not restrain himself from inquiring.

"Oh, I'm positive he has," Ralph answered in his equable unhurried manner, "although I can't be sure."

"I would have shown it to him first, Ralph, but I didn't think anyone there but you would be interested."

"Bruce, I can't emphasize too strongly how high you rate with us. Especially after this. Nothing succeeds as planned—my God, what a concept. All of us want you working with us as soon as possible after the people above us decide whether they want you working here at all. Will you come?"

"As what?" said Gold, who knew already the answer was ardently yes.

"Oh, I don't know," said Ralph. "We probably could start you right in as a spokesman."

"A spokesman?" Gold was abruptly doubtful. It sounded like something athletic. "What's a spokesman?"

"Oh, Bruce, you must know. That's what I've been when I haven't been doing something else. A government spokesman, an unnamed spokesman, an administrative spokesman—it's a little bit like a source. Haven't you been reading about me at all?"

"Oh," said Gold quickly, defensively. "Now I know."

"I do get into the papers often. That's one of the nice things about being an unnamed spokesman. In a month or two, we can move you up."

"To what?"

"Well, if nothing else, to a senior official. As a senior official, you'd be free to hold background briefings any time you want, every time we schedule them. There's no limit to how high you will go. Bruce, this administration is made up almost entirely of people who pushed their way in."

Gold sensed an innuendo at which he perhaps ought to take offense. "I'm not very pushy, Ralph," he said softly.

"That will be a big plus for you, Bruce, that you're not pushy. Like so many others."

"So many other what, Ralph?"

"So many others who are pushy," Ralph went on with such uninterrupted affability that Gold concluded he had been unfairly sensitive. "Could you start immediately?"

"How much money would I make?"

"As much as you want, Bruce. No one comes to Washington to lose money."

Gold's next question carried a twinge of pathos. "Would I have to be unnamed?"

"Just at the start. After all, if we want to use you as an unnamed spokesman, it wouldn't do if everyone knew who you were, would it?"

"I guess not."

"Next week, why don't you come up here for a day to talk the whole thing over?"

"Up?" said Gold, feeling a bit disoriented.

"Oh, I'm sorry." Ralph laughed quietly. "I mean down. I've been talking to so many legislators from the South I can't help feeling that they are the bottom of the world, and we're the top."

"Say, Ralph, *that's* pretty good," Gold told him. "I'd like to use it in a piece, if you don't mind."

Ralph was flattered. "Of course not, Bruce. But don't use my name. You can imagine the trouble I'd be in if I were quoted."

"Don't worry," Gold reassured him. "I'd much rather present it as my own."

"On the other hand," said Ralph, sounding touchy, "I would like some credit for it. After all, I did think it up."

"But how could I do that?" Gold was confused. "How could I give you credit for it in print if you don't want your name mentioned?"

The answer arrived in a second. "Couldn't you say it came from a spokesman?"

"Sure. I could do that."

"Fine, Bruce. That will make all my families very proud. Andrea Conover blushed like a schoolgirl when I gave her your regards. She'd love to see you again."

"When should I come?" asked Gold.

"I'll phone you on Monday or Tuesday, or Wednesday, Thursday, or Friday. You know, Bruce," Ralph pointed out, "the only daughter of Pugh Biddle Conover is no one to sneeze at."

Gold had no intention of sneezing at her.

"WELL?" BELLE studied him closely when he returned to the kitchen to finish his dinner. Dina watched him too.

"I may have to go to Washington next week. They want my opinion about something."

Belle was no dope. "Is it about a job?"

"That was supposed to be secret," he admonished her again.

Belle shrugged. "Who will I tell? Your family?"

Dina's face glowed. "I would tell Leo Lieberman. I bet that would make his father jealous."

"Suppose it falls through," Gold asked, "and I get nothing?"

"I would tell them," said Belle, "that you turned it down."

"That I refused to compromise my integrity?"

"Sure," said Belle.

"Me too," vowed Dina.

"Yes," he admitted. "It's about a government job." Later that evening in their own room he said to Belle, "I thought you didn't want me to take a job in Washington. You said you wouldn't go."

Belle answered, "I'm not going."

"You won't change your mind?"

"Absolutely not."

They slept in separate beds, with a night table in between. He moved into hers.

IV
Nothing Succeeds as Planned

GOLD finished his martini, feeling so consumedly braced he was almost offended that the woman with whom he was lunching was his sister.

"Esther told me you're writing a book about Jews," said Joannie. Cold poached salmon would follow for Gold, with cucumber salad and green mayonnaise. They were lunching at the St. Regis and she would pay. She was a tall, suntanned woman with bright clothes, a springy figure, and hair expertly streaked.

"Esther?"

"She calls about every two weeks," said Joannie. "And has nothing to say. Jerry isn't happy about your book."

"Is that why you're in New York?"

She shook her head. "He wants to know why you can't write a book about something else."

"I ain't got that much choice, Joannie."

"Toni," she corrected.

"What's he worried about?"

"We spend a lot of time in California trying to get each other to forget we're Jewish. That's one of the reasons his family changed their name."

"To Fink?"

"It used to be Finkleman. Jerry gives a lot to both political parties. He thinks he's got a good chance now of being a judge."

"Jerry's not a lawyer, is he?"

"You don't have to be a lawyer out there to be a judge," Joannie explained. "At least that's what they tell him when they come for money."

"You belong to every temple in lower California," Gold derided.

"That's civic, not religious," she countered. "We make it a point never to pray." She picked without appetite at her small salad. "I saw Pop yesterday."

Gold was loath to ask. "How was he?"

"Quiet." Her smile was rueful. "He still thinks it's his fault I left home. He says you're all trying to make him buy a condominium in Florida so he'll stay there all year. I told him to do what Sid says."

"We're seeing him tomorrow," Gold said joylessly. He put his silver down and felt his face turn warm. "Jesus Christ, Joannie—"

"Toni."

"—you don't know what it's like having him around. He thinks we're still a family and he's still the head. He bosses me around like I'm a goddamned kid. I don't have time to go to family dinners three or four times a week and neither does anyone else. We don't like each other that much. We've all got families of our own now and other people we want to see. You ought to have him out in California for a while."

"Jerry can't stand him."

"He knows that," said Gold, in the same tone of protest. "Neither can Gussie's children, so they can't go to Richmond either. He can't just keep telling us whose house he's coming to whenever he wants to and who's going to drive him there and back and who else has to be invited. Christ, I think we've seen more of each other the past few months than when we were all packed together in those five rooms over the tailor shop. Each year he comes up earlier and each year he stays later—this year for the Jewish holidays. Shmini Atzereth. Have you ever heard of it? Neither have I. I swear he's making his goddamned Jewish holidays up."

Joannie laughed. "Don't you think that's funny?"

"No. And neither would you if you had to take so much of him and the crazy lady."

"Gussie is cute."

"She's crazy as a loon."

"She's sweet to me. And smart, too."

"She's losing her marbles," Gold sulked. "Both of them. Every time I see them they lose another marble."

"She gave me some good Southern advice," Joannie related. "She told me to get myself a dog. If a married couple has no children, she said, they find themselves with nothing to talk about if they don't have a dog. She also warned me not to sit facing each other when we're eating home alone, and to avoid noisy foods, especially breakfast cereals that snap, crackle, and pop, and meats that require excessive chewing." Her imitation was marvelously exact. "Well," Joannie continued, her mood clouding, "we have no children and we don't have a dog, so we've got nothing to talk about but his real-estate and insurance business and all the people he doesn't like. We sit opposite each other when we eat and are sick of staring into each other's face. And he does make a god-awful lot of noise when he chews, and I do too. If we didn't have a radio or television set blasting away at dinner and breakfast when we eat home alone I think we'd both want to die. Dinners are over in six minutes and seem like an eternity."

Gold was uncomfortable, hedged in suddenly by pity and embarrassment. She was still his kid sister. He bent forward and touched her hand with his index finger.

"Listen, Joannie—"

"Toni."

"Your name is Joannie."

"I changed it legally when I became an actress."

"Did you ever act?"

"I couldn't. I'd get jobs as a chorus girl sometimes, but I couldn't dance."

"Stay for Rose's birthday party Sunday. Come to the house."

She said no at once. "There's someone in Palm Beach I want to see before I go back. I don't like them in a crowd. I had dinner with Rose and Max and Esther last night, and I'm meeting Ida later. I spoke to Sid. Muriel I can do without, but I telephoned her anyway. I think I slowed down her poker game. Is she any better to Victor?'' Gold indicated she was not. "Rose is getting deaf, I think."

Gold was relieved to have his impression confirmed. "And Max's speech is slurred. Did you notice that?"

"He drinks a lot during the day. Rose told me."

"He shouldn't be drinking at all," Gold said with surprise. "She never told me."

"You probably never asked. She says it keeps him calm."

"He was always nice to us," Gold remembered. "He was our first in-law."

"How would *you* feel," Joannie asked, "if you had to work in a post office for over forty years and then found yourself scared because you would soon have to retire?"

"Not good," admitted Gold. "And I'd be drinking a lot more than I do."

"Lousy. God—neither one of them has ever had another job. That's one of the reasons I got out of Coney Island so fast. I couldn't stand the thought of being poor. My friend Charlotte—the one I ran away with to go into beauty contests—her father was a shoemaker. Imagine having a father who's a shoemaker or a tailor today."

"Did you ever win a beauty contest?"

"I'd come in third or fourth. I wasn't heavy enough."

"Did they mention the kids?"

"Don't you ever ask?"

"That's a subject we avoid."

"Norma's in San Francisco living with a lay psychologist now, doing social work and still finishing her education, if you can believe her, and I don't. They say Allen is a musician somewhere in Spain or North Africa, but you and I both know he's a junkie and probably gay, although they don't. One day soon a letter will come and we'll all find out he's dead. Rose thinks it may be because she went to work. She cried a little. Max too."

"That's why I don't ask," said Gold. "Tell her I said it isn't her fault. The same thing happens to kids whose mothers don't work."

"You ought to see them more," Joannie said.

"I don't have that much to say to them. And Esther makes me nervous, ever since Mendy died. She clings."

"To what?"

"To nothing. She could go live with either one of her kids. They both want her."

"Not like us," said Joannie.

"Not like us. I wish she'd marry that guy Milt."

"He hasn't asked her. She also tells me," Joannie said, "that you might be going to Washington to work in the government."

"That's a long shot, I think. How will Jerry feel about that?"

"It depends." Joannie responded pleasantly to his sarcasm. "If you get in the papers a lot, he'll approve. Otherwise, he'd rather brag about you as a college professor."

"I'll try to oblige," Gold joked. "Tell Jerry not to worry about the book. Very few people read books and almost nobody reads mine. I certainly won't mention him and I'll try not to use anyone like him as an example."

"How about me?"

"Jesus, I don't know, Joannie—"

"Toni."

"I've got five sisters, one brother, three children, a wife, father, stepmother, and more in-laws and nieces and nephews than I can keep track of. It's hard for me to deal with any subject without coming close to some of them. If I do they're embarrassed, if I don't they feel snubbed. My problem is that I've got to write about the Jewish experience in America and I don't even know what the Jewish experience is. Did Mom ever talk to you about sex?"

"I was only nine when she died."

"What'd she die of?"

"It was after an operation."

"Was it cancer?"

"I don't think so. You better ask someone else."

"What about her neck? She wore it bandaged a lot, didn't she?"

Joannie was unsure. "I don't remember that. You'll just have to ask. We were the two babies. If you want to know what my Jewish experience is, I can tell you." Gold felt a chill blow through him. "It's trying not to be. We play golf now, get drunk, take tennis lessons, and have divorces, just like normal Christian Americans. We talk dirty. We screw around, commit adultery, and talk out loud a lot about fucking."

Gold drew back in horror. "I wish you wouldn't talk like that to me," he chided her gently, almost pleading. "It makes me uncomfortable."

"That's part of *your* Jewish experience," she said.

"Do you screw around a lot?" he asked.

"Not since I married Jerry," she replied, and teased, "I do worse. I eat pork."

FROM the very outset, Julius Gold had been distinctly aloof to the idea of a condominium. Gold wore a topcoat and muffler and put on leather gloves as Sid's car pulled to a stop at the curb in Manhattan Beach. Harriet's winter coat was buttoned to the neck. Her head was covered in a knitted cap pulled down over her ears. Sid carried a light raincoat.

"Brrr—it's cold," said Gold.

"Freezing," said Harriet. "It's turning icy."

"I don't feel it," said Gold's father, with a vacancy of expression that was eloquent with disdain. Julius Gold was dressed in a baby-blue cardigan and a thin summer sport shirt. He padded about in velvet slippers of navy blue monogrammed in gold with two interwoven letters on each. "Maybe in the back it's warmer," he said without inflection.

Wordlessly he led the three through the bottom floor of the house to the open sunlit porch. In one direction was a brilliant view of the sea. In the other was Sheepshead Bay, bobbing with moored charter fishing boats. The breeze that occasionally stirred was salutary to the extreme.

"Should I get you some blankets?" offered Gold's stepmother with exquisite kindness, seating herself on a bench. She wore a flat straw hat with colored cotton balls dangling from the wide brim and she looked gaily demented.

Sid lay back in a chaise and turned his face blissfully skyward. It was time to begin.

"The city," said Harriet, clucking in elegy. "It's deteriorating rapidly."

"I haven't noticed," said Julius Gold.

"There's lots of crime."

"Not around here," said the game old man. "I ain't been mugged once."

"In the subways," droned Sid. "In the streets."

"We don't go there."

"How are the garbage pickups?" asked Gold.

"Splendid," answered his stepmother, who seemed to have it in only for him. "You may be wondering what it is I am knitting. It may be that I am knitting you an afghan. To keep you warm on frigid days like this."

Gold took off his coat. Harriet unbuttoned hers and removed her hat.

"We wouldn't notice things like garbage," Gold's father elaborated. "We don't have much."

"We eat so little," said Gussie.

"I got sons who take me out to lunch," said Gold's father. "And daughters who want me in their homes for dinner every night."

"Sometimes we're too tired to go."

"Get them something to drink," Gold's father ordered Gussie. "Serve *them* in the chipped glasses, not me."

Sid asked for beer, Gold for club soda. Harriet would wait for tea.

"Look at my two sons." Julius Gold spoke with distaste. "Fat and skinny." Gold was basking in this compliment when his father added, "Hey, stupid—why don't you put on some weight? You look like a string bean."

Gold, reacquainted with his destiny, heaved a fatalistic sigh. "It's the style now. Ain't you heard?"

"People will think I ain't got what to feed you."

"Ain't there anything I can do to please you?"

"No."

With almost palpable reluctance Sid said, "I heard about this condominium." He rose, wheezing, and chose a chair closer to his father. "It sounds like a good buy."

"In Lauderdale?"

"Hallandale."

"I like Miami Beach."

"There's a good one there too."

"So?" The old man fished in his pocket for a match for his cigar. "Buy it."

"I meant for you."

"For me?" One would have supposed from his father's pure surprise that the subject had not been broached before. "What are you bothering me with condominiums? Go find me a good apartment to rent. Like always."

"It makes more sense to buy your own home, Pop."

"My own home?" His father's voice was mocking. "How many acres?"

"Thirty-five thousand," said Gold.

"Do I have to share?"

"How many do you need? You ain't growing wheat, you know."

"No acres, Pop," Sid resumed. "It's an apartment in a building. But it's yours and Gussie's. You can stay in Florida as long as you want." Sid was perspiring now from more than the heat.

"I stay there now as long as I want. And I've got my money in blue chips. Why don't you buy it?"

"I would," said Sid, "if I lived in Florida."

"I don't live there," his father replied with asperity. "It's for a vacation I go." In a milder tone, he said, "Well, Professor, what do you think?"

"I would do what Sid says."

"I'll go look," Julius agreed.

"When?" Harriet wanted to know.

"When I go. It's still warm."

"Pop, it's turning cold," Sid cajoled. "Two years ago you had pneumonia when you stayed to November."

"Bronchitis."

"It was pneumonia."

"It was flu."

"And it led to pneumonia. Pop, it's a blue-chip investment, as good as gold." At that moment the teakettle whistled. Harriet followed Gussie inside. "Pop, don't tell Harriet," Sid continued furtively. "But I'll lay out the money. Try it. If you like it, buy it from me. If the price goes up, you get the profit. If the price goes down, I'll take the loss. What do you say?"

"That sounds fair," was the old man's conclusion. "But I'll have to think it over."

Gold covered a laugh at Sid's involuntary gasp. "Pop," Sid pleaded, "we've got to find a place for you."

"I got the money?"

"You got the money."

"Then I'll do what you say, Sid," Julius capitulated, with resignation and trust. Gold felt a twinge of compassion at the old man's docility. "But first we gotta go look, don't we? We'll go together?"

"We'll go together," Sid promised. "When?"

"Any time you say. When's the graduation?"

Sid was bewildered.

"What graduation?" asked Gold.

"Your daughter's, dummy." The women returned hastily, drawn by this outcry of contempt. "My favorite grandchild. Dina. You remember her? Ain't she graduating soon?"

"In five years," Gold told him with a steely voice. "If then."

"Don't they change schools any more when they're thirteen?"

"Not in private school. And this one may not make it that far. Your favorite grandchild ain't exactly no ball of fire in class."

"In that case," said his father, "we gotta go look. But I ain't promising to buy. Sid, you name the day. We'll go any time you say, after the holidays." *Vay'z mir*, Gold grieved. Again the holidays? "No, sirree, me and Gussie—we don't like to get on no plane before the Jewish holidays."

Gold bolted from his chair. "What holidays?" he demanded. "When is this Shmini Atzereth of yours, anyway?"

His father's scrutiny was denigrating. "That *was*, already, you dope. A week ago, before Simchas Torah."

"Then what holiday? What are you waiting for now?"

"Shabbos Bereishes."

"Shabbos Bereishes?" Gold was dumbfounded. Even in his own voice those words sounded unbelievable.

"Sure, you skinny *shaygetz*," his father began in a modulated tirade. "It's what comes after Simchas Torah, you damned fool. *This* they want to work in Washington? You did nothing Simchas Torah? You wanted me to get on a plane before Simchas Torah? You want me now to leave my family before Shabbos Bereishes? Some sons I got. *Ich hub dem bader in bud.*"

"I'm not sure," said Gold's stepmother, "that I understand your local Yiddish."

"He has us both in the bath," Gold translated tersely, and tried to ignore Sid, who was witnessing his chagrin with enormous mirth. "Pop, you're an atheist," Gold protested. "You wouldn't even let Sid and me be bar mitzvahed."

"But a Jew," his father retorted, and held up his thumb. "A Jewish atheist."

"You wouldn't let Momma light candles Friday night."

"Sometimes I did."

"And now all of a sudden you know all the holidays. What is Simchas Torah? What does Simchas Torah mean to you, anyway?"

"Simchas Torah," his father answered coolly, "is when they finally finish reading the whole Torah in the temple."

"And what's Shabbos Bereishes?"

"Shabbos Bereishes," replied the old man, and drew on his cigar with a smile, "is when they begin again."

From Gold came a cry from the heart. "For how long?"

"A year," said his father, flicking the ash from his cigar over the railing. "And when they finish, again comes—"

"Shabbos Bereishes?"

"You said it, Goldy boy. But don't you worry," his father added and came to his feet with a jaunty spring. "I ain't gonna ruin your winter. You think I'm gonna spend a year up here in this crummy city when I can buy a condominium in Florida? You want me to invest in real estate? I'll invest in real estate."

"When?" Harriet asked again.

"After next Saturday. Shabbos Bereishes. It's a promise. Let's go eat now. Gussie, get my shoes. Change your hat."

Gussie returned in a creased felt hat with a broken turkey feather and she looked like Robin Hood. To Gold, the smell of the sea at Sheepshead Bay was a powerful call to clams on the half shell, shrimp, lobster or broiled flounder or bass.

"Let's go to Lundy's," he suggested. "It's right here. We'll have a good piece of fish."

"What's so good about it?" said his father.

"So"—Gold declined to argue—"it won't be so good."

"Why you getting me fish that's no good?"

"Black," said Gold.

"White," said his father.

"White," said Gold.

"Black," said his father.

"Cold."

"Warm."

"Tall."

"Short."

"Short."

"Tall."

"I'm glad," said Gold, "you remember your game."

"Who says it's a game?"

Gold was almost sorry he laughed, for Harriet stabbed him with a venomous look. She glared at Sid, who was chuckling. Sid ignored Harriet and winked at Gold companionably.

"Sid," Julius Gold said worriedly, walking with small, shuffling steps, as they neared the car, "you'll tell the waiter, won't you? Give him a big tip before. Let him know we're important. Tell him all my life, even when I was poor, I never liked eating off no broken china."

GOLD was tense as a wound spring the evening of Rose's party, waiting for the last of his guests to leave before the first had even arrived.

"I'd like to make a toast," said Gold's father jovially. "To my host and youngest son. Sid said it ain't nice to insult you in front of your wife and daughter, so I won't say nothing." Everybody laughed but Gold. "You'll really give up teaching?"

"In a minute."

"That feeling, I bet, is mutual." His father leaned his head to the side in fascinated admiration of his own riposte and began to hum.

"I'm glad I'm not in his class," Harriet said cattily.

"He flunks students," Dina told her in awe.

"Not any more," said Gold. "It's easier to pass them along and never have to see them again."

Gold congratulated himself on having set the bar up in the foyer. He tarried alone as long as he respectably could, then filled almost to the top a short, wide glass of bourbon and let fall inside it a single cube of ice.

"Isn't it lucky," mused Sid, as Gold strolled into the living room, "that we found ourselves on a planet where there's water?"

Gold felt his chest turn to stone and watched the luscious slice of bronze-rimmed lake sturgeon on his plate alter for an instant into something as unappealing as a raw sardine.

"Why?" asked Victor.

"Listen to Sid when he talks about water," directed Gold's father drowsily. "If there's one thing Sid knows, it's water."

Gold glanced at his father but found no evidence of complicity. He shifted his fork from the sturgeon to a mound of red caviar. He was confident he could count on Ida, even Irv, to trap Sid on this one, to argue that we did not "happen" to find ourselves on a planet with water but would not have evolved as a species had there been none.

"Otherwise," Sid answered Victor, savoring first the smell and then the taste of a smoked-salmon appetizer on a rounded wedge of soft brown pumpernickel, "we would all be very thirsty." He looked toward Gold with a challenging smile and continued with disarming ease. "After a big meal of turkey, or steak, or roast beef, or lobster, not only wouldn't we have water to drink, we wouldn't even have soda. Or tea or coffee. Because they're all made from water."

And where, Gold wondered, would the turkeys and steak and roast beef come from, you shithead? And the lobsters, with no water? He waited for Ida to eviscerate Sid.

But Ida, he saw with a shock, was listening as raptly as Milt, Max, and the rest. Those black militants in her school district had a point, Gold decided: Get her the fuck out.

Sid forged ahead boldly, testing Gold's self-discipline to the maximum. "We would have to drink wine or beer instead," he commented, placing half a hard-boiled egg in his mouth. "You see, wine and beer are made from grapes and hops," he explained. "And we'd probably have plenty of grapes and hops, I bet."

Gold was not altogether certain what, anatomically, a gorge was, but he knew that his was rising. He had waited too long. He knew from experience the arsenal of retaliations Sid held ready for any contradictions from him. Delivered with an unctuous humility that could kill, they might range from a hurt and affecting "So I made a small mistake," to a proud "See what a college education can do?" The others would not find credible for a second the charge that all Sid's errors were diabolically intentional. Gold feigned insouciance. Having taken a vow of silence, he kept it.

And Sid settled back with an air of victory, finished the last hors d'oeuvre on his plate, and began cracking walnuts from one of the heaping bowls set out by Belle for adornment now and nibbling later.

The crisis past, Gold, having resisted the temptations of Sid, now succumbed precipitously to the attraction of chopped liver, and spooned smoked oysters and more red caviar onto his plate as well, then added a slice of cheese and another slice of sturgeon and some cold shrimp. He went to the bar for more bourbon. Max, his drooping cheeks red, was drinking Scotch for the occasion, while abstemiously avoiding everything else so far except some sliced carrots and a few buds of raw cauliflower.

When Gold returned to the living room, Sid said, "It's really a miracle, isn't it, when you think of it. So many planets—six or seven or eight—how many planets are there now, Bruce?"

"Forty-two."

"Forty-two planets," Sid continued with no change of expression. "And this is the only one with water."

"It's a lucky thing," said Victor, "that we found ourselves on this one."

"I feel sorry for all those people on the other planets," said Gold in the same wry frame of mind.

"Are there people on other planets?" asked Ida.

"If there are," said Sid, "I'll bet they sure are thirsty."

Rose had been flabbergasted when she'd arrived with Max and Esther and found the others present for her party. Immediately she began to cry. She was laughing as well and trying to talk above her own uproar in a voice that quickly grew hoarse. "Oh, Belle! Belle!" Again and again she flung herself upon the shorter woman in a grateful and crushing embrace. Max was beaming, his care-worn face reflecting greater happiness than Gold could associate with him since the days of his engagement and marriage. Gold was dumbfounded by Rose's reaction and stirred with a tenderness foreign to him. Rose was a large, wide woman. He could not re-member her laughing, crying, or talking so freely. At the death and funeral of Mendy, Esther's husband, she had wept noiselessly, and was still doing all she could to bolster Esther in her widowhood. Her broad, darkly freckled face, awash now in rejoicing, was all at once the face of an aging woman. Esther looked still older. Sid looked younger than both, and all three were starting to resemble each other eerily, their dissimilar faces collapsing into old age along the same predestined patterns of decline. Someday he would look like them too.

All but Joannie were present, even Muriel, who had set aside still another grudge against Ida and sacrificed a poker evening with her South Shore Long Island friends. Muriel had always been embittered and self-centered—the *farbisseneh* one, his mother would say, an observation made more in woe than reprimand. Gold guessed she'd been quarreling with Victor again on the drive into Manhattan. Gold harbored suppositions about Muriel that he preferred not to enlarge upon. Gold had lain with too many married women to be blind to all signs.

The main courses were turkey and roast beef. Had Ida or Harriet been hostess, there would have been a ham as well. Two large sections of prime rib had arrived unexpectedly from Victor at the beginning of the week as a spontaneous gift. Everyone agreed that Belle and Harriet cooked the best roast prime rib of beef in all creation. Not for them the bland juices of the Anglo-Saxons. They knew what to do with garlic, paprika, salt, and onions. Harriet came with two deep dishes of the mashed sweet potatoes and marshmallows that Gold adored, two crumb coffeecakes, a cranberry mold, and one bottle of sparkling domestic wine. Always at family gatherings now, the women, excepting Gold's stepmother, vied or cooperated in the preparation of certain foods they made— or thought they made—uniquely well, and were encouraged—or presumed they were encouraged—to bring to the brunches, lunches, and dinners served at the homes of the others. With so many women at work, friction was inevitable and hurt feelings the rule.

Harriet excelled at baking and was forever miffed upon arriving with two or three of her cheesecakes, moist chocolate cakes, or coffeecakes to find a deep-dish fruit pie, cookies, and a high whipped cream or chocolate layer cake already purchased or, at

Muriel's or Ida's, two specially ordered gâteaux St. Honoré, along-side which all other efforts necessarily paled. Esther specialized in stuffed derma and noodle puddings; living alone now, she was expanding into potato and cheese blintzes and experimenting with dishes other than derma, unaware that with chopped liver and stuffed cabbage she was encroaching upon Ida's traditional territories and that with chopped herring she was transgressing against Rose, who was unmatched in the family with all edible things from the sea, as well as with soups, matzoh balls, and other varieties of dumplings. Rose suffered the unintended affront in silence, Ida chafed vocally, Esther shuddered in repentance. No one would contend with Belle at icebox cake. Nothing was more humiliating to one than to telephone with an offer to bring something and be told the assignment had been delegated to another. Muriel, the youngest of the sisters still in the East, concentrated on gourmet variations of standard, sometimes canned, American foods—tuna fish, either in a crêpe, a grilled pizza crust, or a blistering casserole; chicken salad with capers and fragrant herbs; salmon mousse; and a specialty of hers nobody had quite taken to yet, Jewish corned-beef hash made with almost no potatoes and with hamburger meat and tomatoes rather than corned beef, which looked, even before the ketchup she insisted be added, like a monstrous scarlet meat-loaf. Muriel often added minced anchovies to coleslaw and salads she bought. Ida hated anchovies and staunchly maintained they made her want to vomit. Muriel would tell her to go ahead. Muriel frequently wondered aloud whether Ida's and Irv's combined in-comes totaled more than Victor's, assumed her question was its own proof, and took it for granted that Ida was therefore lording it over her. Ida's children were college-oriented. Muriel's daughters were not: instead they were prodigies of inside knowledge about designer-labeled dresses, shoes, pocketbooks, and luggage. It was Ida, typically, who first detected that all Muriel's dishes for her family were built on basic ingredients that were cheap in the marketplace or, because of Victor, free. To the everlasting glory of all, Gold felt, not one had ever attempted to serve him stuffed breast of veal. There was unofficial agreement in the family that Rose was the best-natured, Esther the slowest-minded, Harriet the least sociable now, Ida the pickiest, Belle the most dependable, and Muriel the most selfish. Joannie was best-looking, although this rarely was mentioned. Muriel, who wore large bracelets and rings, had arrived at the party with yet another of her scarlet meat loaves of corned-beef hash to add to the turkeys and standing ribs of beef already there. And all but Gold's stepmother would have to eat some with cries of ecstasy or risk inciting Muriel to sniffs of disparagement for Esther's noodle pudding or Ida's Swedish meatballs, and to the reiterated charge that others in the family had always plotted against her. With Ida born just ahead, and Gold just behind, Muriel, sandwiched between these two achievement-powered phenomena, had not experienced the privileges of youngest child long enough to know there were any.

"Dinner," said Dina.

"And I brought nothing," Rose lamented.

"The party's for you," Max consoled her.

"It was a surprise," scolded Ida.

GOLD WAS in for another blow in the dining room, for Belle had given to Esther copies of Lieberman's magazine, and Esther had just finished laying one out at every second plate, the pages open to the title page of "Nothing Succeeds as Planned" with the repulsive dark portrait Lieberman always used because he had purchased it years before from some scrounging, alcoholic illustrator for only twelve dollars and eighty-five cents. When Gold beheld the magazines, he knew what it was to wish, literally, to fall through a floor. His head reeled and he clasped with both hands the back of his chair as he felt his knees buckle. Oh, Esther, you poor benighted fool, he mourned in pity and forgiveness. He dropped his eyes from her blissful face and snow-white hair as a troubled murmuring rose about his ears.

"It's another story by Bruce," Esther repeated to all who grunted inquisitively.

The ovation, to the extent that one occurred, was a standing ovation only because Esther was standing while she clapped her hands. Her mouth was trembling with an uncommon palsy that seemed to shake her lower jaw now and again and that gave to her chalky face an appearance of heightened shyness. Many of her lower teeth were part of a bridge. It was with a discerning air of protectiveness that old Milt glanced from Gold to Esther and took a loyal position beside her.

"Isn't that nice?" Rose applauded too. Belle, catching Gold's eyes, offered a helpless shrug. Dina lingered evilly instead of escaping into her room as prearranged.

"Another screw," explained Gold's stepmother to Gold's father, "has come loose."

And another marble, Gold replied to himself, has rolled out of your fucking skull. Some at the table had already overshot the pages of his article and were engrossed in the sexual help wanted ads at the back.

"And after dinner," said Esther, "he'll autograph all our copies if we ask."

"Please, Esther," Gold begged. "You're embarrassing me."

"And then," Esther went on, finally sitting down, "we'll all have to go home and read it."

"Fat chance," said Harriet.

"Will someone pass me some turkey?" said Gold.

"We'll have to buy another bookcase soon," said Muriel. "Where's an ashtray?"

Ida, shorter, scowled up at her and fanned the air free of cigarette smoke. "At least he's closer to the front this time," she noticed.

"You get more money for that?" asked Irv.

"For what?" Gold's words were clipped.

"For being near the front?"

"No," said Belle.

"He gets paid?" asked Victor.

"Yes," said Belle. "Victor, take some roast beef. Everybody start eating. Please."

"There's plenty of everything at both sides of the table," instructed Ida. She held a platter of newly sliced rye bread with black seeds directly under Gold's nose. "Take some bread, Brucie. It's your favorite kind."

"I thought you told us to stop calling him Brucie when he turned twenty-one," Muriel corrected Ida.

Gold declined the rye bread with a shake of his head. The aro-

matic burnt allure of those black seeds nearly split his heart in two.
He would forgo the roast potatoes too, butter-yellow with charred
pan burns and darkly flecked with succulent particles of shriveled,
greasy onion embodying now the concentrates of all those piquant
seasonings that had blended together with the flavor of prime rare
beef. Self-denial, like the self-punishment of jogging, made him
feel virtuous and savagely bad-tempered.

"I just don't get it," said Max in thoughtful doubt. "This title, I
mean."

"In my opinion," ventured Dina, "it's a big mistake." She was
eating off her plate as she stood. Having asserted all week that she
would not remain with *that* family, she now evidently found it
impossible to tear herself away.

"Sure," said Milt. "A mistake. What you meant to say, I think,
was that nothing succeeds like success. Right?"

"No," said Belle.

"What I meant to say," said Gold, slipping into the plush conversational robes of the pedagogue-prophet, "is that nothing succeeds like failure. If you take the long view, the only outcome we
can ever rely upon is failure."

"I can't afford to take a long view," said his father. "I'm a very
short person."

"Would you care to elaborate on that, Professor?" asked Sid,
his mouth full.

"If you'd take the trouble to read it," Gold began, chewing.

"Oh, Daddy," interrupted Dina, "no one's going to read it."

"Dina, will you get the hell out of here already, if you're going?"

"Nobody's eating Esther's noodle pudding," said Belle, in a
diversionary alarm.

Like earth-moving equipment, arms reached forth over the table
simultaneously for helpings of Esther's noodle pudding.

"Nobody's settled my hash," said Muriel.

"And I brought nothing," lamented Rose.

"Harriet takes the cake," said Belle.

"And Belle chimes in," Ida said.

And now Dina fled.

"Are you telling me," questioned Irv, holding at a stop the dish of mashed sweet potatoes Gold awaited, "that if I set out to drill a patient's tooth to put a filling in, I haven't succeeded?"

Gold was indulgent. "Irv, you ain't filling teeth because you like to drill holes. If you fill a tooth to make money to buy a car that's going to conk out on you tonight in the tunnel going back to Brooklyn, you haven't really succeeded in what you planned, have you?"

"That's kind of farfetched, Bruce, isn't it?"

"Well, I ain't exactly writing about drilling teeth. Will you pass those sweet potatoes?"

"I think fairness requires," said Ida, "that we all read the article before we form an opinion."

"That will be the day," said Harriet. "And I'll believe he's going to Washington when I see it."

"Harriet, will you please shut up?" Gold pleaded. "For once?"

Harriet said to Sid, "I always told you he was spoiled."

"Not by me," bragged Muriel. This statement was superfluous. Muriel had accepted Victor's proposal of marriage, her first from anyone, after working as a salesgirl in Macy's for eight months, and had not thought of spoiling anyone but herself, since.

"Bruce wasn't spoiled." Ida's celerity in coming to Gold's defense was always sufficient to leave him feeling undermined. "He was given advantages because he showed he would make the most of them. Like I was. There's no need to be ashamed of him just because he writes things nobody understands."

Gold's cheeks were afire with escalating anger. "Irv, will you pass those goddamn sweet potatoes, please?" He speared a slice of roast beef. "Victor, throw some corned-beef hash on my plate, will you? And two of those roast potatoes, with onion, onion. Ida, give me a couple of slices of that bread."

Victor, pleased to comply, said, "She made the corned-beef hash with filet mignon."

Gold was starving and had no appetite. If I ever marry again, he despaired . . . and was interrupted by his father, who coughed to command attention, leaned toward him angrily, and declared:

"This thing that you did was an insult with this guy to me and the whole family. He was rich?"

Gold was flabbergasted. "What thing?"

"With this guy." His father's face was stern.

First Gold blinked. Then he said, "Which one?"

"You know which one," his father began in a harangue. "Don't ask me which one. I'll give him which one, that idiot. You went to school with him, didn't you?"

"Lieberman?"

"Who else, you cartoon? I have to tell him which one." Victor giggled, and Sid was regarding the assault upon Gold with a smiling and benign countenance. "How come—" and here Julius Gold adopted a pose of elegance and bent his head far back for no better purpose, it seemed, than to look horizontally past his knob of a nose—"how come they lived in Coney Island if they were so rich?"

Gold was puzzled. "They weren't rich."

"His father was better than me? What did he do?"

"He candled eggs. He was in the egg business."

"I owned factories," Gold's father maintained. "I built gun turrets in the war for the Bendix people. I was in defense." He slowed, nodding. "They gave me once a small citation for efficiency because I had a small factory. I had a coat business and was in real estate. I had a leather business from which I was able to retire with an income. Ask Sid. Long ago I was in furs, spices, ships, import and export." His look grew distant and he seemed to be maundering. "Once I owned a fine apartment house in a bad neighborhood, but the banks took it back from me. I owned tailor shops, always the same one, but it was hard to make a go, so I kept getting out. I had a big grocery store on Mermaid Avenue before it closed. I was ahead of my time with my supermarket. Once I owned a store with surgical appliances for people with operations, and I knew how to talk—believe me, I knew what to say to people when it came to selling. 'Have I got an arm for you!' I would say to one. 'Who sold you that eye?' I would ask another. I was the best in the whole world, but I couldn't make a living so I went into finance and was a commission man on Wall Street in the Depression when no one could sell a single share of stock, not even me. I was in building, when no one was building. I was a draftsman before anyone even knew what a draftsman was. A lot of people still don't." His eye fell upon Gold accusingly. "An egg candler is better than me?"

"Did I say that?"

"So how come," said Julius Gold, "you work for him, and he don't work for you?"

Now Gold understood. "I don't work for him. I'm a free-lance writer. He's an editor."

His father appeared ominously pleased. "Did you write this or did he?"

"I did."

"Did he pay you or did you pay him?"

"He paid me."

"That sounds like work to me," said his father with sovereign scorn. "Do you wish you was him, or do you wish you was you?"

"I wish I was me."

"Does he wish he was him, or does he wish he was you?"

"He probably wishes he was me."

"Sid?"

"He may be right, Pop."

"Ah, what do you know?" said the old man, shaking his head at Sid in disgust. "You're just as dumb, sitting there like a dope all these years with your laundry machines. Like American Tel and Tel, still with their telephones. You never had no plan. I told you a hundred times, you got to have a plan." His father found a cigar. "By you, he may be right. By me—" his father struck his match— "money talks. The man who does the paying calls the tune. He's paying, you work for him, he's better, a son of an egg candler yet when I built turrets for the Bendix people, and that's it. *Fartig.*"

"Oh, Pa, I'm forty-eight goddamn years old," Gold started to strike back angrily.

"Don't you swear. I never allowed such language in my house."

"It's my house and I do. I'm a college professor and have a Ph.D. I write books. I go on television. I get paid for making speeches at colleges and conferences. And you still talk to me like I'm a child or some kind of imbecile. All of you! There are people in Washington who want me to go there."

"As what?" responded his father with a jeering laugh.

"As a tourist," joked Max, and Gold felt the fight go out of him. Oh, Max, Gold wailed silently, not you too.

"To see the Washington Monument," chortled Milt, in the loudest utterance anyone there had yet heard from him. He was starting to feel at home as Esther's suitor.

Inwardly Gold was close to tears. Soon, he reflected despondently, I will be making recommendations whether to bomb or not to bomb. Here I am hopeless. "Okay, you're right and I'm wrong," he surrendered abjectly to his father, who nodded. "I wish we were talking about water again."

"Ask Sid," said his father. "If there's one thing Sid knows, it's water."

Esther, obliging, asked, "Sometimes when I look out my window in winter, I see ice flowing up the river—why is that?"

"That's because ice is lighter than water," answered Sid, "and it's floating up to get to the top of the river."

For an instant Gold was speechless. Blood rushed to his face. "Do you really think," he demanded in a cold fury, "that the ice is flowing up to get to the top of the river?"

"Isn't it?" asked Sid.

"Do you really think that up is up?" Gold blurted out, pointing northward angrily.

"Up isn't up?" said someone.

"Sure, it's up," said someone else.

"What then, it's down?" answered still one more.

"I meant north," Gold corrected himself with a shout. "Do you really think that something is higher just because it's north?"

Sid preserved a tranquil silence while others championed his cause.

"Of course, it's higher. They got the mountains there, don't they?"

"That's why people go in the summer."

"It's cooler."

"North is always higher on the map," Ida pointed out.

"I'm not talking about a map."

"That's why the water always flows down to the middle of the map," said his father with belittling arrogance. "Where it's wider. Where there's lots of room."

"And I suppose," Gold sneered at them all, "that if you took a map off the wall and turned it upside down, all the water would run off."

"Oh, no, silly," said his sister-in-law.

"There's no water on the map."

"He thinks there's water on a map."

"A map is only a picture."

"I know it's a picture!" Gold shrieked in fear. "I was being ironic. I was asking a question, not making a statement!"

"But turn the *world* upside down," suggested Sid with an air of craftiness in the intimidated lull that ensued, "and then see what would happen."

"Nothing!" roared Gold.

"Nothing?" said Sid.

"The North Pole would be the South Pole," said Muriel.

"The Big Dipper would spill."

"We'd go south to get cold."

"Niagara Falls would fall up."

"And he calls that nothing."

"Nothing would happen!" Gold heard himself screaming. "Uphill would still be uphill, God damn it, there is no top or bottom when it comes to planets, and I'm leaving here right now and never coming back—what is it, what is it, what is it, what is it?" he cried with shrill and perfervid impatience at whoever had been thumping him on the shoulder.

"It's for you," said Dina.

"What is?"

"The phone call." Dina rolled her eyes upward in martyrdom. "It's that man in the White House again. You can take it in my room."

The will to live left Gold. The delusion possessed him that Ralph and rulers in all the capital cities of the world had been witness to the disgraceful scene just completed. Television cameras had recorded it. Woodward and Bernstein would write a book. He was ruined.

DINA HELPED him to his feet. Ida steadied him. He prayed for clemency as he walked through the kitchen to Dina's bedroom.

"Ralph?"

"Just a minute, darling," said a woman's voice as warm and rich as flowing honey.

"Bruce?"

"Ralph?"

"The President of the United States has definitely decided that he wants you to work with him," said Ralph. "He will see you in the White House tomorrow morning at seven-thirty. You will have a chance to get to know each other."

"I can't come to the White House tomorrow morning," Gold croaked. "I've got a ten o'clock class."

"You'll be back in time," said Ralph. "The appointment is only for a minute and a half. If you leave for the airport now you can catch the last shuttle."

"I can't leave now. It's my big sister's birthday party."

"The President would send his own plane but his wife is using it to go shopping. You could charter a private plane."

"I don't know how. Ralph—will the President be angry if I don't come tomorrow?"

"Not angry, Bruce. But very disappointed, although he won't know. I'll simply put somebody else into that minute and a half and he probably will never notice the difference."

"I could come Wednesday," Gold begged.

"He'll be in China."

"Will you please get off the phone?" Gold's daughter hissed from the doorway like the deadliest of adders. "I'm expecting a call."

"Get the fuck out of here," he answered in kind with his hand muffling the phone, "or I'll kill you."

Dina skipped merrily away. "They want him to come to Washington," she sang out.

"But come anyway," Ralph decided, "and we'll talk. Andrea will probably want you for dinner. Stay at an excellent hotel, in case you're recognized. Unless, of course, there's someone here who might want you in his home as a guest."

Gold waited without breath for five full seconds before saying he'd stay at a hotel. In something of a stupor he returned to the dining room.

"Was it really the President?" asked Rose in a whisper.

"And he wants him to come right away," said Esther to Harriet, who was looking chastened.

"An assistant," said Gold.

"The President has lots of assistants," Harriet remarked churlishly.

"Well, this is his best one," Ida informed her.

"I can't wait to visit Bruce in Washington," said Muriel, shaking ashes from the cigarette jutting from her mouth, and Gold was stricken with something more numbing than dismay. "Maybe we can all go together, with the kids."

"That should be nice," said Rose. "Won't it, Max?"

"Maybe he can get me a raise."

"Bruce," Ida reprimanded him sharply, "if you're going to Washington there's something I must tell you. Esther, Rose, Max, Irv, Muriel, Victor, and I all think you're getting too thin."

"He was always too thin," derogated his father. "I told him too thin—but he wouldn't listen. When he wears pajamas it's only one stripe."

"What was it Sid used to tease him about?" asked Emma Bovary.

"Go out for the fencing team," said Echo. "He was so skinny they'd never be able to hit him."

"Remember the time they wouldn't let him sing in school and he came home crying?" asked Natasha Karilova.

"And how funny he looked in eyeglasses?" responded Aurora with equal merriment, and Gold returned from his daze and realized he'd been giving the names Emma Bovary, Echo, Natasha Karilova, and Aurora to his sisters Muriel, Ida, Rose, and Esther. There were just too fucking many of them. With a fork gripped like a dagger, he stabbed brutally for the last remaining end piece of roast beef as Belle and a few of the other women began clearing the table.

"When you going?" demanded his father.

"Wednesday," grumbled Gold, and masticated seriously.

"For how long?"

"He has a class on Friday," said Belle.

"You taking Belle with you?"

"No," said Belle resolutely. "I have to work at the school Wednesday."

"It's too soon for that," said Gold.

"What kind of job you getting?"

"I really can't tell you yet. You wouldn't like it anyway."

"Of course not."

"So let's talk about something else."

"Sure," Sid said. "Let's talk about vultures."

Gold's face froze. "Why?"

"They're like the lilies of the field."

"Sid, you bastard—"

"Apologize!" screamed his father, snapping erect. "Apologize, you bastard, for that filthy word you just said."

Gold walked into the kitchen.

Rose was bawling again. "I can't help it," she explained to Ida. "It's the first party I ever had."

"Rose, what do you mean?" Ida said. "We were always having birthday and Christmas parties."

"Even I had them," Gold recollected.

"I was the one who made them," Rose exclaimed joyously, with another outburst of tears.

Esther nodded. "Poppa was always busy and Momma was always working and sick a lot. So Rose was the one who made the parties."

"And Esther helped," said Rose. "But I never had one for myself."

"I thought it was about time," said Belle, carrying a cup of coffee to Rose. "Happy sixtieth."

Gold had difficulty swallowing. "Rose," he said, clearing his throat, and took coffee for himself. "I'm trying to remember things. Remember the time Sid lost me and you had to come to the police station to get me?"

"Not me. I was selling custard and malteds on the boardwalk. Esther went."

"Boy, was there hollering in the house that night," said Sid, taking, as he entered, a bite-size piece of Danish pastry. "I told them you ran away."

Gold was staggered. "How could you do such a thing?"

"Listen, I was the oldest," laughed Sid. "It wasn't so much fun taking care of all of you. I used to like girls, remember?" He cast a glance backward to assure himself of Harriet's absence.

Ida understood. "I never liked it when I had to take Muriel and Bruce to school."

"I never liked it when I had to take care of Bruce," said Muriel.

And Gold had not enjoyed having to take care of Joannie.

"You know what they did for her birthday at the office?" Max said grouchily. "Nothing."

"I don't care." Rose nullified his grievance with a good-natured toss of her hand. "They didn't even know. Listen, I'm so old I'm glad they let me stay."

"That's why I'm afraid to go looking for a job," said Esther, and those nerves in her jaw were quivering again, giving to her meticulously clean chin the look of something easily broken.

"Remember how hard it was when we started?" Rose sipped her coffee. "I guess we had lots of fun even then. It took me two years to find a steady job."

"I found one sooner when I got out of high school," said Esther.

"You were so pretty," said Rose. Esther's eyes misted over. "But I was always big as a horse," Rose went on. "Boy, was it hard. Jobs were scarce then, especially for Jews. A lot of the ads had lines that no Jews should apply."

"I was one of the first Jews in the Post Office," boasted Max dolefully.

"Victor's older brother was one of the first Jewish cops," said Muriel. "The rest were all anti-Semitic. That's why he quit and went into the meat business."

"Every morning," said Rose, "the four of us, me and my friends Gertie, Beatie, and Edna, would go into the city to look. We were only eighteen. We would have to go to the agencies mainly, because they were the ones who had jobs to give, and they took a nice percentage of the pay. It was not an easy time for Jews, what with first the Depression and then Hitler and all those anti-Semites here, and one big agency, I forget the name but they would let us wait around all day so we'd have a place to stay, would every once in a while announce that all Jews could go home, there'd be no work for us that day. All we even wanted was part-time work or a temporary job. So after that whenever I filled an application with an agency I would put down Protestant. I didn't even know what Protestant was but I knew it was good. They all knew I was lying, with my looks, but they didn't really care. At least then they could send me out. At one of the employment agencies I finally got a temporary job for three weeks. Some job. The interviewer at the department store told me she knew I was Jewish. But she gave me the job anyway. Maybe she couldn't get anyone else to take it. The store was all the way in Newark, New Jersey, but it paid five dollars a day. It cost ten cents each way for the trolley and the train to go into the city and maybe a quarter more for lunch and a drink in the afternoon. It cost me an extra nickel each way to go into New Jersey with the Hudson Tubes. I would give my pay to Momma each day but most of the time she wouldn't take it all. She'd put some of it in my drawer for me to save." Rose, Gold reflected, was already ten years older than Momma had lived. "Sid was working at the Brighton Laundry with all those horses he was afraid of. Remember those horses, Sid?"

"I sure do. 'Watch out for those horses,' Mom would tell me every time I left the house."

"She worried all day long," Rose remembered. " 'Where does a Jew come to a horse?' she'd say, and shake her head so miserably. She worried about me too every day until I got home. It took me two hours to get to Newark from Coney Island and I had to stand in the department-store window and display some kind of a brush and mop with wax. It was a real bad day for me from the first one on, because people would stop and look. I didn't like being looked at but that was what I was being paid for. Then I remembered we had relatives in Newark, most of Momma's family lived in New Jersey, and I was so ashamed that one of them would pass and see me. I worked all day with my heart in my mouth. But five dollars a day was a lot of money then and would pay for a lot of new days of looking for work when that job ended. When I mopped I could do it with my back to the window but with the brush I had to look out at the street. I still don't know if any of them saw me but I was so afraid. I can still remember the lunch all four of us had every day we went into the city to look for work. There was a big cafeteria on West Forty-second Street. I think the name of it was the Pershing. Every day we ordered one order of corned-beef hash and four coffees.''

''Was it as good as mine?'' asked Muriel.

Rose threw her head back and raised her hands. ''It was awful. We hated corned-beef hash, not yours, but it was the only thing that could be divided in four easily and was cheap and filling. We would all chip in for a pack of cigarettes and take five each. Then after lunch we would split up in twos and stand on the employment lines at the department stores or go back to the employment agencies to wait. There was Civil Service, but we didn't think we were smart enough or that they had any jobs we wanted. All we knew was typing and salesgirls. And we didn't want to leave home. In those days people didn't want to move away.'' Gold remembered her two children with a pang. But Rose, in the momentum of narration, was oblivious to the connection. ''So we kept looking and then I got, before the law office, a job in one of the stores on Fourteenth Street, Hearn's. Selling behind the counter, and would probably still be there yet if the head of the floor wasn't a fanny pincher, and this used to kill me and the other girls too. So we made up and stood in a bunch one day and when he came squeezing through with his hands down I stuck a pin in him. He never knew who did it, but I felt he did or would find out and I was so afraid I knew I couldn't stay there so I left when Momma said it was all right and began looking again. We walked miles all over the city every day just to save an extra five cents in carfare, but we were a happy bunch and had fun, corned-beef hash and all, and I made myself a promise one day that if I ever found a decent steady job I was never going to leave it, so when I found this steno job at the law firm, I stayed, and I've been there all this time. I never wanted to have to go looking for a job again.''

''Forty-two years,'' Max sulked, but with that same touch of muted pride. ''And they start new girls out now at almost the same salary she's making.''

''I don't care,'' Rose answered heartily. ''They let me leave when I had the babies and let me work part time when I had to. I'm still afraid they're going to make me leave, and I'll have to go looking again."

"Now?" Max scoffed. "Now you wouldn't have to."

"I just hope I can stay until you can retire too. Maybe then we can get a condominium in Florida also, near Poppa and Gussie."

"Are in-laws allowed?" asked Irv, pushing through. "I want some coffee too."

Belle shooed them all outside the kitchen. When Dina, flanked by Esther and Belle, carried in the birthday cake, Gold felt like crying and feared he might run from the room. He was thankful the lights had been darkened for all those flickering candles. An extra one had been added for good luck.

"My Rosie," said Gold's father proudly, as all made ready to depart and she came to kiss him goodbye. "She was always the best one. She never gave me a minute's trouble."

"So fucking much in character," Gold grumbled. "To judge the whole human race by how much trouble we gave him."

She was also the one who had gotten least. Even Esther had fared better: little Mendy, though scrappy and opinionated, had been devoted to Esther and had left money at his death two years earlier, and both her children, one in Boston and the other in Philadelphia, were upset that she still chose to live alone near Rose rather than with one or the other of them.

There were more large presents than Rose and Max could handle. Irv and Victor helped pack them, while Gold went back and forth for shopping bags. To Muriel's gift of a marked-down alligator purse Victor had added a dozen shell steaks and a pickled tongue. The grandest prize in the bunch was a Caribbean cruise, with spending money included. Sid had paid most but all had chipped in and therefore Sid could tell Harriet that the present had come from the family. The Caribbean would be warm, whereas Europe would remind them of their son and California of their daughter. Neither Rose nor Max had ever been out of the country. They had not even been on a plane.

"I sure get a kick," Irv said to Gold, "out of the way you guys kid each other along."

Gold was appalled. Ho-ly shit. Was *that* the way they saw it?

"You three are a riot," Milt agreed.

By the time they were leaving, with all of the women but his stepmother and Muriel having pitched in, the dining room and kitchen had been cleared and the last pan scrubbed, and the last load of dishes was already groaning in the dishwasher. Gold, when a final worried hush fell, was able to allay their deepest fear and send them away in a mood of jubilation.

"Bruce," Esther found nerve enough to ask at the door, while the others waited with glummest concern, "if you go to Washington, you wouldn't ever do anything to make us ashamed, would you?"

Gold was almost afraid to inquire. "Like what?"

Here Esther's courage failed, and others took over.

"Like ever vote Republican?"

"Never," he answered.

"Or help one get elected?"

"Of course not!"

"Not even if he was Jewish?"

"Especially."

"Thank God," said his stepmother.

"That Aunt Rose," said Dina, sitting cross-legged on Belle's bed. "I never saw her so happy. Did you ever hear her laugh and talk so much?"

"I'm glad I made the party," Belle said.

So was Gold. Belle was a good wife, and Gold guessed he might miss her if he ever decided he wanted one.

EVERYTHING in Ralph Newsome's office in Washington had a bright shine but the seat of his pants. Gold had been greeted at the elevators by a young girl with a pretty face who turned him over to a stunning woman near thirty with straight black hair and a sheer, very expensive dress that clung bewitchingly to her incredibly supple figure, who conducted him at length to Ralph's secretary, a sunny, flirtatious woman of arresting sensual warmth who won his heart instantly with her seductive cordiality and caressing handshake. Everything in view gleamed with a polished intensity that made electric lighting, on these premises, seem superfluous.

Ralph had aged hardly at all. He was tall and straight, with languid movements, freckles, and reddish-brown hair parted on the side. What Gold remembered most clearly about Ralph was that he never needed a haircut or ever looked as though he'd had one. He wore a tapered, monogrammed shirt and his trousers looked freshly pressed. He was still, somehow, the only graduate of Princeton University Gold—or anyone Gold knew—had ever met.

"I hope you had fun last night," Ralph opened innocently. "This town is just bursting with good-looking women who will do almost anything for a good time."

Gold curtly answered, "I was tired when I got in. I wanted a rest."

This was a lie. Rather, he had spent the evening roaming dismally from one public room of his hotel to another, hoping in vain that someone might recognize him and take him somewhere else to girls as lovely as any one of the three who'd just welcomed him.

"Gosh, Bruce, I'm happy to see you again," Ralph said. "It's just like old times again, isn't it?" Gold was silent. It was not at all like old times. "The President will be pleased I'm seeing you today, if he ever finds out. You sure do boggle his mind. He has a framed copy of your review of his *My Year in the White House* under the glass top of his desk in the Oval Office so he can reread it all day long during vital conversations on agriculture, housing, money, starvation, health, education, and welfare, and other matters in which he has no interest." Ralph was in earnest. "I'm told he already has a blowup of your proverb 'Nothing Succeeds as Planned' on a wall of his breakfast room right beside a quotation from Pliny. It's a daily reminder not to attempt to do too much."

Gold was guarded in his reply. "I'm glad," he said and hesitated. "There's still much about his book I don't understand."

"That's one of the things he likes best about your review. He was afraid you might see through him."

"See through him?" Gold shifted his feet uneasily.

"Well, we all knew he really didn't have much to write about his one year in the White House, especially since he was so busy writing about it. He probably wants you here as soon as you can make the necessary arrangements, although he probably doesn't want you making any yet. That much is definite."

"Working as what?" asked Gold.

"As anything you want, Bruce. You can have your choice of anything that's open that we're willing to let you have. At the moment, there's nothing."

"Ralph, you aren't really telling me anything. Realistically, how far can I go?"

"To the top," answered Ralph. "You might even start there. Sometimes we have openings at the top and none at the bottom. I think we can bypass spokesman and senior official and start you higher, unless we can't. You're much too famous to be used anonymously, although not many people know who you are. Got anything else in the works?"

"I'm doing a book for Pomoroy and Lieberman and there's a short piece on education I have in mind."

"How I envy you," Ralph murmured. Gold eyed him with hostility. "What's the book about?"

The question gripped Gold by the throat. "About people in America, Ralph, about Jewish people."

"I gather you're in favor. I would rush that one out while there's still time."

"Still time for what?"

"Still time to risk it. The article on education should help. We'll be organizing another Presidential Commission on education soon and you'll be appointed." Ralph buzzed his intercom. "Dusty, darling, bring in our file on Dr. Gold, will you?"

"Sure thing, honey." The beautiful woman gave Ralph a folder containing a pad on which was written absolutely nothing. "Here you are, sweetheart."

"Thanks, love."

"She's gorgeous," said Gold, when she left. "And Dusty is an exciting nickname."

"That's her real name. Her nickname is Sweets."

"You didn't call her Sweets."

"In a government office?" Ralph chided benevolently. "Now, let's see where we are." Ralph addressed himself to the blank pad and wrote *spokesman, source,* and *senior official.* "We considered beginning you as a press aide, but one of the first things the boys from the press would want to know would be where does someone like you come off being a press aide. Would you like to work as a secretary?"

"It's a far cry from what I had in mind," said Gold stiffly. "I can't type."

"Oh, not *that* kind of secretary," Ralph laughed. "I mean—" he groped—"what do you call it? The Cabinet. You wouldn't have to type or take shorthand. You'd have girls like Dusty and Rusty and Misty to do that for you. Would you like to be in the Cabinet?"

Gold was more than mollified. "Ralph, is that really possible?"

"I don't see why not," was Ralph's reply. "Although you might have to start as an under."

"An under?"

"An under is a little bit over a deputy and assistant, I think, but not yet an associate. Unless it's the other way around. Nobody seems sure any more."

"Could I really begin as an undersecretary?"

"In Washington, Bruce, you rise quickly and can't fall very far. How would you like to be Secretary of Labor?"

Gold, on firmer ground now, hesitated deliberately before evincing repugnance. "I think not."

"I can't say I blame you. How about Secretary of the Interior?"

"That sounds rather dark."

"I believe they work with coal mines. Transportation?"

Gold made a face. "That smacks of labor."

"Commerce?"

"It sounds a little bit like peddling."

"You're showing excellent judgment. What about Ambassador to the U.N.?"

"Don't make me laugh."

"What do you think about Secretary of the Treasury?"

Gold pricked up his ears. "What do you think?"

"It has more tone."

"What would I have to do?"

"I think I could find out. Harris Rosenblatt would know. Most of them are very rich and seem to care about money."

"I care about money."

"But they know about it."

Gold declined with regret. "I'm not sure I'd be comfortable. I'm supposed to be something of a pacifist and a radical reformer."

"But a conservative radical reformer, Bruce," Ralph reminded. "That's true."

"Imagine what a blessing it might be to have you in the Department of Defense."

Gold had an inspiration. "How about Secretary of Defense?"

"That's good, Bruce. Especially for a pacifist."

"But I'm only a pacifist in times of peace."

"We'll put it down." Ralph added to his list. "And then there's head of the FBI or CIA to consider."

"Would I have to carry a gun?"

Ralph didn't believe so and wrote those down too. "These are all good, Bruce. Someone with your flair for publicity could probably get your name in the newspapers almost as often as the Secretary of State."

"What about Secretary of State?" asked Gold.

"That's a thought," said Ralph.

"Wouldn't I have to know anything?"

"Absolutely not," Ralph answered, and appeared astounded that Gold even should ask. "In government, Bruce, experience doesn't count and knowledge isn't important. If there's one lesson of value to be learned from the past, Bruce, it's to grab what you want when the chance comes to get it."

Gold asked with distress, "Is that good for the world?"

"Nothing's good for the world, Bruce. I thought you knew that. You've more or less said the same in that last piece of yours. Now, Bruce," Ralph continued awkwardly, "I have to be honest. You might have to get a better wife."

"Than Belle?" Gold was elated.

"I'm sorry." Ralph was solemn. "Belle would be okay for Labor or Agriculture. But not for Secretary of State or Defense."

"Belle and I have not been close," Gold confided.

"In that case I'm happy," said Ralph. "Try someone tall this time, Bruce. You're rather short, you know. It would add to your stature if you had a tall wife."

"Wouldn't a tall wife make me look smaller?" inquired Gold.

"No," said Ralph. "You would make *her* look taller. And that would add more to your stature and make her look smaller. Andrea Conover would be perfect."

"I'm seeing her tonight. Is she tall enough?"

"Oh, easily. And her father is a dying career diplomat with tons of money and the best connections. Propose."

"Tonight?" Gold demurred with a laugh. "I haven't seen her for seven years."

"So what?" Ralph laughed back in encouragement. "You can always get a divorce. Andrea's doing a great job with the Oversight Committee on Government Expenditures. She's the reason we

can't make personal phone calls any more. You know, Bruce—"
Gold rose when Ralph did—"these are really our golden years,
that period when men like us are appealing to all classes of women
between sixteen and sixty-five. I hope you're making the most of
them. A lot of them go for your kind."

"My kind?" Whatever currents of euphoria had been coursing
through Gold's veins congealed.

"Yes," said Ralph.

"What do you mean by my kind?" Gold asked Ralph.

"The kind of person you are, Bruce. Why?"

"As opposed to what other kinds, Ralph?"

"The kinds of person you aren't, Bruce. Why do you ask?"

"Oh, never mind," said Gold and then decided to take the inky
plunge. "Lieberman thinks you're anti-Semitic."

Ralph was stunned. "Me?" His voice was hurt and astonished.
"Bruce, I would feel just awful if I thought I ever did or said a
single thing to give you that impression."

Ralph was sincere and Gold was contrite. "You haven't, Ralph.
I'm sorry I brought it up."

"Thank you, Bruce." Ralph was placated, and his handsome
face fairly shone with grace when he grinned. "Why, I copied your
papers at Columbia. You practically put me through graduate
school. It's just that I really don't feel Lieberman is an especially
nice person."

"He isn't." Gold laughed. "And I've known him all my life."

The strain gone, Ralph said, "Let me take these notes to Dusty
and have her type them up. We've really covered a lot of ground
today, haven't we?"

Gold was not certain, but never in his lifetime had he felt more
sanguine about his prospects. He glanced out the window at official
Washington and caught a glimpse of heaven. Through the doorway, the view of the open office space was a soothing pastoral,
with vistas of modular desks dozing tranquilly under indirect flu-
orescent lighting that never flickered; there were shoulder-high
partitions of translucent glass, other offices across the way as im-
posing as Ralph's, and the dreamlike stirrings of contented people
at work who were in every respect impeccable. The women all

were sunny and chic—not a single one was overweight—the men wore jackets and ties, and every trouser leg was properly creased. If there was a worm at the core in this Garden of Eden, it escaped the cynical inspection of Gold, who could find detritus and incipient decay everywhere. Gold could look through a grapefruit and tell if it was pink.

"You'll like it here, won't you?" said Ralph, reading his mind.

"Is it always like this?"

"Oh, yes," Ralph assured him. "It's always like this when it's this way."

Gold succeeded in speaking without sarcasm. "How is it when it isn't?"

"Isn't what, Bruce?"

"This way."

"Different."

"In what way, Ralph?"

"In different ways, Bruce, unless they're the same, in which case it's this way."

"Ralph," Gold had to ask, "don't people here laugh or smile when you talk that way?"

"What way, Bruce?"

"You seem to qualify or contradict all your statements."

"Do I?" Ralph considered the matter intently. "Maybe I do seem a bit oxymoronic at times. I think everyone here talks that way. Maybe we're all oxymoronic. One time, though, at a high-level meeting, I did say something everyone thought was funny. 'Let's build some death camps,' I said. And everyone laughed. I still can't figure out why. I was being serious."

"I think it's time for me to go," said Gold.

"I'm afraid it is. I'd give just about anything to lunch with you, Bruce, but I can't pass up the chance to eat alone. It's a pity you can't stay through the weekend, although I can't see how that would make any difference. Alma would love to have you out to see her terrarium, but Ellie would be upset."

"Alma?"

"My wife."

"What happened to Kelly?"

"I think you mean Ellie."

"Yes?"

"She got a year older, Bruce. And there was that thin scar from her Caesarean. Ellie would prefer that Alma and I don't start entertaining as a married couple until people first find out I've been divorced." To the blond woman outside his office Ralph said, "Dusty, please tell Rusty and Misty I'll be showing Dr. Gold to the elevator myself. Ask Christy to step inside my office. Tell her I'm horny."

"Sure, love. Bye, sweetheart."

"Who's Christy?" Gold asked.

"The nice-looking one. I don't think you've seen her."

"And what's all this Dr. Gold shit?"

Ralph lowered his voice. "It makes a better impression. Everyone knows professors don't make much money and doctors do. Oooooops—there goes one. Did you see that beautiful ass? Bruce, give my love to Andrea. You might find her a trifle prudish, but she's really as good as gold. It wasn't easy being the only child of Pugh Biddle Conover with all those riches and horses. They ride them, you know." Ralph pronounced this last detail as though describing a tasteless and unhealthy practice. "And give my love to Belle too. How are the children?"

"Fine. One is still at home."

"That's too bad," said Ralph. "Let me give you some good advice, Bruce, from an unofficial opinion of the U.S. Supreme Court. It was seven to one, with the other member abstaining because he was under heavy anesthesia. When you get your divorce, don't fight for custody of the children, or even visitation rights. Make them all ask to come to you. Otherwise they'll think they're doing you a favor by letting you spend time with them, which you will quickly discover they are not."

Nearing the elevators, Gold could contain his curiosity no longer. "Ralph," he said, his fingers clenching nervously, "what do you do here?"

"Work, Bruce. Why?"

"I need some assurance, Ralph, don't I? Before I start making changes, don't you think I ought to find out a few things?"

"I don't see why not."

"What kind of job do you have?"

"A good one, Bruce."

"What do you do?"

"What I'm supposed to."

"Well, what's your position exactly?"

"I'm in the inner circle, Bruce."

"Does that mean you can't talk about it?"

"Oh, no. I can tell you everything. What would you like to know?"

"Well, who do you work for?"

"My superiors."

"Do you have any authority?"

"Oh, yes. A great deal."

"Over who?"

"My subordinates. I can do whatever I want once I get permission from my superiors. I'm my own boss. After all, I'm not really my own boss."

"Well," said Gold, "what are my chances?"

"As good as they ought to be."

"No better?" Gold inquired facetiously.

"Not at this time."

"When should I get in touch with you?"

"When I call you," said Ralph. "Pugh Biddle Conover can help while he's alive," Ralph shouted into the elevator car as the doors were closing.

Gold's mind was shimmering with fantasies of approaching eminence as the car descended. Secretary of State? Head of the CIA? A voice inside cautioned, *Zei nisht naarish.* Where does someone like you come off being Secretary of State? What's so crazy? he answered it brashly. It's happened to bigger *schmucks* than me.

By the time he was outside, only one disquieting thought survived. He'd been fawning.

SEVEN years back, when Gold had his fellowship at the Senator Russell B. Long Foundation and she was a research assistant doing advanced work in home economics, Andrea Conover had been too old for him. Now, nearing thirty-five, she was just right. Gold was no longer attracted to very young girls. With everybody doing everything to each other now, Gold had only his middle age and his large reputation as a minor intellectual to recommend him as a lover. It was all he wanted. He had never really liked going down.

Andrea was taller than he remembered. Or he had grown shorter. She paid for the drinks and dinner with a credit card, shyly confiding she would charge the expense to the Oversight Committee on Government Expenditures. Gold wondered what in the world she saw in him. She was easily the most beautiful woman he had ever been with, the richest, his first society girl. Her hair was blond. She had blue eyes, a small, straight nose, a broad forehead. Her complexion was light, her skin unmarred. To Gold, who was still shepherding the last of three children through orthodontia, her splendid teeth were of transcending symbolic importance. Her posture and muscle tone were good.

"You must learn to think more of yourself," he told her at one point during dinner, and took her hand lightly for a few seconds. "After all, if you are not for yourself, who else shall be for you?" A self-conscious prudence deterred him from attributing the paraphrase to Rabbi Hillel.

Andrea was timid and deferential, and he was not certain how to proceed with a woman of such quality. In the taxi outside her condominium he asked if he might come up for a drink. She consented with evident relief, grateful, it seemed, for his preemptive move. The apartment was large for a single person, even for one so tall, and the unexpected good order suggested the daily ministrations of an efficient cleaning woman. The furniture was ghastly, the pieces outsized.

"It was left this way when I bought it," he was pleased to hear her explain.

Gold took it as propitious that she seated herself on the sofa near him after bringing him his cognac.

"All that year together at the Senator Russell B. Long Foundation," she said with some bashfulness, sipping her vodka, "I thought you didn't like me."

"Really?" said Gold. "I always liked you. I thought you didn't like me."

"I always liked you."

"You should have said something."

"I thought you hated me. I never thought you even noticed me."

"Oh, come on."

"Really, Dr. Gold—"

"Call me Bruce," he interrupted.

She blushed. "I'm not sure I can."

"Try."

"Bruce."

"You see?" he laughed.

"You're so much fun."

"Why did you think I hated you?"

"Because you knew I liked you," she answered.

"I didn't know you liked me," he said. "I thought you hated me."

She was moderately overwrought, as though charged with something heinous. "Why would I hate you?"

"I don't know," said Gold, and noticed his hands moving about restlessly. "I had so little to offer a single girl like you who was so sensitive and intelligent and even had her own Ph.D."

"I wouldn't have cared," she said in soulful apology. "I was so impressed with you. Everyone was. You were always so quick and domineering and sexy."

"Sexy?" Gold was astounded.

"Of course. All the girls there thought so."

"Do you still," asked Gold, "think I'm sexy?"

"Oh, yes." She blushed again.

Gold wondered what to do next. He laughed loudly and punched her lightly on the arm, as one good fellow to another, and then brushed the back of his fingers against her cheek as though in unpremeditated extension of his jocular disbelief. Her reaction surprised him. Instead of stiffening or withdrawing, as he more or less expected her to do, she leaned into his hand and continued bringing herself toward him on the sofa. In a moment they were kissing. Brandy splashed on his knees as he blindly divested himself of his glass and took her in his arms. Her fingers were clasping the back of his head. Again, he was at a loss to proceed with a girl like her. He moved his lips about her ears and neck as though in thirsting search of an erogenous zone. A waste of time, he knew from experience. Erogenous zones were either everywhere or nowhere, and he meant to write about that someday, too, when neither Belle nor his daughter would be scandalized by his knowledge. With a guilty start he realized his mind had been wandering, and refocused his attention upon Andrea. He clutched her all the harder to compensate for moments lost in digression and feigned a gasping shortness of breath. Moaning softly, he kissed her eyes and waited for something to happen. Andrea dropped her hand into his lap and took hold of his penis. Then he knew he had it made.

GOLD WOKE up in love and a believer in miracles. Andrea did not seem to mind his scrawny chest and sinewy, hairy legs and arms. He showered and, after breakfasting with just a yellow towel knotted faddishly about his waist, began to dress lazily. Gold had made the coffee, while Andrea sliced overripe bananas into breakfast cereal. At his suggestion, she added raisins. On his next trip, he would bring her a coffee grinder, a pound of his favorite blend of coffee beans, and a French drip coffeepot of ceramic. Gold could cook when he had to. He would introduce her to Irish oatmeal.

"Will you want to see me again?" she asked from her dressing table.

"Of course," said Gold.

"Lots of men don't."

"Lots of men?" Gold, sitting on the edge of her bed, paused with a sock halfway up his ankle.

She nodded, turning faintly pink. "I don't mean lots in here. But lots of men take me out and say they'll call me and then they never do."

"Why not?"

"I don't know. Do you really want to see me again? I'll understand if you don't."

"I'd like to come back next week."

"You could stay here with me in the apartment," she said. "I won't be in the way."

"I was hoping you would ask."

She was pleased. He was mystified. "I'm so glad you liked me," she told him. "Was I all right?"

"Andrea, you must never ask that," he instructed. As a matter of fact, she had not been all right, but Gold was far too astute to delve into that can of worms now. "And I think I'm in love with you."

Gold was struck afresh by the number of stunning tall women who fell in love with shorter men like himself who were rapacious, egotistical, and calculating. Andrea might not be expected to know he was rapacious and calculating. Surely, though, she must suspect he was shorter. The explanations that came most readily to the fore were anything but complimentary to either of them. Was it possible that someone so self-assessing as himself had qualities of attraction he was not aware of? It was possible, for Andrea in the nude was as gorgeous as he'd imagined, and she seemed to adore him.

In morning light her eyes were lavender. Her legs were long and straight, her hips small, her grip strong, and all her fair flesh was imbued with a golden tinge that contrasted beautifully, he thought, with his own swarthier pigmentation. She loved his darker color. She was charmed by the hair on his chest. He watched with the possessive air of someone special as she slipped a tasteful print dress over her head and shook out her hair. That she was rich added an extra dimension of vitality and eroticism to the quixotic passion he felt for her. Nothing equals the foot for ugliness, Gold remembered Ernest Becker had written in *The Denial of Death*, but hers, both bare and shod, were as unremarkable to him as his own.

"When I was young," she ruminated aloud, adjusting a thin gold necklace, "I wanted to be a model. I guess I still do. Not a fashion model. A sex model." She applied makeup sparingly to her lips and eyes. "I wanted to be a cheesecake model or pose in the nude. Then when all these obscene newspapers and magazines began coming out, I wanted to be a pornographic model or act in dirty movies. I used to sit in front of a mirror for hours and practice sucking dicks. For the camera, I mean. Like those models in cosmetic ads. I got to be quite good at it, I think. Would you like to see?"

"I have to go back to New York," he replied in the steadiest voice.

"It's just a small motion of the mouth."

"I have a one o'clock class."

"It only takes a second, silly," said Andrea, and made a small motion of her mouth above her cylinder of pale lipstick. "Isn't that good?"

"Yes," said Gold. "That's quite good."

"I was such a ninny as a child, the only child of Pugh Biddle Conover," Andrea went on. "I didn't know anything until I left home. I had to go to *two* finishing schools before I was ready for college, and then to three colleges. At Smith the other girls would talk about sex all the time, and I didn't understand. I remember I never could figure out why anybody would want to suck a rooster."

Gold was immobilized. In less than two days in Washington he was learning to handle with numb amazement the many bizarre surprises to which he perceived he was going to be increasingly subjected. "I can see," he said, "how that might be confusing to someone who did not understand." He straightened his other sock and put on his shoes.

"Once I found out, of course," said Andrea, "I took to it all like a duck to water. Last summer I was at the swimming pool at Daddy's estate with this new beau, and he did the strangest thing. I was scraping a callus off the bottom of my foot with a callus scraper. He stood up suddenly and said he never wanted to see me again, and he drove away without packing his things or even saying goodbye to Daddy. Do you know why?"

Gold came up behind her and stroked her shoulders. "Were you near each other when you were scraping off the callus?"

"We were together at the pool."

"Does it make a noise?"

"Like sandpaper."

"I might have done the same thing."

"I don't know things like that."

"I will teach you."

Andrea pressed his hand to her lips rapturously. Gold wondered if she was crazy. "Sometime soon," she said, "if you still want to see me again—"

"I will want to see you again."

"Would you like to come out for a weekend to visit Daddy before he dies? It's really a lovely estate."

"What is your father ill with?"

"He won't say. Six years ago he bought an electric wheelchair, and he's been confined to it ever since. Every weekend he has mobs of people out to ride and shoot."

"Shoot?"

"Quail and pheasant. Sometimes rabbit and deer."

"No people?"

"Not yet. I think you'll enjoy meeting my father."

"I shall spare you," said Gold, "from ever meeting mine."

"**N**O one in our family," observed Gold's father that evening from the most comfortable chair in Gold's living room, "has ever had a divorce."

"Why not?" asked Dina.

"I don't allow them, that's why," the old man said. "Golds don't get divorces. We have death sometimes, but no divorces."

"Are you and Mommy ever going to get a divorce?" Dina inquired of Gold.

"Over my dead body," answered Gold's father.

"We'd rather have death," Gold added dryly, staring through bloodshot eyes from one speaker to the next.

In a day that had opened in glory for Gold and gone downhill steadily, the low point had been touched with his finding company for dinner. Rose and Max had traveled into the city because of a growth in her breast that had proved upon examination, thank God, to be an easily aspirated cyst. Belle, who accompanied them to the cancer specialist recommended by Murshie Weinrock, had invited them back to the apartment. Irv drove in later with the others. Gold's nerves were ragged. He had work he wanted to continue.

"When you starting in Washington?" his father asked.

"I have to go back next week. To find out."

"That's what I thought," jeered Julius Gold in satisfaction. "What kind of a job would they give to a Jew like you?"

"Admiral."

"Then me they would make a commodore," the old man shot back, "with all the sailing you done."

"How much you done?"

"I came by boat from Antwerp all the way from Russia with Sid and Rose from that Tsar Nikolai. You?"

"Okay, Commodore," Gold sighed with a strained smile. "We're all tired. Can you be a little quiet tonight?"

"He'll be quiet a long time," said Gold's stepmother.

Gold's father elevated himself half out of his armchair and screwed his face up into almost a point. "What's that mean?" he demanded.

"Well, in my family in Richmond," answered Gold's stepmother, concentrating on her knitting and looking weirder than usual in the large pink gingham bonnet she had worn all through the meal, "whenever a child would tell a parent to be quiet or still, the parent, usually the mother, would reply, 'I'll be quiet a long time.' Meaning, of course, that she would soon be dead and would do no more talking."

A moment of shocked silence passed before his father growled, "Well, I ain't no mother. And I ain't doing no dying so soon. So please be quiet."

"She'll be quiet a long time," said Dina.

"Thank you, child."

Gold's father turned away from his second wife with an expression of profound disgust and told Gold, "You'll come to the house Sunday for lunch. Sid too."

"Not this weekend." Gold shook his head. "I've got papers to correct and an article to finish."

"Another article?"

"Another screw," said his stepmother, "seems to be coming loose."

Gold wanted to kill her.

Irv grinned with the rest. "What's this one on?"

"Education."

"Are you for or against?" asked his father.

"Against."

"It's about time you got smart. It ain't done you so much good.

Then you'll come next Sunday. I got questions about going back to Florida.'' He glanced about the room irritably and demanded, ''Why ain't Sid here?''

''Maybe he wasn't invited.''

''Why wasn't he invited?''

''Maybe you didn't ask us to.''

''I have to ask?''

''I asked,'' said Belle. ''They had someplace else to go.''

The old man absorbed this information desolately. Rose was yawning and Max murmured that it was time to leave.

''Not so fast,'' objected the old man. ''I got a couple of dead *faygelehs* I want to watch on television tonight.''

Irv swore he would get him back to his own house in time.

Gold shot into his study before the last had gone and began separating his school work from his personal work while bluntly measuring the impact of the divorce he was considering. Belle could take care of herself. His father would be hurt, Sid wouldn't mind, his sisters would grieve. His stepmother could hang herself. His children could go fuck themselves—let their therapists worry about them. The boys were not bad, now that they were both out of the house. Dina was hell, one affliction he might reasonably have been spared, he felt, as his twelve-year-old daughter strolled in and said:

''Mom's really pissed, ain't she?''

''I haven't noticed.'' Gold did not look up.

''Don't shit me,'' said Dina. ''She don't want you to go to Washington, does she?''

''I'll let you know when I find out.''

''Balls, Dad. Listen, you better be goddamned careful what you put in any more articles you write. That crap on child rearing you had in the *Ladies' Home Journal* last year didn't do me no good.''

''That was intended as a joke.''

''Nobody got it.''

''They'll get this one.''

''What's it called?''

'' 'Education and Truth *or* Truth in Education.' ''

''I don't get it.''

"Take a walk."

"How come I got to go to school if you don't believe in education?"

"It gets you out of the house."

"I'd really like to get out of this house. Living with you and she ain't no bed of roses, you know."

"Get good marks for a year," Gold urged. "And I'll sneak you into boarding school on a scholarship. Let me write your papers for you."

She shook her head. "Not a chance. I ain't ready for all that teen-age sex yet. I saw what you did to my brothers as soon as they went away. You turned their bedrooms into a study and a library."

"There's always room when they come home."

"On the floor. You ain't getting rid of me that fast. I told Lieberman's kid you're going to work in Washington."

Gold smiled in anticipation. "What'd you say?"

"I told him the President was giving you a job as a mayor or governor."

Gold flung down a pencil. "Oh, Jesus Christ. Don't they teach you nothing in that fucking school I send you to?"

"They try," Dina granted philosophically. "But I'm too smart for them. Listen, Dad, I'm warning you. You write anything about me in an article again and it'll be your ass."

GOLD HAD written the opening paragraph of his article on education on the plane ride back from Washington and had completed most of the first draft in his classroom that afternoon instead of teaching. He had stacks of student blue books that would eventually have to be read. Dyspeptic and much put upon is how Gold would have described himself to a biographer if ever one should appear. Arriving at the college from the airport by cab late that morning, he was exactly in that physical and mental state. Already his remembrance of having made love to Andrea appeared to belong to an unrecoverable past.

He was unshaven and unprepared. He threw nearly all of his mail away. He acknowledged with a surly nod the greetings of colleagues, who were astonished to see him.

Gold never spent more time on campus than he had to and never went to faculty meetings. He posted a liberal schedule of office hours but did not keep them. Student conferences were by appointment only, and he never made any. Gold's favorites were those who dropped his courses before the term started. He disliked most the ones whose attendance was regular and whose assignments were completed on time. He was no more interested in their schoolwork than in his own. He arrived in the classroom five minutes late and, to the consternation of all, distributed examination booklets.

"Today," he began right in, "we're going to have one of those surprise examinations I may have mentioned. Write an essay in answer to a question that would lead you to discuss the high points of the work we've covered so far."

"What's the question?" asked a girl in front.

"Make one up. You'll be judged on the merit of your question as well as the quality of your answer. Begin."

Gold emptied his attaché case. There, still in a rubber band, was a bundle of blue books from his other undergraduate class, essays, he remembered with a sinking heart, on the psychology of sociology in contemporary American literature and on the sociology of psychology in English novels of the nineteenth and twentieth centuries. They had been written for a course devised by him with no better intent than to lure people into literature from psychology and sociology on the mistaken assumption they would be mastering all three disciplines simultaneously with no greater expenditure of labor or time. Soon, he perceived, he would have this new set of blue books to lug around like a millstone. Lacking anything better to do, he reread the opening paragraph he had written on a yellow pad on the airplane, was tickled by his felicity of thought and word, and took up a pen enthusiastically. His progress was rapid. He was about to move into the concluding section of his piece on education and truth when he was brought to a halt by the first of his students to finish, a pale, gangling young man wearing a woven skullcap of patterned circles.

"Mr. Epstein?" he called softly as the boy tiptoed past.

"Sir?"

"What high school did you go to?" They spoke in undertones.

"The Herzliah Yeshiva."

"Oh, yes. I know it well. That's in Brighton, isn't it?"

"No, sir. Borough Park."

"Have you ever heard of a holiday called Shmini Atzereth?"

"Yes, sir. It comes right after Yom Kippur."

Gold clicked his tongue in disappointment. "How about Shabbos Bereishes?"

"Last week. That's a calendar day, though, Professor Gold, rather than a holiday."

"Do something for me, Mr. Epstein. Give me a list of all the Jewish holidays and calendar days this year. And maybe in some way I'll be able to repay the favor soon."

"Yes, Professor Gold, I'll be glad to. I hope you won't mind if I tell you I'm very disappointed in the course."

Gold sighed sympathetically. "So am I. What's *your* complaint?"

"It's called 'Monarchy and Monotheism in Literature from the Medieval to the Modern.' "

"Yes?"

"But it seems to be a course in Shakespeare's history plays," said Mr. Epstein.

"We'll be moving on to the major tragedies soon," Gold answered breezily. "All but *Othello* and the Roman plays. In *Othello*, unfortunately, there is no monarch, and the Romans were not monotheistic."

"The course description in the college catalogue isn't accurate," Epstein complained.

"I know," said Gold. "I wrote it."

"Was that fair?"

"No. But maybe it was intelligent. We feel that anyone interested in literature ought to study Shakespeare and we know that few students will do so unless we call it something else."

"But I'm not interested in literature. I'm interested in God. I became an English major because the English Department seems to be offering so many courses in theology and religious visionary experiences."

"You were misled," said Gold. "If I were your adviser I would have forewarned you."

"You are my adviser," said the boy, "and you're never in your office."

Gold averted his eyes. "I'm always in class, though. If you'd like, I'll allow you to drop the course."

"Should I switch to the Department of Religion?"

"No, don't go there. You'll be reading Milton and Homer. Try Psychology if you're interested in God. I believe they've latched on to religion now."

"Where are the psychology courses?"

"In Anthropology. Soon everything is going to be in Urban Studies anyway, so you might as well major in that. But do it soon. Otherwise you might find me there in a year or two and have to read Shakespeare's history plays all over again."

Gold was praying hard that Epstein would drop his course before he had to read his essay.

Gold prayed also for an endowed chair in the Urban Studies Program that would double his salary while halving his course load. Gold had little doubt he would succeed in Washington if once given the chance, for he was a master at diplomacy and palace intrigue. He was the department's deadliest strategist in the conflict now raging to attract students to subjects in liberal arts from other divisions of the college and to subjects in English from other departments in liberal arts. Gold wrote the most enticing titles and descriptions for the college catalogue, and no one was more successful at originating popular new courses. Gold was the architect of an illicit and secret policy of détente that permitted members of the German Department to give courses in remedial English to Hispanic and Oriental students in exchange for votes on critical issues at faculty council meetings. Italy and Spain were reeling as a result, Classics was deserted, and France had been isolated. Russia was in decline, along with History, Economics, and Philosophy. China was reduced to a flash in the pan: only the courses in Chinese cooking enjoyed flourishing enrollments. In the most successful maneuver of all, Comparative Literature had been walled off from texts in translation, while Gold and his English Department were free to pillage the continent at will for such triumphant creations of his as "Dante, Hell, Fire, and Faulkner"; "Through Hell and High Water with Hemingway, Hesse, Hume, Hobbes,

Hinduism and Others: A Shortcut to India''; "Blake, Spinoza, and Contemporary American Pornography in Film and Literature''; "Sex in World and American Literature''; and "The Role of Women, Blacks, and Drugs in Sex and Religion in World and American Film and Literature.'' It was now possible, in fact, thanks to the enterprise of Gold, for a student to graduate as an English major after spending all four years of academic study watching foreign motion pictures in a darkened classroom without being exposed for even one moment to any other light but that of a movie projector. As a result of these progressive innovations, the English Department was one of the few on campus with swelling registrations and a demonstrable need for a larger faculty, a need filled in part by professors of German teaching remedial English to natives of Hong Kong and Puerto Rico. Gold had made peace with the Hun and enjoyed the high regard of his superiors.

Gold himself was saturnine and subdued in the misanthropic pleasure he obtained from these accomplishments. His job was secure. He was esteemed by his colleagues and did not like that. He soon would be given tenure and didn't want it. He would rather feel at liberty. Gold possessed an advantage at the college similar to one he enjoyed with his family: if he did not talk, his relatives assumed he was thinking; if he did not go to faculty meetings, it was taken for granted he was engaged in more important matters. Like a paramecium feeding blindly and incessantly, the English Department, under Gold's initiative and supervision, had stealthily been subsuming more and more areas of the Urban Studies Program through a schedule of courses he'd invented called "Recent American Realistic Problem Literature of the City.''

Gold had no clear idea yet what Urban Studies was about. But he knew he could do that shit as well as anybody else.

GOLD, WHO adamantly repelled conversational overtures on planes from everybody but attractive women, had plunged into his *New York Times* that morning with hawklike predacity as soon as he was seated on the shuttle returning him to New York. He had called Andrea from the airport in Washington and knew he would phone again from LaGuardia to say he missed her still. He quickly found himself at one of the important sections of the newspaper that interested him the most, the social page. Life in the city had gone spinning on without him. He read:

> "It's to die," bubbled Jan Chipman jammed on a banquette with her sister Buffy Cafritz, the Carleton Varneys and the Harold Reeds. "I wouldn't believe that my husband would sit on a floor to watch a fashion show."

Gold could believe it. With fingernails curving like claws, he separated the paragraph from the page and placed the ragged clipping between the leaves of his memorandum pad as frugally as a European bus conductor making change. He would use it, perhaps in his book on Jews. A fragment of political news on the front page kicked over in his memory, and he turned back to read:

> In Indianapolis this morning, the President defended himself against a charge that he was a weak President who allowed himself to be "pushed around." "People who live in glass houses shouldn't throw stones," he retorted at a news conference.

Gold tore it out. Undoubtedly his President needed him. Business conditions were the same, he saw in the financial section, the verities of the free marketplace eternally unchanged, although he had to read the key sentence a second time to be sure:

> Now, however, some analysts believe that the Federal Reserve Bank has stiffened its credit posture because of the growing danger of an economic recovery.

In education, the paper recorded a 55 percent increase in crimes in schools:

> The number of reported acts of crime
> and violence in the city's schools, in-
> cluding assaults on teachers, has risen
> sharply this fall. This improvement fol-
> lowed a sharp upward trend in crime
> during the school year ended last June.

Gold was filled with inspiration suddenly for a brilliant opening to his "Education and Truth *or* Truth in Education." He wrote:

> Education is the third greatest cause of human misery in the world. The first, of course, is life.

Here he had to pause. He had no idea of the second. Death was tempting. Death after life was either very good or very bad. It was glib, and might be mistaken for wit. He decided to chance it. He was on his way with another telling piece that might bring him to the attention of an admiring multitude larger than he had yet enjoyed. He closed his eyes and smiled. Gold was never invited to fashion shows. Soon he would be. He wondered if Mr. Chipman had enjoyed sitting on the floor the evening earlier and if he was eager to do so again. He was saddened that any reply by Buffy Cafritz to her sister had gone unreported and was probably lost for all time. Gold was good at daydreaming and gave himself up to the contemplation of what it would be like to work with Ralph for the President, marry Andrea, share her apartment in Washington, fuck her richer and even more attractive friends, serve on a Presidential Commission on education, and be an overpaid professor of Urban Studies. It was to die.

V
Education and Truth *or* Truth in Education

"**B**RILLIANT!" was a word Andrea Biddle Conover employed to praise Gold's "Education and Truth *or* Truth in Education." "Trenchant" was another, along with "pithy," and Gold rated her animated approval brilliant, trenchant, and pithy. It was not Gold's method to show new work to anyone but editors. Never, however, had he been so intimately involved with a woman of such stunning ways whose academic credentials surpassed even his own, an undergraduate degree at Smith, a master's at Yale, her doctorate from Harvard, and a lectureship in England for one year at Cambridge University in her field of home economics.

Gold discovered during his second tryst in Washington that Andrea Biddle Conover's white terry-cloth bathrobe was too voluminous for him. The large sleeves could be cuffed back over his spidery hands and forearms, but the abundant folds of the skirt were treacherously long and twirled and dragged behind him in a disorderly train. He saw also with disquietude that his present circumstances would not afford him the money and the time to return to Washington as frequently as he would like.

"If you never want to see me again," she volunteered, "I'll understand."

That insistent pledge was beginning to jangle. "I do want to see you again," he assured her with passion. "I would like to spend whole weekends with you. It's just that I'm in this awful limbo right now. Ralph doesn't want me to call him at the office, and he doesn't want me to call him at home. He tells me you won't let anyone get personal calls on government telephones."

"I would let him get one from you, silly," she sighed.

"He might be annoyed," Gold reflected disconsolately.

"Or I can listen in for you."

"You can listen in?"

"Of course, silly," Andrea laughed, beaming at his disbelief. "On everybody." This was the third time, Gold noted, that she had carelessly addressed him as silly. Here was another trait of personality he would soon rigidly have to modify and he found himself looking ahead, with some feelings of vengefulness, to assuming more broadly the role of mentor and disciplinarian.

"You know, Dr. Gold—"

"Bruce," he corrected.

"Bruce—" Andrea glowed each time at such testimonies of minute observance—"maybe my father can help. But he'd want to make sure we're close. A lot of times he helps men and then they never want to see me again."

"How much closer can we be?" Gold cried, and stumbled on the lagging fringe of her bathrobe as he hurled himself across her living room to embrace her.

Gold was enamored. Andrea was captivating in all moods and states of dress and at all times of day. While Gold made improvements in his essay, Andrea, enchanting in eyeglasses, read and graded his student blue books, penciling comments faintly that he could later copy in ink. He pictured an endless and untroubled idyl. Andrea was fascinated by his Irish oatmeal and had responded with gratifying exclamations of rapture to his freshly ground blend of mocha, java, and French roast coffee beans. An entirety of bliss lay in store. She would grade all his papers, balance his checkbook, and write out his alimony payments. In spring he would make her *matzoh brei*.

WITH MAGNIFICENT self-restraint he kept the article down to four thousand words and mailed this abbreviated, droll presentation of his ideas to an editor of the *Times Magazine* who had been soliciting a piece from him for almost a year and who rejected it overnight with the gratuitous recommendation he reduce it to eight hundred words, improve the title, and submit it to a different section of the newspaper, the Op Ed page. Gold knew then he would hate that man till his last breath. He reduced the piece to twelve hundred words and, as directed, submitted this shortened version to the Op Ed page, where it was received with a cry of delight by an irrepressible young editor who pronounced himself blessed to receive so pregnant a work from so revered a source and then requested Gold to cut four hundred words and change the title.

"An affirmative statement would be superior to all that enigmatic coyness, which is not worthy of you, Professor Gold, not worthy of you at all. Use your last sentence as the title instead."

Gold condensed the piece further by four hundred words but stuck to his title and received a check from *The New York Times* for one hundred and twenty-five dollars. Less than a week after his few paragraphs appeared, two letters stimulated by his piece were published. The first was a note of genial accolade from a nonagenerian in Massachusetts who said he had not read a book or a poem, looked at a painting, or given a thought to anything but his income and his health since graduating from Williams seventy-eight years earlier and had not in that time suffered a second's regret or sense of loss. The second was a vituperative attack from Lieberman, who declared Gold "morally nihilistic and iconoclastically desecrating," denounced him for "insultingly promulgating challengingly contrary predications that all we loyal, good Americans must unprecedentedly disapprove of," and scornfully defied him to rebut these charges "if he dared!" Gold loved seeing his name in the papers this second time and was rejoicing as well in the two phone calls he'd already received. The first was from a leader in the State Senate, who requested Gold's support of an education bill denying financial aid to any community in New York containing poor people.

"The beauty of the bill—and I'm sure you'll agree, Dr. Gold—is that it will help force most families on welfare out of New York State."

Gold held back. "I know a better way," he said wryly. "Why not change the welfare laws to give money to all poor people who live *out* of the state instead of those who live in?"

"By God, Gold!" Gold, in his time, had produced many a favorable response. He had never been witness to a better. "I think that's the best political idea I ever heard. Will you come to Albany and help push it through?"

"I'm afraid not."

"Then I'll take all the credit myself!"

The second call was from Ralph. "I thought of phoning you immediately, but the idea never entered my mind. We're going to send you up to Congress to argue our position for us. You've given us just the ammunition we need to end all federal aid to public education."

Gold felt terrible. "Ralph, that wasn't exactly my plan," he interposed timidly. "I was trying to improve education, not destroy it."

"Well, Bruce, nothing succeeds as planned," Ralph informed him instructively. "If we can keep our educational systems just as bad while lowering the cost, we would be improving our educational systems a good deal, wouldn't we? Bruce, you won't have to say anything you don't believe when you talk to Congress. Just tell the truth."

"The truth?"

"Even if you have to lie."

"I suppose," Gold reflected, "I could do that."

"The President will be tickled. He was particularly impressed with your statement—oh, what genius you have—that an ignorant citizen is the best citizen."

Gold gave a start. "That was meant to be ironic, Ralph."

"I'm afraid we all missed that, Bruce."

"Lately," Gold complained, "all my sarcasms are being received as truths."

"That may be," consoled Ralph respectfully, "because like all brilliant artists, you are in closer touch with reality than you know. Your appointment to the new Presidential Commission on Education and Political Welfare is now assured. We'll issue the announcement next week, right after we have your piece read into the *Congressional Record* with a few changes we have in mind. Only if you approve, of course. I'd like to cut about two hundred words and take your closing sentence and use that as the title. Then I'd like to have the authorship read Dr. Bruce Gold."

Gold objected with sadness. "I'm not a doctor, Ralph," he pointed out.

"You're a Ph.D."

"So are you, Ralph. How would you like it if people started calling you doctor?"

"I'd hate it, Bruce. But I'm not German."

"Neither am I, Ralph," said Gold. "My parents were Russian."

"What's the difference?"

"Between Russian and German, Ralph?" asked Gold.

"Oh, you know what I mean, Bruce, don't you?"

"I'm not sure that I do, Ralph. In what way are Russian and German the same?"

"They're both European, Bruce. I thought you knew that."

"I did," said Gold, still depressed. "Not even Anton Chekhov is called doctor."

"It's only for the *Congressional Record*, Bruce," Ralph cajoled. "Nobody reads that but the typesetter, and he's usually blind."

"Ralph, I would look ridiculous and pompous. Kissinger was called doctor, and you know what people thought of him. No, Ralph, I can't allow it."

"I'm afraid I have to insist."

"It's my nature to resist insistence."

"Then let me persuade."

"In that case I consent."

"Bruce, I can't tell you how inspired we are that you're coming to join us. You're already setting a standard of accomplishment that all of us are trying to equal. We call it the Gold standard."

No laughter followed from Ralph.

And none, therefore, came from Gold. "Ralph, how much will it pay?" Gold finally found bravery to ask. "I may have to take a leave from college."

"Nothing, I'm afraid."

"Nothing?"

"Just expenses. Up to a thousand dollars a day."

Gold came closer then than ever in his life to yodeling. "That seems like a lot," he remarked with staid objectivity.

"It doesn't go as far as it used to." Ralph sounded sympathetic and ashamed. He muffled his voice a bit when he continued, "Of course, you can submit a false diary of expenses and perhaps keep a little. If anybody is listening in, I am making that suggestion only as a joke. But don't tell Andrea. She's scrupulous as a hawk when it comes to government money. Right, Andrea? Some of these Presidential Commissions go on forever."

A thousand a day forever appeared to Gold a return that was more than paltry.

His piece was read into the *Congressional Record* by a Representative from Louisiana Gold had never heard of. The morning following, Gold was astounded upon opening his *Times* to find his article published there again under a different title, accompanied by an explanation below:

CORRECTION

Last week the *Times* published an essay mistakenly called "Education and Truth *or* Truth in Education" and erroneously naming the author as Bruce Gold. The author should have been identified as Dr. Bruce Gold, who has recently been appointed to the new Presidential Commission on Education and Political Welfare. Because of the widespread interest in Dr. Gold and his views, the *Times* is pleased to make this clarification and republish his essay under its correct title, "Say Yea to Life!"

Another check arrived from *The New York Times* for one hundred and twenty-five dollars. Gold loved getting money in the mail more than anything else in the world, he guessed, and seldom was unhappy on days some came. He wondered with cheerful whimsy whether there might be another letter in the paper from Lieberman.

LIEBERMAN had put on weight and gravy stains since Gold had lunched with him last. He had lost more strands of his carrot-colored hair. "Did you read my piece in the *Times?*" he asked.

"What piece?" asked Gold.

"My letter demolishing your article," Lieberman replied. The tables in the delicatessen were small and close. "I notice you didn't try to rebut me. I had a devastating reply all ready for you and the whole cowardly Eastern liberal establishment."

"Publish it in your magazine," said Pomoroy.

"Nobody reads my magazine," said Lieberman with abruptly deflating morale.

"Put it in your next autobiography," said Gold. "I'll probably be a famous government figure by then."

There was something akin to hatred in Lieberman's glare. "How many people are there on this Commission?"

"Eight," said Gold. In truth there were twenty-five.

"I want you to know," said Lieberman with the starchy courtesy of protocol, chewing his cheeseburger messily, "that I'm going to have to oppose you. I'll write devastating articles and editorials in my magazine."

"Nobody reads your magazine," reminded Gold.

"I have friends in Washington."

"No, you haven't," said Pomoroy.

"There are people there who know who I am."

"It's why you have no friends," said Gold, savoring as always Lieberman's tormented display of jealousy and resentment.

Now it was Lieberman's round to lie. "Frankly, I wouldn't even take a job like that," he said with a gloating snort, and spit chewed bits of ground meat and melted Cheddar cheese onto the sleeves and lapels of his woolen jacket. He rubbed them into the fabric with his thumb. Then he licked his thumb. "Not unless I could be chairman of the Commission, write the report, and have direct access to the President whenever I felt the situation warranted it. You have my permission to tell that to Ralph."

"Ralph will be inconsolable," said Gold.

"But I'm willing to listen to reason."

"There will be dancing in the streets."

Pomoroy, saturnine and somber as ever, sipped unflavored yogurt from his spoon aseptically as though from a medicine dropper, glowering at Lieberman like a man nurturing a concealed grudge.

"Where's my book?" Pomoroy demanded of Gold, touching at last on the purpose of their meeting.

"*I've* started a new one," intruded Lieberman.

"It's almost done." Gold paid no attention to Lieberman either.

"By which you mean, I take it," said Pomoroy, "that you haven't started."

"There's not much point in beginning until I've finished, is there? That will only create a need for revisions later. I like to know what conclusions we've got before I set out proving them."

"Do you know?"

"Just about," said Gold. "I know there've been a number of good books on this same subject of the Jewish experience I can steal from in total confidence."

"*I* was going to tell *you* that."

"I may need more money. I've put aside my novel, you know."

"You'll have to show me some work."

"I'll show you copies of the books I'm going to steal from."

"Don't you believe in original research any more?" Pomoroy's tone was only faintly caustic.

"Unmistakably," Gold answered. "That's why I'm always so willing to use other people's."

"I wonder often," Pomoroy deplored with a sigh, "if editors and writers and thinkers of the past ever engaged in sordid conversations like this one. Then I remember what I know about them and realize they did. Seriously, have you any idea when you might have it done? I don't take things like this lightly any more.''

"No," Gold replied frankly. "Give me another month or so to sort things out. I'd like to introduce some unique and significant personal elements, if I can figure out what they should be.''

Gold ate his fruit cup and cottage cheese without appetite. Lieberman had ordered a jumbo cheeseburger, a combination lean pastrami-corned beef-tongue-turkey-chopped liver-and-Swiss cheese-tomato-and-Bermuda onion sandwich, a plate of French-fried potatoes, and a chocolate malted milk. "I wish I had you guys' metabolism,'' he had muttered earlier. "Then I could be skinny too." Lieberman still ate with both hands, ingesting and ejaculating food simultaneously while talking without interrupting himself to swallow or breathe. He had eaten his soup with his spoon in both hands. He held his jumbo cheeseburger in both hands.

"I can finish my book in a month and it will be better than his," Lieberman said.

"How can you have such a high opinion of yourself," Pomoroy asked Lieberman, "when all the people who know you have such a low one?"

Lieberman, chewing pensively, turned the question over in his head as though the interrogation were a petition for counsel instead of a slur.

"I'm the editor of one of the biggest little magazines in the country."

"With a circulation of sixteen," said Gold.

"Who belittle you," said Pomoroy.

"I know more," said Lieberman, "and have a better education than over ninety-nine percent of the American people, which means, probably, more than a hundred percent of all the people in the world."

"So do we," said Pomoroy.

"It ain't enough," said Gold.

"It ain't?"

"Not for you," said Pomoroy. "Do you realize, Lieberman—"

"Please call me Skip."

"Do you realize, Lieberman, that you are probably the only person I've met of whom I've never heard anyone speak well?"

Lieberman weighed that information gravely. "Never?"

"Bruce, you grew up with him."

"Not really," said Gold. "Our families lived for a while on the same block. It was a long block."

"You went to elementary school with him, didn't you?"

"Only for a few grades. His family moved to Brighton Beach."

"But you went through high school together."

"He was one year ahead."

"But you know him a long time. Have you ever heard anyone speak well of him?"

"No," Gold answered truthfully. "Skip was always lacking in charm, talent, wit, intelligence, and social ability."

"You're both mistaken," interposed Lieberman. "I was always the best student in my class."

"The second best, you liar," said Gold. "I was the best."

"I went to Columbia College on a scholarship."

"No, you didn't," Gold corrected him again. "And neither did I, although we both say we did. And you were never a member of any Communist organization, so stop taking credit for having resigned from one."

Lieberman, who had never been a Communist, was always tremendously complimented now when singled out as a former one, although he was not quite so complacent when detected at anniversary and testimonial dinners for reactionary groups calling themselves conservative at which celebrated anti-Semites and neo-Fascists were speakers or among the other guests more honored than himself. Lieberman, puff-bellied, jowly, large, and double-chinned, was all for sending in the bombers and for standing up to everyone all over the globe. He was not afraid of war with Russia or China. He was afraid of Pomoroy and Gold.

"I'm a vastly improved writer now," Lieberman pleaded for approbation with an onset of hope. "I'm taking a much braver stand with vocabulary now in foreign policy and using lots of epigrams and paradoxes." Producing from somewhere inside his soiled and rumpled clothing a copy of the next issue of his magazine, he swept open the pages until he at last found the one he wanted, his regular feature boldly headlined "An Outspoken Editor Speaks His Mind, by M. G. Lieberman, Editor." "Listen to what I've got coming up," he cried with excitement and prepared to read. "No more rhetorical questions," he exclaimed and began, " 'What, then, shall we say to those who argue this may lead us into war? *I* say, unflinchingly, then let us have war.' How's that? I express nothing but opprobrium and scorn for the failure of nerve of all the members of the cowardly Eastern liberal establishment. That's a phrase," he could not hold himself back from footnoting, "I got from Henry Kissinger."

"You got it from me," indignantly corrected Gold, who had lifted the quotation from an uncomplimentary assessment of the former Secretary of State in *The New Republic* that, in union with the wild surmise of his father, had prompted Gold's earliest suspicions and helped guide him toward the covert and remarkable hypothesis that Henry Kissinger was not a Jew.

" 'Our will to resist is waning while that of Russia is on the wax,' " Lieberman pressed on. "And here's another good one. 'If we are willing to go to war every time our vital interests are at stake, then *I* say we must go to war every time our vital interests are *not* at stake, to make sure that friend and foe alike understand we will.' After all," reasoned Lieberman in smiling paraphrase, his tiny eyes running appreciatively over his columns of type, "what's the point of building nuclear weapons and bombers if we're never going to use them? That's wasteful, and here—here's where I run out of patience for people without fiber enough for the many sacrifices we must stand ready to make and the casualties we might suffer. What's wrong?" Lieberman recoiled in frantic perplexity from the two stony gazes of which he unexpectedly discerned himself the repulsive object.

"If you don't stop talking that way," Pomoroy admonished softly, finishing his last slice of apple, "we won't let you hang around with us."

Tears were standing suddenly in Lieberman's eyes. "I'm sorry," he said and hung his head.

Lieberman's feelings were so sorely injured that he ordered cheesecake with strawberry topping for dessert with his coffee.

"Whom," asked Pomoroy, when the waiter had come and gone, "do you mean by we?" He looked at Lieberman through his large tortoiseshell glasses with eyes that were quietly incensed.

Lieberman took a long time making his guess. "The government."

"The government is a singular noun," said Pomoroy. "*We* is a plural pronoun. You've fallen into this disgusting, jingoistic habit of saying *we*, *us*, and *our* when talking about the country, the government, our forefathers. Your forefather was a chicken-plucker in Russia."

"In Moravia," Lieberman corrected.

"Who is this *we* that must stand ready to make the sacrifices and suffer casualties?"

"By we," said Gold, "he means them. That shitblower."

"I can change!" Lieberman sought to assure them with a flourish of his hands. "I can be flexible if I have to."

"I know how flexible you can be," Pomoroy accused sardonically, and Lieberman colored. "I saw your name in the papers again at another one of your fucking fascist dinners. My imagination fails me," Pomoroy went on with as much wonder as reproof. "What goes through your mind when you sit there listening to those anti-Semitic speakers. What do you think of?"

Lieberman lowered his eyes. "I do my multiplication tables," he answered shyly.

"Do you applaud?" asked Gold.

"No," answered Lieberman. "I swear, I literally sit on my hands through the whole meal."

"How do you eat?" inquired Gold.

"I was speaking figuratively."

"Then why did you say literally?" said Pomoroy.

"Don't words mean anything to you?" said Gold.

"I have to go pee."

"There goes a man," said Gold, "without a single saving grace. He hasn't the dimmest idea he's a buffoon."

But Pomoroy was not so easily diverted. "So you're going to

Washington," he said with a gaze Gold found difficult to meet. "What will that do to the book you owe me?"

"Enrich it immeasurably," Gold answered none too comfortably. "How often does a Jew from a poor immigrant family find himself in an important position in the federal government?"

"Too often," said Pomoroy, and began to cry. "My father's senile. He doesn't know who I am any more and says queer things when I visit him in the nursing home. He calls me Doc and Judge and doesn't know why I've come. A blind man beat him up with a cane last week, and he doesn't even know it. He's got diabetes and may have his legs cut off, and he won't understand what's happened. I can't leave him there and I can't bring him home. I don't want to break up my marriage because of him. I don't know why I even visit. I don't have any close relatives or friends, and I've got no one else I can talk to but you."

"I've got lots of close relatives and I have no one I can talk to either," said Gold. "My father's eighty-two now and won't go back to Florida. I don't want him to get sick here. I've been holding my breath now for fifteen years waiting for something to happen to him. I'm afraid it will and I'm afraid it won't. He picks on me, and I'm still afraid of him. He's picked on me all my life. Everyone in my family babies me. They treat me like a jerk. There's nothing I can do about it without being mean. Shit, I'm indebted to all of them, but guilt doesn't change anything. My older brother went to work while I went to college and gets more and more jealous of me. I can't shut him up unless I lose control of myself, and that's what he wants. My big sister Rose had a surprise party for her sixtieth birthday and it nearly broke my heart when I found out she'd never had a party before. I felt like crying when they sang 'Happy Birthday,' but I don't feel close to her. She's had the same office job for over forty years and has been scared every day she was going to lose it. Her husband boozes and is starting to get sick. Everything I do they have to be told about."

"Why do you put up with it?"

"I don't want them to think I'm stuck up. I'm glad my mother's gone now. I wouldn't want to have to watch her suffer. I don't love Belle. Family life is a bore. So is writing and teaching. My kid

sister in California is forty-five and I think I may still be in love
with her. I don't feel close to anyone in the world. Everything I do
now is boring. I want to marry money. Wipe your eyes. Here
comes the Moravian *putz.* I'm sorry about your father.''

"Whose sad story is this?" Pomoroy covered his face with a
large white handkerchief as though dabbing just his mouth. "Why
don't you write a book about that if you're really looking for some
unique and significant personal elements?" he said when he had
recovered his composure.

"Everything came out all right," Lieberman reported waggishly,
retaking his seat with the patrician comportment of one who fan-
cies himself the cynosure of adulating regard.

"You mean an autobiography?" asked Gold. Through the corner
of his eye Gold watched Lieberman turn stiff.

"No, not an autobiography," said Pomoroy. "But instead of a
general approach to the Jewish experience in America I'm suggest-
ing a work from your own vantage point. I like the idea of Luna
Park, and Steeplechase, tailor shops, and beach peddlers. Was
Steeplechase really such a funny place?"

"That was the subtitle. There wasn't even a steeplechase
there."

"It must have been interesting to grow up in Coney Island. I'm
willing to gamble the same advance on it. I can sell ten to fifteen
thousand copies of any book you write. If we get lucky on this, we
might sell fifty thousand."

"I'd need more money," said Gold, "for a second start."

"You'll get no money," said Pomoroy, "because you haven't
made a first. Look, Bruce, I'm willing to pay to give you an opportunity to try for something true and honest with real merit and
distinction."

"What's my incentive?" bantered Gold.

"Go fuck yourself."

For some moments Gold had been vibrantly conscious of a gut-
tural noise droning inside Lieberman as though striving to press
past his larynx. It tore from him now in a hoarse expulsion of
breath.

"And what," seethed Lieberman, snapping off his terminal consonants as though they were aspirating lashes of a whip, "about me?" His face was gray with virulence and reminded Gold of a dented aluminum pot.

Gold could not decide if Pomoroy's look of surprise was feigned. "What about you?"

"I lived in Coney Island too, you know," said Lieberman. "You haven't even read the beginning of *my* newest autobiography yet, and you're already publishing his."

"Oh, Lieberman, Lieberman, Lieberman," Pomoroy chanted in dismay. "Yes, I've read your newest autobiography and it's no better than your others or those pretentious beginnings of novels you used to send around. Lieberman, Lieberman, a cat has nine lives. You have one. Lieberman, really—four autobiographies for this one little life of yours?"

"This one is different," insisted Lieberman. "I think the story of my life would be of widespread interest. This one is an affectionate memoir. I forgive a lot of people, even both of you. The critics will love it because I'm so forgiving. There are lots of warm memories of you and Gold when we were at college together."

"I have no warm memories of the period," Pomoroy told him.

"Be sure to include in your warm memories," said Gold, "how little interested we are in what you have to remember about us."

"Lieberman, what a dull four lives you've led," said Pomoroy. "Who in the world cares *how* you felt about the Spanish Civil War or the Hitler-Stalin pact? You were eight years old at the time."

"Eleven," said Lieberman, "at the time I broke with Stalin. And my opinions were no better and no worse than the opinions of some of the best thinkers of the time."

"They *were* the opinions of the best thinkers of the time," Pomoroy retorted. "So who needs them now from you? You still have nothing new to write about."

"And if you did," said Gold, "you wouldn't know how to write about it."

"I still can't write?"

"No."

"So why do you try?"

"Why don't you stop?"

Lieberman's underlip came out trembling, a facial reflex to adversity he had brought with him through childhood.

"It took courage," Lieberman declared, sniffling. "It took courage on those boardwalks in Coney Island and Brighton to argue history and political theory with all those old Europeans."

"On which side?" asked Gold.

"On any side that would be to my advantage," Lieberman answered proudly. "That's something I wish you'd talk to Ralph about," he entreated, placing his hand on Gold's arm. "I don't think they appreciate how loyal I can be. I can switch positions overnight on any issue they want me to." Gold felt vaguely fastidious as he withdrew his sleeve from Lieberman with an ascetic frown and brushed away his touch.

"How can he talk to Ralph on your behalf," Pomoroy asked with mischief, "if you won't let him go to Washington?"

Lieberman was disconcerted. "Maybe I will."

"You won't devastate me?"

"I'll have to think about it." Lieberman arrived at a proposal. "If I let you go to Washington, will you promise to help me there?"

"I don't see why not," said Gold.

"I've come to believe," said Lieberman, "that government might be my true vocation. Frankly, running a leading little intellectual magazine isn't as good as it might sound. It doesn't bring in much money and has no prestige. And by now I'm getting tired of making up all those rhetorical questions. I would like," he disclosed with a smile, "a position with the Administration of very great influence and authority."

"No–oo," said Gold with extravagant amazement, "shit."

"I know I would do very well."

Pomoroy was not so sure, he said, as he gathered in the separate checks. Lieberman took a hard roll from the breadbasket and exploded it between his hands with a report that made their jittery waiter leap and caused a number of people lunching nearby to start from their chairs in panic. Even as the last of the two sections were stuffed into his mouth, his stubby fingers were active as sightless slugs scavenging the four corners of the table for crumbs that he pasted to his lips like rhinestone spangles. Gravely he rubbed his nose with his wrist and said, "Why do you think I might not do well in Washington?"

"You've got no brains," said Pomoroy.

"Or ability," said Gold. "And of course, you've got no friends."

"But you're my friend," Lieberman remembered.

"Not really." Gold drew back from him with aversion.

Pomoroy said, "Bruce might be your only contact in Washington."

"If you don't devastate me."

"If I let you go," said Lieberman, "will you be my friend?"

"I could try."

"Will you help me get a secret CIA grant that I can use to publicize my magazine and build circulation?"

"Hitch your wagon to my star."

SHOULD I try to keep count of the plots that are thickening, Gold marveled to himself as he drove toward Brooklyn with Belle, I surely must fail, for their sum increases even while I am busy totaling them. Like the President endeavoring to chronicle events of his office that unfold more swiftly than he is able to describe them, or like Tristram Shandy relating the helter-skelter circumstances of his birth and his life. Nearly four volumes must pass before he even can come from the womb, and he falls farther and farther behind. Gold was indifferent in his appreciation of *Tristram Shandy* as a literary work but had won high marks when a graduate student for his paper propounding innovative reasons for an enthralling admiration he had never been able to feel. At hand in Gold's future was an inspiring weekend meeting with Andrea's father, that celebrated diplomat and famous old country gentleman, and perhaps even a warm friendship with the President of the United States, who was struck with such wonder by Gold's words that he now kept a framed enlargement of Gold's maxim "Nothing Succeeds as Planned" on the wall of his breakfast room beside a quotation from Pliny. If only the world could know. Gold intended to learn from Ralph whether it was Pliny the Elder or Pliny the Younger. Gold had trouble telling one Pliny from the other and, when drunk, mixed both up with Livy. He had rented an automobile for the afternoon.

Belle rode in silence beside him in an uncompromising attitude of indomitable submission that discomforted him tremendously. Her pudgy round face was expressionless and her head was high.

To oblige him, she had worn some thick sweaters and a heavy coat. They were calling on his father again, but his hopes for soon excavating the stubborn despot from New York and exiling him to Florida were slim. They would have to rely on wind and respiratory infection rather than persuasion. Gold's overall displeasure with Belle was exacerbated by her passive compliance with everything he secretly schemed. He was dependent on her resistance to connive against her at his best and could not defend himself against such aggravating tolerance and resignation. The breakup of their marriage would have to be completely his own doing. He would carry himself away like a dead weight. Why would she never fight or say anything wrong at home or do anything wrong outside? Why was she always so fucking kind and practical and so good to the children and his family? He brooded upon this plight like the victim of something atrociously unfair.

On her lap with her purse was a double shopping bag holding scoured pans and glistening bowls from Rose's party that she was returning to Harriet and Esther.

"Why don't you put them in back?" he had suggested earlier.

"I'd rather hold them here."

Belle judged him the poorest of drivers, he knew, and she reminded him now of a hausfrau ready to abandon the car with all household goods in an instant should his incompetence bring them to collision.

By the time he came out of the Brooklyn-Battery Tunnel, almost all necessary conversation between them had been concluded. He made another attempt to be sociable.

"Should I take the Belt or go down Ocean Parkway?"

"Whatever you want."

He chose the Belt Parkway. He was in surly humor. Heavy, threatening clouds hung low in the air and the spectacle of their shadows darkening the choppy water flooded his heart with acidulous promise and contentment. Nothing pleased him more than the prospect of cold rain.

"What were those phone calls this morning?"

"Barry called from Choate," said Belle. "Noah phoned from Yale."

"Collect? Can't kids write letters any more?"

"They each want money."

"Send it."

"Don't you want to know how much?"

"No."

"Or what for?"

"Not yet."

"Barry wants to go to Moscow for Christmas with a group from his school."

"Good. I can probably get him a travel grant if he'll promise to major in Russian when he grows up."

"Noah wants to take a share in a ski lodge."

"Skiing? I have to pay for his skiing?" Gold nearly disapproved. He had never gone skiing. For that matter, he had not gone to Yale.

"He says if we don't let him do it, he'll come home every weekend."

"We've got no room."

"We have the study and the library."

"I've got my work spread out in both. You know how busy I am these days."

"He could stay downtown in your studio."

"I don't want him in my studio. Send him the money."

"Have we got it to spare?"

"I'll make it in Washington. If we ain't got it to spare we couldn't send it, could we? You interrupted me before, didn't you?" he pointed out primly.

"How?" Belle spoke with some surprise.

"You asked me if I wanted to know why they wanted the money and I said not yet. Then you told me anyway."

"How is that interrupting you?" Belle wanted to know. "You weren't talking."

"I was thinking. I was about to say you're much better than I am at managing money and handling the children and can make decisions like that without asking. You broke my train of thought."

"How can I tell when you're having a train of thought?"

"If in doubt," he said, "always assume I am."

Gold waited in vain for a fractious response, understood there could be no answer at all if she heeded his instructions. If she heeded his instructions he might never hear from her again. Belle revealed no stronger sign of objection than a slight, knowing smile. If all her existence depended on it, he sensed, she would give him no tangible cause for anger. Gold had an uncanny conviction that they could see into each other's minds with altogether too much clarity. They discussed little, yet knew everything. She assaulted him relentlessly with patience and placid silence. This is who I am, her upright bearing seemed to say to him with defiance now. I was not a beauty when you married me, and I couldn't become one if I tried. He could have his divorce any time he wanted it. All he need do was take it by himself. Obedience and acceptance were the cruel weapons with which she persecuted him, total surrender was her strategy of attack, and he was hard put to withstand her. He had Scotch kippers in mind to fly to Andrea the following evening, and maybe slab bacon as well. Or should he withhold the bacon for a subsequent treat? Andrea would never go for herring, he believed, but smoked mackerel would charm her.

Following the smooth parkway as it curved with the shoreline to the east, he soon saw in the distance on his right the gaunt structure of the defunct Parachute Jump standing on the narrow spit of land across Gravesend Bay and recalled, with some pride in his upbringing, how that Parachute Jump, the hit of the World's Fair in New York in 1939 or '40, was moved to the Steeplechase boardwalk afterward but had never proved adequately perilous for success to an indigenous population trained on the Cyclone and the Thunderbolt and on the Mile Sky Chaser in Luna Park. Now it looked forlorn: no one owned it and no one would take it away. Like those haunted, half-completed luxury apartment houses in Manhattan whose builders had run out of money and whose banks would not supply more, gaping with dismal failure and aging already into blackest decrepitude before they ever shone spanking new. A moment later came the skeletal outline of the giant Wonder Wheel, idled for the year by the chilly season, the only Ferris wheel left in Coney Island now that Steeplechase, the Funny Place, was bankrupt and gone. Hard times had descended there as in other places.

Where Luna Park had last whirred in bright lights on summer evenings over thirty years earlier there now rose a complex of high, honeycombed brick dwellings that looked drabber than ordinary against the lackluster sky. On the overpass spanning Ocean Parkway Gold turned his head for a speeding glimpse of Abraham Lincoln High School and bemoaned for the thousandth time the vile chance that had located him in classes there the same time as Belle and gulled him into a mismanaged destiny of three dependent children and a wife so steadfast. If a man marries young, he reasoned aristocratically in the self-conscious mode of a Lord Chesterfield or a Benjamin Franklin, as Gold himself had been minded to do, it will likely be to someone near him in age; and just about the time he learns really to enjoy living with a young girl and soars into his prime, she will be getting old. He would pass that precious homiletic intelligence on to both sons, if he remembered. If only Belle were fickle, mercenary, deceitful. Even her health was good.

He turned off the parkway past Brighton at the exit leading toward Sheepshead Bay and Manhattan Beach. The slender crescent on the southern rim of Brooklyn through which he'd driven was just about the only section of the area with which he was familiar. Almost all of the rest was foreign to him and forbidding. His thoughts went back to a ramshackle street he'd passed minutes before on which stood the same moldering antique police station to which he'd been brought as a small child the day Sid had abandoned him and gone off with his friends. What a heartless thing to have done. Gold must have been numb as he waited in the precinct house. If they asked him his address he might not have known it. The nearest telephone to his house then was in a candy store at the trolley stop on the corner of Railroad Avenue. Just a few years later he was earning two-cent tips for summoning girls from their flats for calls from boys phoning for dates. Brooklyn was a big fucking borough.

SHORTLY afterward, Gold found himself flushed and over-heated on the porch of his father's house. Instead of the cloudburst he'd counted on, there was a bracing surfeit of fragrant sunshine. He unfastened the buttons of his coat. Harriet removed her ear-muffs and Sid said, "It's really amazing, isn't it? About vultures, I mean."

And Gold, hearing this, suffered a further plummeting in spirit of a kind that might have resulted from a corresponding loss in blood pressure. He had no inclination for resistance. As always, Sunday for him was a gray spell of inertia to be endured in torpor unless one worked as a professional football player or, like Andrea, had horses to gallop and foxes to hunt. On Monday he would meet with Ralph and sleep with Andrea. Tuesday morning he would prevail in a convocation of luminaries as splendid in individual magnitude, perhaps, as any convening that day in all the land. Here, in the webwork of his origins, he had to listen to Sid smack his lips over the last of his glass of beer and continue lackadaisi-cally, "It's really one of the great miracles of nature, isn't it? The way vultures, or gizzards, as they sometimes are called—"

"Buzzards," growled Gold, without looking up.

"What'd I say?"

"Gizzards."

"How strange," said Sid in an imitation of surprise. "I meant buzzards, of course—how vultures are able to locate dying animals from five or ten miles away—even though all of them, from the moment they're born, are always totally blind."

Now Gold's head came up with an involuntary flip, and he stared at Sid as though through a mist. "Says who?" he snarled, without wanting to speak at all.

"Aren't they blind?" asked Sid.

"No."

"What makes you think they aren't?"

"I would know if they were," said Gold.

"From where?" scoffed his father. "From his college?"

"Sid knows more about science than he does," sulked Harriet.

"Sure," said his father. "Sid invented things. I was in business. Now I'm retired."

"I'd like another beer," Sid said. Esther rose with upsetting alacrity to serve him, making everyone feel unbearably sorry for her. "How would you know?" Sid asked Gold.

"I'd have heard," Gold insisted moodily. "Like I know about termites and moles. Termites and moles are blind. Vultures aren't."

"He isn't talking about termites and moles." Harriet addressed her annoyance with Gold to the others. "He always has to correct him."

"Moles make hills." Gold's stepmother delivered herself of this wisdom while knitting and purling her wool as usual with her long needles that almost never were idle. Today, a pinprick of a scarlet pimple glowed like blood against the very pale skin on the side of her nose. Her freshly washed gray hair was slightly askew, and she looked to Gold like that demented figure in the painting of Pickett's charge at Gettysburg. "And some people," she added, with a glance at Gold laying to rest any doubt whom she meant, "take those molehills and make mountains of them."

"Even the Bible says so," Sid announced as Gold silently gnashed his teeth.

"The Bible?" Gold grew alert as a leopard. He had given university courses in the Bible, although he had never succeeded in reading either of the Testaments wholly and had found incomprehensible much that he had read. The value of the celebrated Book of Job remained a mystery to him, the text overblown and the knowledge colloquial, and that of the Song of Solomon hardly less confounding. "Where in the Bible does it say that?"

"Three things have no answer for me," Sid sang out resonantly as a cantor. "The way of a bird with its prey, the way of a corn on its cob, and the way of a man with a maid. Right?" The cropped interrogation was submitted to the others in a simplehearted appeal to reason.

Gold could believe his ears well enough but not much else. "Oh, horseshit," he grumbled and then spoke louder. "You're misquoting."

Sid affected innocence. "Nobody's perfect, kid," he said with a throb of contrition.

"And where does that say anything about vultures being blind?"

"Oh, kid." Sid set his glass down and began drying his hands one upon the other. "You went to college, didn't you? Use your head. What would be so special about it if vultures could see? Would that be worth a mention in the Bible?"

"Of course not," said his father.

"Bruce isn't really fighting," Esther apologized for him with more than the usual flutter in her voice.

"He's only making conversation," said Belle.

My origins were humble, said Gold to himself in a dogged auto-biographical obsession as though he were dictating his, or Henry Kissinger's, memoirs. My family was impoverished and I had no advantages. Actually, we were not impoverished and I had plenty of advantages but not as many as I subsequently demonstrated I deserved. Performance was delayed by early hardship. My light was eclipsed by a bushel. Everything I received I earned for myself, except what I got from my father, my mother, and my brother, and from all four of my older sisters. I had nothing going for me but my brains, which I believe I inherited from people other than those persons purporting to be my parents. There is ground for supposing that I am of nobler lineage than first strikes the eye and that I have been lost among these honest, but poor, working folk as the ill-fated victim of sundry circumstantial misunderstandings too tangled for unraveling. My older brother, Sid, with whom I've been acquainted all my life, is the eldest of seven children, a solid business success with a layman's interest in nature and mechanics who is liberal with his funds and compassionate and easygoing in his dealings with others and is also a fucking nitwit imbecile who treats me like shit and makes me talk about vultures.

IN CONTRAST to her belligerent, dark temper now, Harriet had greeted him earlier with an effusion of conspiratorial warmth. Taking him aside for a confidence, she had said, "Esther thinks Milt might ask her to marry him soon. You have to help. She asked Rose to ask Ida to find out from Sid if there would have to be any sex."

Gold curled up inwardly. "Where do I shine in?"

"You can find out things like that," she informed him in peremptory explanation. "You're an English professor. Sid knows about science."

"Come outside," his father called to them then with unconcealed ill will. "It's nice now on the porch."

This reassuring news of the weather seemed a death knell to their chances for the day, and Gold felt in the veins of his extremities the wet coldness of slush.

"I warned Sid," Harriet revealed, hardening her expression in hostile preparation for the conflict ahead. "If they don't leave for Florida by the end of this week, I will, with my daughters and my grandchildren."

Gold was not altogether easy in league with this cranky, thrifty woman past sixty with whom he had been at odds in one way or another for more than thirty years. In contrast to the fit and virile image he had of himself, Harriet appeared at least a generation beyond her years, closer in age to his father than to him. He noticed how pinched and weary she looked about her narrow eyes and mouth, how the pores of her face had enlarged, and how her artificially brown hair had thinned. Recalling the libertine escapades of Sid and his friends in the past, Gold wondered how Sid felt about Harriet now. He knew she had troubles. Her gallbladder had been removed, a younger brother of hers had died of cancer just a few years before, a daughter was back from Pennsylvania on another visit, with her children, and there were inescapable signs of serious discord in the marriage. Sid volunteered nothing. Sid rarely talked of his children, and when he did it was almost always with unconscious overtones of criticism and disappointment. All his life he had been closemouthed with the family, perhaps in wounded reaction to the continual early strife with their father, who was as raucous in petty displeasure as in volcanic wrath, and as overwhelming in both as in his chronic flights into passionate humming or unrestrained outbursts of singing. His songs extended from simple Yiddish ditties to hearty imitations of American operetta and Gilbert and Sullivan learned from the family radio and to tearful renditions of ballads of fractured love affairs that were the newest contenders for the top of the Lucky Strike Hit Parade. "Ipana for the smile of beauty" became an intolerable, embarrassing utterance he gave in repetitious salute to neighbors and to patrons of his tailor shop or made aloud to himself; "Sal Hepatica for the smile of health." "When Nature forgets, remember Ex-Lax," was another.

Julius Gold adjusted his eyeglasses now, the frames colorless in these recent years of suave refinement to blend with the wiry and wavy curls of his thick white hair, and blew smoke from his cigar as he held the door to the porch open. Sid already was entombed in a posture of relaxation too slumbrous for combat.

Harriet began militantly. "So how did you enjoy your stay in New York this year?" she asked with pointed civility.

"I'll let you know," he answered, "when it's over."

Harriet's offensive buckled right then. Gold's father was wearing a turtleneck shirt of navy blue and a neutral cashmere sport jacket that Gold appraised as costing easily above two hundred dollars. A corolla of a dotted navy-blue handkerchief blossomed from his breast pocket. The son of a bitch looks better than I do, Gold moped. In ten years he'll be wearing cowboy suede with fringed yoke and sleeves, and I'll be drab as Sid. A far cry indeed from the era of the dingy tailor shop in which the old man would go dashing about insanely in vest and flapping shirtsleeves with pins sticking from his mouth, a tape measure flying from his shoulders, and a plaque of marking chalk in his hand.

Gold faked a shiver. "The paper said something about snow."

"Not mine," said his father.

"In North Dakota," said his stepmother.

"Two people we know," said his father, "dropped dead from the heat last week in Miami."

Grimly, Harriet prodded Sid. "Wasn't there something you wanted to talk about?"

"Crime?" guessed Sid.

"It's really bad," said Belle.

"Bail doesn't work," said Gold, expatiating. "If you make it low, habitual offenders are right back on the streets. If you make it high they're punished without having been found guilty. The concept is archaic when crime is a commonplace and the presumption of innocence no longer rests on safe probability."

His father's fingers were drumming. "We got just as good now in Florida," he said as though Gold had not spoken at all.

"Prices?" tried Gold, as a shot in the dark.

"They're so high in New York," said Harriet.

"We can afford them," said his father.

"We don't need charity," said his stepmother.

"Just what we get from you and Sid," said his father impudently to Harriet, "and from the rest of my children. Even my daughter in California sends me money. Joannie."

"It's to die," said Harriet, giving up again.

"In other words," asked Sid with a grin, "you and Mother here can't find anything wrong with New York City?"

"It gets a little cold sometimes," his father conceded after a pause, "around February or March, but otherwise it's okay. It's the Empire State."

Gevalt! grieved Gold. "You can't stay here that long," he blurted out. "Two years ago you and Mother—"

"I'm not your mother," Gussie reminded him tartly.

"Sid?" said Gold.

"Pop, it's really starting to get too cold for you and Mother and much too damp."

"Not here," said Julius Gold.

"What are you talking about?" Gold's voice was shrill. "You're surrounded by water. You've got the bay in back of you and the whole ocean in front."

"We like," said his stepmother, "the briny smell of the sea."

"It's a dry cold we get here," said his father.

"And a very dry damp."

"Why is it," Gold demanded, "that he can call you Mother and I can't?"

"Because I like him," answered his stepmother with no change of expression.

"That's a good one," laughed his father.

Gussie was aglow with triumph. "Hold this for a minute," she said and held her knitting needles and band of wool toward Gold. He had to stand to accommodate her, and he clasped them all tightly in mortal fear something might fall. "I want your help. As you can see," she said with her slightly musical cackle, "you've left me holding the bag, haven't you?" She wedged her straw tote bag up beneath his elbows. "There."

"What should I do with it?" asked Gold.

"The minute isn't up yet," she said.

"That's another good one!" said his father.

Momenyu, Gold cursed his fate, and would have flung something heavy at someone, had he not felt hogtied by the responsibility of holding her wool. He spoke to his father threateningly. "I won't have much time for you from now on, you know. I'll be busy in Washington. And I've got my teaching job to look after and my books to write."

"And Sid and I," Harriet joined in, "will probably be going away on a long vacation. Maybe even to Florida."

"Stay in my place."

Sid covered a smile. "Pop, you don't have a place. That's why you got us here, to talk about buying a condominium."

"Sure, I told you the condominium," the old man recalled agreeably. "We'll talk about it at dinner."

"Dinner?" Gold's voice cracked again. "We're here for lunch."

"I thought for lunch we'd go to a nice Chinese restaurant nearby for dinner. Sid, you told them on the telephone? I never ate on no chipped china at home, I don't have to take any now from that bunch of lousy chinks. Why's he standing there with that wool like an idiot?" he inquired about Gold.

"The minute, I think, is up," said Gold's stepmother, and snatched back her wool and bag. "It's mine, you know."

Tatenyu, thought Gold, and threw himself into a chair. He turned to his father and challenged, "You're just about out of Jewish holidays now, aren't you?" The old man was disturbed by this audacious incursion into a territory of data which heretofore had been monopolistically his own. "You've got nothing more coming up until . . ." Gold slid from his pocket a typewritten list and found the entry he sought.

"Until Hanukkah," interrupted his father, turned partly around to shield himself from observation. "Which doesn't come . . . until the end of December."

Gold rose without noise and looked over his father's shoulder. His father was consulting a schedule of Jewish holidays similar to his own. With slips of paper in hand, the two confronted each other in joint amusement.

"Where'd you get that?" demanded Gold.

"From Taub in Miami," said his father. "Where'd you get yours?"

"From Epstein in 'Monarchy and Monotheism.' You going back?"

"We're practically packed." Gold sat down. "But not before the big party," his father reported in a pugilistic resurgence of will, and Gold promptly stood up. "No, sirree. And hurt my children's feelings? Not me."

Sid was soonest to recover from this newest disclosure. "What party?"

"Our anniversary party," the old man announced with exuberance. "You all forgot? Me and Gussie, we got our tenth anniversary coming up soon. And we don't want to make anybody unhappy by going away before the party you're making."

"When is it?" challenged Gold. "What day?"

Julius Gold was stricken with an odd look of discomposure and glanced for succor at his wife. Gussie gave an agitated shake of her head and declined to speak.

"November fourteenth," said Belle. "On a Friday."

"Sure," said Julius Gold. "November fourteenth, on a Friday. And we ain't going to miss that party for anything, are we?"

"Not," said Gussie Gold, "for all the wool in China."

A guiding star directed Gold to sit mute.

"Is there much wool in China?" Harriet rushed in acidly with an air of nasty superiority.

"Oh, yes," said Gussie Gold. "More than anyplace in the world. They import it to clothe the large population. Almost one out of every four people in the world is Chinese, you know, even though many of them might not look it."

Gold's father grunted at Sid in a touchy undertone. *"Emmis?"* He was discontented when Sid nodded.

"This means," Gold's stepmother went on informatively, "that of the seven of us here today, almost two of us are Chinese, even though we may not look it."

This time Sid shook his head and Julius Gold dug his teeth into his cigar and puffed it into a blaze.

"Who," asked Belle, "is making the party?"

"I ain't decided yet," said the old man, blowing smoke. "Maybe Rosie because she's near. Maybe Esther because she's all alone and has the time. Maybe Muriel because she knows we don't like her and maybe won't be so jealous if I let her. Maybe Ida and Irv because they got money, even though they don't like to spend it. Maybe Sid and Harriet, because Harriet here always looks so happy when I come to the house to visit, don't she? Where's Ida and Irv and Rose and Max, anyway? I invited them. Why ain't they here?"

"I told you," said Sid.

"Irv had a chance to play tennis," Belle explained to him again. "Max went to see his brother."

"Where's Esther?" he asked with crankiness. He suddenly looked sleepy. "What's she doing in the house so long?"

"She's setting the table," Gold's stepmother answered unself-consciously. "She asked if she could help set the table for lunch, and I told her she could."

Gold's father spoke with puzzlement. "We ain't eating lunch here. We're eating in a Chinese restaurant."

"She didn't ask me that," said Gold's stepmother, "so I didn't tell her."

At this reply, Gold's father peered with disfavor at his second wife as though scrutinizing a kink in an otherwise normal chain of events. "Go tell her to stop," he said with uncommon quietness, and conversed with himself indistinctly until she had gone into the house, when he observed wistfully to his sons, "Your real mother was better than her. She was sick a lot, but she never stopped working."

To so touching an encomium a reply seemed a sacrilege. Sid changed the subject.

"Pa, I want to go to Florida this week and find a good place for you to live after your anniversary party."

"I might want to stay longer here."

"You can't stay here longer," Harriet said with more severity than she likely had intended. "We haven't the money."

"Why can't I use my own?"

"We've got the money," Sid retorted sharply to Harriet. "So please don't say that again."

Harriet bit her lip. "Now you're starting fights," she accused the old man.

"I?" said Julius Gold with a hand to his heart. "I'm starting fights?" Indignation was prominent on every feature. "Not me. I don't start fights. You got the last person in the world. It ain't my fault your daughter's marriage is breaking up, is it? Don't blame me no one ever told her how to be a good wife. I'm not the one who told her to marry that noisy nobody in Pennsylvania just because his family has department stores. Did I tell Esther to marry that crazy Mendy?" he said as Esther reappeared then, lucklessly, and was brought to a standstill, her pitiful smile petrified upon her lips. "I knew he wouldn't live long, with that temper of his. Always blowing up at me, over nothing. It ain't my fault she's a widow now and I have to be embarrassed with my friends because my daughter got no husband. So ugly he was with a face like a monkey—they had better in Barnum and Bailey. What are you crying about?" he reproached Esther with surprise. "Go back inside if you want to make noise like a baby. Here, take these dirty glasses while you're going. One of them's cracked. You didn't even invite me up to the funeral, she thinks I don't remember, don't she, but I know more than she thinks. You thought I'd never say anything about it, didn't you?" he gloated. The mask was off! Gold was gaping at him with incredulity. The raw cruelty of the mad tailor of Coney Island had not lessened. The man had merely aged. A monster, Gold breathed furiously to himself, first with a vicious look toward Belle and next with a savage glower at Sid, a fucking monster! "Gussie, get my topcoat," his father requested with disinterest and fatigue in a steep alteration of temperament that was inconceivably abnormal in a person not wholly insane. "We'll soon go eat. And straighten your hair or something. Your head looks crooked." He struck a note about halfway between a groan and a cry and held it on pitch in a low hum until she had left, when his voice flowed into words without a break from the long, distressful drone. "Am I wrong? Or does she sometimes talk like she's crazy?" No one there would argue he was wrong. "If Jews got divorces," he philosophized, "I sometimes think I might want one."

"Jews get divorces," said Belle, the only woman present he had not yet insulted.

"Not real Jews. Not Golds. Not this Gold." For one moment longer the old man was sanctimonious and serene. Then he opened fire again. "Maybe someone like their spoiled daughter comes home to her parents with her children to get a divorce. Or maybe someone like your college-educated husband here got something like that in mind when he goes off to Washington on a fishy job and leaves his wife behind and maybe don't even ask her to come. But not me. What's the matter?" he asked in surprise with that same phenomenal resilience of personality of someone unregenerately self-centered. "Why's everybody look so angry? It's a party, ain't it?"

Sid answered cautiously. "You've been saying some pretty awful things, Pa."

"I? I say awful things?" The old man's hand covered his heart once more as he dismissed the accusation with a fixed smile and a dogmatic shake of his head. "Not me. I'm not the one who says things. Do I ever say anything about Ida and the way she bosses around that puppy dog of a husband or what Muriel does to that dummy Victor?" He was panting with displeasure and his eyes were hot and glaring. "Did I ever once say anything about how you used to sneak away to Mexico with those skinny dress models so often even your smart wife here would know, or how my younger son here keeps downtown an apartment for his who-ers he calls a studio and never once invites me to sleep there but makes me ride all the way home at night into Brooklyn?"

"Will you shut up?" screamed Gold.

"I wouldn't lay my head down on one of your filthy mattresses!"

"Can't you please shut up?" screamed Gold again with an urge to take him in his hands and tear him apart like a turkey.

"I? I should shut up? What am I saying that's so terrible? To a father you say shut up? Sid was big as a football player when he was young, but I still gave him plenty all his life. Once I even chased you away for a whole summer, didn't I?" he remembered, chuckling.

"You sure did," said Sid.

"Look how warm it gets when the wind stops. Why's everybody so quiet? I don't like to go eat with a bunch of sourpusses. Gussie, make somebody laugh," he ordered as she reappeared with his topcoat.

Gussie tried. Her shiny skin paling almost to translucence, she approached Gold with her tote bag closed and proffered the tip of a fabric protruding from the opening.

"It's yours. I finished. Take it, my son."

"What is it?" Instinctively Gold put his hands behind his back.

"A sock."

"One sock? You knit me one sock?"

"I only have two hands. Last May I saw a hole in your sock. If I'd seen a hole in both socks I would have knitted you two."

"What'll I do with one sock?"

"Maybe you'll lose a foot," said the old man and clucked appreciatively. "Take it, go on, bigshot, take it."

Gold, overmastering caution, took hold of the corner of cloth and pulled—and pulled—and felt he might have continued pulling until the earth stood still, for out of the straw bag waggled a serpentine section of that knitted band of wool she had been diligently spinning like a spider for all the years she had been his stepmother. It was not a sock, it was a practical joke, and there was simpering.

Gold forced a smile, cursing her horrendously in silence, and said, "Oh, Mother, Mother, that is a hot one. You really are funny."

"I'm not your mother," was the swift retort.

"She got him again," cheered his father, rising.

"It's your fucking fault," Gold bristled at Sid as the group milled from the house toward the two automobiles at the curb. "Next year move them into my neighborhood with all those niggers, nuts, and welfare kooks and then see how long they stay. Listen, I want some advice," he whispered, drawing Sid farther aside. "I need some help and I think you can give it."

"You name it. Anything you want, kid."

"You could begin by not calling me kid."

Sid was moderately abashed. "I didn't know that bothered you." He rubbed his knuckles across his chin in a movement of meek self-mockery. "I guess I'll always think of you as my kid brother, no matter how old we get. I promise I'll never do it again, kid. What else?"

Gold tolerated the unpremeditated lapse with resignation. "I may need this for my book." He circled Sid as though by inadvertence to hide his face from the others. "A Jewish guy goes out of town for a while, to Washington, let's say, and wants to stay with another woman. Is there any way he can protect himself against calls from his wife?"

Sid was on the mark. "Check into a hotel," he answered with joyous affinity. "Telephone the switchboard every evening to hold all calls. Telephone again the next morning to see if there've been any. Return all calls from your hotel room."

"I think I'd be afraid."

"Oh, no, kid, don't ever be afraid. That's the worst. You got a nice girl there?"

"It ain't for me."

"Too bad. The worst thing ever is to be afraid." Sid's eyes were glittering in spirited recall, and he ambled casually around Gold to turn his own back to the others. "I used to spend weeks in Acapulco when I was supposed to be in Detroit and Minneapolis. Once I spent four nights right here in Manhattan when she thought I was in Seattle."

"You got caught once in Acapulco, didn't you?"

Sid nodded with a soft bronchial laugh. "Her uncle was in Mexico at a druggists' convention. But it didn't matter, and I wasn't afraid. When she ordered me out of the house, I went back to Acapulco. When she moved out with the kids to her mother, I moved into a hotel suite in New York and had parties with Sheiky, and Kopotkin the machinist, and Murshie Weinrock. Mursh was an intern then and brought nurses. When Harriet smashed an ashtray, I broke a dish. She pushed over a chair, I pushed over a whole breakfront full of china. Once she saw I was never going to be afraid, it turned out to be a pretty good marriage, I think."

Sid never had said so much about himself or ever appeared so merry and animated. Gold heard him with fascination. Science, machinery, fearsome dray horses at the Brighton Laundry, now marital infidelities with farcical catastrophies at home—the only subjects on which he'd ever heard his older brother dilate. There had to be more underneath such disciplined reticence.

In an access of powerful fresh feelings, Gold proposed, "Sid, let's have lunch together when I get back from Washington. I'll take you to a good uptown restaurant where we can see some writers and theater people."

"I'd like that," Sid exclaimed with such shocking modesty that Gold could do nothing but stare. "We've only done that once, I think, when you got out of college. We're all very proud of you, kid, you know," he disclosed, to Gold's added surprise. "Not everybody's got a college professor in the family."

"You sure as shit don't show it," Gold said with a smile. Harriet was honking the horn from her seat in Sid's Cadillac. "Sid, why'd you stop running around? Old age? Health?"

Sid argued he was only sixty-two. With a blush, he confessed, "I began to be afraid."

In Gold's car Esther started crying again. "It wasn't that we didn't *want* him at the funeral," she explained, while Gold tried paying no attention. "We were trying to save him the trouble."

"How come," Gold asked Belle, "you remember their anniversary date and they don't?"

Belle smiled. "I made it up. I picked a Friday so they could pack on Saturday and leave on Sunday."

Gold approved. Both women alighted at the Chinese restaurant on Kings Highway and Gold accepted like a godsend the solitude in which he found himself for the quarter hour needed to park and walk back.

"NOBODY," SAID Sid without warning as Gold was lowering himself to his chair, "knows the mouth of the Nile." He had ordered a family dinner for twelve.

"The source," said Gold and finished sitting down.

"What'd I say?"

"The mouth."

"How droll," said Sid, his face in flower with trickery and delight. "I'm not myself today."

"Yes, you are, you rotten fuck."

"He said please pass some soup and duck," screeched Belle with admirable presence of mind.

"And *everybody* knows the source of the Nile," muttered Gold, eyes focused rigidly on the food already there.

"Everybody?"

"I don't know it," disagreed his father.

"I don't believe I know the source of the Nile," said his stepmother.

"I don't know it," said Esther.

"Everybody who wants to take the trouble to find out."

"Do you know it?" teased Sid.

"Yes," said Gold. "Which one? There are two Niles."

"Two Niles?" The women spoke as though with one voice.

Gold was unwary. "Yes. A Blue and a White."

He looked up with concern at the sinister stillness that fell and perceived from the ineffable solemnity on the faces pondering him that he had blundered into another disastrous pit. Commiseration mingled with anxiety in the gazes of the women, and tears of pity were mounting anew on the lids of Esther's eyes. Oh, Sid, Sid, you treacherous, malicious, infantile motherfucking bastard, he chanted to himself in a litany of misery. You have bushwhacked your baby brother again.

"Two Niles?" his father was already growling irately, spilling hot tea onto his lap from his trembling cup. "A Blue and a White one? What in hell's the matter with him?"

"Can't you tell when he's joking?" Belle interceded with not too much faith.

"Is anything wrong?" asked the tall, well-muscled manager with menacing inscrutability, arriving to insure that nothing in his restaurant ever would go amiss. A second contender for the world karate championship glided noiselessly up alongside in formidable allegiance.

"Not at all," Sid hailed them both jovially. "We'd like a couple of more orders of pork. The soup is superb."

Gold, face to face with futility, used the intermission to escape his predicament. "Never mind my Niles," he put it bluntly. "What about your condominium?"

His father was taken off guard. His jaw dropped and his cheeks quivered.

"Yes," said Sid, joining forces with Gold.

"Why can't I stay here?" asked Gold's father, and added winningly, "I'm no trouble."

"Pa, I want you to buy that condominium."

For one moment more the old man glanced wildly about in hectic disorientation. Blood rushed alarmingly to his whole face, and he choked with such anger and violent confusion that he seemed to be fighting for each mouthful of air. Words would not come. In torrents of fury and frustration, he began poking with a bent finger toward the table in imperious spasms, his walleyed gaze rolling from the people seated on one side of him to those on the other. At the first motion of his arm, the ancient reflex abiding in the others leaped into life, and everyone present lunged with terror for the closest dishes of food to pass to him. Gold pushed plates of duck, spareribs, and rice toward him with both hands. Esther, who was sitting nearest, gave him the enormous bowl of wonton soup. Gold spied the hairline crack in the porcelain an instant too late to scream and foresaw with an intuition that defied any possible doubt just what would follow. The crash when the bowl shattered on the floor was even more hideous in reality than in his despondent imagination. The manager returned in a moment with a visage of awesome force and authority, joined this time by three unsmiling warriors with onyx eyes and closely shaven heads and a jittery Oriental woman with bright lipstick who carried a very long, thin pencil.

"Is anything wrong?"

"Chipped china?" inquired Esther.

"*Vehr Gehargit!*" the old man roared in reply to the baleful Chinese manager when he at last found his voice, stabbing his forefinger into the tall man's stomach and driving him back. The man blanched as Julius Gold, still thrusting toward him, shouted, "I don't want no condominium! I live here, not there! It's for a vacation I go!"

Sid was already on his feet, gushing twenty-dollar tips and magniloquent apologies like a fountain. Fuck him, steamed Gold, dispensing ones and fives with the readiest of hollow laughs to dumbfounded children and parents at tables nearby. He should be locked up! In a prison, not a hospital! In handcuffs! To the walls of a dungeon he should be chained, that crazy fuck of a bastard, fifteen feet off the ground!

In time the floor was mopped and they progressed through the meal to the pineapple, ice cream, and fortune cookies in near total silence under the harrowing pretense that nothing untoward had intruded. The haggling that did ensue was concise. The old man was not returning to Florida until he was good and ready. Sid guaranteed a visit from at least one branch of the family every month for no less than five days. Nothing doing. Every three weeks for seven days? We'll see about that.

"Fuck him!" Gold ranted to Belle in the car going home. "Let the son of a bitch get bronchitis again and start coughing his lungs out. Let him start complaining he's lonely because we don't come visit."

"You'll be in Washington," Belle said laconically.

And fuck you too, Gold fulminated in silence with an evil squint at his wife. You're goddamned right I'll be in Washington. At midnight he was on the telephone to California pleading with Joannie to come to New York to try to take charge. She was having trouble with Jerry, and a lawyer had warned her not to desert the domicile.

"He broke the soup!" Gold insisted tragically in recapitulation. "He broke the goddamned soup! I think this must be the worst day in my life. Then, in the restaurant after he broke the soup I got the weirdest fortune cookie anyone ever heard of. When I finally got back home someone had turned all the one-way signs around as a joke and I couldn't get close to the house to drop Belle off or back to the garage to bring my rented car in. Gussie said she made me a sock—''

"One sock?"

"She only has two hands. And it turned out to be that same strip of wool she's been knitting since we know her and everybody laughed at me. Nobody who knows me treats me with respect."

"We're your family, Bruce. Do you want us to call you doctor too?"

"Not just them. Everyone around here treats me like a *schmuck*. Even Chinese fortune cookies. Yesterday at the gym I ran into Spotty Weinrock, this guy we grew up with in Coney Island, and he said Belle was a dumpy broad and talked to me like I was still a jerky little kid in school. Belle's not dumpy, is she?"

"Yes," Joannie said after a small hesitation. "She is."

"Well, what's so bad about dumpy?"

"I didn't say it was bad. Some women are slim and tall, like I am, and some are short and . . . well."

"It ain't her fault she's dumpy, is it?" Gold was peevish. "We're born that way. It's not my fault I'm short, is it?"

"You aren't short," Joannie defended him. "You're average."

"Average ain't good enough."

"What did your fortune cookie say?"

Gold's whimper was a malediction against fate. "Everybody else got normal ones. I never even touch the damn things. They made me." He re-created for Joannie now how, only after concerted importuning by the others, he had broken open the fortune cookie he had picked and extracted from inside the stoic message YOU WILL HURT YOUR FOOT. "And they all thought it was so funny."

"*What* did it say?"

" 'You will hurt your foot.' And then they all made me pass it around and started laughing at me again. Joannie, what's wrong? What's that noise? Holy shit—what the hell are *you* doing?"

"Laughing," she said. "I can't help it. I think it's funny too."

BETWEEN the locker room in the Businessmen's Club of the YMCA and the staircase to the indoor track two floors above were a television lounge, a sleep room, showers, some massage tables, a steam room and sauna, and a small exercise room that normally was unoccupied when Gold stopped by in the mid-afternoon for his warm-ups and clandestine weight lifting. The familiar form of Karp the chiropodist, a member, was planted on a wooden stool in the aisle of the locker room with his bald head drooping almost into his lap, much like a man praying to God against impossible odds. He mumbled something somber in greeting that Gold obdurately refused to hear as he turned around him toward his locker deep inside the row. Gold's demeanor at the Y was habitually unsociable, his countenance that of someone introverted and choleric. When Gold walked back in his gym clothes, Karp reiterated his sacerdotal incantation in exactly the same dirgelike cadence. Gold growled "Hi" and continued past. As Gold proceeded through the carpeted hallway toward the staircase to the track, a tall shambling figure wearing just a bedsheet over one flabby shoulder emerged from the sleep room with a semiconscious smile and began laughing at him.

Gold halted with a scowl. "What are you doing here?"

"I belong," said Spotty Weinrock, chuckling steadily and staring down at Gold with an expression of drowsy merriment that instantly put Gold at a disadvantage. "What about you?"

"I've been a member for years." Gold was arrogant in establishing seniority. "What do you do here?"

"I sleep," said Spotty. "Mursh said I ought to start going to a gym for my health. So I come here a few afternoons a week for a nap. I read *Variety* and the fashion papers in the sauna and sometimes I lay myself down for a massage. Mursh was right. I feel much better since I've been coming here. What do you do?"

Gold had been listening as though in a dream. "I jog."

"You? That's something. How've you been?"

"Fine," said Gold. "What's it your business?"

"I know why you're snubbing me," Weinrock said with good humor. "I owe you thirteen hundred dollars."

"I'm not snubbing you. I don't think of you at all."

Weinrock responded to the slight by beaming even more offensively in enjoyment of Gold's sally. "I can pay you back now. Call me at my office and I'll take you to lunch. How's your old man?"

"What's it your business?"

"He still alive? My mother was asking about him only last week."

"He's fine," retorted Gold. "How's your old man?"

"Mine's gone, Bruce. I thought you knew that."

"You only owe me eleven hundred," Gold said in apology. "I couldn't spare it the last time you asked."

"I forgot." Weinrock rubbed his half-closed eyes with both fists. "Those old folks are really something, ain't they? I still get a kick out of my fucking mother. She couldn't speak a word of English but she learned how to call me Spot when I was eleven years old because I worked for your father. She's okay now." Unjust, Gold lamented for more than the first time, how everybody's parents but his own turned easier and more manageable in advanced age. "How's your brother Sid?"

"Fine," said Gold.

"Your sisters Rose and Esther?"

"They're fine. What do you care?"

"I'm interested. And Ida and Muriel and Kitty and Betsy?"

"I've got no Kitty and Betsy."

"I forgot."

"What are you laughing about?" Gold wanted to know. "What's so fucking funny?"

"Fishy Siegel tells me you're going to work in Washington for the President. It's in the papers."

"Fishy Siegel don't read the papers."

"His brother Sheiky does. You still married to that dumpy broad what's her name?"

"Yeah," Gold answered aggressively. "You still married to that skinny giraffe with the big teeth?"

"Oh, no," said Spotty Weinrock. "I got rid of her."

Gold was balked again and said, "Gimme the money you owe me, you cocksucker."

"Is that how a college professor talks?"

"You filthy prick," raged Gold. "You come to a gymnasium to sleep and read and lay on a massage table? And you don't like the way I talk? Where's my money?"

"Call me at my office." Weinrock was chuckling once more. "So you're going into politics in Washington and cash in big, huh? And all of us guys in Coney Island thought you'd never amount to anything."

"I look at it," said Gold, "as performing a useful service to society."

"That's what I'm laughing about," said Spotty Weinrock.

Weinrock was gone when Gold came down from the track half an hour later after running three miles and looked for him. All the bones at the bottoms of both Gold's feet felt broken. Karp the chiropodist repeated:

"The Angel of Death is in the gym today."

Gold's guard was down and this time the words penetrated. "What?"

"The Angel of Death is in the gym today."

"What are you talking about?"

"Another man dropped dead here this morning."

"On the track?"

"On the squash court."

Then what the fuck do I care? was the thought reverberating in Gold's mind as he strode to his locker to strip for his shower.

"I've been reading what you've been writing in the *Times* and that other magazine," said Karp when Gold returned wearing shower sandals and carrying a plastic bottle of herbal shampoo and his green soap dish, ''and I would like to differ with you on one or two points if you will first take the trouble to define your terms for me.''

Almost two minutes went by before hot water came up from the boiler in the basement. Twice the soap slipped from Gold's hands as he showered and he dropped his bottle of shampoo once. In adjacent stalls in the shower room two old men, deaf to melody, insensible to tempo, and oblivious to each other, were singing different songs industriously. Gold's head began to ache. He was a pound and a half heavier on the scale than he wanted to be. He would have welcomed a prodigious bowel movement.

''How do you feel about municipal tax-exempt bonds,'' asked Karp the chiropodist, ''as an investment, as an economic phenomenon, and as a social inequity? Do you have an opinion?''

Gold's pulse rate was down. Dressing at his locker, he assessed the damage to his flesh, bones, and systems from the track. Again the toll was heaviest on his right side. A rigid ache toward the rear of his neck there descended into his torso like a railroad spike. His shoulder, elbow, and breast were throbbing, and his liver felt swollen and seemed heavy as a cast-iron mass. There was a fiery, very fine twinge in his left kidney and a snag in his right hip that he hoped might grind away. His appendix was sore, as were his groin and right testicle, and there was stiffening compression in the leg muscles below from his buttock to his calf. It would not surprise him to be told he had cancer of the thighbone. A toe had bled beneath the nail. Physically, he was in peak condition.

''Personally, I'm opposed in principle to tax advantages of that kind,'' said Karp the chiropodist as Gold took his coat from the rack. ''But I hold to the view that attempts at correction will produce dislocations in other areas of the economy that will prove more harmful than the injustices we remove. Who do you think will play in the Super Bowl the next three years and how do you feel about the effects of television on revolution and the quality of conversation in the nuclear family? Don't you have an opinion?''

An old handball player several rows down complained in a high-pitched voice, ''This is supposed to be the Young Men's

Christian Association, isn't it? But you don't find so many Christians around here any more, do you?"

"It's hard to be a Jew," said Karp to Gold. "Do you agree?"

Gold shut the door of the telephone booth. Weinrock Fashions had changed to Spot Modes.

"Mr. Weinrock is out in the market," the frail voice of an immature girl said when Gold had given his name. "May anyone else be of assistance to you?"

"What market?" asked Gold.

The girl hung up in panic. Karp the chiropodist was standing in wait near the exit and jeered, "Aaaah, you don't know what you're talking about."

Gold made for the elevators in a weary hobble. Both kneecaps were tender. There was pain in one ankle and he walked with a limp, in premature fulfillment of the mystic prophecy in the Chinese restaurant that came to him the following day.

VI

You Will Hurt Your Foot

"**H**AVE you left Belle yet?" said Ralph. "In that case, please give her my love. Do it soon, though, if you hope to propose to Andrea and marry her before your appointment is announced. Now these Commission meetings tomorrow morning can be of great importance to you, Bruce, because they're of no importance to anyone else. Do whatever you want as long as you do whatever we want. We have no ideas, and they're pretty firm. Seize control. This Administration will back you all the way until it has to."

GOLD ARRIVED for his first Presidential Commission meeting punctually at eight-thirty the following morning as though borne to his destiny on a tide of optimism and felt his poise crumble when he found nobody there. At ten, an enticing, buxom woman with black hair in a ponytail entered with several young assistants to supervise the physical arrangements and was staggered to discover someone else already present for an official meeting slated to convene but an hour and a half earlier. Her name was Miss Plum. She had much makeup on her comely face, and a necklace of green Mexican beads lay languorously between her breasts. Gold cursed his poor judgment in arriving on time. He prowled nervously to and fro in the marble hallways and neighboring side rooms like a creature in fear of ambush, praying feverishly for his allies on the Commission to join him. In a while a coffee wagon rolled into the anteroom, closely stalked by a celebrated, superannuated career diplomat in striped pants and morning coat, who, stretching upward on his toes for improved range, was plucking avidly at the raisins and glazed almonds on the pastries he still had spryness enough to reach.

The hour was past eleven when his remaining twenty-three colleagues arrived in chattering clusters so concentrated that all could have alighted from the same chariot. The walls resounded with hearty salutations from which Gold was excluded. People tended to look and move right through him as though he were made of something nebulous. All were addressed by title. Eventually, Gold was introduced to a defeated mayor, a deposed old judge who could hardly see, a retired naval commander, an apostate clergyman in splendid vestments, and the ex-athletic director of a large university who wore a sweatshirt, whistle, and billed cap and was called Coach. Even Gold had a title: his title was Doctor, and as far as he could tell, he was the only member of that superior group with a job—as a doctor, although it was only as doctor of philosophy, and in English literature at that.

He was distressed from the outset by how little attention his presence excited, and his powers of speech were vitiated by his dread of being considered inferior. He began to wonder if he were the only Jew. Introductions were performed by Miss Plum with effulgent cheerfulness and inviting sexual warmth and there was much lewd laying on of hands by the more elderly men who had worked and resided in Washington longest and were most in keeping with the customs. Miss Plum had been divorced four times, and Gold could tell she was not a virgin. Overshadowing all was a handsome, silver-haired former governor of Texas with a chiseled cleft in his chin and a reputation for emanating authority.

"I'm glad to meet you, Dr. Gold," the Governor said crisply when Miss Plum finally brought them together. The flat blue eyes resting on Gold were friendly as ice. "People tell me you're a genius."

"Who?" Gold blurted out, repenting the blunder even as he was committing it.

"You can't be much of a genius if you don't even know that," said the Governor, turning away. "Good morning, Mayor, you're looking marvelous. So is the Deputy and the Chief. Have you seen the Admiral?"

"He's with the Consul and the Chancellor, Governor. Enjoying a word with the Widow."

"Who is the Spade?"

"He's our new Token Black. A brilliant scholarship student at Oxford."

"He knows his place?"

"At the foot of the table. They tell me, Governor, you might be back as a Secretary soon."

"Ho, ho, ho, Solicitor-General." The Governor advocated caution with a reproving shake of his finger. "You must have been eavesdropping on the Major or the Coach. I do know I'm up for an Under."

"The Ambassador certainly looks healthy again since he lost Vietnam, Chile, Greece, Cyprus, Turkey, Pakistan, China, Africa, Thailand, and the Middle East, doesn't he?"

"He bounces back every time. The tougher the losses, the tougher he gets. Look at that vitality."

All turned with love to glance past Gold at the active old Ambassador, who, in a world of his own at the coffee wagon, was busily stuffing cakes into the pockets of his morning coat, striped trousers, and pearl-gray weskit.

Gold was stung again by their indifference. He would either have to forgo the society of such people or get used to stinging, and he knew already it was going to be the latter.

He was eager for the chance to excel and take charge when he heard Miss Plum suggest softly that all move inside the conference room and begin. In his briefcase were notes for an opening statement that would start with remarks from Montaigne and Erasmus and end with a likable summation from Cardinal John Henry Newman that would win him the enduring loyalty of the Roman Catholic episcopacy in America, provided he were never examined closely on abortion, transubstantiation, the Resurrection, or papal infallibility. Coach was named Permanent Temporary Chairman and the Governor said:

"Let's adjourn."

"Till when?" screamed Gold as the room cleared.

"You'll be informed, hon," Miss Plum crooned, placing a gentle hand on his neck. There was perfume in her breath and the scent of freshly soaped flesh floated from the low neckline of her dress. "It isn't necessary to work eight hours to get your thousand a day."

Gold could have fucked her right there. Sympathetically she guided him out through a darkened alcove lined with telephone booths, where she took his hand and curled her fingers ever so lightly toward the tips of his own. Gold drew Miss Plum inside a telephone booth and pressed her against his member.

"Not here," she said. "It's against the law."

"Then where?"

"Anywhere. Andrea's apartment."

"Oh, shit." Dejection superseded lust. "You know Andrea?"

"She tells me you're great."

"I'm not. Andrea doesn't know."

"She tells me you're powerful and domineering and rates you an A plus. Power turns me on."

"It's a known aphrodisiac. But power corrupts."

"Don't I know it."

"I love you, Miss Plum."

"Felicity."

"But breathe that to a soul and I'll break your head."

Felicity Plum scheduled another session for the following day just to see him again that much sooner.

By then, Gold had learned in Washington that the CIA was recruiting mercenaries to fight in Africa. He learned this at breakfast from his morning newspaper when he read:

> CIA DENIES RECRUITING
> MERCENARIES TO FIGHT
> IN AFRICA

In Congress all the preceding day, members of a coalition of right-wing Republicans and Democrats had been taking the floor to extol the CIA for recruiting mercenaries to fight in Africa.

GOLD WAS stern in his determination not to be outdone again as he arrived with the others for the second meeting of the Commission with an expression of almost belligerent impudence. Even Miss Plum had a title now, he noticed; her title was Dear. Gold casually lifted a licentious hand to her shoulder and found hairy, cold, wrinkled flesh and fossilized bone. The old blind Judge had got there first.

They convened earlier than the preceding day. Coach gaveled the session to order and the Governor said:

"Let's quit. We've already spent more time on these problems than I think they deserve."

There tore from Gold a feline wail of protest. "No! Please! We haven't spent any!"

"And it's more than enough," said a quondam Attaché. "We've done as much as we're going to. Let's get out."

"We haven't done anything!"

"And in record time, too," clucked the Ambassador. "I was once on a Presidential Commission that took almost three years to do nothing, and here we've accomplished the same thing in only two meetings."

"We have computers now," said the Widow.

"I agree with the Governor," said the retired Naval Commander. "And I command we conclude the work of this Commission by unanimous consent."

"I agree with the Commander," said the Governor.

"All in favor say aye."

"I object," said Gold.

"One objection, the rest ayes," said Coach. "The motion is carried by unanimous consent. Can I drop you at the reception, Governor?"

"I'm going to the brunch."

"Then I'll see you at the lunch."

"I'm so glad it's over," chortled the Ambassador, "even though I'm sorry. I love the expense money so—" he made fists of his hands and tapped them together—"and all these free cakes."

"But we can do so much more," Gold pleaded. "We haven't even called any authorities."

"Gold." The Governor pronounced the name quietly and the others fell silent. "Everyone here is an authority." Even seated the Governor projected that extra impression of size that placed him head and shoulders above all the rest. "In about three minutes, we are going to leave this room. Any reporters outside will come to me first because I'm the most important one here and can emanate emanations of authority that have been commented upon the world over. I'm *famous* for them, dammit! I'm going to notify them that the business of this Commission is concluded and that we've done all we could under most difficult circumstances—that the people will understand when they read our report. Now if you want to tell them something else, you do that. But you will be giving insult to me and the rest of these fine people who have worked together with you cheek to jowl and hip to thigh, and you better believe right now that sooner or later I'll have your pecker in my pocket, along with all the other peckers I've collected in a successful political career that has been a surprise and a joy to my teachers, my family, and my friends. Now do you want to tell me I'm wrong?"

Gold did not.

"I'm obliged to you for that," said the Governor. "Gold, you a Jew, ain't you?"

No hell could be worse, or with more finality seem eternal, than the instants Gold needed to reply to that deafening question. The cutting word was pronounced as though the letter *y* had sneaked in before the vowel, and Gold also took note of the Governor's declension into a cruder syntax. He prayed with passion for the voice of some Arthurian champion to supervene; his prayer was answered with the silence of a tomb.

"I'm Jewish, sir," he replied with a flippant dignity invented for the purpose, "if that's what you mean."

"What in hell else do you think I mean?"

"I was not," said Gold, "totally sure."

"It don't make a sparrow shit's worth of difference whether you are totally sure or are not totally sure, and the sooner you learn that fact the safer your pecker will be. Hey, boy!" The Governor abruptly moved his gaze to the black student at the foot of the conference table. "You a nigger, ain't you? You understand what I mean when I say you a nigger, don't you?"

The student squared his shoulders. "The ones I don't like are those Northern liberals who say one thing and mean another. I know where I stand with you and you know where you stand with me."

"Where do I stand with you?"

"Wherever you want to, Master."

The Governor redirected his attention to Gold with a patronizing sigh of impatience. "Now, Gold. Everybody here is a somebody, and I don't know why you're being so captious about who it is you are. He is the Spade, she is the Widow, I am the Governor, and you're the—"

"Doctor!" yelled Gold in time to ward off a crushing repetition of that denunciatory term. "The Doctor!"

The Governor's manner was transformed into one of self-interest. "You an osteopath or something, Gold? A faith healer? A chiropractor?" He flexed his arm and massaged his shoulder. "I may have a pinch of bursitis that could use relief."

"I'd like him to examine my foot," said the Coach, unlacing his shoe, while the Judge waved wildly for Gold's attention and tapped his breastbone as though suffocating while fumbling with the buttons of his shirt as the Consul stuck his tongue out toward Gold with a cough and the Ambassador rose, bent his asshole to Gold, and began dropping his striped pants.

Gold's cries now were of terror mingled with desperation. "Of philosophy!" he yelped, slapping his brow. "I'm a Doctor of Philosophy! A professor. I'm a writer!"

"Then fuck my bursitis," said the Governor with an emanation of authority of the kind for which he was justly renowned and an air of expeditiousness for which he was also applauded universally. "You write the report. Can I drop you at the reception, Widow?"

"Thank you, Governor, but I'm praying with the Bishop."

"Then the Envoy and I will see you at the ball park."

"What should I write?" Gold broke in helplessly.

"Anything you want," said the Governor, and the Ambassador cheered "Hear! Hear!" "As long as it doesn't contain a single thing anyone here might take exception to." A look of mercy crept into his eyes and he spoke with benevolence. "Gold, a Jew always needs friends in Washington, because he doesn't really belong here. Don't argue—listen. You oblige me in this and I may help you get some.''

Relief was Gold's first emotion and his fires of initiative were damped. ''How would you like me to write the report, sir?'' he asked.

''Make it short,'' the Governor advised, ''and make it long. Make it clear and make it fuzzy. Make it short by coming right to each point. Then make it long by qualifying those points so that nobody can tell the qualifications from the points or ever figure out what we're talking about.''

''I think I know,'' said Gold, ''what you mean.''

The Governor was mollified. ''Let me give you five good rules of behavior I got from my momma the first time I left our dirt farm for the great big city of Austin. My momma, bless her heart, instructed me, 'Don't make personal remarks, never tell a hostess you enjoyed yourself, don't force anything mechanical, never kick anything inanimate, and don't fart around with the inevitable.' Now, Gold, it appeared that in disputing with me you were drawing very close to farting around with the inevitable. I hope I am mistaken.''

''It was certainly not my intention, sir,'' said Gold, ''to fart around with the inevitable. Or to force anything mechanical. I will never kick anything inanimate.''

The Governor placed his huge hand upon Gold's shoulder in a gesture of fraternal pardon. ''Understand that nobody in this room ever wants to read our report. That's another reason you must make it too long to be published in total in that damned *New York Times*. Otherwise, some of these nosy journalists might be pestering us for years with questions we don't know the answers to about matters we have no interest in. Will I see you at cocktails, Mr. Special Prosecutor?''

''No, Governor. We're going straight to the banquet with the Comptroller and the Queer. Will you be at the ball?''

''The Mrs. and I will be detained at the orgy. But perhaps at the supper.''

''If I'm able to get there. I'll be shooting the shit with the Adjutant and the Bailiff. Let's say hello to the Crook and goodbye to the Champ."

"I am not a crook," said the Crook.

Gold was sorry it was over and missed them dearly. Working in concert, they had accomplished in just two meetings what had taken others as long as three years: nothing. He had served on his first Presidential Commission, and oh, the joy—the intoxicating ecstasy of being insulted and condescended to by people of established social position who ignored, abused, or despised him, the gratification in being admitted into such company as an insignificant status-seeker to be overlooked and snubbed, interrupted when he did try to speak and banished with such grace from each conversation he attempted to penetrate. They were occupied with brunches, lunches, and orgies at which his presence was not yet desired. They went to the ball park with Widows and Prelates and had good seats. How he envied their sense of belonging and their impervious stupidity.

"Invite a Jew to the White House (and You Make Him Your Slave)" was a snide attack on Lieberman he had planned writing after the latter's invitation to the White House for supporting a war. How close, as Ralph had discerned, Gold often came by whim, jealousy, and blind intuition to the fundamental truths of his world.

And how pleasing the custom of allowing people to wear like plumes the titles of the highest position they had held. If I were President, thought Gold—*when* I am President, he amended in fanciful contemplation—everyone will be appointed to some good government position one day and asked to resign the next, so that all in the land—regardless of race, occupation, family, creed, or financial station—can go through life called Ambassador, Judge, Major, or Secretary, instead of Esther, Rose, Irv, Victor, Julius or Sid.

GOLD WAS jarred from his reverie by news from Miss Plum that four reporters had lingered outside in hopes of obtaining some truth from him.

They could hardly have been younger, and they came flocking

about him for light like moths around a dark bulb. One was a tall pretty girl with a small face and straight blond hair who asked in a tone of nagging disrespect as querulous as any of which Gold had ever been the target just what he and the others were trying to pretend they'd accomplished. Gold decided to seduce her.

"Frankly, my dear, I don't know," he began in a practiced mode of disarming modesty, but could get no further. They had flown.

"That was terrible!" Miss Plum rebuked him severely in a panic that brought a strained ellipse of unsightly tension around her voluptuous mouth and beads of sweat to her cheeks and forehead. "You're *never* supposed to say that!"

"That was great!" cheered Ralph on the telephone before Gold could slink from the building in solitary disgrace. "Cables of your declaration are already out to our embassies in computerized code."

"What declaration?"

"Your motto is now a mainstay of official policy."

"What motto?"

"Your instinct is infallible, your words poetic, your modesty endearing. Bruce, you boggle my mind. Rush right over now to our next press briefing. An executive order has been issued to sneak you in."

"You were wonderful," cried Miss Plum, pressing close, but Gold no longer loved her and knew he would never wish to hold her against his member again.

HE ARRIVED for the White House press briefing not a moment too soon and found a place against the wall with an uninterrupted view of the lectern just as the Press Secretary said:

"I have an announcement to make. As you know, this President conducts an open Administration and is committed to total truth. In keeping with that policy, I have to announce that I have no announcement to make. Nothing's happened since yesterday."

There was a dumbfounded pause in the room before a veteran newsman up front asked, "Nothing?"

"That is correct. There is no news today."

"No news?"

"No news."

"Not a thing?"

"Not a thing worth talking about."

"Is that just for Washington, Ron?" asked a voice at the side. "Or is that true of the rest of the country as well?"

"Just for Washington. We don't care about the rest of the country."

"You don't care about the rest of the country?"

"That is correct."

"Does that mean there'll be nothing in the newspapers about the President?"

"That's right. Unless you want to make a story out of that. Can we move along?"

"Your announcement leaves me somewhat at a loss, Ron, so let me go back several years. Some time ago, Ron, the former head of the CIA, Richard Helms, appeared to have lied under oath to at least one Congressional committee. Yet he was allowed to remain as Ambassador to Iran instead of being indicted for this crime and brought to trial. Can you comment on that?"

"No. This Administration does not feel it appropriate to comment on matters that are under investigation."

"Are you saying," asked a woman quickly, "that the matter *is* under investigation?"

"I didn't say that."

"But isn't that the implication of what you did say?"

"I don't know."

At this reply a collective gasp of amazement filled the room and was followed by a tempest of excitement in which one voice at last rose above the rest.

"What was that?"

"I don't know."

"Could you say that again?"

"I don't know."

"You don't know?"

"I really don't know."

"Holy cow! Ron, Ron, would you mind repeating that one for the mike. I want to be absolutely sure I have it on tape."

"Certainly. I don't know."

"Thank you, Ron. That was swell."

"Is that reply for attribution? Are you willing to let yourself be quoted on that?"

"I don't know."

"You mean you don't know whether you're willing to let yourself be quoted saying you don't know?"

"That is correct."

"Can we quote you on *that* one?"

"I don't know."

"Ron, is there anyone else in a position of authority in government, or anywhere else, who ever said, 'I don't know'?"

"I don't know. Those are the words of Dr. Bruce Gold, who teaches college in Brooklyn, New York, and may soon be coming to work for the Administration."

"In what capacity, Ron, would Dr. Gold be coming to work for the Administration?"

"I don't know. May we move on?"

"You remember Henry Kissinger, don't you? What was your opinion of him?"

"Second-rate."

"That was his opinion of Richard Nixon, wasn't it?"

"Make that third-rate."

"That's something that's always puzzled me, Ron. If Richard Nixon was second-rate, what in the world *is* third-rate?"

"Henry Kissinger."

"You rate Henry Kissinger *below* Richard Nixon?"

"Only in intelligence and wit. In character and credibility they're about the same."

"On this subject of credibility, Ron. You remember that Richard Kleindienst was caught lying under oath in connection with his appointment to Attorney General. Now, this is perjury. Yet he was allowed to plead guilty to just a misdemeanor and to continue practicing law. Can you tell us now why Richard Kleindienst, like Richard Helms, was afforded this lenient treatment normally denied to other criminals?"

"I don't know."

"It's a little fishy, isn't it?"

"It's fishy as hell."

"Is that for attribution?"

"Of course not. Who's next?"

"Now that so much time has passed, can you tell us the real reason—it's a lot of Richards, I know, that we're dealing with now in the criminal element but I hope you will bear with me, Ron— Gerald Ford found it necessary to pardon Richard Nixon for all the sex crimes he committed while in office?"

"Did Nixon commit sex crimes?"

"I don't know. But wasn't that the effect of pardoning Nixon for all crimes committed while he was President?"

"I don't know."

"This Administration has decided to fight inflation by raising prices to lower demand to reduce prices to increase demand and bring back the inflationary high prices we want to lower by reducing demand to increase demand and raise prices. Isn't that pretty much all your present economic policy amounts to?"

"I don't know."

"Ron, are you sure you don't know or are you merely guessing?"

"I'm absolutely sure I don't know."

"What are you willing to predict will happen to unemployment and the economy in the short-term period ahead?"

"I don't know."

"You don't know what you would predict?"

"That is correct."

"Is there anyone in government who does know?"

"What I would predict?"

"I withdraw the question."

"How about our overseas alliances? If just about all are based on bribery, coercion, and subversion and other corruption of one kind or another, what stability will they have in a genuine crisis or when a government changes?"

"Lord, I don't know that."

"Well, is there anyone in the Administration who does know?"

"What?"

"Anything."

"Would you repeat that question?"

"Anything."

"Is that a question?"

"Is that an answer?"

"I don't know."

"I forgot my question."

"I'll withdraw my answer."

"Well, how about the President? Doesn't he have any intelligent opinions about what's going to happen at home or abroad?"

"I don't know."

"Ron, please. Pretty please. Can I have that one again for the television camera? I'd like to zoom in on you just before you answer. Hold your answer until you see us zooming in."

"Sure. I don't know."

"That was peachy."

"Ron, I have to ask you this about the President. Is it that you really don't know or that you don't want to say?"

"I don't know."

"You mean you don't know if you don't know or not?"

"That is correct."

"Thank you, Ron," said the senior correspondent in the first row. "You're to be congratulated. This has been the frankest and most informative press briefing I've ever attended."

"Oh, I don't know."

RALPH phoned the next morning while Gold was making breakfast to tell him the President wanted to see him to congratulate him personally. "He tried phoning you at your hotel, but the switchboard told him you weren't taking any calls."

"I'm staying with Andrea," said Gold. "Registering at the hotel is a way of protecting myself."

From Ralph came a low whistle of homage. "You're deep, Bruce. That's exactly the safeguard we all should use to protect our most vital secrets. Be at the White House at eleven. Use the servants' entrance."

Gold followed directions and was ushered upstairs through a pantry into a private waiting room just as Ralph emerged on tiptoe from a private inner office and led him back out. The appointment was canceled. The President was asleep.

"He's taking a nap," whispered Ralph.

"At eleven in the morning?" cried Gold.

"The President," Ralph explained, "is a very early riser. He is up at five every morning, takes two sleeping pills and a tranquilizer, and goes right back to bed for as long as he can sleep."

"When does he work?" asked Gold.

"What do you mean?" said Ralph.

"When does he work?"

Ralph's chief emotion was perplexity. "I still don't get it."

"When does he do what he's supposed to be doing? As President?"

"Twenty-four hours a day," said Ralph. "The poor man is probably working right now, even while he's napping. You've been promoted, you know. He meant to tell you that."

"To what?" Gold exclaimed in surprise.

"We haven't decided, but it's a big step up."

"From what?"

"We never found out, did we? You can just about have your pick now, unless you can't. That much is official, although it has to be approved, and it must remain secret until we announce it, in case we decide we won't. You're way past a spokesman and a source now."

"Will I make more money?" Gold wanted to know.

"As much," said Ralph, "as you can get away with, although the competition is always strong. You know, Lyndon Johnson and Jack Javits were not the only ones to get rich while serving in government. I bumped into Harris Rosenblatt and found out what the Secretary of the Treasury does," said Ralph as they settled down comfortably in his office. "People of your religious beliefs inevitably do well there."

Gold cleared his throat. "I have no religious beliefs, Ralph."

"You know what I mean, Bruce," said Ralph. "I was trying to phrase it with tact."

"I'm very grateful for your tact."

"There's something mysterious happening with Harris Rosenblatt, Bruce," Ralph said with a furrowed brow. "Each time I see him he looks more and more like someone like me and less like someone like you."

Once more Gold found difficulty speaking. "In what way, Ralph, does Harris Rosenblatt look more and more like you and less like me?"

"He gets taller and leaner, Bruce," Ralph answered simply and honestly and seemed unmindful of the frostiness with which Gold had spoken. "And he stands up straight. You remember how short and flabby he used to be. And he seems to be getting paler too. I saw Andrea at a party the other night and I'm worried about her also. Didn't she used to be taller?"

"Taller?" Gold searched Ralph's eyes for some beam of shared intelligence. "Taller than what?"

"Than she is. I'd check if I were you. You wouldn't want her to get too short, would you?"

"Too short for what, Ralph?"

"For you, Bruce. I don't think it would add much to your stature if your second wife turned out to be as short as Belle, would it?"

"I'll ask, Ralph, when I have the chance. What does the Secretary of the Treasury do?"

"He reassures the business community."

"I could do that," said Gold.

"Sure you could," Ralph agreed. "And promises to hold down deficits. He doesn't actually hold them down, you understand, but merely promises to. He also looks after the financial interests of himself and his friends so they can continue to live on the level they're used to."

Gold was losing interest. "I'm not so crazy about my friends," he confessed, "and I'm trying to improve the level I'm used to."

"Your heart wouldn't be in it."

"I've been giving second thoughts to Chief of NATO, Secretary of Defense, Director of the CIA or FBI, and even to Secretary of the Army, Navy, or Air Force, if it isn't too late."

"No, of course it isn't," said Ralph, "unless, of course, it's already too late. Did we come to a decision on Health, Education, and Welfare?"

"I'm only interested in my own."

"What about Housing and Urban Development? It helps to know what it's like to be poor—"

"I've been poor."

"—and identify with the underprivileged."

"Count me out."

"How about Attorney General, Bruce? That one really packs a wallop."

"I have an open mind," said Gold. "I think I could really get behind such issues as busing and integration now that my own children won't be affected by them. But don't I have to be a lawyer to be Attorney General?"

"I don't think so. Not as a matter of law."

"Could you find out?"

"I'll ask the Attorney General."

"Let's pass it up."

"How do you feel about the State Department?"

"It's where I think I'd fit in best."

"The President may think so too." Ralph, rising, stretched contentedly. "I know I can just about guarantee that you'll get the appointment you choose as soon as you want, although I can't promise anything. So please don't hold me to that."

Although there was nothing but pure friendship in Ralph's voice, Gold determined he might bear closer inspection. "Ralph, I find myself listening to things here that I can't believe I am hearing."

"I know just how you feel." Ralph ran his hand through his auburn cowlick. "Now that I've been in Washington awhile, I'm willing to believe almost anything."

Gold wondered if he was being too abstruse. "Ralph, I'm hearing them from you."

"From me?" Ralph spoke with frank surprise. "Bruce, you can believe what I tell you, because I will never lie to you. Everything I've promised has come to pass, hasn't it? Tell me how you're handling your job at the college."

"I've promoted all my students into the Honors Program," said Gold, "and assigned them term projects. I may never see any of them again."

Ralph gasped approvingly and tapped the side of his nose with his finger. "You're deep, Bruce, deep indeed. I doubt there's a problem in government you won't be able to solve with ease. All that remains is for you to leave Belle and marry Andrea. It would be so much better, Bruce, if you did that before your confirmation hearings begin. It's always bad for the country when someone waits until *after* he's made it big in government before dumping his old wife for a better one. That may be acceptable ethics for a Senator or Congressman, but you're much bigger than that now."

"I am?"

"I thought you knew that," said Ralph, "although there's no way you could have found it out. Leave Belle, Bruce. Do the right thing."

Gold was slightly cowed. "Leaving a wife is not so easy, Ralph."

"You say that to me?"

"And how do I know Andrea will marry me?"

"How can she refuse when you tell her about your promotion?"

"How can I tell her when it has to be a secret?"

"Oh, you can give her a hint," said Ralph. "She's probably been listening in anyway. Have you met Pugh Biddle yet? He's special, you know, and so is his estate in the hunt country. What are you working on these days?"

"I still have to do that book on . . ."

"Jewish people?" Ralph showed off.

"Jews," Gold said bravely. "Although it's more in the nature of a personal history now. And I'm organizing material for a humorous book on David Eisenhower and a serious one on Henry Kissinger, although it may turn out the other way around."

"How will you treat Henry Kissinger?"

"Fair."

"I never liked him either. Oh, yes, the President asked me to find out from you if Russia will go to war if we reduce our military strength."

Gold looked at Ralph through the corner of his eye. "How should I know?"

"Could you find out?"

"From who? Ralph, doesn't anyone here have an idea?"

"Oh, we have lots of experts. But the President feels your guess might be as good as anyone else's."

"I'll ask around."

"You're aces, Bruce," said Ralph. "The President will be grateful."

"Ralph," said Gold, with skepticism predominating again over a multitude of other concerns, "do you ever really see the President?"

"Oh, yes, Bruce," Ralph answered. "Everybody sees the President."

"I mean personally. Does he see you?"

"The President sees a great deal, Bruce."

"Do you ever see him to talk to him?"

"About what?" asked Ralph.

"About anything."

"Oh, Bruce, you can't just talk to the President about anything," Ralph chided. "The President is often very busy. He may be writing another book."

Gold persisted rationally in the face of a gathering fog of futility. "Well, Ralph, if you did have something of importance to discuss with the President, could you get in to talk to him?"

"About what?" Ralph asked again.

"About whatever you had that was important—no, don't stop me—like war, for example."

"That's not my department," Ralph said. "That's out of my area."

"What is your area?"

"Just about everything I cover, Bruce."

"What do you cover?"

"Everything in my area, Bruce. That's my job."

Gold was struggling to keep his voice down. "I've been trying to find out, Ralph, just what your job is."

"Well, I'm glad I've been able to help," said Ralph, pumping his hand. "Please give my love to Belle and my best to Andrea, or my love to Andrea and my best to Belle, whichever seems more appropriate."

Gold stood wearily. "And you give mine," he said, "to Alma."

Ralph looked blank. "Which Alma?"

"Isn't Alma the name of your wife?" Gold demanded.

"It's also the name of the girl I'm engaged to," said Ralph. "She's almost a full year younger. Bruce, take my advice. If a man is going to leave one wife to marry another, it's better if he divorces the first before he marries the second. I've tried both ways. And leave them quickly, before they start getting those tumors and hysterectomies. Yes, it's always practical to leave your wives while they're healthy and young enough to attract another husband to pay the medical bills and make those dreary hospital visits. Oh, yes, I'm supposed to find out if there is anything disgraceful in your life that would be embarrassing to us if it were made public?"

"Like what?" Gold watched him shakily.

"I haven't any idea."

"Then I have to say no."

"Have you ever done anything worse than the rest of us?"

"Absolutely not."

"Then you're in the clear." One would have guessed from his serenity of expression and the deep breath Ralph took as he stared out the doorway at the banks of desks on the office floor that he was contemplating a fertile meadow and inhaling breezes enriched by privet and honeysuckle and astir with the seasonal hummings of countless bucolic copulations. "Isn't this breathtaking," he exclaimed. "It's been said, Bruce, by two out of three of our most dependable think tanks, that if someone stood in this doorway of mine long enough, sooner or later he might see the President walk by. Would you care to wait?"

Gold looked at him askance, doubtful once more that he had heard his Protestant friend aright. "I have to propose to Andrea."

"The President will be pleased."

GOLD was nervous and faintly giddy all through dinner. Preserving his outward calm, he artfully inculcated Andrea again with the need to forbear discussing their relationship and sexual intimacies with people like Miss Plum or anyone else. Andrea attended him with a credulous sort of rapture that had him feeling superbly gifted and slightly alarmed. He was not used to wielding such hypnotic influence over anyone he revered.

The Scotch kippers and Lithuanian rye bread he had brought from New York had gone down well, and Andrea would find out from contacts in the Commerce and Agriculture Departments if Arabian mocha coffee beans could be obtained anywhere in the world or if they were extinct. He preferred the Arabian mocha to the French. Gold put the last of the saucers in the dish drain and moved into the living room, where Andrea awaited him on the sofa in a recumbent attitude that summoned to mind the painting and the marble statue of Madame Récamier, her head resting lightly on her hand and her fine, lithe legs extended atop the cushions of the couch. His breath was swept away again by the lavender expanding radially from the clear, sea-blue circles surrounding her pupils. Her face was the loveliest into which he had ever peered, and he questioned anew why he occasionally was so bored. Her fingers played affectionately with the dark hairs at the back of his neck.

"Ralph thinks," he said, kissing her, "that we ought to get married."

An influx of color made her cheeks shine. "I think so too."

"He feels it would be good for the country," said Gold, suffused with an embarrassed shyness that he did not believe descended on people past the age of fourteen and which he made Spartan effort to suppress. "I'm going to work for the government, you see. It's absolutely definite now, although I can't be sure."

"I've always wanted to be married to someone with a high position in government," said Andrea. "To someone I admired who would want to see me again."

"I was given a big promotion today."

"From what?"

"I can't say," he told her mysteriously.

"What will you do?"

"I'm afraid I'm not able to tell you that either."

"I bet I can guess," Andrea teased and began tickling him. "A spokesman?"

"Oh, no," Gold replied immodestly, chortling with her. Both were frolicking. "I've already been promoted well beyond that."

"A source?" She played the game zestfully. "Higher than a senior official?" she continued as Gold kept shaking his head. "Then I bet I do know," she said, growing serious. "Chairman of the Joint Chiefs of Staff? Secretary of State? Attorney General? Chief Justice of the Supreme Court?"

Gold put a finger to her lips. "That's close enough, my darling," he told her firmly. "It has to be secret. But I think we can begin making plans for marriage. I feel we've always sort of wanted to. I know I've always had a crush on you."

"You're so much fun."

"Bliss!" he cried in ecstasy when he saw his proposal of marriage accepted. "I have never known such!"

So was it done. Both took it for granted, Gold surmised afterward, that in one way or another he would separate himself from Belle, for neither made mention of it then.

In bed later she said, "You don't have to do that. I almost never come."

By every imaginable standard, she was ideal.

GOLD broached the subject at home discreetly. There was a cowardly procedure for leaving a wife, and he had the substantial advantage of a studio apartment into which he could move with a minimum of dislocation.

"I've been seeing a doctor, a psychiatrist again," he began evasively. "For overwork."

"Yes?" said Belle.

"I've been under a strain, with my teaching and my writing and all my work in Washington."

"So you told me, just a few days ago."

"See how things slip my mind? He thinks it's important that I get away somewhere by myself for a while and pull myself together."

"Sure," said Belle.

"Well, I can't really take a vacation now. So he suggested I might start sleeping at my studio when I'm in New York, one night a week, maybe two, sort of live there three or four nights a week when I'm in town, until I sort of pull myself together."

"Okay," said Belle.

"Belle, you understand? You understand what I'm telling you?"

"Sure," said Belle.

"And there's all those times I like to get up in the middle of the night and start typing, and I don't always feel right about doing that here."

"Okay."

Against such limp opposition his courage flagged. He felt a melancholy letdown at the thought she might not care.

"So you see," he explained, with a warble of woe gargling in his throat, "we'll really be living apart some of the time. Separate. Separated, sort of." She said nothing. "You understand?"

"I understand."

"At least until I can pull myself together."

"How long," asked Belle, "will it take to pull yourself together?"

"Nobody knows."

"Do you think," asked Belle, "you'll be able to pull yourself together in time for your father's anniversary party next Friday?"

"Oh, sure," Gold acceded with a hardy spirit of cooperation far from consistent with the neurasthenic condition he had described. "I'll still be coming here often for dinner and mail and to have my suits cleaned and pick up my laundry. I'll need my old dark suits for Washington and some of those old white shirts."

"Otherwise, he might want to stay in New York longer to help you pull yourself together."

"I'll be in Washington a lot."

"I bet he would even go to Washington to help you pull yourself together."

"I'll be at the party," said Gold, "and anywhere else I'm needed until they go back. Belle, you're sure you don't mind?"

"Why should I mind?"

"That I'll be out at my studio almost every evening and sleeping out of town so much? Sometimes whole weekends?"

"To tell you the truth," said Belle, "if you didn't tell me, I wouldn't know."

"You wouldn't know?"

"It's how you've been living for years."

GOLD'S daughter, though only twelve, was less easily deceived that nothing ulterior was afoot.

"You're moving out, ain't you?" she charged, with acumen rare in one so fresh in years.

"No, I'm not." He made a face at the scornful laugh she discharged. "I'm merely packing things I'll need at my studio for my work and have to take with me to Washington."

"Don't shit me," said Dina. "You're getting a divorce."

"That's no way for a little girl to talk."

"Don't you care what happens to me?"

"No."

"Why'd you have me if you didn't want me?"

"Who knew it would be you?"

"What's that supposed to mean?"

"Ask somebody else."

"You really are the pits."

"Do some homework now, or go outside and play."

"There's another woman, isn't there? I can tell. You probably think you want to marry her, don't you?"

"Not one word of that is true," said Gold.

"Bullshit. I know you've been screwing other women all my life. You think I don't know what goes on in the world? You might as well tell me. I've got a right to know. I'll find out anyway."

"Mind your own business."

"And what am I supposed to do? Come visit you on weekends?"

"Don't even call."

"You fuck. I ought to go into therapy just to spite you. I'll get thrown out of school. I'll bleed you dry."

"You'll go to a public clinic," Gold warned with a sudden chill, for Dina generally made good her threats. "One session a week. In a group."

"I hope she gives you the clap and the syph."

"Go shit in your hat."

HAVING SEPARATED from Belle and talked the matter out fully with his daughter, Gold decided to stay for dinner and spend the night. He was more comfortable home than at his studio, where the strident music from the Haitian whores next door came through the walls nightly as though the partitions were made of tissue.

SCRUPULOUSLY consulting his wristwatch, Gold, inflated with a growing sense of himself as a dignitary whose fortunes were on the rise, stepped gingerly past the unadorned reception room at the magazine and threaded a fastidious path through a creaking corridor congested perilously with leaning heaps of unsold back issues, attaining at the farthest end the office that still was the shabbiest and scruffiest and mustiest of any in which he had ever set foot. He could not think of a runner-up. An old feather duster as dirty as anything existing outside a garbage dump or an abandoned tenement ruin lay atop a shambles of yellowing old *New York Times Magazine* sections from which Lieberman perpetually plagiarized most of his new editorial ideas. Gold glanced balefully at the repellent object.

"I use it to clean," Lieberman apologized.

"Clean?" Gold repeated in a tone of aloofness intended to bulwark a distance between them of at least an arm's length. "What can you find to clean that's filthier than that?" He could not remember milking so much satisfaction from the relative standings in their relationship since that fruitful spring far back when Lieberman was rejected for a Rhodes Scholarship, a Fulbright Scholarship, a Guggenheim Grant, and a library card on successive days of one week. "Get it the fuck out of here if you want me to sit down there and sign anything."

Lieberman had responded jealously to Gold's ascendant fame by producing another of his manifestos. Gold read:

MY CALL FOR AN END TO COMMUNIST
RULE IN ALBANIA

"As you can see," said Lieberman, "I'm allowing a number of my colleagues in the intelligentsia to cosponsor this manifesto with me. We want fifty dollars from each signer to run advertisements in the most influential publications in the world, including mine. We're shooting for a thousand important people and I've decided to let you be among them. I personally have guaranteed to produce five hundred."

"How many have you now?"

"None." His manifesto continued:

WE DEMAND

1. POLITICAL DEMOCRACY IN ALBANIA.
2. FREEDOM OF THE PRESS IN ALBANIA.
3. RELIGIOUS TOLERANCE FOR THE ALBANIAN PEOPLE.
   WE WILL NOT BE DENIED!!!!!!

Gold read no further. "I won't sign it."

"Will you give fifty dollars?"

"I won't give fifty cents. Since I became a neoconservative, pragmatic progressive, concerned Democrat for a Coalition for a Democratic Majority, liberal reactionary, and enlightened Republican I am no longer accustomed to paying my own money to advertise my political principles. And neither are you."

"Why won't you sign it?"

"I'm not sure it's wise," said Gold with that incandescent contentment that often glowed in his heart when he contemplated the failures and frustrations of his contemporaries. "I'm about to be appointed to an important permanent position in Washington."

"You're *what?*" Lieberman drew back the corners of his mouth and seemed for the moment on the brink of attacking Gold's head with even his hind teeth. "You must be joking."

"I have not been more in earnest."

"Washington? Where do you shine in? Why should you be in government and not me? I had dinner at the White House once."

"With four hundred other people."

"With my wife. You never did. You want the Albanian people to be without political democracy just because *you're* getting a job in government? Don't you care what happens to them?"

"No," said Gold.

"I'll ruin you for that," Lieberman threatened. "I'll issue another manifesto."

"Easy, Lieberman," Gold cautioned gaily. "Let cooler heads prevail. If you're going to use manifestos, why aim them at little Albania? Launch them at Russia and China. Why waste manifestos? Once you bring Russia and China to their knees, I'm sure the little fish like Albania will fall into line."

"You're funny," Lieberman muttered bleakly. "But someone has to start somewhere. What kind of a job will you get in Washington?"

"I couldn't tell you if I wanted to," said Gold. "But I've already received a promotion."

"It's that big, huh?" Lieberman was impressed.

"And confidential."

"You can't trust even me?"

"My lips are sealed."

"When will we know?"

"I can say no more."

"You must have powerful friends in Washington now, huh?"

"Many. I was at the White House to meet the President."

"For dinner?" challenged Lieberman.

"At brunch," said Gold. "There were just Ralph and me. It was brief. We all have so much to do. I was chosen to write the Commission report, you know."

"What will you say about me in it?"

"Nothing," said Gold, "at which you will take umbrage."

"I'll give you all the help you need," offered Lieberman, and asked for some himself. "I bet you can do a lot for me now, can't you?"

"I believed you would get around to that," said Gold. "But is it, I must always ask myself, in the best interest of the country?"

"I think it is," said Lieberman. "That's the main reason I've been shifting all my editorial policies around in support of the Administration.''

"I'm not that sure the Administration is aware of all your editorial shifting around," said Gold.

"You could tell them." Lieberman seized his arm. "Bruce, what's it like in Washington?" Gold wrested his arm free and began rubbing at the grease stains and clumps of dust left on his sleeve by Lieberman's fingers. "What do you do there?"

Gold gave it to him with both barrels. "I fuck girls, Lieberman," he began explosively with a sadistic delight he could not bring himself to forgo. "Blond girls, Lieberman, blond, the blondest girls you ever saw. All of them beautiful. The daughters of millionaire oil barons and newspaper publishers. Lumber barons, potentates, steel tycoons. Magnates. You should see them, Lieberman, oh, you should see them. All are nineteen or twenty-three and will never grow older. They love Jews. Do you hear me, Lieberman? They love Jews. And they don't have enough of us there to go around. We're at a premium. They're crazy about us, Lieberman. Are you listening? Do you hear? Wealthy widows. They think we're brilliant and dynamic and creative, instead of just jumpy, nervous, and neurotic. They don't know, Lieberman, they just don't know. You should get them, Lieberman, by the armful, you should get them while you can."

"Take me with you!" Lieberman blurted out tearfully, and raised his eyes to Gold's face with an imploring look. "Get me a job!"

"I'm not convinced," Gold informed him coolly, "that what the government needs at this juncture is another Russian Jew from Brooklyn."

"Moravian," Lieberman corrected promptly.

"You've got no experience," said Gold. "I'm afraid I must go."

"Then get me a CIA grant." Lieberman chased after him through the winding path in the corridor with the agonized puffing of someone in a seizure.

Gold pinned him with an icy stare. "Won't you feel your intellectual integrity is compromised if you take money from the government secretly?"

The effect of this question was to reunite Lieberman with his vaunted moral authority. "Absolutely not," he replied with great asperity and hauteur. "There is nothing wrong with accepting money for supporting positions I would advocate anyway."

"And what are the positions you will advocate?"

"Whichever ones they want me to."

"Good day, my man."

"Bruce," Lieberman wheedled, attempting to obstruct Gold's exit, "why don't you and Belle come over the house for dinner with me and Sophie some night?"

"Because I don't want to," said Gold, and began working adeptly with scissors, pencil, and Scotch tape—his tools of preference for scholarship and research—as soon as he'd taken a seat by himself in the rear of the plane transporting him back to Washington and Andrea. He had clippings to mount on pages to classify in folders. Within minutes after takeoff he was surveying with complacency an ingenious sequence of three front-page headlines constructed from different issues of the New York *Post*:

Judge to Utah:
SHOOT HIM JAN. 17!

The Gilmore Ruling:
KILL HIM!

GILMORE DEAD!

A climax was missing. He made one up.

Court Orders:
KILL HIM AGAIN!

To these he inventively appended on a separate page two old headlines from the New York *Daily News* having nothing whatsoever to do with each other:

Ford to New York:
DROP DEAD!

And:

Mayor to Sanitation Men:
PICK UP THAT GARBAGE!

These he deftly rounded off with two strips of Scotch tape on a
scrap from *The New York Times* he had been carrying in his wallet
for ages and had feared misplacing:

> QUOTATION OF THE DAY
> "I told them I didn't like what was going
> on. I told them to shape up or ship out."
> Mayor Beame, expressing displeasure
> with Sanitation Department officials
> over the condition of city streets.

Although he wasn't sure how, Gold knew already he would fit
these somewhere into his book on Kissinger, David Eisenhower,
or the Jewish experience in America. He found himself next with
two more jokes by Henry Kissinger for the collection of public
witticisms by the former official which Gold, uncharitably, had
been amassing for years. He reread the first:

> Secretary of State Henry A. Kissinger
> made a little joke yesterday while pass-
> ing out local Monday morning quarter-
> back awards. The outgoing Secretary
> quipped that he had turned down a
> tryout offer from the New York Jets to
> become a possible successor to the Jets
> quarterback, Joe Namath. "I didn't
> think New York could handle two sex
> symbols in a row."

The next was hewn from similar wood:

> This week's going-away present for the
> go-go Secretary: honorary membership
> in the Harlem Globetrotters, plus a Trot-
> ters' basketball uniform. Kissinger ap-
> provingly noted that his new uniform
> bore the number 1. Said Henry: "The

numeral accords with my estimate of
myself. My only worry is how I will look
in short pants."

Gold fiendishly planned using both in a morbid and depressing
chapter on Kissinger's humor. Neither reflected the ironic, fatalistic mockery of either the Talmud or the *shtetl*, and Gold greatly
preferred as humor a joke *about* Kissinger circulated by the Danish
news agency Ritzaus:

> Kissinger, it seems, obtained a length of
> top-quality tweed cloth that he wished
> made into a suit. Tailors in Washington
> and New York, after measuring him,
> said there was insufficient material for
> trousers and a jacket that would fit. In
> London, France, and Germany, where
> he went on diplomatic missions, the
> same warning was repeated by the best
> tailors in these countries. Then he came
> to Jerusalem and was told by a Jewish
> tailor to leave the material and return in
> ten days. When Kissinger came back
> after meetings in Egypt, Arabia, Syria,
> and Iran, he was astonished to find not
> only a suit that fit him perfectly but a
> vest, an additional jacket, and two extra
> pairs of trousers all made from that same
> length of material. "How is it possible,"
> asked Henry Kissinger, "that in New
> York, Washington, London, Paris, and
> Germany I was told there was not
> enough material for even a suit, and here
> in Israel you were able to make so
> much?"
>   "Because here in Israel," said the
> Jewish tailor, "you are not such a big
> man."

Gold now was down to his two last pieces of Kissinger data. The
first brought a wry laugh, for the story, though small, had appeared

on the front page of the *Times* and seemed to have been written
with a certain subtle facetiousness:

KISSINGER IS HONORED
BY U.S. JEWISH GROUP

Secretary of State Henry A. Kissinger
paid an emotional farewell to leaders of
the American Jewish community yesterday at a luncheon given by the Conference of Presidents of Major American
Jewish Organizations.

"I have never forgotten that 13 members of my family died in the concentration camps," Mr. Kissinger told the
hushed audience.

From luncheon at the Pierre, he went
to a dinner at the Waldorf, to receive the
Great Decisions Award from the Foreign
Policy Association.

Among the greatest of those Great Decisions, Gold surmised
perniciously, was the decision to leave those Jews at the Pierre for
dinner at the Waldorf. Now he was left with just one clipping that
still remained a vexing enigma after many months, and he pored
over it three, four, five more times with drawn brows:

3 ON HELSINKI PANEL
CURBED BY KISSINGER

Secretary of State Henry A. Kissinger
withdrew permission today from three
Administration officials to accompany a
Congressional fact-finding commission
to check on how the controversial Hel-
sinki agreement is being carried out.

Instead, Mr. Kissinger instructed
them to travel with five members of Congress only as far as Brussels for a briefing by officials of the North Atlantic
Treaty Organization and the Common
Market.

Gold read it a sixth time to no avail. He could not remember why he had saved it. Desolation reigned in his emotions for another minute or two before he pensively turned over the clipping and saw:

DIRECT FROM MANUFACTURER TO YOU!
TOP QUALITY SHEEPSKIN COATS!
UP TO 40% OFF!
VISIT OUR SHOWROOM NOW!
WE WILL NOT BE UNDERSOLD!

Gold smoothed the clipping carefully and preserved it in his wallet. His work for the day concluded, he opened his *Times* and found:

POLICE BLOTTER

The Citibank branch at 1 Park Avenue South, at 32nd Street, was robbed of $1,290 by a man who passed an obscene note to a teller.

In the business section he came upon a second obscene note of financial news that seemed to him not entirely unrelated to the first:

SIMON REPORTED PLANNING
RETURN TO SALOMON BROS.

William E. Simon, the Secretary of the Treasury, is planning to return to Salomon Brothers, the New York investment banking firm he left on January 1, 1973 to join the Nixon government.

William R. Salomon, managing partner of Salomon Brothers, said he hoped Mr. Simon would rejoin the firm. "Because he has been Secretary of the Treasury, Mr. Simon obviously would be more important to us than he was before."

At the time he was tapped by former President Nixon, Mr. Simon was, ac-

cording to published reports, earning $2
to $3 million a year. Mr. Simon has been
the Ford Administration's best articula-
tor of the President's economic philosophy.

_____

REMEMBER THE NEEDIEST!

Gold's ambivalent feelings were easily sedated when his disgust
with the voracious materialism of his society was quickly overcome by the consideration that, when his government service was
concluded, he too might be more important to Salomon Brothers.
As the wheels of the plane touched ground his attention was riv-
eted to a caption of more fortuitous worth than any he might dare
improvise in even his most extravagant fantasies. He read:

MORAVIAN PUTZ

Gold turned aside for an instant and sucked in his cheeks. His
eyes had not, as he first had feared, deluded him. He read more:

MORAVIAN PUTZ
Correction
Several inaccuracies appeared in the
article "Christmas—the Other Bethlehem" (Travel News, Nov. 7). The
correct information follows: The
Christmas-scenes display known as the
Moravian Putz will be put on view Dec.
5 in the Christmas Education Building
behind the old Moravian Chapel on
Church Street in Bethlehem, Pa.

In the air terminal, he bought a stamp and begged an envelope
and dispatched the clipping headlined "Moravian Putz" to Lieberman with the unsigned scrawl: "Does this mean you?" He has-
tened to a taxi with a lively spirit he felt nothing in the world could
dispel, and then he arrived at Andrea's and saw he was mistaken.

SHE was leaving for a weekend away with a man she had been seeing till the time of their secret engagement. Words failed him when she resumed packing after kissing and pinching him perhaps a dozen times and vowing she would love him always for returning to her so quickly. Gold reached deep inside himself for understanding and patience. When away from her field of home economics, he knew, she was often ingenuous in a way strangers might call obtuse.

"Darling, we're going to be married," he explained.

She remembered. "It's the reason I felt I should see him. I want to say goodbye."

"You want to say goodbye?" Gold affected a phlegmatic calm. "What's the matter with the telephone?"

"We were already on the telephone, silly," Andrea replied with a somewhat sprightly titter and gave no evidence she saw Gold wince. "We made the date on the telephone."

"Why couldn't you say goodbye on the telephone?"

"It seemed so cold."

"It has to be warm?"

"It's just for the weekend," she reasoned.

"You told me you'd love it if I came back for the weekend."

"I do!" she exclaimed. "It makes me so happy to know you're here. You mustn't be so small-minded, Brucie."

"Please don't call me Brucie," he reproved her and wondered if she realized she was bruising his most vulnerable feelings. It was

228

not in such fashion that Gold was accustomed to hearing himself addressed by his wife or girl friends, and he accordingly held himself apart from any display of friendly emotion. "Where will you stay?"

"At his house. Or maybe a motel. He used to like motels."

"Is this one of those men who didn't want to see you again?" He watched her nod. "What made him change his mind?"

"He's a great admirer of your work."

Gold's pose of reserve broke. "Oh, shit, Andrea," he moaned, shaking his head in grief and bewilderment. "Are you telling *him* about our sex life too? We've got to keep this relationship secret."

In the dreary silence that ensued Gold remembered the food he had brought with him from New York and went morosely into the kitchen to unpack the two heavy shopping bags. Andrea followed in silence.

"It's only my body I'm giving him, darling," she attempted to placate him after a minute. "After all, what is that?"

Gold felt his eyes glaze. "Only?"

"That's all." Her manner now was hectoring and amused. "What difference should it make to us what he wants with my body? You'll have my mind."

"I've got my own mind." Not for the first time did Gold feel himself estranged from the mores of a generation other than his own.

"You've got a body too." She was relying on gentle good sense to cajole him.

"Not like yours."

"Let him have it if he wants it," she urged. "It's only bones, and flesh, and organs, and places."

"Your body," said Gold, "is one of the things *I* look forward to having."

"But you will, darling, whenever you want. You can have it too, even right now if you make it fast." She glanced at her watch.

"Unshared," Gold emphasized loudly, with a look of uncompromising disapproval. "I want it to belong to just me."

"Oh, Brucie—"

"Don't call me that."

Andrea clung to the arm of her chair and laughed. "I really think you're attaching too much importance to the whole thing. It seems to me you've got the sexual attitudes of a middle-aged man."

There was something in her tone less than the adulation and total acquiescence he had come to expect from her as his due. "I *am* a middle-aged man," he said coldly. "What kind of sexual attitudes would you expect me to have?"

"But it isn't necessary to be so fussy and old-fashioned about it, is it? Why can't he have my body if he wants it? A lot of men want my body."

Gold was bowing in flinching rhythm to each repetition of "body," as though the subject were too painful to discuss. Not for this, he told himself, was he leaving his wife, provoking the enmity of his children, offending his family, and forsaking for the time all other erotic relationships, but for money, beauty, social position, political preference, and a stupendous magnification of sexual prestige, and when he remembered, his damaged feelings were assuaged and his damaged pride repaired, and his paramount objective was one of reasserting his supremacy over her or see it forfeit forever. He began his rebuttal with formality.

"When we first met at the Senator Russell B. Long Foundation," he reminded her, "I was Dr. Gold. When we had coffee or lunch together, or occasionally cocktails and dinner, I was always Dr. Gold. When we made love together the first time not long ago, I was still Dr. Gold. Even when I telephoned you the next day to tell you how happy I was and how much I wanted to see you again, I was Dr. Gold. Now that we're secretly engaged to be married, I'm fussy and silly and ridiculous and old-fashioned. When did I stop being Dr. Gold and become small-minded and narrow-minded? Why didn't you notice it before?"

"It didn't matter before."

"What did matter?"

"That you were Dr. Gold," she said. "And you were always so quick and sinister and articulate. I was so impressed with you. All of us women were. I'm still so impressed that you're Dr. Gold to everyone here. And you aren't even a doctor?"

Gold spoke with mistrust. "What do you mean by that?"

"A real doctor."

"I have my Ph.D."

"Oh, Bruce." She laughed again. "*Everyone* we know has a Ph.D. I have a Ph.D. But you're the only one we know that's called *Doctor*. It's so thrilling to be in love with a doctor who isn't a medical man. I can't tell you how happy I'll be when we're married."

Gold took a calculated risk. "I'm not so sure that we're going to be married," he said, and watched the smile fade from her face.

"You're angry, aren't you?" she replied with uncertainty, and her eyes filled with tears. "I didn't think you'd care. Oh, darling, I don't want to fight with you over this big stupid body of mine. I wish I didn't have it. It's always been so much trouble. If you're going to be so jealous about it, maybe I won't give it away any more after we're married."

"Had you intended to?" asked Gold with curiosity and surprise.

"I took it for granted we would both want to be free." She was ready to capitulate. "If it means so much to you, I'll break the date. Should I?"

Gold drew upon a lifetime of experience to find the words with most telling effect. "I don't want you ever to see him again."

He could not have done better. She smiled in sweetest subservient contentment and pressed his hand to her cheek with a lambent look of love. It was obvious she had never been favored with such chivalry before.

"I'll tell him I'm not going."

Gold, in this first test of power, had reestablished his primacy and was prepared to be lenient. "I was looking forward to spending the whole weekend with you," he admitted tenderly, kissing her hand.

Andrea started violently. "The whole weekend? What will we do for a whole weekend?"

Gold kept his temper under excellent control. "When we're married, Andrea," he told her in the bedside tones a mother might use to a backward daughter, "we'll be together for more than just whole weekends, you know."

"But then we'll have so many things to keep us busy. Houses to rent and furnish, parties and dinners to go to, trips to make. What can we do for a weekend now?''

Again Gold's answer was inspired. ''Couldn't we drive out to your father's estate tomorrow? You can go riding while he and I get acquainted.''

''I'll tell him we're coming.''

"MY daughter tells me," said Pugh Biddle Conover, "that you have the sexual attitudes of a middle-aged man." He spoke from his motorized wheelchair in the spacious wood-paneled library overlooking many of his gardens and many of his gardeners.

This was a comment for which Gold, though drastically self-vigilant, had not made provision. His first trauma of the afternoon had occurred two hours earlier after driving with Andrea through the Virginia hunt country to the splendid, immaculate manor house possessing the breadth, though perhaps not the equivalence in height or depth, of the celebrated palace at Versailles, and deducing from an unavoidable aggregation of visual clues that none in the multitude of elegant and wealthy weekend guests normally in attendance at Conover's had yet arrived. In place of the festive bustle of activity he had anticipated there prevailed a ghostly and quiescent inertia. Scores of uniformed retainers of countless occupational gradations were everywhere in view, but the long driveways and innumerable garages were empty, and Gold could spy no evidence that other people were expected. It was the largest abode in which he ever had stood. Close to seven full acres, Andrea had revealed, as they approached in her yellow Porsche, were under roof in the main house alone.

"I'm sorry she spoke to you about that," Gold was able to mutter at last.

"Lord knows I didn't ask her to," Conover replied with a rich, soft laugh, and Gold gazed with fondness at his spare and dapper host. "Although that's much to your credit, I'm sure." Conover was a blooming, compelling figure of indeterminate age, a man of slight, wiry build in worn corduroy and cavalry twill, with white wavy hair and a small pointed military mustache. A paisley kerchief of deep red was knotted rakishly about his neck, and he projected the opulent assurance and panache of a ruler secure in his reign and his revenues. It occurred to Gold that Pugh Biddle Conover was the healthiest and handsomest moribund valetudinarian upon whom he had ever laid eyes. The bracing, astringent odor of horse liniment clung to him like a virile ambience, and he had the pink, unlined face of someone who has never known vicissitude or expects to. Gold was hungry with admiration. "I confess," said Conover, chuckling, "that I haven't any idea what she meant by that. Do you?"

"I haven't, either," said Gold, "and I'm greatly embarrassed that the subject even has come up. Andrea didn't used to be so outspoken." Gold was gratified by the easy terms on which they were already conversing. "When I first met your daughter several years ago at the Senator Russell B. Long Foundation, she was interested in me even then but she said she was much too shy to show it."

"She was lying," said Conover with robust good humor. "Andrea has never been too shy to ask for anything, even millions. I'm afraid she doesn't always demonstrate good judgment in every area of intelligence and is far too tall, but I don't suppose we can do much about those failings now. I had a deathly fear you might want to talk to me about sex too. Or about marijuana or other drugs you both use."

"There was never much likelihood of that," Gold boasted. "And I don't use drugs."

"My mind is more at rest. It's another trait for which you are to be applauded, Mr. Goldberg. So far it seems you are utterly without fault, doesn't it?"

"Gold, sir."

"Sir?"

"My name is Gold. You called me Goldberg."

"Indeed," said Conover, cogitating. "Learn this, my boy, be-

fore you grow old, that learning is better than silver and gold.
Silver and gold may fritter away, but a good education will never
decay.''

In other company Gold might have delivered a more disputatious
reply than the one he permitted himself. ''I will always keep that
in mind, sir. As you may know, I've invested a great deal of myself
in my own education, and I've written a number of articles and
books on the general subject.'' Conover was silent and Gold
looked at his watch.

''You're ill at ease,'' said Conover after sipping from the glass
of bourbon Gold had poured him from one of the cut-glass de-
canters that stood close by. ''I can tell from your face.''

''Andrea said I must always be frank with you,'' replied Gold,
and was emboldened to continue by Conover's signal of concur-
rence. ''And that you would think less of me if I pretended to take
no notice of your illness or infirmity. May I ask what's wrong?''

''What illness or infirmity?'' Conover inquired with surprise.

''Your disability.''

''I have no disability,'' Conover retorted with testiness. ''What
the devil are you talking about?''

''You use a wheelchair,'' Gold found himself protesting defensively.

''It's easier than walking,'' Conover said. ''You rolled here by
automobile, didn't you?''

''You see a physician.''

''Only when ill, Mr. Goldfarb. I see a mechanic for this infernal
wheelchair much more often. Would you care to whiz around a bit
while we wait for Andrea to return? You have misgivings. Your
expression betrays you.''

''My name is Gold, sir, not Goldfarb.''

''There are gold ships and silver ships but the best ship is friendship.''

''Pardon?'' Gold squealed, leaping upward a few inches as
though snatched from a preoccupation. ''No, no, no, no, sir.'' He
recovered quickly as Conover obligingly made ready to repeat. ''I
was merely expressing astonishment at the wisdom of your
words.''

"Old truths are the best truths, Mr. Finegold. I think you'll always find that so."

"My name, sir, is Gold," Gold corrected a little less tolerantly.

"Fine." Conover nodded weightily and looked up at him with a smile. He resumed after a moment in his quiet mellow voice in which the rounded vowels of the South were euphoniously inter-blended with the distinct consonants of the best English tutors and preparatory schools. "I hope you will not allow an occasional extra syllable from an aging mind to be the cause of any serious misunderstanding between us."

"Certainly not, sir!" Gold assured him with candid fervor and stepped back a pace to feast his eyes again upon his host. More than ever, Pugh Biddle Conover appeared the quintessential gentleman-statesman of his maudlin ideal. Pomposity was absent. A keen and cultivated intelligence presided. He was good as gold.

Conover asked: "Would you like to geld some horses?"

It was a decision Gold had not in his lifetime been forced to make. "Why," he gulped, "would I wish to do that?"

"For the pure thrill," Conover answered exuberantly. "It's sexual, you know. I can place some lively colts at your service if you like. I'll have my niggers whet a sterile blade."

"I think not," said Gold, with faltering confidence, "if I can demur without offending you."

"The choice is yours," said Conover with disappointment, "although I think you're missing a rare chance. Some of them have such big balls. You seem surprised. I can tell by your gasp."

"I think I will have that drink, sir."

"I'll have another spot too, if you'll be so good. Oh, a much larger spot than that, Mr. Goldstaub. You pour so sparingly, Mr. Goldsmith, one might think it were your own. You people don't drink much, do you?"

Gold raised his eyebrows. "We people?" A monstrous notion that had been with Gold nearly every day of his adult life was now bulking in his thoughts. "What do you mean, sir, by *we people?*"

Conover answered amiably with no loss of equanimity, as though blankly unmindful of any uncomplimentary nuance. "I

mean you people who don't drink much. There are people who do,
Goldstein, and people who don't—"

"Gold, sir."

"—and those who don't, don't, do they? I swear on my life I
intended nothing less innocent than that. Your health, you dog,"
toasted Conover with a sudden surge of vitality. "You have questions in mind. I can tell by your twitching."

A knowing light in Conover's small, sharp eyes was adding to
Gold's uneasiness, and he felt the ground shifting beneath him in a
way one sometimes experiences in dreams. He longed again for
Andrea's return. "I was under the impression," he said nervously
with a careless veneer he hoped might be misconstrued for insouciance, "that you always had a great many friends here on weekends."

"They're not my friends," said Conover with charm, "but
they're the best I can do. They come when I want them to and they
stay away when I want to be alone."

"If I'd known you wanted to be alone this weekend," Gold
offered debonairly, "we would not have come."

"If you hadn't come," said Conover, looking squarely at him,
"I would not have wanted to be alone. I'm a great admirer of your
work, Mr. Gold," Conover continued unpredictably in a way that
was keeping Gold off balance, "although I've been much too feeble
to read any. I hear only praise."

"Thank you, sir," said Gold with heartiness and elation, freed
from much of the strain cast upon him intermittently by what he
now perceived to be an endearing instability in the mental state of
his prospective father-in-law. "And I, sir," he ventured, "have
always admired you."

"I said I admired your work," the spruce little man stressed
waspishly, "not you. The truth is I don't like you at all. If you
wish to know, I find you pushy."

"Pushy?" Gold's voice was cracking.

"Yes."

There was little room left for circumlocution. "Are you saying
that," he asked with a sickly feeling, "because I'm Jewish?"

"I'm saying it," said Conover, "because you seem pushy. But

since you raise the point, I don't like Jews and I never have. I hope I am not offending you."

"No, no, not at all," said Gold, feeling miserable. "These things are better brought into the open."

"Especially," said Conover, "when they cannot be concealed. You'll be marrying far above you, you know."

Here was a topic for which Gold had prepared. "Lots of people marry above them," he began articulately, "although that may not be the reason they marry. They often marry for . . ."

"Yes?"

"Love." The word caught like a barb in his palate and emerged through his nostrils with the timbre of a high note from a clarinet.

"Is love your reason?" asked Conover acidly. "Or are you choosing a wife appropriate for the new career in Washington toward which you presently think you are directed?"

"I couldn't love a woman who wasn't appropriate."

"Then love is not exactly blind, is it?"

"It shouldn't be at my age. Should it?"

"I don't really care," Conover conceded with a sigh. "Andrea can take care of herself and always has. Ten or fifteen years ago I would have been too busy with my own pleasures to notice. Thirty years ago I would not have allowed it. Forty or fifty years ago when I had no daughter and still possessed some democratic ideals, I would have championed her marriage to an inferior. Now I'm beyond all prejudice and it's merely a nuisance. A middle-age Jew is better than a nigger, I guess, and not much worse than a wop or a mick. Or somebody bald! Oh, I think that's what I dreaded all my life more than anything else," Conover went on shrilly with a manic volubility that began to take Gold's breath away. "I don't think I'd be able to stand it if Andrea came to me with a husband who was bald. I feel ill. Ill, do you hear? Ill, you idiot!" As Gold, struck dumb with amazement, stared helplessly, Conover allowed himself to be racked with a perfunctory cough and then studied Gold as though expecting to learn something from him. "Oh, God!" he cried in a tone of repugnance and began to beat the side of one fist lightly against his chest. "My medicine. Oh, oh! I must have my medicine. Quick, you gaping fool. You Jew nincompoop—can't you get me my medicine?" Gold cast his eyes about the room frantically in a manner famished for illumination. "Never mind!" Conover screamed at him. "Bring me whiskey, whiskey, in the tumbler—the large one, you miser. Fill it up, up, goddammit—it's my whiskey, not yours. To the top, the top. Ah, that's better. Hey-hey. Ikey-kikey, where's your bikey? I'll survive, I think. You've saved my life, my bravo," he exclaimed with regenerated conviviality, "and I'll drink to your health. Sit on the tack of ambition and you will surely rise. You have something in mind. I can tell by your pallor."

"You aren't being very courteous to me," said Gold with an affected air of urbanity, "as *you* people are supposed to be. After all, I am a guest."

"But not of mine, Goldfine," Conover responded merrily. "And I'm not a host. You're part of a formality here today, and so am I. Andrea will do what she wants no matter what I say. She has money of her own and much more coming and she has no need to fear my displeasure."

"I have money of my own," Gold said.

"I do doubt it compares to ours," said Conover with sarcastic politeness.

"I really don't care much about Andrea's money," argued Gold, "although I'm sure you won't believe that."

"*I* don't care about it at all," said Conover, with a laugh, "since none of it is mine. All of it descends to her from grandparents and great-grandparents, too many to count. There was a time, I'll admit, when I entertained great expectations of inheriting all of hers in the event she predeceased me, but now that I've aged, she might as well live. My sentiments shock you. I can tell by your nausea. But I do love money, Mr. Finestein, more than anything else in the world. I doubt there's a creature walking the earth who loves money more than I do. I don't crave it greedily, because I've always had plenty, but I value money much more than health. I am ailing and I'm old, no matter what lies I tell. Let the Fates propose, 'Take perfect health for many more years, but we'll give you nothing,' I would turn it down in the blinking of an eye. If an angel appeared on my deathbed to beg, 'Forsake your wealth while you still have time and you can live for decades as a pauper and in eternal Paradise afterward,' I would answer, 'Be off, you feathery fool. Spend at least a million on my tomb and each of my cenotaphs.' I'd much rather die in splendor. After all, Mr. Goldfedder, health won't buy money, will it? Philosophizing drains me of energy,'' Conover said and replenished his strength by emptying his glass. ''But I do treasure the company of someone like you with whom I can engage in intellectual discourse as an equal.''

Nothing but the malice in Conover's eye suggested he was intending anything different from a compliment.

''My name, sir, is Gold,'' Gold reminded him once more with an exasperated sigh. ''And I do wish you would remember it.''

''I remember it,'' Conover countered with a smile, smoothing with a pinky his trim mustache, the flush shining higher in his neatly formed cheeks like a thermometer of malevolent satisfaction. ''My mind is as clear as any in the world when I'm not having one of my fits. I won't object to the marriage since it would do no good, and I won't stand in the way of your career, although I can't for the life of me see what business a Jew has in government except to gain social recognition. There've been no good ones, have there? It's hard enough for a Protestant, isn't it, and we have the knack.''

Gold would not be deflected into a dispute on comparative religion. ''It is my belief, sir, that I might make the same kind of contribution in public service that people of my—ah—ethnic denomination have made in other areas.''

''I have four acres of stables, Mr. Goldfinger, with less horseshit than that,'' Conover replied pleasantly. ''You have black and thinning hair too, I see, among your manifold other shortcomings, but I believe it will last as long as you do, if I am any connoisseur of scalp. If Andrea had to marry a foreigner I would have preferred someone like Albert Einstein or Artur Rubinstein or even Arturo Toscanini. God, what glorious heads of hair they had. But not Joe Louis or Ignace Paderewski. You're better, I guess. I don't think I could stand a Pole as a son-in-law. Son-in-law? Oh, what a sickening term, sickening. Don't you understand yet? Sickening!'' Gold poured him more whiskey. The adventure was over, the romance was gone. The bracing odor of liniment rising from Conover was metabolized liquor, the gleam of acuity in his penetrating eyes a flame of gifted lunacy. Gold was confronting another old kook. "Your health, you weasel," Conover shouted with vigor, and swallowed deeply. "May all your troubles be little ones. I always knew Dean Rusk would never amount to anything, or Benito Mussolini. Too bald. Ah, Andrea, my child. You've come just in time. I have trouble making conversation with all of your boyfriends, but this one is practically a stone."

Andrea was radiant and refreshed after her ride and her bath and looked almost blindingly beautiful. She kissed each of them lightly, saying, "I think you're being rude, Daddy."

"I'm feeling poorly, Daughter dear," Conover said in a whine. "I wanted my medicine and he wouldn't give me any, not a single drop. May I have some now? No, let him get it. Faster, faster, you kike filly-fucker. To the top, the top, dammit, I'm paying for it, not you. Ah, that's better, my health is restored. Bless you, my lad. Never circumcise a bus. They're not Jewish. Arabs wash feet. McGeorge Bundy is the warmest human being I ever met."

"Daddy dear, I think you're babbling."

"I may be failing fast. Your health, sir, and to our everlasting friendship. I never met a man I didn't like till you. May your life be as bright as Edison's electric light."

"Finish your whiskey." Andrea held the glass steady for him. "Your mind is still wandering."

"Hip, hip, hooray. Let's call it a day. Daisies are yellow and so is cheese. What is a kiss without a squeeze? You're touched, Mr. Gold. I can tell by your blush."

"I'm mulling it over."

"How wise you are, how wise you be. I see yo_____ _____se for me. For God's sakes, it's been awful for all ____ circle, ____ feed you. Have Simon whip them if th__se dinin___ up his wheelchair, whipped him____ ___sive ebo__ from the room without fu____ ___ separate ___

Gold and Andre___ nated by can____ large eyes w___

different elevations half a mile apart, and Andrea led Gold to his. A *mezuzah* was on the doorpost.

"Please don't fuck me here," she pleaded.

Gold was incensed. "If you ever use words like that with me again," he answered, "I may never want to fuck you anywhere."

It was his only victory of the day. His room was large, the bed was good. He had the consolation of knowing he had suffered the worst. Things might improve on the morrow.

HE AWOKE at daybreak and waited for sounds indicating others were astir. Past nine, he could bear his solitude no longer and crept forth into the morning in a spirit of cautious dejection. He descended the magnificent curving oak staircase with the mournful cast of a sacrificial victim whose moment for the spotlight had come. The house was inundated by a stillness that seemed eternal. Conover had horses that did not whinny. His dogs did not bark. If there were roosters or cows on the baronial grounds, they did not crow or moo. Doors did not close, toilets did not flush, wood did not creak, leaves did not rustle, and footsteps did not fall. At the base of the staircase a portly old Negro with woolly hair stood in the silver-and-black Conover livery and indicated with a slight bow the direction Gold was to follow.

Maids with dusters and porters with chamois cloths were silently cleaning and polishing wood, brass, pewter, glass, and porcelain. Passing in awe and disbelief down the center hallway of the main floor, Gold came at length to an enormous breakfast room containing a buffet of a size he did not know could exist outside the whimsical visions of novelists with extraordinary powers of devotion. Legions of servants, all of them black, in color of skin as vision race, were on duty at fixed posts under the canny supernasty-look inal white spinster who was herself subordinate to a plantation overseer glowering cruelly, even at Gold. The The serving staff was present intact.

he moved along than sixty-five feet long. Only the ge, quail, square ered. His line of march was clear a trance. There were turkey, t with. There were heavy hams. Too much, too much, was the cry of his soul. His fingers trembled and he could hardly look. Mute figures with high cheek-bones waited expectantly to serve him. There were pans of biscuits and baskets of eggs, rashers of bacon and kettles of fish, creamers and crocks and gallipots brimming, compotes and hoppers and casseroles steaming, dry cereals in bushels and hot ones in caul-drons, platters of sausage and trays of beef, kegs of butter and bins of cheese, urns of fresh milk and jugs of hot coffee, and condiments in cruets, flagons, and flasks. On a crested salver of silver em-bossed with the head of a pig was the eyeless head of a cooked pig. There were basins of fruit and bushels of washed fresh vegetables, and smoking tureens of stews of hare and venison. Glowing like a Christmas fire near the end of the table was a firkin or two, perhaps a whole kilderkin, of fresh wild raspberries, each perfect as a ruby. Gold took only coffee, a cannikin of orange juice from a beaker, and a sample of honeydew melon from a trencher with a trowel. Tables had been set with silver and linen for five hundred persons. He was the only guest.

He sat facing the door and prayed for a sight of Andrea. How long could she sleep? Never had he longed for the arrival of a human being so much as he now missed her. The loudest noises in all Christendom seemed to roar in his mouth or flow from his person. His prissy sips of juice and coffee were as hurricanes and wild cataracts in their sound, and his mincing swallows were the thundering explosions of erupting primeval volcanoes. He feared he would make himself deaf. Each contact of cup with saucer was a vibrating crash of cymbals of which he was positive all thirty-eight staring people there to serve him were critical, although they said nothing to him or to each other. The awkwardness he had felt at first was nothing compared to the sensation of their unanimous and unmitigated disapproval which oppressed him now. Whenever he lifted his eyes to glance at anything a somber form materialized at his shoulder as though by witchcraft and poured another ref coffee. Finally Gold addressed the servant nearest him in th est voice he could find above an immoral whisper.

"Miss Conover? Do you know what time she com
breakfast?"

"Miss Conover was here at five, sir. I believe she's gone riding."

"Mr. Conover?"

"Mr. Conover never comes down for breakfast when he has overnight guests. He can't stand them the next day. More coffee, sir?"

Gold had already finished seventeen cups. He left through the French doors opening onto the gardens and aimlessly strolled along the wall of the building. In a minute he came upon Pugh Biddle Conover on a patio, ensconced in his wheelchair like a monarch on a throne. He was dashingly clad in a glove-leather shooting jacket of plover gray and this time the bandana about his neck was of frisky blue. In his hands was a full decanter of whiskey he was examining lovingly in the morning sunlight. His face lit up when his eyes fell on Gold.

"Ah, good morning, dear fellow," he greeted him warmly. "Did you sleep well?"

"Indeed I did," Gold responded with eagerness to the unexpected clubby sociability of his host. "The room was a castle and the bed was superb."

"I'm sorry to hear that," said Conover cheerfully. "Enjoy your breakfast?"

"Immensely."

"Too bad," said Conover, and Gold welled with sorrow again. "You miss my daughter, don't you? I can tell by your tears. She's probably out riding. You don't ride, do you? Your kind usually doesn't."

"My kind?" Gold sucked air deep into his diaphragm and followed Conover inside a small study. "Whom again, sir, do you mean by my kind?"

"Oh, you know, Goldenrod," said Conover with the same chipper good humor that was not in character with the phobic dislike with which he was now regarding Gold and made no serious effort to suppress. "There's a kind of person who rides and a kind of person that doesn't, and those who don't, don't, do they?"

"Jews? Is that who you mean?"

"Jews?" Conover repeated, happily cocking his head. "Italians and Irish Catholics. You keep speaking of Jews as though that's all we have to think about. Is that the only thing you have on your mind?''

"You give the impression it's very much on yours."

"Perhaps it is, this weekend," Conover retaliated with the aim of a marksman and the sleek proficiency of a well-bred asp. Dropping all restraints, he now leaned forward with a gloating leer. "Your grandchildren might ride, if you make or marry enough money. But your children don't, because you haven't. Look at how much the Annenbergs and Guggenheims and Rothschilds have been able to do for their children and how little you can do for yours. How does it feel, Dr. Gold, to know you've already failed your children and probably your grandchildren as well—to realize you've already deprived these innocent descendants of yours of the chance ever to enter good society?''

Gold echoed him with disdain. "Good society?"

"Yes, Shapiro, you know what I mean. I'm in it and you're not. My family is and yours isn't. You have aspirations and regrets and feelings of inferiority and I don't. What are you doing in here with me?" he demanded suddenly with eyes screwed up into an expression of ferocious surprise and annoyance. "We don't have to talk to each other this much, do we? What the devil do you want from me, anyway?''

"I want to marry your daughter," said Gold. "I'm here to ask for her hand in marriage."

"Take it and get out," said Conover. "Go read the Sunday papers or something until Andrea gets back. Do the crossword puzzle."

"I have your blessing?"

"If you leave early."

From the doorway Gold hit back. "I am hopeful, sir, that in the fullness of time, you will come to love me."

"DADDY LIKES you," Andrea said, in her tiny golden sports car, slicing back through the hills to Washington with the speed of sheet lightning, and Gold was bound to the conviction that she was out of her fucking mind. "I can tell. You can't imagine how cold and sarcastic he can be to people he doesn't like."

"I can imagine," said Gold wanly.

"And then they never want to see me again. Please don't be angry." She was visibly upset by his sullen demeanor. "I'll do anything you say."

"Do ninety-five." She braked considerably and the needle of the speedometer came down below a hundred. "He was rude and nasty to me, Andrea. Why wasn't he polite? Why wasn't he deferential? Doesn't he know I'm up for a job in government?"

"He's dying, darling. Isn't that better?"

"No!" Gold exclaimed guiltily, recalling with aversion how inconceivably callous and accepting some of these Christians always had been about their dead. The old Greeks set pyres flaming as soon as they could chop the wood and clean and oil the bodies. The Jews had them in the ground in forty-eight hours. Some of these gentiles remained on such good terms with their deceased that they kept them on display at home for a week, often in back parlors adjacent to kitchens and dining rooms. "For God sakes, Andrea," he added in a more reasoning tone, "what has that got to do with the way he treats me now?"

"It's true, though, isn't it?" Andrea was eager to explain. "Won't it be much easier for us after he's dead?"

"But you're not supposed to say it." Andrea was abject and Gold began to enjoy the generous wrath roiling within him. "Goddammit, why wasn't he quailing? I'm going to be on the President's staff, and he ought to know what that means."

"More work?"

"Less work. Power. Raw power. Brute, illegal power. I'll misuse it to ruin him and make his life miserable. I'll tap his telephones. I'll have the FBI ask insinuating questions about him. I may be a balding little foreigner from New York to him but—"

"He likes your hair."

"Not as much as Arturo Toscanini's, does he? Horsepower. I'll plant microphones and secret agents in his stables and catch him gelding. The IRS will question him over every deduction. I'll unplug his wheelchair and leave him out in the sun to poach. I'll be an unnamed source spilling leaks to the press that your old man's syphilitic. Ha! The eminent Dr. Bruce Gold's new father-in-law is not dying of whatever he's supposed to be dying of. He's got syphilis and syphilis has got him. How will that sit with all his horsey friends back there once they learn he's got the syph? Your fucking father was insulting to me from beginning to end," he went on, smiling faintly in anticipation of the irony to follow, "and I'm going to have my revenge, if he helps me get my job. He didn't treat me with respect, Andrea. He has no respect for me."

"Neither does your own father."

"My father knows me. Yours doesn't. He isn't coming to our wedding."

"He said that too."

"Neither will mine, or my sisters." Gold rested his chin on his fist with a dull laugh. "I think we're going to have a very small wedding, whether we want one or not. If we get married at all."

Andrea's lovely face trembled. "Don't say that, Bruce," she pleaded, improving his spirits vastly. "I'd be so miserable if you didn't want to marry me just because of my father. I never scrape calluses from my feet any more unless I'm alone."

"Watch the road!" Gold shrieked as she put both arms on him in a supplicating hold. "You're doing a hundred and eighty again!" Andrea slowed the car to a hundred and thirty-five, and his heartbeat decelerated in ratio. "Andrea, I have to ask you this and I don't think I know how. But didn't you used to be taller?"

"Taller than what?"

"Than you are now, I guess. Ralph saw you at a party and he seems to feel you're getting shorter."

"Than what?"

"Than you used to be, I imagine."

"I haven't noticed if I am. Maybe I only looked shorter because you're getting larger."

"I wasn't there."

"Would it make much difference if I were?"

"Not to me." Gold's answer flew from him too readily to leave him altogether secure in its accuracy. "Although Ralph seems to be concerned. But if you are getting shorter, don't you think we ought to know about it before the marriage and try to do something? After all," said Gold, feeling rather expansive, "you wouldn't want to get too short, would you?"

"Oh, no. Not too short. I'll look into it if you want me to. I'll measure myself or see a specialist. I'll do anything you want."

"I'm glad we agree on that," said Gold. "You told your father I have the sexual attitudes of a middle-aged man, didn't you? Why do you have to talk to people about our sleeping together?"

"I only say very good things about you."

"That isn't the point, really." He snickered morosely. "You told Miss Plum I was great and your father I have the sexual attitudes of a middle-aged man. I guess that makes me a great man with middle-aged sexual attitudes, doesn't it?"

"I can't help boasting about you," Andrea answered. "Please don't be angry with me. I'll do anything I can to make you happy. I'll be your slave. You can make believe you're my master and tie me up in chairs and beds with ropes and belts and chains."

"Andrea, what are you talking about?" cried Gold with instinctive horror, hoisting himself from the low-slung seat as though his ass were on fire and pivoting on his hip to gape at someone so unlike the girl he supposed her to be that it took a larger stretch of imagination than he could command to recognize her.

Andrea misread the message in his response and continued spiritedly, "Or I can pretend I'm a young Victorian maid from the provinces who's poor and you're my wicked employer in London who can make me do everything perverted you like, with whips and costumes and riding crops. You can bind my buttocks or hands."

Gold gazed at her in utter stupefaction. "Why would I want to do that?"

"To have your will with me. I can eat your foot."

"Don't do me no favors!" Gold objected with frightened vehemence, and repented at once that he had spoken so resolutely. In afterthought, her ideas did not seem altogether that degenerate, and he began to pay attention to the visions conjured up by her words. Andrea as a slave or bound-up Victorian maid was not half bad.

"I was only trying to make you happy," she defended herself. "When I was going with this economist at Georgetown University—"

"I don't want to hear it," Gold interrupted with a bedraggled wave of his hands. "Andrea, why must you tell me things like that?"

"I've always believed in the truth."

"Well, stop, for God sakes," he ordered. "What's so special about truth?"

"Do you love me?" she asked.

"With all my heart," he lied.

"Then let me do something to please you. There must be something you'd like."

Gold concentrated with a pout. "I'd like to eat out for a change," he decided. "I'm getting tired of cooking every night."

Andrea left the car with the doorman of the restaurant.

"Good evening, Miss Conover." The towering captain of waiters spoke directly to Andrea over Gold's head. "Would you like to be seen? Or would you prefer someplace secluded where you can do whatever you want to with each other?"

"Both," said Gold.

They were seated in a booth against the rear wall with phallic sconces illuminating only their brows and eyes. Gold was seized with a clammy terror when Harris Rosenblatt joined them almost immediately and looked from one to the other with piercing inference.

"This is Andrea Conover," said Gold. "She and I were at the Senator Russell B. Long Foundation together and we happened to run into each other here in Washington."

"I believe I know your father well," said Harris Rosenblatt even before Gold had finished. "How is Pugh?"

"Just about the same," answered Andrea.

"I'm sorry to hear that." Harris Rosenblatt's voice came down in register a bit with condolence, but he continued in the same workaday manner, as though all three were about to run out of time, "Were there many people out this weekend?"

"Almost none."

"Promise him I'll try to drive out to see him the next time I'm in Washington. What is it that's wrong with him, anyway?"

"No one can find out."

Gold's confusion and chagrin on discovering Harris Rosenblatt on such knowledgeable terms with Pugh Biddle Conover were beyond description. He had experienced the contradictory sensations of recognizing Harris on sight and requiring several instants to place him. Despite Ralph's disconcerted observations, Gold was unprepared for the physical changes in his former schoolmate that he would have thought biologically incredible. Harris Rosenblatt had grown lean with rectitude and tall and ramrod-straight with probity and that manifest puritanical social self-righteousness that is by no means rare in the financial world. He had grown a high forehead somehow. He had a Norwegian nose. Dark, vertical clefts scored his face from eyebrows to chin and the gaunt muscles of his cheeks held any inclination to smile or laugh imprisoned in a vise of solemnity. His words were to the point and his eyes had the look of a person with a propensity for uncovering people who did not measure up to standards. Before retreating from graduate school under the pressure of impending failure, Harris Rosenblatt had been a rather obese and epicene figure of smaller than average stature with a rotund and fleshy face and a shapeless pelvis and a puffed-out chest. Finance changes a man that way. Humor would be wasted upon him and Gold guessed he'd be even drearier and thicker than before.

"How's Belle?" Rosenblatt boomed at once, affirming the veracity of this analysis.

"Okay," said Gold and dropped the subject like a live coal. "You're looking wonderful, Harris. You've grown so thin and tall. You must be on a fine diet. You've lost much weight, haven't you?"

"Oh, no, I haven't lost weight."

"You haven't been on a diet?"

"No. Not on a diet."

Gold's wonder was increasing. "Have you grown taller?"

"Oh, yes, much taller." Here Rosenblatt somehow let it be known he was pleased. "I've grown a lot since the last time we met. I'm a much bigger person now than I have ever been. I've learned a great deal and I'm much better in many ways."

"What have you learned?" Gold was curious.

"I'm not sure," Harris Rosenblatt replied. "But I used to be a very proud person. I'm not any more. I've learned what it is to be humble, and I'm very proud of that." In the silence that came in the wake of this, he again shifted his glance restively between Andrea and Gold. "Someone told me you and Belle aren't together any more."

"There's not a word of truth in that," said Gold.

"I was very disappointed when I heard that. I believe I got that information about you and Belle from a reliable unnamed source."

"I've been doing a lot of work here as an unnamed source," Gold answered with nervousness and haste, "so it may have come from me. No truth to it at all."

"I'm pleased to hear that about you and Belle. There's much too much of that sort of thing going on now to suit me. It isn't good for the family, it isn't good for the children, and it isn't good for the country. It may be good for the economy but it just doesn't suit me for the short term or the long term and it certainly is not good for the budget. I'm happy to hear that you and Belle will be staying together, and Selma will be happy too."

"What's new in money, Harris?" Gold inquired as soon as he found himself with the chance. "Are we going to revaluate or devaluate and what will that mean to income and purchasing power?"

"I have no idea. We have other people in our firm who deal with matters like that. I specialize in municipal bonds and government budgeting."

"Well, what's going to happen there?"

"I don't know," said Harris Rosenblatt smartly as though delivering an apt recitation, and bestowed upon Gold a look of approval that clearly was to be appreciated as a rarity. "That's a remarkable phrase you coined there, Bruce, remarkable, and I'm sure that everyone in business and government is grateful to you. It boggles the mind how minds like mine used to boggle at mind-boggling questions like that before you gave us those three marvelous little words, *I don't know*. I can see why the President wants you. I hear good things about your report."

Gold veiled his surprise. "It's still in a preliminary stage."

"Good news leaks out. When will it be ready? I look forward to reading it."

Gold decided to have a crack at it. "I don't know."

"Good," came the plaudit from Harris Rosenblatt. "I must go now. I have early appointments tomorrow with the Treasury Department, the Office of Management and Budget, and the Federal Reserve Board. I can tell you what I'll tell them tomorrow and what I told them at the White House yesterday and today. It's the soundest advice I can prescribe for the country and the soundest advice I can give to any individual." Harris Rosenblatt made his pronouncement while rising, and stood as upright and rigid as the column of a temple. "Balance your budget or you will rue the day. If you want to dance you have to pay the piper, and the man who pays the fiddler is the one that calls the tune."

"Harris," said Gold, holding on to the edge of the table as though for dear life, "you really say that to people?"

"In just those words." Pride rang triumphantly in Harris Rosenblatt's voice, and his enunciation too, Gold noted now from the hardened *r*, had taken on the meticulous polish of a tenth-generation Midwesterner. "And they listen wisely. I can confide this much to you. I think every effort will be made to balance the federal budget and I think there's a very good chance we'll succeed."

"What will that mean?"

"What do you mean?" Gold's question evoked in Harris Rosenblatt an expression of stark incomprehension.

"What will it mean to things like prices, taxes, income, and unemployment? What effect will a balanced budget have on the economy and social welfare?"

"I don't know." Harris Rosenblatt was pleased with his response and paused with pride a moment to allow it to sink in. "We have other departments in our firm with knowledge like that. I just specialize in budget balancing. Good evening, Miss Conover. Give my best to Pugh Biddle and tell him I'm looking forward to coming out again soon and hunting the fox, eh? Remind him I'll want that dog he promised me. He said he would give me a good one to shoot. Bruce, now that you're becoming well known, why don't

Selma and I get together again for dinner with you and Belle? We
used to have such good times together with you and Belle. Be sure
to give my love to Belle,'' he clanged as loudly as the old Coney
Island trolley car and trundled away in an aftermath of echoes.

''Who's Belle?''

Gold was already at the starting block. ''My ex-wife,'' he said
and sprinted ahead nimbly. ''We still have some details to talk over
before the divorce becomes final. What did Rosenblatt mean when
he said your father would give him a good dog to shoot?''

''Probably one of Daddy's jokes. You know how funny he can
be. How long will it take to get your divorce?''

''Ralph says it can be done in an hour in Haiti once we reach an
agreement.''

''I wish we were already married and you didn't have to go
back.''

''I wish I had that government job already and I wouldn't have
to go back,'' Gold declared in a voice charged with bitterness. ''I
was hoping your father would offer to do more.'' Andrea looked
hurt and Gold was stricken with self-reproach. ''I wish the two of
us could sneak away from everyone now on a secret honeymoon.
I'd like a vacation with you more than anything but I don't think I
can afford it.''

''We can use my money,'' Andrea promptly offered.

''I won't allow that,'' Gold heard himself state even quicker. His
spontaneous avowal of principle sounded much more final than he
expected it would, and disgruntlement followed hard on its foot-
steps. ''Dammit, why doesn't somebody rich invite us to Acapulco? I'll bet Kissinger didn't pay.''

''You have to be important *before* you get those,'' Andrea explained with a laugh. ''I'm happy you even thought of it. Much of
the time I'm afraid you won't want to see me again, even after
we're married.''

''Why would I marry you,'' asked Gold, ''if I didn't want to see
you again?''

''To help you get the government appointment,'' she answered.
''That's why I want to wait until *after* you have it before we decide.
I don't think we could be happy if you were only the Secretary of

Agriculture or a speechwriter, could we? But I love the thought, if only you could afford it.'' She squeezed his hand in both her own. His hand was in his lap.

''I can raise the money,'' he decided recklessly with a surge of joy, recalling the money owed him by Spotty Weinrock and all the rest he could borrow from Sid. ''We'll sneak off to Acapulco together and tell nobody. It will be dangerous, but what the hell— that will make it more exciting.''

''You're so much fun.''

''I'll start making plans. We'll leave as soon as I get my father back to Florida.''

GOLD HAD trouble sleeping. Andrea would not lose a wink in a cataclysm. With envious petulance he listened to her breathe, deploring the defect in his character that left him destitute of that flatness of viewpoint and narrowness of mind without which it is impossible for any strong ideological belief to flourish. That a dunce like Harris Rosenblatt should find adherents in Washington raised questions about the sanctity and durability of government and American society that no amount of patriotic reasoning could subdue. Andrea sighed in her slumber with a stirring that did not cease until she had backed into contact with him again. They both slept nude. Her tawny flesh, fuzzed with silken, yellow hairs, was gorgeous in the rippling overlaps of muted light and shadows. It dawned upon him then that she could not really know in her deep and tranquil repose it was he who was there beside her. Sadness overcame him and he lost contact with the present. Sid had spurned him. Stinting in conversation with everyone at home, what fraternal comments he had for Gold as a child seemed mainly criticism and belittlement. So much older in years, Sid was like a second father, and both these elders were disgraced by his early need for eyeglasses. No matter how brightly he excelled in elementary school, Ida was always exhorting him to do better, dumbfounding their immigrant mother, who could not believe he was as habitually delinquent as the reprimands signified. Even when his grades were perfect her praise was a rebuke. No, he's very good, Gold could still hear Ida trying to impose her dictum on the hapless, uncomprehending woman, but there's no reason he shouldn't be perfect, instead of like Muriel.

"Hey, kid, you ought to put on some weight or you'll never make a team," Sid would say to him often. For one year Sid had been on the high-school football team as a substitute. Then he gave it up to work in the laundry. "Go out for fencing when you get to high school. You're so skinny they'll never be able to hit you. I bet you could stand under a shower without getting wet."

In music class he was converted into a listener and not permitted to sing. The teacher staggered back with a look of nausea the first time she massed the children for song at the front of the classroom and some sound of unbelievable ugliness landed without pity on her sensitive and unsuspecting ears. She flew into a frenzy of action as though confronted with a dire emergency. By a rapid process of plucking and grouping, she narrowed the source of the offending voice down to eight students, then four, then three. The accusing finger fell at last upon him. "And you, Bruce," she announced with what little breath remained to her, "can be a listener. We need listeners too, don't we, class?" Her bosom heaved with enormous relief.

Thereafter, he would sit and listen two or three hours a week while the others stood and rehearsed for the performance they would give one Friday at the weekly assembly. Once, Miss Lamb, the teacher, after commending the singers at the conclusion of a session, thoughtfully had all of them turn and clap their hands at him for being so faithful and true a listener, and this became a ritual at each of the music classes. Gold was dumb as a log at every music session, and his head felt as heavy. Even fucking Lieberman was a bass.

And then his fucking crackpot of a father, Gold recalled with a surge of nostalgic grief that oozed from his heart to form a lump in his throat, at last was proud of him and bragged outrageously to customers in his tailor shop and to neighbors up and down the street. "In that whole class, there is just one listener," he would announce to Gold's speechless mortification, exhibiting one finger high in the air, "and that listener is my son." With no warning his father would then soar melodically into the five most celebrated notes from *I Pagliacci* and terminate abruptly. "See how good he listens?"

"Me and Fishy Siegel are altos in our class," Spotty Weinrock stopped him once to say, approaching in a limping walk with one foot on the sidewalk curb and the other in the gutter. "What are you?"

A clock tolled three. A child was crying. Scores of memories of that melancholy nature flowed through Gold's mind as he lay in bed with Andrea and forgot she was there, and Bruce Gold, Doctor of Philosophy and Professor of English and related disciplines, Presidential appointee-designate, near the half century of his life, sought refuge at night in the fantasy of his childhood that he was not really Bruce Gold and that his family was not really his family, his background was not his background, and his station in life was not his station, that he was of better heritage than anyone but himself had yet supposed, and had been unfortunately misplaced all his life as the result of some incomprehensible series of errors and misunderstandings that were on the brink of correction. A computer was already deciphering them. Justice would be done. Everything was destined for improvement. Men and women of beautiful and most noble lineaments would appear in sandals and silken robes to claim and redeem him. The land would rejoice. A child had been found. He might even be a prince. The people who attended him with such devotion and bliss were all multimillion-aires.

"You are not Bruce Gold," they assured him soothingly. "These people are not your people and these relatives and friends are not your true relatives and friends. You are Van Cleef and Arpels," they said. "You are a stunning, sparkling jewelry store on Fifth Avenue, and it's all yours. The wealthiest people come from everywhere to shop in you." Gold held fast to his dream, and his trust in the inevitability of this outcome for him had lessened only slightly over the decades of maturity. "Please come in, Mr. Van Cleef and Arpels," they cooed, "and be at home, for it all belongs to you. You are a group of dazzling and distinguished jewelry stores with branches in Beverly Hills, Palm Beach, Paris, and other lovely cities and have secret contacts in Antwerp. People of what little royal blood survives come in homage on soft foot-steps and pay you money. The finest, most beautiful persons in all the world are your subjects and your suitors. You are not a listener any more," they whispered. "You are not," they lullabied, "even a Jew."

Gold moved his lips to reply but no words came. He was asleep.

VII

Invite a Jew to the White House (and You Make Him Your Slave)

BRUCE Gold still could not understand how any Jew of right mind and good character would have put himself in the service of Richard Nixon, and he could think of none who had. Those Jews who did work in that administration were possibly the only educated adult witnesses in creation who failed to recognize in Vice President Spiro Agnew's malignant assaults on the press a mischievous campaign of camouflaged anti-Semitism. Or else they did, and affected not to.

"Invite a Jew to the White House (and You Make Him Your Slave)" was the defiant title Gold gave to the invidious diatribe he wrote in the fit of smoldering pique into which he had been plunged by Lieberman's invitation to the White House in return for supporting American combat activities in the war in Vietnam. In a spurt of creative activity motivated as much by hostile emotion as by principle, Gold had completed a powerful first draft at near-record velocity. Unflinchingly he delved back from the present to President Eisenhower and the Rosenberg trial for his earliest models of that docile subservience endemic to the breeds of craven, watchful opportunists he was inspecting at length with such intrepid vindictiveness and excoriating contempt. Gold was no longer keen to publish his "Invite a Jew to the White House (and You Make Him Your Slave)." If he did, he might never again be invited to the White House.

"Would you be interested in something important in the Department of Agriculture if something should open up there first?"

asked Ralph when Gold dropped by once more to bid him another disappointed goodbye.

"No."

"I hardly blame you." Ralph slipped into his jacket to stroll partway back with him. "Imagine the absurdity of a social order in which the overproduction of food becomes an economic catastrophe. How much easier things would be if we nationalized all our basic resources. And how lucky we are that most of the country doesn't know that."

"You talk," said Gold with eyes narrowing warily, "almost as though you believed in socialism."

"Oh, I do," said Ralph, "with all my heart. And every day I thank my stars that others don't and allow people like you and me to live in such extraordinary privilege. You've been here before, haven't you?"

Gold glanced across the avenue at the meadow inclining upward to the base of the Washington Monument. "On a peace march," he admitted. "But that was very late, Ralph, when a lot of people had turned against the Vietnam war. You were on one too, I believe."

"I was on all," said Ralph, and Gold had the disquieting feeling he was being probed. He did not believe Ralph for a second. "I hated that war, Bruce," Ralph went on without noticeable change in his breezy spirits, "and just about every one of those government officials under Johnson, Nixon, and Ford who conspired to keep us in or raised no public objection to help get us out. What swine! It may be the one thing in the world I feel serious about, that and marriage. The lies, Bruce, oh, the lies. Forget the horror if you will—fifty thousand Americans killed, hundreds of thousands maimed, a million or more Asians—but who can forget those lies? They're guilty, Bruce, of atrocious war crimes, all of them, and I feel they ought to be hanged by the neck until dead. I certainly don't think they should be forgiven too quickly or that any of their names should be forgotten so soon." Gold maintained his silence stolidly, thanking God it was Ralph, rather than himself, who was voicing these stringent sentiments. "I'm not just talking about Jews like Walt Whitman Rostow and Henry A. Kissinger," Ralph resumed after an interim sufficient for Gold to endorse or dispute these views if he were disposed to do either. "I also mean people with names like Ball, Brown, Bundy, Bunker, Clifford, Eagleburger, Haig, Humphrey, Kleindienst, Laird, Lodge, Lord, Martin, McNamara, Mitchell, Moynihan, Richardson, Rockefeller, Rusk, Valenti, Vance, Warnke, Ziegler, and Javits.''

"Javits?'' The word erupted from Gold in an expulsive reflex. "Javits was Jewish, Ralph.''

"Jack?''

"His real name was Jacob.''

"Why wasn't he called Jake?''

"Because that's how some people are.''

"A Republican?'' A momentary smile flickered quizzically over Ralph's amiable, blameless features, forcing Gold to squirm. "I must say that a Jewish Republican has always seemed to me somewhat tainted and droll.'' Gold could hardly dissent. In any such galaxy of the incongruous he would also include Jews on ski slopes, tennis courts, and horseback; and those in polka-dot bow ties had always impressed him offensively as specious and profane, and flamboyantly unconvincing as both Christians and Jews. Heavy drinking, adultery, and divorce were other alien cultural peccadilloes he could list, but he preferred leaving himself out of it. "It's another reason I distrusted Kissinger from the start and always found him something of a clown,'' Ralph continued with a quiet laugh. "You know I'm not anti-Semitic, Bruce. But I must admit I was tickled when I learned that Kissinger had gone down on his knees with Nixon in the Oval Office to pray on the carpet there. Do Jews kneel when they pray, Bruce? I didn't realize that.''

Gold was not positive. "I don't think so.''

"Maybe that's why they wear those prayer rugs around their shoulders in church—'' Ralph pursued the subject unheedingly— "so they can fall to their knees on a moment's notice and pray on a carpet whenever they want to.''

"They're shawls, Ralph, not rugs,'' said Gold with the devout wish they might talk of something else, "they're in temple, not church, and we don't kneel when we pray or use prayer rugs. Arabs do.''

"Then why did Kissinger?''

"Because he's Kissinger, that's why,'' Gold answered with acerbity. "It was probably easier, that's why.''

"I must admit I detested him," said Ralph. "I have to confess I always thought of Kissinger as a greasy, vulgar, petulant, obnoxious, contemptible, self-serving, social-climbing Jewish little shit."

Gold, who'd been nodding along as slavishly as a faithful dog to the syllabic tempo of Ralph's adjectives, now came to a rather sudden stop.

"Ralph," he inquired in a most tentative manner, "are you absolutely sure you're not anti-Semitic?"

"Because I hate Kissinger?" Ralph dismissed the preposterous imputation with a good-humored shake of his head. "Oh, no, Bruce. I wouldn't know how to be anti-Semitic if I tried. By the way, Bruce, one word to the wise—people here might get the idea you're clannish if you keep on defending him so loyally."

"I was not defending him!" shouted Gold with ferocity at the fantastic charge he was partial to the person in the universe he probably liked least. "I was merely wondering," he said with strained composure, "whether you say that because he's Kissinger or because he's Jewish."

"Because he's Kissinger, Bruce," Ralph answered artlessly with an ingrained seriousness that would have convinced the most skeptical of the purity of his thoughts. "How could I possibly be anti-Semitic? I'm indebted to you for so much. I used your research to get through graduate school."

"And got better grades," Gold remembered.

"I used your paper on *Tristram Shandy*."

"And got yours published, without giving me credit."

"I couldn't do that, Bruce, without getting us both expelled. I'm even using your hotel room now every time you come to Washington."

"And having more fun, probably, than I am."

"You'll find a telephone message there from Lieberman asking you to talk to me. And another from Belle reminding you of your father's anniversary party Friday. I thought you left Belle."

"I did," said Gold, with some shifty disturbance of mind. "The problem is that I'm not entirely sure she knows I've gone."

There was no way to overstate the look of awe with which Ralph all at once was gaping at him. "Deep, Bruce, oh, you are deep," he explained in a devoted whisper, tapping his nose excitedly. "My God, if I'd been clever enough for that I might still be playing with all of mine. No, it's better to be free of them before they start getting their backaches and polyps. Please give your father my love, Bruce. And try to convince yourself there's no such thing as anti-Semitism any more. Why, we've even got a Jewish FBI man now. Would you like to meet him?" Gold thought not. "I'm afraid you'll have to, Bruce. He's on your case."

"My case?"

"And handling it brilliantly," said Ralph. "He's the one who uncovered that stunning comment of yours that Harvard and West Point together have afflicted civilization with a greater number of harmful blockheads than all other institutions in the history of the world, combined."

Gold surveyed him with shock. "That was a joke, Ralph," he exclaimed in frightened protest, and then a feeling of dismay swept over him. "Oh, shit, Ralph—has someone from the FBI been investigating me already?"

"He's one of our best men. We call him Bulldog."

"He should know I wasn't serious. Ralph, I made that remark nearly ten years ago at the University of Oklahoma when I was kidding around in a question-and-answer session."

"It happens," said Ralph, "to be true. And one of our most closely guarded secrets. I know you were thinking mainly of officials, but throw in the whole Yale graduate body and you've got it just about right. You must have known you'd need a security check and a thorough physical exam. Under current guidelines you can use any Jewish specialist or get your checkup free at Walter Reed Memorial."

"I'd rather use Murshie Weinrock."

"The FBI will be in touch. And from now on, let us see anything new you write before you publish it."

"For clearance?"

"For ideas. With so many people doing so much pontificating these days, it's become just about impossible for anyone to say anything new that doesn't immediately sound trite and dishonest. That's where your real contribution to the country can be, Bruce. We'll need something good soon on blight."

"Blight?"

"Urban, not elm."

"Are we for it or against it?"

"Neither," said Ralph. "But we have to make some kind of pretense, and the President will want something fresh."

Gold rose spontaneously to the occasion with that aptitude for the expedient that occasionally was mistaken by others for brilliance. "I may have just the thing," he volunteered. "There's this section of my book I'm preparing for Pomoroy and Lieberman on the decline of Coney Island that uses roller coasters, carousels, and fun houses as metaphors for social cycles. I can easily expand it to embrace all the violence and decay of our inner cities. I can make it funny."

"That sounds like just the thing," Ralph rejoiced. "Send us a copy. And next, maybe you can give me a hand with the Washington Monument."

Gold found himself peering sideways at Ralph again. "In what way, Ralph?"

"It's been bothering me, Bruce, ever since I got here." Ralph scratched his head mournfully. "It reminds me of something, and I can't for the life of me remember what—not a phallic symbol, but something else."

"An Egyptian obelisk?"

"Oh, Bruce, what a mind you have, what a mind-boggling mind!" cried Ralph, looking absolutely astonished. "You know all you need to know, don't you? It just boggles my mind how you keep boggling my mind. Incidentally, Bruce, what does boggle mean? I've been looking it up everywhere but can't seem to find it in any dictionary in the world, and no one I ask is sure."

Gold said, "There's no such word."

"Really?" Ralph found this curious. "How are we able to use it if it doesn't exist as a word?"

"Because that," said Gold, "is how people are."

THE INTERVIEW took place an hour later in Gold's hotel room. The Jewish FBI man had hair like wrought iron and a neck and face that seemed to have been grown in a foundry.

"Greenspan's the name, Dr. Gold," he began without loss of time, "Lionel Greenspan. May I be frank?"

"Sure, Frank."

"You're a *shonda* to your race."

"Pardon?" Not in Gold's memory had so ingratiating a pleasantry of his fallen so flat.

"You're a *shonda* to your race," Greenspan repeated. "I say it more in sorrow than in anger."

"What are you talking about?"

"I have to be frank," said Greenspan grimly. "Dr. Gold, is your wife, Belle, a Communist?"

"No, why?"

"Then how come you're fucking all these other women?"

Gold sat down slowly. He was familiar with practical jokes. This was not one. "I like it." For the next few moments only the sound of their tense breathing could be heard. "And there aren't so many."

Greenspan had recourse to a leather-bound memo pad. "There's this gentile girl you're secretly engaged to, there's this married woman in Westchester who sneaks into the city once a month on a shopping trip, there's this Belgian exchange student in Romance languages at Sarah Lawrence who—"

"That was last year!"

"And then we have Felicity Plum."

"Miss Plum?" Greenspan nodded with a critical look which Gold indignantly returned. "I never fucked Miss Plum."

"She says you did. She tells everyone you're great."

"I'm not. Greenspan, it's a lie. I never even touched her."

"You held her against your member twice."

"Once."

"I have it twice."

"You have it wrong. Greenspan, can't you make her stop? A story like that can ruin me."

"We can only try," said Greenspan solicitously. "We have the duty of guarding your reputation as well as your person. But I want to be frank. Professor Gold, there'll be nothing we can do if she decides to write a book and gets a lucrative contract."

"I'll sue the shit out of her," vowed Professor Gold, "that's what I can do."

"You're reaping the whirlwind," Greenspan philosophized, and then charged at Gold alarmingly with his hands lifted. "Mend your ways, I beg you, before it's too late," he broke out in a quavering voice. "Do it for my sake, if not for your own. Oh, Dr. Gold, if I could only tell you how many times my heart was broken, over and over again, by that *momzer* Henry Kissinger. Please don't put me through that again. How sick I was when he raised his voice to Golda Meir. How I wept, wept, Dr. Gold, when I found out he went down on the floor—without even a hat on, I betcha—to pray with that *shaygetz* Nixon." Now Greenspan was brandishing a fist in anguish. "With his own people he don't go to temple, but on his knees he goes down on a carpet to pray with that *vontz*. Dr. Gold, I suffered. I'm not making a joke. I must be frank."

"Am I cleared or ain't I?" Gold interrupted wearily. "Greenspan, stick to the goddamned point."

"I'm not sure. It's why I say you're a *shonda*."

"You're going to disqualify me for fucking girls? I'm not the first, am I?"

"Not just for fucking girls, Dr. Gold," Greenspan justified himself decorously. "You're vulnerable to blackmail in the interests of a foreign power by anyone who knows all the facts."

"Who knows all the facts?"

"The FBI knows all the facts."

"Is the FBI likely to blackmail me in the interests of a foreign power?"

"You pass," Greenspan said with reluctance and snapped his pad closed. "Since you're almost a government official, it's almost our duty to protect your life. Call on me for help if you find yourself in danger."

"How can I reach you?"

"Talk to the wall." Greenspan went for his gun at Gold's blistering look of reproach.

"Say that again?" dared Gold.

"You can talk to the wall. Here, I'll show you." Greenspan came zigzagging back with his large, hard head hanging forward and called, "Testing, one, two, three, four. Do you read me?"

"I read you clearly, Bulldog," came a voice from his stomach.

"I've got a bug in my belly button," explained Greenspan. "It looks just like skin. I'll see you very shortly," he concluded in a way Gold found sinister. "Have a good time at Muriel's and I hope when we meet again it will be on a happier occasion."

"Muriel's? What's at Muriel's?"

"Your father's tenth anniversary party. Leah thinks it's nice that you're having a tenth anniversary party for your father and stepmother, when they've only been married six years, five months, and nineteen days. Leah is my wife now for twenty years, four months, and eleven days, and in all that time—in all that time, I'm not boasting, Dr. Gold, but simply stating a true fact—in all that time I never once lusted for another woman. I remember my own dear departed father." That memory detonated in Greenspan a final shot at bathos, and he came blubbering back toward Gold with a face drenched in revolting piety and goodwill. "If you won't do it for me, at least do it for your sweet old father. Give up sex," he entreated with outstretched, shaking arms, "and go back to your wife. Adultery might be all right for *them*, but not for us."

"Brush up on your Bible, Greenspan," Gold told him. "We found it first. We were even fucking sheep when we couldn't get Canaanites and Philistines."

Greenspan answered coldly, "You're a *shonda* to your race."

"You're a credit to yours."

"Our race, Dr. Gold, is the same."

"Beat it, Bulldog," ordered Gold and began talking to the wall the second he was alone. "Get me Newsome," he burst out angrily. "Tell him it's an emergency." Ralph was on the phone in a minute. "Ralph, that fucking cocksucker Greenspan has been following me everywhere. He knows everything about me."

"Did you pass? What did he say?"

"He wants to be frank. For Christ sakes, you should have given me warning. If I'm going to be subjected to the degradations of public office, I at least want the office. Or you and the President will get shit from me on blight, Ralph, I'm warning you now."

"Please don't quit us," Ralph begged. "Not while the President is having all these terrible problems with inflation, unemployment, disarmament, and Russia."

"I haven't even been hired."

"You've already been promoted."

"To what? Give me a sign, Ralph. Say something public or I might have to start meeting those fucking classes of mine again. I hate teaching. No one knows I'm playing this important role in the Administration. I don't even think Andrea really believes it and she sure as hell won't marry me until she does."

"Would you love a balloon?" asked Ralph.

"I'd adore a lollipop."

"A trial balloon," Ralph explained. "We'll launch one this afternoon and see if it lands in the public eye."

Belle found his name in the newspaper first the following morning and called it to Gold's attention while serving him breakfast. Gold saw no pragmatic need for reaffirming to Belle he'd moved out until he had actually done so; Andrea could not sew or iron and Gold did not have the time. Under "Notes on People," the gossip portion of the *Times* certain to be seen by more of his cultivated associates than any other section of the news, Gold read of unconfirmed rumors from an unnamed source about his imminent appointment to a high Administration post that a government spokesman refused to comment upon and about which a senior White House official professed to have no knowledge he could reveal. "I just don't know," said the senior White House official, when pressed by journalists for details.

OVERNIGHT, GOLD had increased in status prodigiously. Royally he extended his hand for the New York *Daily News* and found:

> Everyone is dressing—or trying to.
> Maggie and Clyde Newhouse have asked
> the ladies invited to their black-tie party
> for Nedda and Josh Logan to wear flow-
> ers in their hair, preferably fresh ones.
> And the Cooper-Hewitt Museum is en-

couraging the male guests at the Regency
Ball to wear whiskers and waistcoats.

Imperiously, Gold drew a line. The Newhouses could go fuck
themselves, and the Cooper-Hewitt Museum could kiss his ass.
Gold wasn't wearing whiskers, and no woman with a flower in her
hair was getting anywhere with him.

"**W**HEN you die," asked Gold's stepmother of Gold's father in a lull toward the end of the dinner party commemorating their sixth-and-a-half wedding anniversary, "where would you like me to put you?"

The aforementioned lull was as nothing compared to the silence that gripped the others now. Even Muriel's vacuous teen-age daughter finally terminated her conceited prattling to wait with dread. At last Julius Gold found the capability to reply.

"What?" he growled incredulously with his eyes straining in their sockets. Every vein in his face seemed swollen to bursting, and Gold was sure it would happen then, apoplexy, right there in Muriel's dining room, instead of a painless demise in Florida, where Sid could close out that whole generation on a single trip with no inconvenience to the others.

"When you die," Gussie Gold repeated to Julius Gold, without lifting her gaze from her knitting, "what do you want me to do with you? Where would you like me to put you?"

It required but an instant longer of calculation for the old man to persuade himself that he could indeed believe his ears. "In the kitchen under the table!" he thundered in reply and, with beetling brow and a gigantic, writhing tremor, twisted away from her in his chair as though from the most frightful misfortune ever conjured up to human sight by some foul destiny.

"Julius, I am being serious," said Gold's stepmother. "How would you like me to dispose of your remains?"

"Never mind my remains, you cockeyed lunatic," the old man roared his reply at her with bared teeth. "And just what makes *you* so sure," he gloated, a note of triumph stealing into his voice, "you're going to live longer than me?"

"I'm younger," she answered securely. "And when I die, I won't have a problem. I have my own burial plot in Richmond, Virginia, and I can always find room, if need be, in the ancestral grounds in the Jewish cemetery in Charleston, South Carolina, although they frequently have moisture there, I'm told—the land is so damp and low, you know—even though all of my relations on the Charleston side of the family have refused to have intercourse with me"—Gold was consoled by some sixth sense that his was not the only countenance that was falling—"since I married your father."

There was an audible halt in all respiration for a moment and then a common resumption of life when she concluded her account with no debauchery more scandalous than the slighting allusion to the low estate in which the old man was held by the Charleston side of her family.

"I got a cemetery plot of my own," Gold's father was already retorting. "I don't need yours."

"I was merely trying to find out, Julius, whether you would rather be laid to rest in your plot or in mine."

"In mine. It's better."

"Have you got room?"

"Sure I got room. I bought for everybody."

Sid bent forward worriedly. "When was that?"

"When I came here and found good work. I bought for the whole family. I bought for Momma and me"—his voice grew faint as his confidence subsided visibly—"and Rosie . . . and you. That was the family."

"That's only four," Ida counted with her flair for the literal. "Mother has one. One from four leaves three."

"It's not enough—we'll have to get more," cried a voice Gold could not place as he sat groaning inwardly with a mental agony no words could describe.

"Don't argue," ordered his father. "I know what I did and I

know what I said. I bought for everyone and that's where you're all going whether there's room or not and that's it. Finished. *Fartig.*"

"I've got a family plot of my own now," apologized Sid.

"Mine wasn't good enough?"

"I've got my own family now, Pa."

"And we want our children to be buried with us," Harriet added with spiteful determination. "And our grandchildren too. Sid, are you sure we have enough? We didn't count on having four children. And we might have to make room for my mother and my sister."

"You can use some of ours. Max has plenty."

"I don't have one. Mendy went with his family."

"Maybe they're holding a place for you," said Milt. "If not, I'd love to have you come with me."

"She's coming into mine," snarled old Karamazov. "All my children are going with me, and all my grandchildren. That's where I want them."

"Well, we want ours with us," said Lady Chatterley. "And our grandchildren too."

"We might not have room, Harriet," said poor Twemlow in an effort to placate both. "And the kids might have plans of their own."

"They're not adding up," said the venerable Chancellor of the Exchequer with the ostentatious vanity of a swain showing off to Esther his perspicacious powers of leadership. "How many have you?"

Cinderella shrugged.

"We have some to spare," said Irv, smiling amenably until tiny Clytemnestra shot him a nasty look with a legible message: She did not want nonprofessional people like Victor or Max lying in peace with *her.* "But we don't. I forgot my brother. Now that he's divorced we might have to let him in."

"His wife got custody?"

"He can come into mine."

"No, he can't, Mr. Dummy," said Muriel, and her daughter sniggered behind her hand at this rude disparagement of her father.

"Your own children come before strangers. And it isn't even ours. The family plot is in your brother's name. Everything's in his name, isn't it, even most of the business?" A dark flood of embarrassment swept over Victor's ruddy face, turning him maroon.

"How many have you got?" Quilp demanded of Gold a second time, and turned into Max.

Gold had none.

"I may need one soon for my mother," politely entreated Sophronia, who'd said scarcely anything else all evening and began to bear an uncanny resemblance to Belle. "I'm sure there's room left with my father, but I've forgotten where we put him."

"We've got to get more!" cried someone shrill.

"It's crazy to buy now."

"Real estate can only go up."

"Now ain't the time."

"We can run it like the opposite of a beef and veal inventory," Victor said, recuperating, and tittered ridiculously. "First one out, first one in."

"It makes more sense to buy," persisted Jarndyce and Jarndyce, and somewhere about here it dawned forcibly upon Gold that there was a nice distinction between "incredible" and "unbelievable" which he'd overlooked all his life. That was "incredible" which merely was unexpected or not most obviously foreseen. "Unbelievable" was something that absolutely, even by the most elastic stretch of faith or the imagination, could not be believed. *This* was *unbelievable!*

In other families relatives quarreled over cash and bibelots; here they bickered over burial plots. Every instinct instructed him he could never introduce a single one, not even Joannie, to Andrea or the glittering new social circles awaiting him in Georgetown, Bethesda, Alexandria, Chevy Chase, McLean, and the Pugh Biddle Conover hunt country of Virginia. They were not coming to his inauguration—that much was sure. He would lie and say he had no tickets. He would noise it about through Ralph that he was a foundling. The children would understand and explain everything. The children would understand and explain nothing, the carping fucks. All they wanted . . . Gold was shaken from his melancholy ruminations when he perceived his father haranguing the room in a violent outburst, strangling with rage and bellowing in indignation simultaneously with each wheezing gasp for air.

"I don't want no more talk about dying and funerals, you hear?" he shouted with finality, pausing to huff with slack lips, and promptly transgressed his own injunction with his inflamed and mottled face aimed mainly at Sid. "You want to know about dying and funerals? I'll tell you about dying and funerals. In my day—" he sputtered to another halt, pointing a trembling finger in blazing frustration while he battled for breath to continue, and found pushed upon him immediately from all sides plates of cakes and cookies and pitchers of coffee and tea, which he batted away with the backs of both hands, emitting wild and sibilant incoherent objections while his arms flapped—"in my day, we didn't push people away from their children and their grandchildren when they began to be old. They died near their homes and their families. Like your mother did. And your mother's mother, she died in my house, and my own mother, in my brother Meyer's house she died when we brought her here. Today you wouldn't even bring me here, would you? She was almost ninety and she couldn't see, and her hands and face shook like Jell-O, but we kept her till the end. With bundles they came and slept on the floor until someplace else they could find, like we did in my brother Meyer's house. You and Rosie should remember, if you want to, and maybe Esther. Your mother's brothers and sisters I took in too, even when I didn't like them. And when they were sick and dying we didn't send them away to condominiums and nursing homes. We stayed together, even when we couldn't stand each other. Some sons I got. Once I could break your back with my belt buckle or a clothes hanger if I wanted to, and I never did. Now I'm sorry I didn't. Now you try to move me here and there like a dumb baby that don't know what you're doing, but I see what you're doing, I still got something up here. I got money of my own and can stay where I want. Only my daughter Joannie in California treats me with love and respect while I'm still alive. Once a month she calls me, without fail. That's when!" His voice rose suddenly with a hard, vindictive laugh. "When I'm *toyt, geshtorben!* Sure, that's when I'll go back to

Florida and you can buy me my condominium, when I'm dead and ready for *d'rerd*, and that's where I want you to put me when I die, in the kitchen under the table!"

The old man's eyes were spilling over with tears when he stopped, and Gold did not think he had ever seen a sicker group of listeners. Gold defended himself against anything like shame or penitence with the lurking suspicion his father himself had not experienced one spark of the feelings he had stirred in the others, and the proof was not long in coming.

"You always said you wanted to retire to Florida," Sid defended himself feebly.

"Now I don't. *Ich fur nisht.*" The old man surveyed them all defiantly with a look of spleen. "I ain't going back till I'm good and ready, which might be never."

"You promised," reminded Harriet. "You gave us your word."

"So what?" answered Gold's father and cocked his head to the side while exploding in a fit of triumphant laughter which ended quite suddenly, and Gold could not imagine a more crafty or disreputable figure anywhere on earth. "Why must I smoke these cheap cigars?" he complained with whining belligerence. "Why can't you buy me a good one for my anniversary if you really like me? And I don't want no more talk about cemetery plots either, no more. That subject is closed."

"My father," began Gold's stepmother with queenly dignity, drawing a very deep breath and pursuing her work with her knitting needles as she spoke, "gave me a rather large and very beautiful cemetery plot as part of my wedding present. That was a nice stitch, wasn't it? Isn't this a beautiful stitch? Look, everybody. Everybody look at my beautiful stitch. There was room for eight of us, and I, in my childish innocence, honestly believed it was enough for a lifetime. Oh, how young and inexperienced I was. I once was a virgin, you know. When my first husband died, my real husband, that is, not *him*, he was buried there, of course, in the place of honor, and I looked forward so to the happiness we would share when I joined him there. Sometimes I could hardly wait. Shortly afterward, my husband's father died, my father-in-law, that is, and simple decency required me to honor my mother-in-law's appeal to put him near his firstborn son when she explained how much it might mean to both, even though they did not get along in life. Well, no sooner was he interred there, it seemed, than she passed away too, and I thought it only suitable that she be placed alongside her husband and my husband. I know I would want that if the situations were reversed. Three of my places were gone in almost the twinkling of an eye, and just as I was catching my breath, dear me, my husband's brother dropped. He was something of a spendthrift and a ne'er-do-well, and since he had neglected to acquire adequate land for himself and his loved ones, and since so much of his family was already there, I thought it a cruelty to turn him away and send him off God knows where to spend the rest of his days with strangers. So I took him in too. Then his wife died, of grief or kidney failure, they say, and next a woman he had been seeing secretly all his life expired of love and loneliness or drink—her physician told us in professional confidence that it is often impossible to tell the difference between the ravages of deep love and cheap whiskey on the vital organs—and had no place else to go. I let her in too, although I'm still not easy in my mind about the propriety of allowing all three to lie in the same bed, so to speak, although it's hardly what we would choose to call a bed of roses, is it? That made six. Well, I can't say how the seventh person got in or find out who he even is, but someone is there—of that there is no doubt—and that leaves room for just one more, Julius, me, which is why I'm trying to find out where you'd like to be. If you do want to come with me rather than with your first wife, I'm sure we can find a lovely spot for you very close by, perhaps even in walking distance, if we begin looking now. I know I would be happy with that, for I'm not sure how comfortable I'll be surrounded by so many in-laws and one person I don't know at all. Please let me know while you still have time to decide. Would one of you sweet children bring me a clean glass of water? I am dry from talking, and I'll need just the tiniest sip if I'm to continue.''

The rush to the doors of the dining room would have demolished a house less sturdily constructed. Gold flew past the kitchen and came to a stop at the bar beside Max, who had to squint to see him. Max, with his diabetic condition, ought not to have been drinking at all. The pouches under the sad man's eyes were tinged with blue and he had the listless and cadaverous demeanor of a man who had given up.

"How are things, Max?" Gold inquired squeamishly.

"Fine, fine, Bruce, very good, good," said Max. "Not so good, I guess. Norma broke up with her fellow in San Francisco and thinks she wants to go back to graduate school to get her degree after she takes another half year off. She was down in Los Angeles a week or month ago and had lunch or dinner with Joannie. I think they had a fight or an argument. She says Joannie was mean to her."

"Joannie wouldn't be mean."

"Maybe Norma was a little touchy, I guess." Max shuffled nervously. "We saw your name in the papers again, Bruce. Rose showed it to everyone in her office. Maybe if the postal rates go up we'll get a really big raise, do you think?" asked this sallow, saturnine, ailing man who had once scored second highest in the state on a Civil Service examination for a job in the Post Office Department and was glorified for one day by a paragraph and picture in the Brooklyn section of the New York *Sunday News*. "Wouldn't you say that was only fair?" He used to give Gold dimes. "It's a nice party, isn't it?"

It was a dismal party—Muriel was a despotic hostess, and she and Ida had been clashing all evening—and Gold sought refuge in one of the many small television dens with which the house was appointed. He was grossly disheartened when Muriel's daughter followed him there with the request that he speak at her high school.

"My teacher isn't sure what you do but she says everyone will be interested in hearing you."

"Please tell her I'm not doing any speaking at this time, Cheray," Gold said tactfully.

The older of the two girls, Simone, had dressed up garishly and departed before dinner to watch television with a girl friend across the street with whom she was dieting.

"Do you like this new purse too, Uncle Bruce?" the younger

asked him now with her thin, somewhat inane, nervous laugh. "Mommy bought it for me also but she doesn't want Daddy to know, so please don't tell him. Or do you like the other one better with these shoes?"

"Why don't you show it to your Aunt Rose and Aunt Esther?" he replied after a lengthy silence. It was painful to Gold to observe how Muriel had influenced her daughters to disparage their father, and he felt compassion for Victor. Like Muriel, both girls were heavily rouged and wore large rings and many thin bracelets on both arms. "They'll know better than me, and I know they'll be pleased."

"They're both so old." The girl made an unpleasant face. "I'd rather sit here with you and learn things. You're young. Mommy doesn't like Aunt Joannie. We haven't seen her for years."

"You should go talk to them anyway, Cheray," Gold chided soberly, "and to Grandpa too. All of them love you very much. And you really shouldn't make fun of your father, especially to other people. He's really a very generous man."

The girl checked him with another gesture of distaste. "He probably doesn't even notice. Do you like this skirt better with these shoes and blouse or the other blue one, Uncle Bruce? Mommy likes us to look nice when we go out with her and her friends." The girl had the jittery habit of masking her mouth with a hand and giggling before disclosing anything she deemed of unusual interest. "I go out a lot with her and Simone on Saturdays now. I even go with them to the racetrack sometimes, but she doesn't want Daddy to know, so please don't tell him. Mommy knows lots of men and women who are much more fun than Daddy, but she doesn't want him to know, so please don't tell him. Where are you going?"

Gold explained he was rejoining the rest of the family and ambled away with a barren smile and the dreary intuition that the day was fast approaching when, at Victor's tearful bidding, he would have to elucidate for Muriel the distinction between a whore and a cunt and illustrate how it was possible to be one without also being the other. And an uncomprehending Victor would beg him to continue reasoning with her to save his marriage, his children, and his home. Muriel, at fifty-two, Gold saw, was copying Joannie at eighteen, and envy, not disapproval, was at bottom of the unrelenting enmity she still bore the wayward youngest sister.

It was a cheerless prospect that met Gold's eyes in the large family room, where Ida and Muriel were disagreeing heatedly over the Academy Awards while his father sat hunched over the tuning knob of the television set like a thwarted ghoul, sounding barbaric mutterings at the giant screen as he scavenged through one channel after another in futile hunt of old movies with dead entertainers he knew familiarly.

"Where you been?"

The gruffness of the question annoyed Gold very much. "I've got a slight headache."

"Where?"

"That's a good one," exulted Gold's stepmother.

Gold cursed the frail figure of the genteel woman vilely without moving his lips. In another corner of the room a more hazardous development was unfolding, and Gold was spellbound when he overheard Esther, Rose, and Harriet remonstrating with Belle to accompany him to Washington each time he went. Then, and perhaps only for an instant, Gold knew what was meant when a mind boggled and could have defined the term for Ralph with exactitude.

"A woman belongs with her husband always," Esther was saying with a throb in her voice.

"If only to keep an eye on him," Harriet stressed insidiously.

Belle was evasive. "I won't like it there. Washington is a high-crime area."

"So is New York."

"I'm used to our high crime. I don't know anybody there."

"Bruce will introduce you to all his friends," said Rose.

Gold felt the moment had arrived to intervene discreetly. "You really shouldn't force her, if she doesn't want to go."

"You see how much he wants me there?" Belle flashed bitterly in one of her rare manifestations of disagreement. The other women sighed in concert and Belle with embarrassment turned her gaze away from one condoling face after another.

"Besides," said Gold with a fake laugh and a burst of ingenuity, "I have to go to Mexico first. Yes. On a secret cultural mission."

"Mexico?" Scales appeared to fall from Sid's eyes, and he sat up with a keen, tense look. "Mexico City?"

"Acapulco."

"Acapulco?" The word issued from Harriet like a primordial snarl. "What's in Acapulco?"

"Acapulco," answered Gold in a baritone of pedantry, "is rapidly becoming the new cultural center for the entire country. My assignment there is officially secret and I can't talk about it."

"In that case, let's talk about something else," said Sid, as though springing in to help, and Gold felt fervently relieved. "Let's talk about geology. *Are* vultures blind or aren't they?"

A blow to the groin could not have brought Gold closer to tears. There was little restraint in his reply. "Sid," he began in a flying start nothing in existence could obstruct, "there are only a few holidays left now and we got six families who want to play host to them, so there ain't enough meals to begin with. There's Christmas and Thanksgiving, the two Passover nights, there's Rosh Hashonah and Purim maybe, and sometimes Easter, sometimes New Year's Day, and here and there a birthday Sunday or anniversary, and that's about all, except for weddings and funerals and the very few Bar Mitzvahs left, thank God. You do this every time, don't you? Now, you do this one more time, Sid, one more time, you fat, vegetating, overfed, lazy, smirking son of a bitch—"

"Victor! Kill him! He's ruining my party!"

"—and this family—"

"Leave him alone!" shrieked Belle.

"—and this family, you imbecilic old prick, may never get together for dinner again, you slimy, sneaky, invidious bastard."

"*I'll* kill him!" decreed his father with patriarchal prerogative, rising too quickly and massaging a hip that buckled. "Two of you run me across to him."

"Muriel, Muriel," pleaded Gold with hands clasped religiously. "I'm sorry to ruin your party, but don't you understand what he's doing? He never liked you either. He's been doing it all my life. He's jealous, that's why. Ida—explain to her," he entreated and annulled the suggestion with a sour face when he recalled that from a diplomatic standpoint, he was selecting the worst of available advocates. "Muriel, it isn't geology and vultures are not blind! Soon he'll be hitting me with three-part statements of misinformation and I'll never be able to catch up." Gold ended with a sob.

"So it isn't geology," said Sid. "I was only trying to change the subject to do a favor for my kid brother."

"And stop babying me, goddammit," Gold exploded and moved in brutally to flay Sid and expose his ignorance to the others once and for all. "Okay, wise guy, we'll see what you know. Morticians!" Gold heard himself exclaim somewhat madly. It was not how he had intended to begin. "Where are they? Why don't we know any? How come we never meet anyone else who knows one? Fish. Do they cook the salmon and tuna before they put it into the can or after? How?"

"It's cooked?" asked his father.

"It's raw?" answered Gold, taking a leaf from his father's book.

"Then you tell us. You're the one we sent to college."

"That's not science," Harriet informed Gold with scorn.

"Sure." Gold's father placidly unwrapped a cigar. "Ask him about hot and cold."

"What's heat?" Gold snapped at Sid.

"The absence of cold."

"What's cold?"

"The absence of heat."

"That makes no sense. One's wrong."

"Which one?"

"It makes sense to me," said Irv. There were nods from the others.

"I like to talk topics," said Gold's father, majestically striking a match.

Gold was undeterred. "Why does a match go out when you blow on it?"

Sid said, "You're blowing away the heated gases that keep the temperature up and the match burning."

"Then why does a log burn brighter when you blow on the embers?"

"The heat is in the embers, kid, not in the gases. You're creating the heated gases when you blow the oxygen on."

"Why does water expand when it freezes, while everything else contracts when it gets colder?"

"It doesn't." Sid grinned.

"It doesn't?"

"It doesn't."

"You damn fool," said Gold with contempt. "You've seen ice cubes in a tray, haven't you? The water gets bigger, doesn't it?"

"It isn't water any more, kid. It's ice."

"Why does the ice get bigger?"

"It doesn't. The tray gets smaller. Metal contracts when it freezes. You should know that."

"Why doesn't the water get smaller when it freezes?" Gold's voice was rising to a shout.

"Because it's ice."

"Why doesn't the ice get smaller?"

"Smaller than what?"

"Than before."

"It wasn't ice before, Bruce. It was water."

"Oh, you're so full of baloney. Why doesn't the human stomach digest itself?"

"It does," said Sid without missing a beat.

"It does?"

"But once it starts it isn't a whole stomach any more and has to stop until it rebuilds in order to start again."

"Why don't you go fuck yourself?" asked Gold. And then instantly invited Sid to lunch on Monday. "I owe you one."

"Make it Wednesday, pal." Sid had Gold by the arm and was leading him from the others to the bar with a grasp not to be resisted. "I've got a meeting with Joannie Monday."

"That's the last time you'll humiliate me in front of your family," Belle finally broke her silence on the drive back to Manhattan.

"Every time I humiliate you," Gold said with detachment, "you tell me it's the last time. How did I humiliate you?"

"With your filthy language. You know I hate it. And why must you fight with Sid all the time?"

"The cocksucker always starts it, Belle, you know that. You're just sore because I might be moving to Washington, aren't you?"

"You can do what you want about Washington. I couldn't quit my job in the middle of the school year anyway."

Gold was still banking on that. "I can fly back every weekend. Lots of Senators and Representatives do that. Okay?"

"If it's okay with you it's okay with me," said Belle. "Like everything else."

"Not like everything else," Gold objected. "You like to think I have everything my way, don't you?"

"Not like everything else," Belle yielded with a shrug. "Have it your way."

"You won't even notice when I'm gone."

"And I won't even notice when you're here."

"If that's the mood you're in," said Gold, "I think I better sleep at my studio. Make up a good story for Dina."

"Why must I do that?"

"So she won't think we're fighting and be insecure."

"Dina says you left me weeks ago but are too lazy to move out and too sneaky to say so, and that you're probably already thinking of seeing a lawyer secretly about a divorce."

Gold slept home and weighed the merits of consulting Sid about his trip to Acapulco with Andrea.

BUT FIRST there was the troubling conversation over drinks with Joannie, who admitted she'd been inhospitable to Rose and Max's daughter in Los Angeles. "She's snorting cocaine and dropping pills and is a living sponge when it comes to other people's money. Norma's over thirty now, for Christ's sake, and thinks she has the rights of a teen-ager. I hate addicts—of any kind. They're always wanting something." And then disclosed, after a distrait and worrisome silence, that she and Jerry were on the verge of separating. "All these years I thought I was doing him a favor—he's such a boring windbag—and now he wants *me* to go. He won't give me enough money to live well and I can't live any other way."

Gold knew he was not much good at comforting people. It dismayed him that Joannie was no longer beautiful. Although she still had the carriage of a tall and graceful woman, her suntanned skin, suddenly, was sandpaper-dry, her lips were thin, her eyes were restless as his own, and the lines in her face were dark and taut.

Gold had another Scotch and Joannie switched to coffee. The friend she would fly to in Palm Beach the following day was an elderly, bedridden man she was fond of who'd been close and very decent to her when she was younger, after she'd run away from home to become a famous beauty queen or movie star. In Key Biscayne was the shoemaker's daughter from Coney Island she'd left with, associated in some way now with a wealthy man with a houseboat on which sybaritic parties of peculiar sorts took place, and Gold began to acknowledge that Joannie might not always have been telling him the whole truth about herself.

"What'd Sid say?"

"Sid promised as much as I need for the best lawyers out there, but I can't really ask him for more than that, can I? What about you?"

"What do you mean?" Gold was taking no risks and looked tremblingly into her face to see what her question might portend.

"How's the book and the job in Washington?" Wryly, she added, "If you get a good one, Jerry might let me stay."

"Both at a standstill," he conceded darkly. Her glamor was perishing before his eyes and he was impregnated with something like disillusionment by the unattractive signs of deterioration in her face and her spirit. "If I get the job, I won't want to write the book. If I don't get the job, I guess I'll have to."

"Do you want to?"

Gold answered with an awkward shake of his shoulders. "I should want to. I could use some stimulating information from someone. God knows I can't come up with any of my own. Did Mom—Momma ever talk to you about sex?" This succeeded in making her laugh. "I mean it. What does a woman from Russia who never even learned English tell her daughters who are growing up here about lust, petting, screwing, morals? What did she say to you?"

"Bruce, I'm younger than you. I hardly remember her. Ask the others."

Now it was Gold who gave a terse laugh. "How could I talk to Rose or Esther about something like that? Or Ida. Muriel's running around a lot as though she's just invented adultery and doesn't seem to care if Victor finds out. I think there'll be trouble."

"Belle sounds depressed," Joannie said neutrally.

"She's worried about her mother," Gold replied without a blush, and skillfully worked his way around that sunken danger. "I can't get over those people, Joannie, Mom and Pop—"

"Toni."

"Can't we stop that shit now?"

She resisted but one more moment and capitulated sadly with a reluctant nod. "Joannie."

"Imagine those old people—"

"They weren't so old."

"—leaving with children from a small town in Russia more than sixty years ago and coming all the way here. How did they do it? They knew they would never go back. I can't go anywhere without hotel reservations and I can't go out of town two days without losing some laundry or luggage or having a plane connection canceled. You travel, don't you? Imagine them."

"Always with credit cards," said Joannie. "And I use Jerry's travel agent."

"I wouldn't move without one," said Gold, somewhat surprised by the ardor of his interest. "But they didn't have any. Who told them? How did they know where to go? Where did they sleep? The trip must have taken longer than Columbus. What did they think and talk about, what did they eat? They were just kids. They had Sid, remember, and Rose was just a baby."

"Ask Pop," urged Joannie.

"Pop," Gold repeated despairingly. "He wouldn't answer me. He couldn't remember if he wanted to and I wouldn't believe him if he did. A native-born American, he was calling himself last week, without even knowing what it means. Soon he'll be claiming he isn't Jewish."

"Not Pop," Joannie stated. "Maybe you and me. But not him."

"I wonder why I never spoke to her more." Curiosity was making him thoughtful and he leaned forward studiously with his head resting in his hand. "I still don't know what she died of, Joannie, and I'm afraid to find out." He felt mawkish but nevertheless went on. "I understand what that means now. I didn't even realize I didn't know until I applied for my first life-insurance policy and they asked. I answered cancer of the thyroid because of that bandage of some kind around her neck, but I've really no idea. The only time I think about it is when I talk to you, and you don't want to find out either."

"Ask Sid," said Joannie. "I bet he remembers a lot."

"Sid," Gold repeated with the grimace of a minute before and stared past her. "Sid won't open up about anything. All he does is make fun of me at dinners. I wish he'd stop. I could kill him."

"He thinks it's funny," said Joannie. "He thinks you enjoy it too."

"Tell him it's not funny and we're both too old for it now."

"Sid's really proud of you, Bruce," Joannie said. "He still kind of takes care of us, doesn't he, even though it kills Harriet now to see him spend anything? He feels very close to us. They all do."

"We don't feel close to them."

"That's the funny part of it," said Joannie with a look of inscrutable melancholy. "They think we're a very close family. They'd be so hurt if they heard us talking this way. Not even you and I feel close to each other any more, do we? Oh, shit, Bruce, what am I going to do? I just know I'm never going to find another husband, and I don't ever want to have to live without one. It's better to have Jerry to fight with than no one, isn't it? I don't want to be another one of those clumsy middle-aged people taking up tennis because I've got nothing else to do." Her eyes narrowed guardedly and she fell silent, swallowing. Gold made no effort to console her. "God," she exclaimed with a cynical amusement when she was able to continue, "I can just see myself. You can add that to my Jewish experience. I just know I'll wind up living with some kid with a motorcycle who plays the banjo and wants to be an actor. Oh, Christ, I'll be smoking dope with nitwits again, won't I?"

Gold, meanwhile, had stealthily withdrawn into the citadel of noninterference he automatically chose whenever threatened by the encroaching personal problems of others. Let Sid handle it, he decided as he parted from his favorite sister with a cursory kiss. A formidable constraint lay between them. Sid could handle them all—Joannie, Muriel and Victor, his father's dying and funeral arrangements. But wouldn't it be awful if Sid died first and all of it landed on him? The ramifications latent in that unthought-of state of affairs were too many to be contemplated by Gold now with anything like equanimity. A thumping vertigo possessed him instead. He leaned a moment against a mailbox to clear his head completely of all traces of that horrendous possibility before continuing along the sidewalk to his studio to check his recording machine for telephone calls.

He felt anything but good about himself and knew it would be in vain to hope for a better nature to assert itself. When Esther was left a widow by Mendy's death two years before, Gold's apathy toward her as an older sister was transmogrified at once into a bristling mood of vigilant suspicion and dislike. He sensed a danger that in one way or another he was going to be stuck. That didn't happen. Remorse took him in its grip shortly afterward when he beheld in Harriet a similar change from the sisterly feeling of more than thirty years to a temperament of miserly reserve that expanded to pervade her relationship with all the members of Sid's family. She too was afraid she was going to be stuck and was taking measures to cut her losses.

Mendy's burial services were the last Gold had attended. Only a small portion of the people filling the Jewish chapel in Brooklyn made the trip out to Long Island for the interment. Gold knew as he stood in the field of carved headstones and allowed his thoughts to roam that even fewer people would come to the cemetery for his funeral. Then he remembered that he had left instructions in his will for cremation without any ceremony or memorial service. Next he remembered that he had also left instructions for the donation of all his organs and tissues for medical use and research. He made a mental note at Mendy's funeral to correct his will. Now he remembered he had forgotten. And he also remembered it would make no difference. Part of the Jewish experience would be to get him into the ground so fucking fast there would be no time to find and read his will.

SID was already at the bar and hailed Gold's arrival with the rosy generosity of mild intoxication. "This is quite a restaurant, kid. I think I've already seen a couple of television actors and a newsman. And what girls."

All Gold saw was Pomoroy and Lieberman leaving. Pomoroy passed in tactful acquiescence when Gold turned away to talk to Sid. But Lieberman veered like a *bulvon* and with his elbows clubbed his way between them to the bar, knocking an ashtray to the floor and blindly plopping a stubby paw smack into the center of a bowl of dried nuts with the atavistic luck of something Neanderthal and hungry.

"I've been getting flak." Lieberman sprayed chewed nuts from his mouth when he spoke and stuffed whole ones in when he stopped. "About that article of yours. I thought it was conventional, safe, intelligent, orthodox neoconservatism. But some people tell me it's nihilistic and negative."

Gold put an open hand on Lieberman's face and firmly pushed him back from the bar. "My brother Sid. This is Maxwell Lieberman. You may remember each other from Coney Island."

"Call me Skip. Are you really saying that nothing anybody does, even us, succeeds as planned?"

"Sure," Sid said good-naturedly while Gold was forming an educated reply.

"Well, I can't see why anyone is making such a fuss about it," said Lieberman. "Is it liberal or conservative?"

"Both," said Sid.

"Sid," said Gold, "why don't you let me talk?"

"Because you never could make up your mind, kid," Sid answered playfully. "Even when he was a child I used to make every decision for him."

"Are you saying," Lieberman demanded of them both in a manner of niggardly disgruntlement, "that every attempt at political and social improvement has been a failure?"

"Nope," said Sid.

"Sid!"

"He didn't say that," continued Sid in satirical high spirits. "He said they didn't succeed."

"Industrialization? The labor movement? Integration? The Constitution? Democracy, communism, fascism? Public education? Free enterprise?" Lieberman was arguing now only with Sid. "Are you saying none of that succeeded?"

"As planned," specified Sid.

"In any way?"

"Ask him." Sid jerked a thumb toward Gold. "He wrote it."

"You read it, didn't you?"

"No," said Sid. "Leave me out of it."

"Well, what about it?" Lieberman demanded in a way that challenged opposition. "Do you really maintain that every action anyone takes to improve anything is doomed to fail?"

"I didn't quite say that."

"He said it wouldn't succeed."

"Sid!"

"What's the difference?"

"A world," said Sid.

"A world?"

"Of difference."

Gold remembered then that he disliked Lieberman and was suddenly delighted by the ease with which his big brother was handling him. In Pomoroy's eyes was that familiar look of careworn pessimism and Gold asked with sympathy, "How you doing?"

"I'm prospering," Pomoroy confessed funereally, as though revealing he was the victim of a malignant tumor of the heart.

"I'm sorry to hear that," Gold commiserated.

"It could be worse, I suppose."

"It could be fatal," said Gold. "You might be president of the company some day and have to stay there the rest of your life."

"Bite your tongue."

"Where else would you rather be?"

"Bite it all the way off."

"I can tell you one thing," Sid announced with authority, paying the bar bill before Gold could get back. "Every action toward social improvement in one direction produces a reaction of equal force in the opposite direction. Right, kid?" Lieberman was frozen in place by this proclamation and appeared, incredibly, at a loss for words. "Let's go eat. So you're going to Acapulco, huh?" were the words with which Sid began at the table after Gold ordered another round of drinks.

"I don't want to talk about that," Gold answered brusquely to close off that line of discussion. "What are we going to do about the old man?"

"I find I get a kind of kick out of him now," Sid said softly.

"I can see that. Harriet doesn't want him around either."

"I don't pay too much attention to what Harriet wants any more," Sid confided gently. "I kind of like him, Bruce, and we're not going to have him much longer."

"How can you like him?" Gold asked. "He's such a pain in the ass. He was mean to you. The two of you were always fighting."

"He was never mean to me," Sid disagreed almost in a whisper. "We didn't fight."

"Sid, the two of you used to fight all the time. Once he drove you away for a whole summer. You ran away from home and went all the way to California."

"That's not why."

"It is, Sid," Gold persisted. "Rose and Esther say so, and so does Ida. Even he likes to brag to people how he drove you away."

"That wasn't really the way it was," said Sid. He avoided looking at Gold. "It was a chance to see the country. He was never mean to me."

"Sid, you ran away," Gold reminded him gently. He wanted to touch his hand. "How old were you?"

"About fourteen or fifteen, maybe sixteen. I know I was still in high school."

"Why don't you ever talk about it?" Gold asked with wonder. "That must have been pretty exciting."

"Yeah, it was, I guess."

"And dangerous."

Sid thought a moment. "No, I don't think it was dangerous."

"You had no money, did you?"

"I had a few dollars. A lot of people were on the road then. I hung around with hoboes for a while and they helped. I worked. A rancher in Arizona offered me a regular job if I wanted to stay. A farmer in California offered me another. I saw Hollywood. But I was glad to be able to make it back when the summer was over. I didn't want to miss school." Sid's eyes were moist and he did not seem to know how close he was to crying. At the same time, his fleshy face was wearing a weird and dull and distant smile, as though his mind were lost in thought.

"You had a fight, Sid," Gold prodded. "That's why you went. And Mom was worried."

"I wrote her twice a week. I sent her postcards. She knew I was okay. Poppa was a very kind and gentle man and was never mean to anyone. He had troubles, you know." Sid's eyes were filling with tears again. His smile broadened and he paused a moment. "There were all us kids and the Depression, and Momma was sick so much, and he was worried a lot and I guess that's why he was so mean."

"You said he wasn't mean."

"He wasn't really mean. Can I have another drink?"

"No, Sid, I don't think so," determined Gold. "You must have all made a lot of sacrifices for me, you and Rose and Esther, didn't you?"

Sid pondered a while and shook his head. "No, kid, it really wasn't that way. We would have had to do pretty much the same thing, even if you weren't there."

"It was a pity you had to miss college," said Gold, trying to catch and hold his gaze. "Didn't you mind that?"

"I wasn't really smart enough for college," answered Sid. "I think that was decided before you were even born."

"But you couldn't have gone even if you wanted to, could you?"

"I wasn't really smart enough."

"You had to give up the football team in high school to go to work in the laundry, didn't you?"

"No, kid, it wasn't really that way. I was only on the freshman team one year. I wasn't big enough for football. I was a lot safer with those horses at the laundry than I was on the football field. Can't we have another drink?"

"Maybe a glass of wine."

"I don't like wine."

Gold ordered wine for himself and another bourbon for Sid. "How old were you when you came here and how much do you remember?"

"About six, Bruce, I think, and I remember a great deal, I guess. I remember—" here Sid interrupted himself to laugh with his eyes half shut, and he choked a moment as though to clear his throat of a rising sob— "I remember one time Pop moved us to the Christian section of Bensonhurst by mistake. He was always making mistakes like that. I think we were just about the only Jewish family there and none of us spoke English."

"Oh, Sid," Gold exclaimed. "It must have been awful."

"It wasn't so bad," Sid answered faintly after considering. "They called me Jewboy most of the time, but they let me play with them, the other kids. They were mainly Irish and Norwegian. Every once in a while they would gang up on me and make me lie down on the ground. They would make me open my fly and show my penis, and they would all spit on it, but if I did what they told me and didn't cry or tell anybody, they would let me play with them again, so I guess maybe it didn't really bother me too much then."

"Oh, Sid, how terrible," cried Gold.

"We only lived there a year," said Sid, "so it didn't happen too many times. I guess Mom and Pop had to put up with a lot worse, there and later, and often from our own kind. A lot of people who got here first didn't want us to come at all. I remember that every year we'd move into a different apartment, everybody did. The new landlord would paint the apartment and give us the first month without rent. I don't know why the old landlords didn't offer the same deal to us every year, because they gave it to whoever came in after us, but they didn't, and at the end of the year we moved again and were back in a Jewish neighborhood and I was going to school. I think I spoke English with a very funny accent, but I was too dumb to realize that until the other boys and girls started imitating me. Even then I didn't understand right away that it was me they were making fun of. I only knew they would start talking funny when they were around me, and then I would try to talk funny like them in the same way, imitating them as they were imitating me."

Gold's pity deepened and he felt moisture fill his own eyes. "Oh, Sid, didn't you feel terrible when you found out? When you understood?"

"No, I don't think so," said Sid. "A lot of us talked funny, it seems to me. I remember I had a tough time figuring out at first how the lunch hour worked at school. Mom would give me a sandwich and an apple in a paper bag, but somehow I got the idea I had to go home for lunch, like at the first school. I didn't know where I was supposed to eat it, and this time we lived too far away. So every day at the recess I would hurry out like I was going home for lunch, and then I would walk a few blocks and hide in some fields nearby and eat my lunch near the subway tracks and watch the subway trains go back and forth from Coney Island to Manhattan."

"Alone? Couldn't you ask your friends? Didn't anyone tell you?"

"I didn't have any friends," Sid said. "I never really had any friends until we finally moved to Coney Island and stayed. And then one day, it must have been snowing or raining pretty hard, I guess, and I couldn't go out, I realized that all the other children had been eating their lunch at the school or in the schoolyard all that time and then playing together in the yard or gymnasium for the rest of the hour."

Gold's heart bled. "Oh, how terrible, Sid. How lonely you must have been."

"I wasn't lonely."

"But you must have been so miserable and embarrassed when you found out."

"I wasn't miserable and embarrassed," Sid said obstinately, and then searched his memory as though weighing the denial that had sprung from his lips. "No, I don't think I was lonely, kid. Everything was kind of new and interesting. I didn't know what was good or bad. I kind of liked it both ways. I liked playing in school and watching the other kids and I liked going into the fields with my sandwich and watching the subway trains. I can tell you a funny thing that happened to me on the boat coming over. It was a crowded boat and pretty dirty and noisy and most of the time I was scared. The first couple of days the waiters brought around oranges with the meals. Well, we had never seen an orange before, I don't think they had them in the villages we'd been in, and I didn't even want to touch it."

"Never seen an orange?" Gold broke in.

"Not in the places we'd lived. Well, one day Mom made me taste a piece and I loved it and wanted more. But the next time we had a meal, the oranges were all gone, and I couldn't get another one."

"All gone?" Gold echoed dolefully. "Oh, Sid, you poor, unlucky kid. You couldn't get another one? You'd never seen an orange before?"

"Where would we see them?" Sid replied. "None of us had. Or a banana or pineapple or anything like that either."

Gold could not quite bring himself to believe him yet. "What's the Jewish word for orange?"

"In Yiddish? *Ahrange*."

"Pineapple?"

"*Pine-epple*."

"Banana?"

"*Benena*. We had no words for them, Bruce. Don't you understand? Those all come from the tropics. Poor Mom had to come all the way to New York to taste a tangerine. She loved them so."

"About Pop—there's another question I want to ask you."

"I know what it is," said Sid, meeting his eyes. "But I wouldn't want you to write about that."

"Pop wanted to be a singer. He decided he was a singer, right?"

"Yeah. Overnight." Nodding heavily as though still drained by the ordeal, Sid went on with an amused sigh. "I think that nearly

killed Mom. It was the only time I ever heard her argue with him.
He wanted to go all over Brooklyn and sing at weddings and amateur nights. Suddenly he was a professional singer. He sang all day
long. For everybody. He began to tell the whole world he was a
famous singer."

"In his tailor shop?"

"In his tailor shop."

"And was he really a draftsman and a junk dealer and an importer and a Wall Street commissions man?"

"Pop did a lot of things," Sid said elusively, rubbing his ear.
"He may have been a draftsman and an importer. I just don't
remember that. But he was bread and dresses and coffee beans and
furs before he fell into that machine shop and the leather business.
Pop was good at leather."

"You had to bail him out, though, didn't you?"

The question added to Sid's uneasiness. "No, kid, it wasn't
really just that way. He was good at leather but lousy at business.
I just sort of helped him organize things."

"Bullshit, Sid. You paid for everything, didn't you?"

"No, kid, I swear it. His business was worth a lot. I just sort of
pulled his assets together and found somebody to buy them, and
then I advised him to put most of the money into an annuity so
he'd always have a decent income and never be dependent on any
of us."

"And the singing?" asked Gold.

"There it was, Bruce." Sid bobbed his head again several times
with a nostalgic air. "All at once. No warning. No working his way
up. Suddenly he was there, Mr. Enrico Caruso. He even walked
around like one, with his head back and his chest out and his hand
on his heart. He wanted to go up on the stage of the movie houses
in Coney Island and sing in the vaudeville acts. And all he knew
from beginning to end was a couple of Yiddish songs. He'd write
away to every radio station and try to get on the amateur hours
and even to the Metropolitan Opera House tryouts. He wanted to
go there in person. Then he tried to get on the air on the Mr.
Anthony show with a problem and hoped he'd be allowed to sing.
He'd make up problems and send them in. It's kind of funny talking

about it now, but it wasn't so funny then. We were afraid. We thought he might really be crazy, and we wouldn't know what to do. We had to hold him back and hide his carfare and tear up his mail. Mom and the girls were frantic. He told all the relatives in New Jersey and Washington Heights and all the people on the block that he was a very famous singer and he gave recitals all day long to anyone who would listen. He wanted to come and sing at my school. You must remember some of this. Maybe it was all that steam from the pressing machine that cooked his brains for a while. I don't know how it passed, but it did, I think maybe the war came along, World War II, and he found himself in that machine shop and forgot all about it. You notice, he never mentions it now. You know, it's nice talking to you this way, Bruce. We haven't had lunch or talked to each other in a long time, have we?''

"That isn't all my fault, Sid,'' said Gold. "You usually don't like to talk much. You must have hated me pretty bad at times, didn't you?''

"Hated you?'' Sid looked up quickly with a sharp intake of breath. His face paled. "Why would I do that? Oh, no, Bruce. I never hated you. I was always very proud of you.''

"You lost me once, didn't you, you bastard?'' Gold recalled for him with a laugh. "How could you lose a little kid like me?''

Sid flushed sheepishly. "I knew you'd be found. I left you near a cop and told you to go up to him. Then I went to the cop and told him you looked lost. You know, you really ought to try to come out and visit Esther more. She's taking things hard, although she doesn't complain.''

"I try,'' Gold said hypocritically. "Sid, you must have resented me a lot back then, didn't you?''

"Oh, no, Bruce,'' Sid said. "Why would I do that? I was always very proud of you.''

"I had such an easy time of it after you had such a hard one. I got those good marks at school and was able to go to college.''

"I'm glad we were able to send you,'' said Sid. "No, I didn't mind that.''

"Didn't you mind having to take care of me?'' Gold asked softly. "I was the youngest boy and the family made such a fuss over me.

Sid, it's okay to say yes. People in a family often dislike each other for much less than that."

"No, I didn't mind." Sid spoke with his face partially averted from Gold's fascinated gaze.

"Aren't you jealous of me now, Sid? Ever? Sometimes?"

"I'm very proud of you."

Gold eased off. "How'd you make it up with Pop when you finally got back from California?"

"I remember that clearly," Sid replied with a kind of wistful pleasure in the recollection, and his eyes grew cloudy again. "I came down the street from the trolley on Railroad Avenue. You remember, they used to have the Norton's Point trolley there. No one was expecting me that day, but Mom was looking out the window watching you and Pop outside and saw me first. Pa was outside the house with you, playing with a new toy he had bought for you, a windup airplane, I think, that really flew. He looked at me. I said hello. I was pretty grimy, I guess. He told me to go upstairs and take a bath, and that was pretty much it."

"No handshake?" asked Gold with a pang. "No kiss? No hug?"

"No hugs or kisses." Sid shook his head. "For years after, Mom would make a joke. 'When you come from California,' she'd say, 'you've got to take a bath.'" Sid chuckled introspectively. "She was so glad to have me back."

But Gold had fastened with astonishment upon a different detail. "He bought me a toy?" he exclaimed. "He was outside playing with me?"

"Oh, sure," Sid said without hesitation. He cleared his throat quietly. "Pop was crazy about you when you were small. We were the ones he was mean to. We were the ones who couldn't stand you."

"Then you did dislike me." Gold pursued the point doggedly. "You just admitted you couldn't stand me."

"Oh, no," said Sid softly. "I never disliked you. I was always very proud of you."

Pity cast a shadow of restraint over Gold, and he ceased trying to untangle the hazy conflicts in Sid's repeated evasions. He felt fifteen years distant from his older brother, and a thousand years wiser. And perhaps, for the moment, equally repressed. There was more to Sid indeed, very much more, but whatever lay secret in him would remain occluded forever beneath the shield of denials Gold would not again make the effort to penetrate.

"Sid, what'd Mom die of?"

"Poor surgery," said Sid with that heartbreaking, incongruous smile that seemed to have no place in a countenance otherwise flooded with the memory of a poignant old remorse. "It had nothing to do with her goiter. She died in Coney Island Hospital. It was a simple gallbladder operation. But the stitches inside opened during the night and she was dead from bleeding in the morning."

"Why can't I remember any of that?" said Gold. "There must have been lots of crying and shrieking in the house when you were sitting *shivah.* We had so many aunts and uncles and so many neighbors."

"You weren't there," Sid told him. "She made us promise before she went in for the operation that if anything went wrong we would send you and Joannie away until everything was over. She didn't want any of the young children around. She thought it would scare you. Mom was like that, you know."

"Was I at the funeral? I can't remember."

"I can't remember."

"Do you ever go to the cemetery?" asked Gold. "To visit her grave? I never thought of doing that."

"Nah, we don't do things like that any more," said Sid with a guilty look flitting across his face. His fingers toyed with his empty whiskey glass. "We used to do it, on Mother's Day, at least, but I can't remember the last time. I couldn't get Harriet to go now, or any of the kids, even if I wanted to. I couldn't even get Pop. I used to try. There's a custom, you know. You're supposed to leave a pebble on the grave when you visit as a sign that somebody's been there and you still remember. Poor Mom hasn't had a pebble on her grave in thirty, thirty-five years. Will you come to dinner at Esther's house this Friday? It means a lot to her when you show up."

"I'll try. Sure, we'll come. Will you try not to pick on me?"

"How?" Sid registered surprise. "I don't pick on you."

Gold smiled tolerantly as though at someone harmlessly incorri-

gible. "Just don't talk science or nature once or make any philo-
sophical statements. Okay?"

"Okay," Sid agreed. "I didn't know that really bothered you.
Sometimes I can't think of anything else to say so I kid around.
Did I embarrass you before with that editor? I'm sorry if I embar-
rassed you."

"Lieberman? He doesn't count."

"I'm sorry if I did."

"You didn't," said Gold. "You were pretty good. The other one
knew you were kidding around and probably enjoyed it."

"I forget sometimes that you're an important person and I
shouldn't act undignified when you're with people you know."

Gold laughed with affection. "It's okay, Sid. And I'm not so
important."

"Yes, you are. We see your name in the paper. You're the most
important person we know. This was nice, kid."

"It was, Sid, and let's repeat it soon," said Gold, feeling absolutely certain they would never have lunch together again.

"Will I see you at Esther's Friday?" Sid asked as they rose. It
seemed important to him.

"If you promise not to tease or pick on me. Do you promise?"

"I won't tease. I promise I won't. I swear."

"Then I'll come."

"THE LILIES," said Sid at Esther's to Gold alone.

"What lilies?"

"Of the field."

"What about them?"

"They toil not, neither do they spin."

"So what?"

"Consider," Sid boomed suddenly out to all the others in the
commanding ululations of an Elijah, after inciting in Gold a sense
of onrushing crisis by the rather brooding manner in which he had
first brought the subject to his ear. "The lilies of the field." Gold's
mind was reeling. "They don't toil and they don't spin. Yet nature,
or God, sees to it that they have enough to eat and grow every
year, and every year they bloom."

"Sid, you promised, you swore to me," cried Gold. Not until

then, he felt, had he ever truly known human nature could sink so far.

"It's just a thought," Sid whined deceitfully with the apologetic meekness of someone defenseless who had just been set upon unfairly.

"A very nice thought," rejoiced Gold's father. "From my favorite son."

"And the Bible too," Gold muttered viciously. "And it's wrong."

"How can it be wrong if it's from the Bible?"

"Sid's wrong, not the Bible."

"And he don't even believe in God," Gold's father retaliated by addressing the others with a snort of ridicule. "Hey, dummy, if there's no God, Mr. Smart Guy Politician, how can there be a Bible?"

"You should listen to your father more," counseled Gold's stepmother. "And maybe you can be his favorite son too."

"How can I listen," said Gold, "when all he does is call me names? He doesn't like me. He never liked me."

"I don't like you either," she informed him with courtesy. "You admire money and you idolize the people who have it. You crave success. Wouldn't it be funny," she went on, and cackled at him with a gleam of satanic wickedness in her eye, "if he isn't even your real father and you've been taking all this criticism from him for nothing all these years? Wouldn't it be funny if you aren't even Jewish? You don't even know the language and the holidays, do you?"

Gold chose a strategy of silence.

"Pyrenees," said Sid when it seemed no one else would speak, "is the only known language in the world that has no words for right or left."

After an instant of indignation, Gold discovered himself responding to the asinine statement with his intellect and smiled with the tired awareness that he probably would never again find it within himself to be angry with Sid for anything. It could be Sid was right. It could also be Sid was full of shit. Gold was as conscious as the next fellow of the mountainous area in the border regions joining

France with Spain; but possibly there were isolated villages with inhabitants to whom what Sid had just said did apply. There could be people far away in the Pacific or in the Indian Ocean called Pyrenees, or Pirenese—Gold could not be sure even of the spelling—just as there were people and languages elsewhere called Portuguese and Japanese. Let someone else pick up the gauntlet, he decided, reflecting peevishly that people thought more respectfully of him in Washington than they did of him here, where he was at the very nadir of repute.

"How do they know which way to go?" asked Esther after an interval allowing for these discursive speculations.

"They know," said Gold's father.

"How do they give directions?" asked Ida.

"They give," said Gold dryly in an effort to make himself agreeable, and his father looked at him with greatest surprise and a tint of admiration, as though scarcely expecting such percipience from so unsatisfactory a source.

"They must be very smart," said Ida.

"Very smart," said Milt.

"Then how come they don't have words for right or left if they're so smart," Muriel belittled Ida, a cigarette jutting from her mouth.

"Because," Ida instructed her shrewishly, "they're so smart they don't need them. And there's a lesson to be learned by all of us from the Pyrenees."

"And from the lilies of the field," said Gold.

"And from my first husband," said Gold's stepmother, knitting a few and purling a couple more, "who always loved a good joke too. I'm a Southerner, you know, with connections in Richmond and Charleston, and ours has always been one of the most respected Jewish families in the South—respected, that is, by other Jewish families. In marrying your father, I married very far below my station, and he married very much above his." Pride glowed like a furnace in Julius Gold's face as he nodded in Olympian accord. "We owned slaves and very large plantations. It's the reason we know so much about wool."

"Cotton," said Gold before he could help himself, and came

close to banging his head with the heel of his hand for his impetu-
ous stupidity.

"Wool, my child," Gussie Gold took him up at once with a
majestic turn of her eye downward. "It was because of the money
we made from our cotton that we could afford so much wool. Even
as a little girl I was able to do my own flocking."

"Flocking?" said Gold.

"I bet she flocked good too," said Gold's father, "better than
you."

Flocking? repeated Gold to himself, and gave way ignominiously
before his father's challenge. Flocking was a subject of which he
had sparse knowledge and ground upon which he was not zealous
to contend with people who had more.

"I can remember," said Gold's stepmother, "my husband's favorite joke. 'If you ever forget you're a Jew,' he would say, 'a
gentile will remind you.' And he would say this over and over
again to all of us until the day he died. It's a joke that you, my pet,
would do well to remember."

"With a stepmother like you," Gold told her with a set smile,
"I won't need a gentile to remind me."

"It's the reason you're having so much trouble with your book,"
she said, bending close with this new verbal thrust.

"Who's having trouble?"

"You'll never be able to write it without me, you know," she
said in ghastly exultation. "How can you write about the Jewish
experience when you're not even sure you've ever had one?
You're not even sure you're really Jewish, are you? Wait till that
gets out. You never even bothered to check, did you?"

"Check where?" Gold demanded. "What are you talking
about?"

"The adoption agency," said his stepmother with a hideous
laugh. "They have to put that down and tell you now. I read it in
the papers."

"What adoption agency? I'm not adopted."

"How do *you* know?" gloated his stepmother, and Gold did not
dare look at her pale face and burning eyes. "You never even went
there to check, did you? You can do that now, you know. You can

get a lawyer and find out. You're not even sure who your real parents are. Maybe I'm your real mother and he's your stepfather. You don't know much about that at all, do you?''

Gold rose from his seat on the sofa beside her with his brain in a whirl and stepped a safe distance away. ''Pop, what's she talking about? I'm not adopted, am I?''

''Get out of here with such foolish questions,'' his father replied without patience. ''If we were going to adopt somebody, why would we pick you?''

''You're not even sure that your mother was your real mother, are you?'' his stepmother harried him tirelessly with fiendish glee. ''How do you know she isn't a fake? You're wasting your money. Every time you go out to the cemetery to visit her grave—''

''I don't go to no cemetery,'' Gold shouted in her face, hoping to stanch her garrulous flow, but the woman only laughed the more.

''—it isn't even her grave. You're preserving the wrong landscaping and putting your flowers on the grave of a stranger.''

''*Gevalt!*'' cried Julius Gold, once more the man of unpredictable wrath. ''Again the cemeteries? This is worse than my anniversary. I don't want no talk about cemeteries and I don't want no one forgetting my anniversary party next year.''

''Your tenth,'' Gold said savagely.

''And I won't have any more anniversaries,'' Esther said and began to cry again. Gold nearly groaned with exasperation.

Rose led Esther into the bathroom and Milt rose slowly to his feet like the man of methodical habits he was and asked:

''Can I get anything for anyone?''

Esther was composed on her return and began telling of Mendy's death with but a hint of the perpetual flutter of excitement that had become as natural a trait of her appearance as her pure white hair and brimming eyes. It was an affecting story but Gold did not want to hear it repeated. He was thinking hard about his mother's grave with a feeling of odium spreading through his system at the knowledge he had never been there. Reason told him it was only a stone he would find.

''He was so healthy and busy and could still work as hard as any of the men at the warehouse or on the trucks," Esther was relating about the short, rambunctious, excitable man with the sloping forehead and massive inferiority complex whose presence only Max and Rose had been able to tolerate without aching stress. "He really did love you, Bruce," Esther went out of her way to maintain with a noticeable absence of vim. "It's just that he always felt uncomfortable because you went to college and he thought you were so smart."

"I don't think he's so smart," cracked Muriel in her tough and abrasive voice, and blew a polluting cloud of cigarette smoke into the room. "If he's so smart, how come he teaches college? I bet even Victor makes more than he does."

Such was the riposte that sprang first to Gold's mind that Victor would have pounded him to death had he made it.

Mendy Moscowitz had been an opinionated, uninformed man who drank beer with his meals and still played handball aggressively at Brighton Beach when the weather was mild. He woke from an afterdinner nap one evening feeling lousy and went back to bed for the night. In the morning he was listless. All day at work he didn't feel right. A week later he was in the hospital with leukemia. He read his medical charts and made certain clamorously that everything prescribed was given him on time. He had books brought and pried free enough information to learn he was fated to die.

"Let it happen," he decided in tears one day. "I don't want to fight."

Esther's hair turned white. He wanted no comforts or treatments not covered by medical insurance.

"I want to leave money," said Mendy. "Let it happen at home. If you don't want me in the house I'll rent a furnished room."

It happened at home. He left the hospital in the first remission and refused to go back with the reappearance of the symptoms of debilitation. When the day came that he was too faint to stand, he stood. Esther phoned Sid. Gold cut classes in Brooklyn. Only Esther held Mendy's arm as the four descended in the elevator. He had dressed in a suit and tie and his overcoat was buttoned to the collar. There was not one word more of conversation. They rode to the hospital in Sid's Cadillac. Mendy would have been proud to know he lasted there only a day and a half. Sid and Esther cried in the car.

"It was such a sunny day," Esther remembered now. "Everything looked so beautiful out."

"Can I get anything for anyone?" asked Milt.

ONCE again Gold found himself preparing to lunch with someone—Spotty Weinrock—and the thought arose that he was spending an awful lot of time in this book eating and talking. There was not much else to be done with him. I *was* putting him into bed a lot with Andrea and keeping his wife and children conveniently in the background. For Acapulco, I contemplated fabricating a hectic mixup which would include a sensual Mexican television actress and a daring attempt to escape in the nude through a stuck second-story bedroom window, while a jealous lover crazed on American drugs was beating down the door with his fists and Belle or packs of barking wild dogs were waiting below. Certainly he would soon meet a schoolteacher with four children with whom he would fall madly in love, and I would shortly hold out to him the tantalizing promise of becoming the country's first Jewish Secretary of State, a promise I did not intend to keep. He would see Andrea's father, Pugh Biddle Conover, one more time before his tale was concluded, and Harris Rosenblatt twice.

His phone call to Spotty Weinrock for all or part of the money owed him had been received with more warmth than he expected. "All you want," Weinrock repeated in his showroom, gazing fully at Gold with a look of amusement and his chuckling undertone of detested indulgence and familiarity. "What do I owe you, fifteen hundred?"

"Eleven hundred."

"Make it two thousand," said Spotty Weinrock generously. "I like to work with round numbers. How do you like the place?"

The curving walls of the showroom guided visitors naturally into a reception area of spare elegance affording a view through glass of an orange room with four modern hand looms at which attractive female designers sat weaving the new patterns of wool his factory in Rhode Island would manufacture. Gold was impressed.

"How's business? Good?"

"Great," answered Weinrock. "If I had a better cash flow I could probably pull out now with over a million bucks clear."

"What does that mean?" asked Gold, who had no head for business.

"I'm in terrible trouble," said Weinrock. "I've got short-term obligations I have to meet, and I never in my whole life knew what an obligation was. I may have to take in more partners or sell out cheap. I could use a thousand for some new winter clothes, but none of that concerns you. I can pay you back all the money you want. What income-tax bracket are you in?"

"What's it your business?" There awoke in Gold at that mysterious question the first ugly writhings of suspicion that he was destined for disappointment.

"I have to know how much to put you down for in the company books." Weinrock's amiable spirits were unaffected. "We can make it as much as you want if you can use more dough."

"What are you talking about?"

"I'm turning myself into a bad debt," said Weinrock, "just for you. And doing a lot of my old friends a favor at the same time. Claim me. For as much as you want. I'm going into bankruptcy. A thousand? Ten thousand? A million? Ten million? Say the word. I'll be as generous as you want."

"Spotty, what are you talking about?"

"You still asking that? I'll explain at lunch, but only if you let me pay. There's a dairy restaurant around the corner that's sometimes pretty good. Let me start," he said to the stocky old waitress who gave them menus, "with a glass of sour milk."

"We got no sour milk," the waitress said. "Everything here is fresh."

"Get me Lupewitz."

"It's not his station."

"Yankel," Weinrock called loudly to a lean, limp-looking waiter resting against the wall on the other side of the room with a rather sepulchral expression. "She won't give me sour milk. It ain't on the menu."

"Sure, the menu," said Yankel Lupewitz with the defeated air of a discontented philosopher of the Schopenhauer school. "I told them the menu, but that's how they are. I'll bring your milk."

"And let me have," shouted Spotty Weinrock, "a glass of strained borscht, the big fruit salad and cottage cheese with a prune, but only if it's fresh Oregon." The waiter shook his head. "Then tell them to put a fresh fig on top instead. And bring me black bread with lots of end pieces. I'm going bankrupt and turning you into a creditor," he explained in a normal voice to Gold. "If you're in the thirty percent bracket I can put you down for a five thousand loss and you'd break about even. If you want to make it more, we'll make it more. You want a million, we'll make it a million. But our figures ought to agree for your tax deduction."

Gold chewed gravely on his herring. "It sounds spotty, Spotty."

"It is."

"How does it work?"

"I'll give you some back-dated promissory notes. Fill them in for whatever you want. When the government auditors ask you why you loaned me the million in cash instead of by check, tell them your wife doesn't like me and you didn't want her to know you were helping me out. If they ask you where you got the cash, tell them you always like to store some in a mattress or safe-deposit box in case the banks fail again."

"A million dollars?"

"It's your money."

"Where did I get it?"

"Be evasive. It doesn't have to be that much. I've done this before. It's one of the ways I maintain my good credit in the industry. By going bankrupt regularly."

"And what happens if they don't believe me?"

"You go to jail."

"I go to jail."

"That's the downside risk," Weinrock answered with a sanguine smile, lavishly buttering an end slice of pumpernickel. "The upside gain is what you get back from the government next April from your income-tax return."

"Next April?" Gold cried with a convulsive lurch. "Spotty, I need that money now for a trip to Mexico."

"I could use some money for a trip to Mexico myself," Weinrock said. "I could also use new winter clothes. Will you let me have another thousand for a good coat and suit?"

"Spotty, are you really going bankrupt?"

"I have to," said Weinrock, grinning again in a way that left Gold chafing at the thought he was being laughed at irreverently by someone of lower station, "if I'm going to pay you back that eleven hundred dollars."

Gold took umbrage at the insinuation and retorted, "Am I your only creditor?"

"You're the only one who's pressing me."

"Pressing you?" Gold exclaimed indignantly. "You fuck—I phone you once in three years. You call that pressing you?"

"You never phone to buy goods, do you?" joked Spotty.

"Weinrock," droned the lugubrious waiter. "Please tell the gentleman we don't allow such language here."

"He don't know, Yankel," Weinrock lamented. "He's going to work in Washington as a bigshot and he thinks it's modern. The fig was good, Yankel. But the bread . . ." Weinrock shook his head accusingly with a tragic frown.

"Sure, the bread," promptly apologized Yankel Lupewitz guiltily. "I told them the bread, but that's how they are."

"Spotty, I'm not going to put you into bankruptcy," Gold relented. "I can get it from Sid. If you ain't got, you ain't got."

"I can get nothing from Mursh," said Spotty. "These fucking doctors all turn into conservatives."

"I have to see him soon for an examination," said Gold.

"Tell him to send cash," said Spotty Weinrock airily. "All I've got left is my clothes, my business, my car, my apartment, my beach house, and my girl friends. After that, I'm just about bankrupt."

Gold said, "You don't look like a bankrupt."

"I can't afford to," said Spotty. "If things were good I could look like you."

Gold's eyes opened wider. "What's that supposed to mean?"

"Seedy and thin. Like a bum. A guy with a pushcart. Old jacket, old turtleneck, old pants that don't match. That may be good enough for your classroom but it ain't good enough for the garment district. No bankrupt could afford to dress that way. You shouldn't have worn those rags into the garment center or into a good dairy restaurant."

"I'm sorry," said Gold coldly, "if I embarrass you."

"What then?" answered Weinrock. "Before you shame me in front of my salesmen, here you shame me in front of my creditors. I will have to make apologies for you."

"You filthy prick," said Gold quietly, losing all patience. "I changed my mind. Give me my fucking money and let me get the hell out of here. I don't even want to finish eating with you."

"Sit, sit," said Weinrock with tranquility, his face wreathing in jocund crinkles, and Gold guessed just then that the healthy tan on his face was the product of the sun lamp at the gym. "I want to treat you to lunch if you'll lay out the money and lend me another five hundred for a good fur-lined raincoat."

"I'll lend you shit."

It was clear Weinrock was going to reproach him. "Filthy prick? Shit? Is that how they taught you to speak at Oxford on your Rhodes Scholarship? You never learned no language like that in Coney Island."

"I never had no Rhodes Scholarship either," Gold mimicked him in a friendlier manner. "I was in Cambridge, and only for a summer. They weren't giving Rhodes Scholarships away to many Jews then. And I wasn't an athlete."

"Like that other one, on the Supreme Court? What's the name of that prick on the Supreme Court?"

"Rehnquist?"

"The other one."

"Burger?"

"Whizzer."

"Whizzer?"

"White." Weinrock's large, soft, slumping body shook with lazy laughter. "Imagine growing up with a nickname like Whizzer and liking it. A judge yet they make of a *naar* named Whizzer."

"Not like Spot."

"What's wrong with Spot?" asked Weinrock with honest ingenuousness.

"It's spotty, Spot." Gold was reveling in the momentary turnabout in advantage.

"I earned it, didn't I? I took out spots in your father's tailor shop for a whole week. Then he fired me."

"You were too slow," Gold taunted. "He still says you're no good."

"My mother says about you," said Weinrock, "that you can take a cow around the world—and you'll still have a cow. Tell me, who whizzes? Show me one man in the world who ever whizzed. If I was ever big enough to be a football player and someone called me Whizzer, I would put my fist through his brain. So now you want the money again, huh?"

"Oh, forget the money—it ain't worth the trouble collecting it from you." Gold glowered darkly for several seconds. "I guess I'll have to write my book. Give me some help and I'll pay for the lunch. I'm doing a book, a serious one." Gold did his best to ignore Weinrock's wondering smile and obnoxious chortling. "In a way it's a big chance for me. It can be a killer if I grind it out right, an abstract autobiography."

"What's that?"

"I don't know yet. But I will by the time I finish. It will be about how much fun it was to grow up in Coney Island."

"Fun?" Weinrock planted upon Gold an expression in which it would have been impossible to choose whether derision or disbelief was the ruling sentiment. "For you? Four-Eyes?"

Gold winced slightly at the derogatory reminder. "That's one of my problems. I didn't do much. I'm supposed to write about the Jewish experience and I'm not sure I ever had one. I have to make up a lot. That's why I need you and some of the other guys, to give me information. Where were you going all those times when you wouldn't let me come along?"

"Sometimes noplace."

"Noplace? Then why wouldn't you let me come?"

"We didn't want you."

Gold swallowed this piece of information like a bitter pill. "That's the kind of thing I need to know, I guess. All I've got is my own memory and experience to work with and it ain't enough. I may be able to knock the whole country on its ass with a big best seller if I get the right kind of help. What was it like for other people in the neighborhood? Like you and Fishy Siegel and Sheiky from Neptune Avenue. You still see Fishy. I don't remember their father or mother. What did his father do?"

"He rode a bike."

"Rode a bike?"

"Sure. With a white beard and a funny hat with buttons and with holes cut out. Like Sharkey's father. Just as crazy."

"Cheez!" Gold was quivering with serendipitous excitement. "See? I forgot all about Sharkey and his father."

Spotty laughed. "Don't you remember the time Sharkey's father disappeared on his bike? The whole neighborhood was looking for him. They had the police. Somebody told him New Jersey was just over the bridge, so he took off on his bike to see his brother in Metuchen there. He made it across the Manhattan Bridge and then started back into Brooklyn on the Williamsburg Bridge and thought he was heading for New Jersey. Halfway across he ran out of steam and went to sleep there with a Jewish newspaper over his face to keep off the sun. When the police called, Sharkey had to get him with Sheiky in the car Beansie had bought from Smokey the Fighter and Scarface Louie without knowing it was stolen, and neither one of them even had a driver's license when they ran out of gas right in front of the station house."

The genial reminiscence was just the spark needed to precipitate in Gold an explosion of loyal and merry attachment to the past such as he had not experienced in years. "Spotty, you bastard, I need you," he burst out. "I forgot all about those older guys. Listen, the next time you go back to Brooklyn to see Fishy or any of the other guys, I want you to bring me. It will be great getting together again."

"Great?" Again Spotty Weinrock scrutinized him closely. "It

was never so great for you before. We do a lot of drinking now. In an Italian bar."

"I do a lot of drinking now too," said Gold.

"Lend me five hundred for some clothes for a little while," said Spotty Weinrock, "or I may not have the time."

"Will you pay this back? I may need it in two weeks."

"The minute you want," vowed Weinrock. "I'll go into bankruptcy this very afternoon if you say the word."

"Oh, never mind that," said Gold. "Now tell me. What was I like as a kid? What did you all really think of me and why?"

"Bruce." Weinrock stopped as he was about to fold Gold's check into his wallet. "You wouldn't stop payment on this if you didn't like my answer, would you?"

Gold was insulted. "Of course not. I don't want flattery. I want information I can use. Tell me truthfully. What was it like growing up with me?"

"Well, to tell you the truth, Bruce," said Spotty Weinrock with his manner of lazy and presumptuous mirth, "we didn't really look at it that way."

"When we were kids together," persisted Gold, feeling he was not getting his general idea across, "when we were growing up in Coney Island, did you and the other guys resent it because I was so much smarter than the rest of you?"

"Frankly," came the congenial reply with an unhesitant chuckle underscoring the words like the accompaniment of a basso ostinato, "we didn't think of you as smarter."

"You didn't?" Gold could scarcely believe he had heard him correctly.

"We thought you were a *schmuck*."

The buoyancy in Gold took a sudden drop. "And now?"

"Now?" said Weinrock with a long vowel. "Ho, ho, now? Now, of course, we're all very proud of you every time we read your name in the paper. But we still think you're a *schmuck*."

"Really?" Gold proceeded with strong resentment. "Well, would you like to know what we used to say about you?"

"I don't even know who you mean by 'we,' " was Weinrock's nonchalant reply. "Who is this 'we' you're talking about?"

"Me and the fellows," said Gold. "The gang."

"Bruce," said Spotty Weinrock. "*I* was the fellows. *I* was the gang. You weren't."

"I wasn't popular?"

"You know that."

"Not even a little?" Gold's voice was husky.

"Not at all. You were an outsider, don't you remember? That's probably why you got so smart in school. You couldn't play ball and you had no personality."

"I didn't?"

"None at all," said Spotty Weinrock. "You did a lot of boasting and sometimes you'd go out of your way to make yourself a pain in the ass."

Very soon, said Gold to himself with a *tristesse* presaging a *cafard*, I will be the most renowned figure ever to come out of Coney Island. I am already a somebody and soon I will be somebody more. And I wasn't popular as a child and had no personality. "Was I as bad," he asked meekly, "as Lieberman?"

Here Weinrock was reassuring. "Lieberman was the worst. Lieberman was a real *zshlub*. I'll bet not even Henry Kissinger was as bad as Lieberman. Hey—" Weinrock paused a moment and turned red with laughter—"imagine how long a Yid like Kissinger would have lasted with the gang at the poolroom on Mermaid Avenue."

"Kissinger," Gold was constrained by fairness to mention, "made a lot of money."

"Not," said Weinrock, "by impressing Jews. He's lucky he found all those gentiles to help him." Gold, with his kleptomania for ideas, was already inscribing a mental note: Kraemer, Elliott, Rockefeller, Nixon, Ford—not a one of these sponsors and patrons of Kissinger was Jewish. "You even," Weinrock continued, "wore glasses."

"Glasses? Everyone wears glasses. Look at you."

"But *then?*" Weinrock sternly shook his head.

"I couldn't see."

"What kind of excuse is that?"

"I couldn't see the blackboard in the classroom and I couldn't see a ball coming at me without eyeglasses when you let me play."

"You couldn't catch it when you did."

"Sometimes I caught it."

"I bet," laughed Spotty Weinrock, "that if your family had dough, they would even have put braces on your teeth. You even started losing hair before everyone else. All the rest of us are still thick and wavy and curly. Gosh, Brucie, you really were a fucking misfit, weren't you? It's a lucky thing you're getting famous. Otherwise, you wouldn't have a thing going for you."

"You're doing very, very much to cheer me up now," said Gold. "Listen, I want to meet you the next time you go into Coney Island to see Fishy Siegel or anyone else."

"You can meet us Wednesday after dinner."

"I was going back to Washington Wednesday. I've got a meeting with a very important Presidential aide and a date with a very beautiful tall girl."

"That's up to you."

GOLD CHOSE Coney Island and squeezed his way politely through a jammed, dark Italian bar on Mermaid Avenue to Spotty Weinrock, Fishy Siegel, and Fishy's son, Eugene, a clear-eyed, curious boy of twenty-four with an engaging, constant smile. Fishy was surprised to see him.

"Didn't you tell him I was coming?"

"I forgot," said Spotty Weinrock.

Fishy Siegel's response to Gold was that same challenging look of insolent reserve that had been the infuriating bane of school-teachers and other supervising adults since the day he walked. Emulating a mannerism of his older brother Sheiky, who'd set him up profitably in a number of illegally interlocking suburban automobile dealerships, he sank both hands into the pockets of his trousers rather than extend one in greeting. Clearly the evening was not going to be remarkable for nostalgia.

"Sid says hello to your brother Sheiky," Gold lied with aplomb to bring about a thaw. "How'd Sheiky ever learn to make all that money, anyway?"

"My name is Wheeler, not Squealer."

Eugene blushed richly. "My mother goes nuts when he does that home."

"I'm not prying," retreated Gold. "I was just wondering how a guy who never finished high school learns about things like mergers, reinsurance, accelerated depreciation, subordinated debentures, and all that other shit."

"Your name is Goose, not Bruce," said Fishy Siegel. "You must be crazy if you think I'm going to tell anything to some scumbag who's going to work for the government."

"Scumbag?" echoed Gold, feeling disemboweled.

"Scumbag," repeated Fishy Siegel with a confidence that dared inquiry. "Can you think of a better word? My name is Tucker, not Sucker."

"Oh, shit," said Gold in a long sigh of fatigue. "I'm getting sick and tired of people who are always running down the government."

"I'm not," chirped Spotty Weinrock.

"Me neither," said Fishy Siegel. "Hey, Eugene, you getting tired? What's it like in Washington, Goldy? I'll buy a round. But no bullshit."

"My name is Meyer, not Liar," said Gold, and waited for the fresh drinks to arrive. These were not people with whom he could be circumspect. "Frankly, I don't know, Fishy. I'm having trouble figuring it out. They say things in Washington that I don't hear anywhere else. They say something funny and nobody laughs. I say something serious and they think I'm joking. I say something funny and they think I'm serious. They don't find anything strange."

"They know they're crooked?"

"They don't know that's strange."

"Neither do the muggers and rapists we got running all over now," said Fishy Siegel vengefully. A few of the Italians close by were muttering affirmatively. A woman in another corner of the room was inveighing against looters and burglars. It seemed to Gold that he and the boy Eugene were the only ones not smoking. "Don't shut me up, Eugene. We got muggers and rapists and murderers running around now like we never had before and they're going to keep running around whether I talk about it or not. Hey, Goldy, do you think I feel like a crook when I juggle my books?

Why should they? Did you think we were criminals when we used to steal school supplies and had to work in the storeroom? Remember the time the box of penpoints fell out from underneath your sweater right in front of Mrs. Prosan? What a *klutz* you were.'' Fishy finally smiled.

''What are penpoints?'' asked Eugene.

''Those are those small metal things that used to go into the bottoms of those wooden pens we'd chew on. You'd dip them into inkwells on your desk when you wanted to write.''

''What are inkwells?''

''Things sure have changed if Eugene doesn't even know what an inkwell is,'' said Spotty Weinrock.

''Don't go by him,'' said Fishy of his son Eugene with insult and boundless love present in the same breath. ''He's dumb. He got married when he was twenty-two.''

''You didn't want me to live with her, either,'' said Eugene. ''You wouldn't give us the money for a house until we got married.''

''I had warts one year,'' Gold remembered. ''All over my fingers, about seventeen of them. I started putting ink on them every day in school and they went away.''

''It's changed,'' said Spotty Weinrock. ''All those stores boarded up closed. Where do the people shop?''

''Sure, it's changed,'' Fishy Siegel grumbled with the impertinent surliness of someone middle-aged who was not used to giving an inch. ''When we were kids the Italians used to try to beat us up. Now we have to hide in an Italian bar when we come here if we want to feel safe. When the Italians move away we'll have nothing. Raymie Rubin's mother was one of the old people killed last year.''

''We had this one Christian kid on our block,'' said Gold, ''and his father used to get us free admission passes to Steeplechase, and then we'd go up to old people and ask for the rides on their tickets they were too scared to go on themselves.''

''Jimmy Heinlein,'' Fishy Siegel recalled. ''His family had chickens. He had a joke. First it was Coney Island, he told me, now it's Cohen's Island, next it will be Coon's Island. He could have thrown in the spics too, they're getting just as bad, but we

didn't know about them then. I told him I'd bust his head open if
he ever told that joke to anyone again, and I must have scared him
pretty good because he never did.''

''He told it to me,'' said Gold.

''Maybe I didn't scare him.''

''What's Steeplechase?'' asked Eugene.

''It was a big famous amusement park around the Parachute
Jump, Eugene,'' answered Spotty Weinrock. ''Steeplechase, the
Funny Place. We had another famous one that was even better,
Luna Park. It had the Shoot the Chutes and the Mile Sky Chaser,
maybe the highest roller coaster in the world. You know something, Fishy. I could have picked up that Parachute Jump in guaranteed working condition for just a few thousand dollars. I think
maybe I could have bought all of Steeplechase for just a little bit
more.''

''Why didn't you?''

''I forgot.''

''You know something about Steeplechase?'' asked Gold in a
tone of significant meditation.

''It wasn't such a funny place.''

''Luna Park was better.''

''The depths of the Great Depression,'' Gold announced with
profundity, and knew already, with a collector's instinct for everything usable, that he would include the proposition in his book
whether it proved viable or not. ''That was the best time of our
lives, wasn't it?''

''Not for me,'' said Spotty Weinrock in sprightly rebuttal. ''The
older I get the more fun I seem to have.''

''Me too,'' said Fishy Siegel. ''Kids don't know how to enjoy
themselves.''

''I'm enjoying myself,'' said Eugene.

''What do you know?'' answered his father. ''You're just a kid.
Why'd you get married, you dope? Nobody gets married any
more.''

''Pop, that was two years ago.'' Eugene smiled.

''What will you do with the baby when you get your divorce?''

''We got no baby. Who's getting a divorce?''

"Everybody, you dumb kid, that's what I'm trying to tell you. Everybody gets divorced now. You hold on to that baby for us, you hear? Or I'll throw you out of the business and won't give you a fucking penny. Let her have the house and car and all the other shit she wants, but you keep that baby for us."

"Hey, guys." Smokey the Fighter, near sixty now, pushed through the people behind and poked in a face with a grizzled stubble of beard, the tip of his nose missing from a historic knife fight in his teens with local gangsters. He couldn't place Gold. "I know I'm getting old now," he related to the others in his deep, gravelly voice. His eyes twinkled and his cheeks were shining. "I feel like nineteen until I look in the mirror, and then I'm surprised. Last summer I was peddling ice cream on the beach and this Italian kid in his twenties tells me to keep out of his territory if I know what's good for me. I couldn't believe it. 'Hey, kid, take care of yourself,' I tried to warn him. 'You know who you're talking to?' I'm still pretty quick with my fists. We moved under the boardwalk and had a fight and he beat the shit out of me—so easily." Smokey put his head back and basked in the memory. "I didn't see a single punch coming. Then I knew I was getting old. And I'm the guy who used to beat up all the other peddlers."

"Not my brother Sheiky," Fishy Siegel contradicted him tersely. "You couldn't beat him up."

"I could beat him up if I caught him," said Smokey. "He was always running."

"But you never caught him, did you?"

"All you guys are doing pretty good, ain't you?"

Fishy wouldn't buy him a drink, so Gold did. Smokey still couldn't place him. Weinrock gave him a cigar.

A pasty, small, sharp-featured man a few places down said, "They're even dumping those welfare families into Sea Gate now, in those big houses there. I guess there are just too many of them and they don't know what to do about it."

"I know what to do," growled a hugely obese man on the seat next to Gold in a harsh, deep voice that seemed to emanate from his stomach and move to his lips without vibrating a single vocal cord. Hip flesh overflowed the bar stool on both sides. "Concentration camps. I mean for *them*," he explained with dainty politeness and a delicate change of tone to Gold and his group.

The bartender reached forward. "Be a good boy, Ant'ony, and don't make trouble."

"Ant'ony, you prick," said the large man's thin friend, "they're white. That's what I'm trying to tell you. They got lots of little kids in those welfare families too, and they don't know what's happening to them."

"Let's get out of here," Fishy Siegel decided abruptly with an air still starkly devoid of friendship or civility, and Gold was impressed by the consistency and sustaining power of that unsociable personality: never in his life had Fishy Siegel evinced human feeling for anyone outside his family. "I want to go home."

"Can I pay?" said Gold quickly. "If you don't mind."

"My name is Mort, not Sport."

Gold was halted a moment by the bleak, charged darkness when he stepped outside alone. The smell of old fires was thick as fog. He had nearly half a block to catch up with the others at the cars. Four springy, dark-skinned bloods in sneakers were coming his way, and he knew in a paralyzing flash of intuition that it was ending for him right then and there, with a knife puncture in the heart. He visualized the newspaper clipping someone else might be interested enough to collect:

PERSONABLE
PRESIDENTIAL APPOINTEE
DIES OF KNIFE WOUND
TO THE HEART
ON CONDESCENDING VISIT
BACK TO
NEIGHBORHOOD OF BIRTH

Society Fiancee Grieves
Further Details Inside

Help the Neediest!

They passed without bothering him, deciding to let him live. His time had not yet come. Where was progress? he wondered. When he was young, there were lots of poor people and the rich were his enemy. The rich were still there and now the poor were his enemy too.

Gold had noted earlier all the boarded-up, ruined shops on the three major lateral avenues of Coney Island and wondered where all the people went now to buy food, have their suits and dresses mended and dry cleaned, their shoes and radios fixed, and their medical prescriptions filled. In his rented car, he drove alone one more time the desolate length of Mermaid Avenue to the high chain-link fence of the private residential area of Sea Gate, where owners of the larger houses were now accepting welfare families, turned left toward the beach and boardwalk, and made his way back slowly along Surf Avenue. He did not see a drugstore. Behind the guarded barriers of Sea Gate, which once grandly sported a yacht club and was restricted to well-off Christians, younger Jewish families now congregated for safety and sent their children to whatever private schools they could. Elderly men and women, as always, probably still crept forth from secret places each morning and prowled the streets and boardwalk for patches of warming sunshine, conversing in Yiddish, and Raymie Rubin's mother had been killed one day on her return. Gold did not pass a single Jewish delicatessen. There was no longer a movie house operating in Coney Island: drugs, violence, and vandalism had closed both garish, overtowering theaters years before. The brick apartment house in which he had spent his whole childhood and nearly all his adolescence had been razed; on the site stood something newer and uglier that did not seem a nourishing improvement for the Puerto Rican families there now.

Gold remembered the summer the city widened the beach and trucks loaded with sand rolled past the house on Surf Avenue all day long from early spring on. In summer on scalding days his mother cautioned each child in her fused vocabulary: "It *brent* a fire in street." Each fall she had a fervent admonition she repeated: They must always go to temple on Yom Kippur no matter where they were in later life; otherwise, people would think they were a "Comminist." She would sit at the window exchanging nods with women at windows across the street and watch for dirigibles, and she told of a time not far back when whole families ran down into the street for sight of an airplane in the sky. She could sing the start of two of the first songs she had learned in America, "Don't Go in the Park After Dark" and "I Didn't Raise My Boy to Be a Soldier." Both were timelier now. The frail, mothering woman with the bandage around her neck never learned to read or understand much English, but she could identify arias from *Carmen*, *Tosca*, *Faust*, *Aida*, and *Madame Butterfly* on the big old Atwater-Kent radio in the living room—bought for her by Sid, Gold remembered now, with money he'd saved secretly from his afternoon work in the laundry and his weekend work Saturday nights and Sunday afternoons at the catering halls. Now how the fuck was she able to learn that?

With the first fragrant, balmy days of March or April, the peddlers would come with their trucks of fruits and vegetables and continue hawking their freshest, ripest produce all through summer. Long Island potatoes were twenty-five pounds for a quarter. The peddlers, all brawny, browned Italians, many with Gypsy sweatbands tied to brows and neck, would fill the air with a special din of raucous shouts among which one of singular mockery always predominated in the echoing aftermath:

> If you've got money, come out and buy.
> Got no money, stay home and cry.

Gold had been hearing that same peddler's cry daily ever since from financial firms, manufacturers, and governments.

> If you've got money, come out and buy.
> Got no money, stay home and cry.

His mind was a ferment of heresies as he turned from the Island and headed home, heresies he knew would not find the light of expression in print or speech from him, and his brain was pumping with fragments of ideas he thought he might use for a lively article on blight or rubbish. Nationalize Rockefellers and extirpate all Houses of Morgan. Rubbish. Rubbish was accumulating along byways throughout the country, and all but demented eccentrics dropped litter anywhere with utmost peace of mind. The Half

Moon Hotel in Coney Island was a skyscraping nursing home now, and enterprising teen-agers were murdering old people casually in the normal course of their youthful depredations. Gold had the clippings to prove it. The nation had nothing better to do with its forsaken aged or unenraptured young. Gold knew something no one else did, but was not going to reveal it: he knew there was no longer anything legal to be done under the American system of government to discourage crime, decrease poverty, improve the economy, or nullify the influences of neglect, and when he got to Washington he would not even try. Why should he be the exception? And he knew something else as a social evolutionist that he might stress someday in his ''Every Change Is for the Worse'' should he ever find time to write it: Gold knew that the most advanced and penultimate stage of a civilization was attained when chaos masqueraded as order, and he knew we were already there.

Office buildings rose as spectacles where there was no lack of office space, and organizations with Brobdingnagian names were sprouting like unmanageable vines and spreading like mold with sinecures and conferments for people of limited mentality and unconvincing motive. Gold knew several by heart from pieces he had clipped:

> Irving Kristol is Resident Scholar at the American Enterprise Institute for Public Policy Research.

> Sidney Hook, professor emeritus of philosophy at New York University, is a Senior Research Fellow at the Hoover Institution of War, Revolution, and Peace.

> Colleagues report that Senator-elect S. I. Hayakawa, the former head of San Francisco State College, has been sleeping through seminars cosponsored by the Harvard Institute of Politics and Library of Congress Research Division.

> Former Secretary of State Henry A. Kissinger has agreed to be consultant at the

University of Southern California's new
Center for the Study of the American
Experience. His salary was not dis-
closed.

Every good place has always been deteriorating, and everything
bad was getting worse. Neighborhoods, parks, beaches, streets,
schools were falling deeper into ruin and whole cities sinking into
rot. They were putting Coney Island welfare families into Sea Gate
now. There were just too many people. Italians, Jews, Blacks,
Puerto Ricans—it was not unlike the great Caucasian migrations,
except there was no place left to go. Assimilation was impossible,
upward mobility a fantasy. Multitudes witnessed the avalanching
decline. Gold's spirits were improving tremendously as this vocabulary of degeneration and decay coursed through his head. It was
the Shoot the Chutes into darkness and dissolution, the plunging
roller coaster into disintegration and squalor. Someone should do
something. Nobody could. No society worth its salt would watch
itself perishing without some serious attempt to avert its own de-
struction. Therefore, Gold concluded, we are not a society. Or we
are not worth our salt. Or both.

Gold had his article.

By nightfall the next day he was secluded in his study at the
apartment with his notepaper and typewriter and his folders of
newspaper and magazine clippings that might prove apposite.

The liar Richard Helms, former Director of the Central Intelligence Agency, had finally been brought to justice for alleged acts
of the felony of perjury and was permitted to plead "no contest"
to trivial misdemeanors instead. In a departure from long tradition,
no notice of the hearing was given to the press. The Attorney
General of the United States angrily denied there had been any
agreement between the Justice Department and Mr. Helms's lawyers to conceal the courtroom proceeding from reporters.

"It is my understanding that there is to
be no jail sentence, that I will be able to
get my pension from the U.S. Govern-

> ment, and there will be no further pro-
> secution," the transcript reflects Mr.
> Helms as telling the judge.
>
> "This court does not feel itself bound
> by any Justice Department agreement
> with Mr. Helms," said Federal District
> Judge Barrington D. Parker at a court
> session attended only by Mr. Helms, his
> lawyers, Justice Department officials,
> and court officers.

And then fined Helms only two thousand dollars for lying under oath about the CIA's secret contributions to the undermining of the democratic constitutional government in Chile. Justice was done.

> Federal District Judge Barrington D.
> Parker told Mr. Helms before sentenc-
> ing, "You dishonored your oath and you
> now stand before this court in disgrace
> and shame."
>
> "I don't feel disgraced at all," Mr.
> Helms later told reporters outside the
> courtroom after the sentencing.

His lawyer, Edward Bennett Williams, gave exemplary display throughout of that special probity and that commitment to justice and light for which the members of his profession have historically been famed:

> In the courtroom, Mr. Williams had told
> Judge Parker that Mr. Helms would
> "bear the scar of a conviction for the
> rest of his life." Outside, however, he
> told reporters that contrary to what
> Judge Parker had said, Mr. Helms would
> "wear his conviction like a badge of
> honor."

A political columnist for the New York *Daily News* called the disposition of the case "an establishment fix, pure and simple."

The Attorney General of the United States was understandably sensitive to the charge he was party to a fix and replied as best he was able: it was not credible to Gold that there should appear in his lifetime still one more U.S. Attorney General with the stultified brain of an ox and the psychology of a corkscrew, but the evidence now before his eyes was lamentably persuasive.

> **BELL DENIES DOUBLE**
> **STANDARD ON HELMS**
>
> Attorney General Griffin Bell angrily denied yesterday that the Justice Department had used a "double standard" in handling the case of former CIA Director Richard M. Helms. Bell insisted that the Justice Department recommendation that Helms spend no time in prison and be allowed to keep his government pension was "fair and just." He denied any double standard of prosecuting rich and poor. "Only the well-to-do go to prison," he said.

This was news to Gold. It was news from which he recoiled in disgust to absorb more about this establishment public servant who had kept his government pension and magically escaped the discriminatory incarcerations systematically meted out in the criminal courts to other members of the well-to-do.

> Richard McGarrah Helms (he prefers not to use his middle name) was almost the epitome of the establishment figure. His father was a corporate executive and his maternal grandfather, Gates McGarrah, was an international banker. He spent two high school years in Switzerland and Germany, where he learned French and German as well as the social graces.

Gold would almost rather be a Jew.
He brushed Richard McGarrah Helms aside for what use he

could make of him later in his book on Kissinger or the Jewish experience and turned to the task at hand with a concentration that was diluted almost at the start by the regretful wish that he were already writing his book. David Eisenhower was writing a book:

DAVID EISENHOWER WRITING BOOK
ABOUT GRANDFATHER'S CHARACTER

David Eisenhower is writing an intimate character study of his grandfather. "I will include the impressions I had of him," Mr. Eisenhower said, "but the more I leave myself out of the book the better."

The timing of the book is just right for him, Mr. Eisenhower explained. "I just got out of law school, and I've always been ambitious in the writing field. The idea sort of occurred to me."

John Ehrlichman, Spiro Agnew, and H. R. Haldeman had written books. Gerald Ford was writing a book:

TALENT SCOUT

He still has 17 days in office, but President Ford has quietly signed up with the William Morris talent agency to represent him when he returns to private life. He will have the same agent who represented Olympic swim champ Mark Spitz and the racehorse Secretariat.

William Morris will get 10 percent on any books the President may write, any lectures he may give, any television deals he makes.

If Gerald Ford could write a book, was there any reason Secretariat could not? An engaging screenwriter named Nancy Dowd was not writing a book:

Although a Smith College classmate once predicted that Nancy Dowd would

> be "our generation's James Joyce,"
> Miss Dowd seems quite content writing
> screenplays in Hollywood. "I wouldn't
> mind writing a novel," she said. "But
> the way you can show behavior in films
> is so exciting."

Gold warmed to Miss Dowd and thought of sending a fan letter because she was *not* writing a novel.

Richard Nixon had written a book.

The President of the United States had written a book about his one year in the White House and might secretly be writing another about his second.

A popular fashion model named Cheryl Tiegs had overcome considerable misgivings and decided to write a book:

> In addition, Tiegs just negotiated a deal
> with Simon & Schuster giving her
> $70,000 plus royalties to collaborate on a
> book. "The problem with writing," she
> sighed, "is that there's not much money
> in it."

Even that fat little fuck Henry Kissinger was writing a book! He was writing his memoirs, after Gold had done most of the work, and, according to separate stories in *The New York Times*, had negotiated for the publication rights with the same frantic subtlety and intrigue of which he had given such striking illustration in public office. Said the first of these stories in the *Times:*

> A NEW SHUTTLE FOR KISSINGER,
> TO PUBLISHERS WITH MEMOIRS
>
> Secretary of State Henry A. Kissinger is
> about to embark on one of his most chal-
> lenging diplomatic journeys—the selling
> of his memoirs. How skillfully he ma-
> neuvers for the rights to his life story
> could mean the difference between
> merely a large advance and the biggest
> advance in book publishing history. The

figures being totted up range from $1 million to $3 million, plus extras.

Mr. Kissinger, who negotiated his own contracts in the past, has never used a literary agent and, according to a well-known knowledgeable source at the State Department, probably will not employ one.

Said the second:

KISSINGER RETAINS LITERARY AGENT

To enhance the value of his memoirs in the marketplace, Secretary of State Kissinger has retained a powerful literary agency to represent him. The agency is International Creative Management.

I.C.M.'s clients include Barbra Streisand, Steve McQueen, Isaac Stern, Peter Benchley, Arthur Miller, Tennessee Williams, Harry Reasoner, Joseph Heller, and Sir Laurence Olivier.

$2 Million to $3 Million Mentioned

According to publishing informants, the "extras" being sought include a lifetime consultancy as an editor, magazine and newspaper columns, television adviserships or appearances, unlimited staff, chauffeured limousines, and other things.

Gold presumed that "other things" included the two shifts of three bodyguards he was later reported hiring at his own expense.

Gold perused the dollar amounts again with a vitriolic misanthropy greatly exceeding that natural jealousy to be found in every man. His own original plans for a book of Kissinger's memoirs were aborted. Deftly he had rearranged his information for a more combustible line of attack, considering he would easily obtain the Kissinger manuscript as soon as photocopies were made for book club and paperback deals. Six months ahead of publication Gold could rebut assertions and positions before they were proclaimed, in a fusillade of debunking articles that would diminish the commercial value of Kissinger's book while enhancing that of his own. Let the shuttling little bastard publish first if he dared! Each of Gold's articles, of course, would find a place in his book. But the big bucks, unfortunately, still would go to the surreptitious former Harvard professor and Secretary of State who was now, as well as a number of other things, consultant to the University of Southern California's Center for the Study of the American Experience, instead of a primary topic of investigation.

It was disgraceful and so discouraging to Gold that this base figure charged with infamies too horrendous to measure and too numerous for listing should be gadding about gaily in chauffeured cars, instead of walking at Spandau with Rudolf Hess, while Gold had to drive rented ones.

Gold, who'd collected everything by and about Kissinger ever published, could certainly do a better job than Kissinger on a book about Kissinger. For one thing, he had an objective antipathy toward his subject possibly lacking, or weaker, in Kissinger himself. Gold strongly doubted that the sneaky man who'd treacherously monitored his telephone calls for eight years and cooperated in the illegal tapping of the family lines of journalists and aides would have the humorous conviviality and that largeness and flexibility of nature to view himself in the comic light of ridicule and loathing he inspired in so many others. Or that he could be anything but oblivious to the despicable character of his small actions and the bloody catastrophies resulting from his large ones. There was the judgment of Anthony C. Lewis in *The New York Times:*

> His agony was at arm's length; there is no sign that the human torment of Vietnam affected him inside, as it did so many others.

There was also a deficiency in imagination likely to circumscribe the value of any study of Kissinger by Kissinger. Asked about his role in the Cambodian war, in which an estimated five hundred thousand people died, he'd said:

> I may have a lack of imagination, but I
> fail to see the moral issue involved.

Whereas another State Department official, William C. Sullivan, had testified:

> The justification for the war is the reelec-
> tion of the President.

Not once that Gold knew of had Kissinger raised a voice in protest against the fascistic use of police power to quell public opposition to the war in Southeast Asia. How honestly would he deal with unfriendly assessments of himself Gold had found: (1) of himself as someone "as shabby as the certified scoundrels in the Nixon administration"; (2) of his policies and record as "marked by ignorance and ineptitude" and likely to be viewed by history as "thin in diplomatic achievement and shameful in human terms"; and (3) of his major achievement, peace in Vietnam, that "Kissinger brought peace to Vietnam the same way Napoleon brought peace to Europe: by losing," and that "If he had his way we would be bombing Vietnam still." Or with that exultant peroration by an editorial writer for *The New Republic* who, responding to the report that Kissinger might soon be working in television and not in government, gave thanks to God that now "he can devote his conjuring talents to television land, where they won't do any harm"? Had Kissinger, as alleged, really longed for "a brutal episode of battle" that would result in a convincing Israeli military defeat? Had he really tried to delay arms shipments to that country during the Yom Kippur war? Were his hopes truly depressed when Israel rallied by fording the Nile and encircling the Egyptian armies on the farther side? Gold had ample documentation of the plain silliness of the prick:

KISSINGER CALLS NIXON "UNPLEASANT"

KISSINGER APOLOGIZES FOR
OVERHEARD WORDS ON NIXON

KISSINGER CRIES IN SALZBERG
AT CHARGE HE LIED ABOUT CHILE

"Power is a great aphrodisiac," this man of vaunted brilliance
and wit had said more than once with an arrogance and naiveté, in
Gold's estimation, that merited contempt. Gold knew from experience that women were a better one. Only a lamebrain, Gold
thought, would state to an interviewer in wartime after his own
efforts at peacemaking had been failing wretchedly for almost four
years, "When I'm talking to Le Duc Tho, I know how to behave
with Le Duc Tho, and when I'm with a girl, I know how to behave
with a girl." It did not seem to Gold that Kissinger knew anything
at all about behaving with Oriana Fallaci, the woman conducting
the interview:

> "No, I don't want to engage in polemics
> on this subject."
>
> "Enough, I don't want to talk of Viet-
> nam any more."
>
> "Oh! No, I shan't answer him. I shan't
> respond to his invitation."
>
> "Don't ask me that."
>
> "That's a question I can't answer."
>
> "I can't, I can't . . . I don't want to an-
> swer that question."
>
> "And don't make me talk of Vietnam
> any more, please."
>
> "But that's really enough about Vietnam
> now. Let's talk of Machiavelli, Cicero
> anything except Vietnam."
>
> "No, I have never been against the war
> in Vietnam."
>
> "But are we still talking of Vietnam?"
>
> "Power as an instrument in its own right
> has no fascination for me."
>
> "What counts is to what extent women
> are part of my life, a central preoccupa-
> tion. Well, they aren't that at all. To me
> women are no more than a pastime, a

hobby. Nobody devotes too much time
to a hobby. Moreover, my engagement
book is there to show I only devote a
limited portion of my time to them."

". . . I've always acted alone. Americans admire that enormously. Americans
admire the cowboy leading the caravan
alone astride his horse, the cowboy entering a village or city alone on his
horse."

"This romantic, surprising character
suits me, because being alone has always
been part of my style, or of my technique
if you prefer. Independence too. Yes,
that's very important to me and in me.
And, finally, conviction. I am always
convinced of the necessity of whatever
I'm doing. And people feel that, believe
in it. And I attach great importance to
being believed."

"I'm not asking for popularity, I'm not
seeking it. In fact, if you really want to
know, I care nothing for popularity. I
can afford to say what I think. I am referring to what is genuine in me. Take
actors, for instance, the really good ones
don't rely on mere technique. They also
follow their feelings when they play a
part. Like me, they are genuine."

"Oh, he's so full of shit, that self-seeking *schmuck*," Gold said
aloud.

"Why I agreed to it," Mr. Kissinger later commented about the
interview, "I'll never know."

Said Mr. Lewis of the *Times:*

[His] jokes have about them the air of
the grave. That we honor a person who
has done such things in our name is a
comment on us.

The transition from Kissinger to blight, rubbish, rot, and moral defilement was a natural one, and Gold was not distracted from his article when his daughter entered.

"You want dinner?"

Gold waved her away without looking up from the work in which he was immersed. In an hour he settled on a title:

WE ARE NOT A SOCIETY
or
WE ARE NOT WORTH OUR SALT

It was a title that sang. The divine fires were burning.

VIII

We Are Not a Society *or* We Are Not Worth Our Salt

"I LIKE the first part of the title but not the second." As Gold watched with a look of cold dislike, Lieberman took a pencil in his fist and drew heavy black lines through the offending words as though gouging them from the page with some primitive stone implement. "There, that's much better, isn't it? 'We Are Not a Society.' "

"It's hardly a blockbuster that way."

"We can build on it. I'm thinking of wearing polka-dot bow ties. How would I look in them?"

Gold knew he would look just awful. "I think you'd look just fine."

"So do I." Liberman sat back in his swivel chair with a face too plainly smug and disrespectful. "Now what is all this nonsense about salt? What do you mean 'worth our salt'? What's that supposed to signify anyway?"

Gold considered walking out the door. "It's a play on words," he defended himself. "In addition to any idiomatic value in the metaphor, I feel that salt is one of those basic, shared commodities that give that kind of cohesion to an aggregate of families in a given area that we commonly call a society."

"Well, why don't you just say it as simply as that?" Lieberman instructed with an intolerable air of authority. "Cohesion is better. Salt is too complex."

"Salt?"

"Especially 'worth our salt.' We'll use 'cohesion' instead. Try to remember, Bruce, that we've got a highly educated, very intellectual, politically concerned group of readers who are always very well informed, and they just won't know what you mean when you say 'worth our salt.' What *do* you mean, anyway? I don't get it. How much is salt worth? And why is it ours? Why not worth our beef?"

"Go on," said Gold.

"We'll call it 'We Are Not a Society *or* Are We Lacking in Those Basic, Shared Commodities That Give Cohesion to Aggregates of Families in a Given Geographical Area That Enable Us to Call Them a Society?' That just about says it all, doesn't it? 'Cohesion' works like a charm. We can put in plenty of sex now and take out all the salt. Just remember, Bruce, that I'm an experienced editor and you're not," continued Lieberman with a bloated sense of superiority. "Sophie and I had dinner at the White House once, you know. And we got there on my merits, not by sucking up to an anti-*Semitt* like Ralph."

"You got there," reminded Gold, losing all control as the fury submerged beneath the rather pacific exterior he was striving to maintain finally achieved the upper hand, "by supporting a war with a bunch of other assholes who were too fucking corrupt to tell Johnson and Nixon they were full of shit. If I had a kid hurt in that war I'd cut your head off now. You yellow hypocrite, I never saw you rushing out to enlist. And your kids would have been deferred along with mine, wouldn't they, if they'd been old enough to be drafted? That gives me a good idea for another article."

"Let me see it first." Lieberman rose, wheedling. "You owe me that much."

"You wouldn't use it," Gold taunted with a curled lip. "It's called 'My Meal at the White House,' by Skip and Sophie Lieberman."

"As told to Bruce Gold," said Lieberman with a look of almost livid hatred, "who has never eaten there."

"But keeps trying. Good day, you prick."

"Good day, Bruce." In the instant they stood motionless and glared at each other, perhaps nowhere else on earth were so powerfully contrasted two old friends who liked each other not at all and who were so intractably in contention on almost every issue.

"You give some thought to improving the title still more while I rewrite the text. Maybe we should be coauthors."

"You change one more fucking word," Gold warned, "and I'll take it back and sell it to another magazine."

"BRUCE, IT'S marvelous," cried Ralph on his hot line from Washington to Gold in his apartment, where the latter was furtively squirreling together the family bankbooks and other testaments of ownership in anticipation of his flight to another domicile when the hour foreclosing further procrastination was at last at hand. "Everyone here agrees."

"They do?" asked Gold in a soaring resurrection of spirit.

"Even the President. The President wants me to tell you he's crazy about it. He asked if you'd be willing to work as a speechwriter."

"No," said Gold.

"I told him that. You're too important in your own right. And you'd be much more valuable to us as an independent voice in our control."

"It would compromise my moral authority," Gold added with a passing chill.

"I'll point that out. He likes your article so much, Bruce, that he doesn't want you to publish it."

"He doesn't?"

"He wants to introduce it in sections entirely as his own," said Ralph, "in speeches, and press conferences, and in his next State of the Union message. He loves your phrases, Bruce. You've been promoted again."

"To what?"

"We'll have that nailed down definitely before you fly back unless we don't have time. He especially loves that worth his salt. What a stunning gift you have. How in the world did you arrive at an image like that? It boggles the mind."

"That's worth *our* salt, Ralph," Gold corrected.

"He might want to change it, Bruce," cautioned Ralph.

"It's already been changed," Gold informed him. "It's out of the article. Cut."

"By whom?"

"Lieberman," said Gold. "He doesn't like salt. He wants to take it all out."

"Salt?"

"He's changing it to cohesion. That kind of cohesion—"

"Cohesion?" cried Ralph in a tone of wounded surprise. "What kind of word is cohesion? He's crazy, Bruce. You mustn't let him ruin it."

"He thought salt was too complex."

"He doesn't know what he's doing," said Ralph. "Cohesion's no good. He just isn't worth his salt."

"Will you talk to him about it?"

"I won't talk to Lieberman about anything," said Ralph. "But he won't have dinner at the White House again while I'm around. We'll have you instead. Then we can have the salt, right? You won't be using it anyway."

Here Gold's inherent tactical sense surged to the fore. "There are other places, Ralph," he began his negotiations. "And I've been thinking about it for my book. Pomoroy's very impressed. *Worth Our Salt*. I'd hate to give that up, Ralph."

"I can see why," said Ralph. "But let the President have it. After all, he's the only President we have."

"It would be worth a lot to him, wouldn't it?" hinted Gold.

"And this President would repay. Maybe that Ambassadorship to the Court of St. James. Or Secretary of State. That one is not bad, Bruce. You travel free and get all the nights out you want. Would you like to be Secretary of State?"

"Let me think about it," said Gold with a sangfroid he'd not known till that moment was an inner resource he could draw upon. "What about that head of the CIA you once mentioned?"

"You could be that too."

"Too? Ralph, is any of this really possible?"

"I don't see why not, if you're worth your salt. Could you handle both jobs at the same time?"

"I don't see why not," said Gold. "I'll take the piece back from Lieberman. Mum's the word, right?"

"Salt," Ralph corrected and laughed. "And remember—the walls have ears."

"I know," said Gold. "I've been talking to them."

"And I'm going in right now and start fighting for you, if I can get an appointment. We'll shoot for Secretary of State, Ambassador to the Court of St. James, head of NATO—"

"I'm not sure I want that one."

"—or Director of the CIA. It's high time you got what you deserved, Bruce, although it may be too soon."

"Thank you, Ralph. You're the salt of the earth."

"Would you say that again, Bruce?"

"LIEBERMAN, I don't like cohesion."

"I won't take salt."

"Then I'm withdrawing the piece."

"You've made a deal somewhere else."

"May God strike me dead," said Gold, supremely content with the terms of the agreement he was forging with the Deity, "if you ever see that article in print in another magazine."

"I wasn't crazy about it anyway," Lieberman retorted with an ugly petulance, and Gold recalled with considerable mental peace an additional explanation for Lieberman's mood of morose and vindictive frustration. But a fortnight earlier, Lieberman had applied with fanfare for membership in a stodgy, obsolescent conservative organization called Young Americans for Freedom and had been rejected because he was too old. He had on a polka-dot bow tie with matching crumbs and grease stains—another wandering Jew, Gold decreed in disavowing lament, converted to a bow tie. He was wearing a shabby leather jacket and looked like a rough beast with slotted eyes on whom it belonged as a hide. "I've got more important things to busy myself with than you and your salt. I want to do something about China, communism, and the grape growers in California."

"What's wrong with China?"

"There's no political democracy there," said Lieberman grumpily, "and no freedom of the press."

"No shit," said Gold with feigned amazement. "What did you have in mind?"

"A manifesto, of course, by me, in the form of a petition, with a list of non-negotiable demands, insisting they change. I'll need supporting names.''

"Count me in," said Gold.

"And a special issue of my magazine in which you and others express my feelings in two thousand words.''

"How much will you pay?''

"Nothing.''

"Count me out.''

Lieberman retorted with the savage fervor of a maddened fanatic. "You want nine hundred million Chinese to be without political freedom just because you won't give up a few bucks? That's a third of the human race.''

"A fourth, you imbecile. What about communism?''

"I want to halt the spread right now on every border in the world. With armed might, if necessary.''

"Whose?''

"I haven't been able to figure that out yet," admitted Lieberman. "But I'm willing to make the people of the world an offer they can't refuse—a preferable alternative they will find impossible to resist.''

"What's the preferable alternative?''

"I haven't been able to figure that one out yet either.''

"What about the grape growers?''

"The workers are on strike. There's been a breakdown of tradition and a loss of respect for the workings of the free marketplace.''

"What do you want to do about it?''

Lieberman was quick to reply. "Government subsidies.''

"To the workers?''

"The growers. To help them beat back the strikers indefinitely and allow them to band together to peg prices at a high level and stabilize the free market.''

"I'll pass on that one too.''

"That's the thing I dislike most about you," Lieberman rebuked him with a snarl. "What shall I say is wrong with you? You'll find it all spelled out in my newest autobiography. You're always afraid to come down solidly on the side of the status quo. It's the reason you're not getting anywhere.''

"Really?" said Gold, and took pleasure in continuing, "I've just been promoted again."

"To what?" Lieberman demanded jealously.

"It must not pass my lips."

"Have you been working in Washington all this time?"

"I've been fucking girls there," Gold answered with a cryptic smile. "I can tell you no more."

"Well, I've been fucking girls too," Lieberman blurted out in challenge. After this, there came a pause from Lieberman pregnant with the expanding weight of a confidence craving release. "If I tell you a secret," he said with uncommon reticence, "will you tell me one?" He persisted with his confession even after Gold said no. "Will you promise never to tell anyone?"

"It will go with me," said Gold, "to the grave."

"I've been getting girls too," said Lieberman, squirming with uneasiness. "I've been answering those sex help-wanted ads we run in the back of my magazine. I can get an early crack at the best ones before they're even published. I've been surprised at how easy it is and how many of them there are. I never knew women enjoyed sex too. Of course," said Lieberman, and here his voice sank confessionally in a mixture of disappointment and apology, "they're not always the most beautiful girls in the world."

"No shit," said Gold.

"No—oo shit," said Gold in Washington when offered his pick by Ralph of Secretary of State, Ambassador to the Court of St. James, Attorney General of the United States, or Director of the CIA in exchange for his "We Are Not a Society *or* We Are Not Worth Our Salt."

"I would go for Secretary of State if I were you."

"But I don't know anything," said Gold doubtfully, "and I've got no experience."

"That's never made a difference," said Ralph.

That part seemed plausible. "Ralph, can I really be appointed Secretary of State soon if I decide I want the job?"

"Oh, I can practically guarantee that," said Ralph, "although I can't be sure. That's as much as I can tell you right now."

"Would the Senate confirm me?" asked Gold. "Most of them don't even know who I am."

"That would work strongly to your advantage," said Ralph. "As you state so eloquently in your article, Bruce, the more we know about any candidate for public office the less deserving he is of our support, and the ideal nominee for President is always someone about whom everybody in the country knows absolutely nothing."

"Ralph," Gold cried, "that was a joke, a sarcasm, a piece of satirical whimsy."

"We see it," said Ralph with a look of grave reproof, "as the absolute truth and are already taking it into our calculations for the future. It's a pity you've had your name in the papers, Bruce, or you might have been our next Presidential nominee. Settle for Secretary of State, Bruce, at least for now. It's a foot in the door."

"What would I have to do?" asked Gold.

"Nothing," said Ralph. "And you would have a large staff to help. You would have a Deputy Undersecretary of State with a map showing the capitals of all the countries in the world and another with the names of the people in charge so you wouldn't have to call up the newspapers to find out. Unless you wanted to keep busy, and then there'd be no limit to the affairs in which you could interfere."

"Could I make policy?"

"As much as you want."

"Foreign policy?"

"Domestic too. If you're quick enough."

"Quick enough?"

"Oh, sure," said Ralph. "Bruce, you know the President as well as I do—"

"I've never met him, Ralph," Gold corrected stiffly.

Ralph appeared baffled. "Didn't he go to your big sister's birthday party?"

"I went. He went to China."

"But I took you to see him in the White House after you did so well at the Commission, didn't I?"

"He was taking a nap."

"Well, you will have to meet him at least once before he can announce your appointment," Ralph advised. "I hope you won't mind that."

"I don't think I'll mind."

"Actually, the best time to catch him is when he's feeling sleepy and wants to nap," said Ralph. "That's when the rush to see him is thickest and you have to be quick. This President is much too busy to spend time on life-and-death responsibilities in which he's lost interest. Although we do suspect," Ralph confided after a fretful glance at the wall, "that he's often off writing another book secretly when he's supposed to be napping. If you approach him with your policy when he's wide awake you might command his attention. Hang in there, if you can, until his eyes turn glassy and he starts to yawn. If you're beside him when he's drifting off, you can get his authorization for just about any policy you want."

"Suppose," said Gold, "it's a bad policy. Suppose I make a mistake."

"In government," Ralph answered, "there's no such thing as a mistake, since nobody really knows what's going to happen. After all, Bruce, nothing succeeds as planned. I wouldn't be worth my salt if I didn't know that."

"Suppose my policy fails."

"Then it fails. Nobody's perfect."

"It fails?"

"And there's no harm done," said Ralph. "It's happened before. But there was no harm done."

"No harm done?"

"We're still here, aren't we?" said Ralph.

The bland insouciance of the reply fell upon Gold with a nasty jar and evoked in him the first faint beginnings of repugnance and an inclination to withdraw. "Ralph," he began after a moment of inhibition, "there's a kind of cynicism and selfishness there that I'm not sure I can be comfortable with."

"I know that feeling of good conscience, Bruce," Ralph answered with a jovial air of patronage, "and I assure you it will fade without a trace when you've been working here a minute or two." Gold breathed more freely. "Just don't delude yourself into thinking you're going to upgrade anything. When your friend Henry Kissinger—''

''He's not my friend, Ralph.''

''I'm glad, Bruce, because I was going to say that when that pushy toad Henry Kissinger first came here, he told his friends the war would be over in less than six months, and he was sulking like a spoiled child when the country took it away from him after five years and wouldn't let him have another to play with in Africa. Bruce, please be Secretary of State. If you won't, we might have to give it to someone else of your religion—''

''I have no religion, Ralph.''

''To someone else of your faith then who—''

''I have no faith.''

''To someone Jewish who might be just like him.''

Gold required no further inducement. He yielded assent in a solemn moment in which words would not do. Ralph was greatly relieved by Gold's dignified handshake.

''Now let's see if we can get it for you.''

Gold stared at him with a renewed sense of shock. ''Ralph, you promised, you guaranteed it.''

''But I didn't say I was sure.''

''As a matter of fact, you did,'' Gold said in reprimand, and hoped Ralph caught the injured tone in his voice. ''You did say you were sure you could get me appointed Secretary of State.''

''Unless I couldn't, Bruce—I always add that in order to avoid misleading people. In your case, I have no hesitation about saying it's a sure thing unless, of course, it isn't. I don't see how you can miss once you're married to Andrea Conover and pass your medical exam, unless you can, but that would be hard, if it isn't easy.''

''Ralph,'' said Gold, with his mind spinning, ''I'm not even divorced.''

There was something about the reproachful eye Ralph fixed upon him that made Gold blush profusely. ''I thought you'd taken care of that, Bruce.''

''I'm seeing a lawyer next week.''

''And the physical?''

"That same afternoon," said Gold. "Belle hasn't a real suspicion I'm even thinking about it."

"That's always the best way," Ralph said approvingly. "But won't she get a glimmer of some kind when you marry Andrea?"

"She doesn't even seem to understand I've practically moved out," Gold said with perplexity, and with the guilty knowledge that he had not. "Ralph, I should have the appointment quickly, before I do anything. Andrea is in love with me, I know, but she won't marry me until I'm somebody important in government."

"I'm not sure you can have that appointment quickly, Bruce, until she does marry you," Ralph answered frankly. "The Conover connection is crucial."

If the Conover connection was crucial, Gold was bereft of alternative. "I guess I'll just have to move all my shirts and underwear out and bring everything into the open with Belle, won't I?" He and Ralph regarded each other in silence. "In a way I hate to do this to her."

"Don't we always?" caroled Ralph with a sigh. "But your country comes first. If you like, Bruce, I can have the Vice President fly to your apartment in Manhattan and explain the exigencies of the emergency to Belle, or the president pro tem of the Senate, or even the minority or majority whip. Anyone you want, Bruce. Just ask."

Gold answered faintly with a sort of inert fortitude, "I'll just have to do it myself."

"This is noble, Bruce," said Ralph without a hint of guile and rose from his chair to his long legs. "And you'll never regret it. Why, you can become the country's first Jewish Secretary of State. You might even be a credit to your race."

"Kissinger was Jewish," countered Gold sullenly, dipping one shoulder to allow what he felt to be an offensive innuendo to go bouncing past like a glancing blow from a javelin. "Or said he was."

"Then maybe you could be the youngest Jewish Secretary of State. I bet your family would be proud of that too."

Gold scowled. "Kissinger was young," he muttered grudgingly

with a note of aggression invading his voice. "But he could have been lying about that too."

"What do you mean?"

Gold knew a notorious idea when he had one and was not about to divulge it.

"He ain't no Jew!" Gold's deranged old father had howled like an ungovernable dybbuk toward the television screen with his hooked finger stabbing pitilessly at the corpulent, comic image of Kissinger descending from his plane with a complacent smile after his devious efforts to blame Israel for the breakdown of Middle East negotiations he had lacked ability to consummate. ("Kissinger," wrote journalist Leslie Gelb in the *Times Magazine,* "had agreed with the Israelis not to blame anyone for the breakdown of his latest round of shuttle diplomacy. No sooner did he get on his aircraft to return home than he started blaming the Israelis.") "No Jew was ever a cowboy! *Ich hub im en d'rerd.*"

And Gold was prepared to develop the thesis that Kissinger was not a Jew in a book of Kissinger "memoirs" he was positive would excite attention and hoped earn him at least a discernible fraction of the *parnusseh* Kissinger was raking in from his own memoirs and the other vocational opportunities opening up on all sides that he oozed into naturally like an oleoresinous jelly. Perfect truth was not of determining importance in the exposition of Gold's theory: he felt mutinously that he had as much right to falsehood, bias, and distortion in *his* memoirs of Kissinger as Kissinger did in his own memoirs of Kissinger and had exercised in public office. In Gold's conservative opinion, Kissinger would not be recalled in history as a Bismarck, Metternich, or Castlereagh but as an odious *shlump* who made war gladly and did not often exude much of that legendary sympathy for weakness and suffering with which Jews regularly were credited. It was not a *shayna Yid* who would go down on his knees on a carpet to pray to Yahweh with that *shmendrick* Nixon, or a *haimisha mentsh* who would act with such cruelty against the free population of Chile:

> I don't see why we need to stand by and
> watch a country go Communist due to
> the irresponsibility of its own people.

Such a *pisk* on the *pisher* to speak with such *chutzpah!* And then plot, with a sneaky duplicity for which he was to grow scatologically abhorred, for the downfall of that innocent democracy. Under oath he dissembled about his role and his knowledge. Gold could detect with his nose a rancid taint of swaggering fascism in such arrogant deeds that did not fit flatteringly the plump bourgeois figure who committed them and was not in concordance with even the most prejudicial historic depictions of the characteristic Jew. Gold still recoiled from the cold terminology of Kissinger's book of 1957 in which he bravely talked of "the paralyzing fear of weapons" and called precociously for a unique brand of diplomacy:

> . . . to break down the atmosphere of
> special horror which now surrounds the
> use of nuclear weapons.

The remedy suggested by the dumb *putz* was limited nuclear warfare. *Zayer klieg*, that *grubba naar*, with his special diplomacies and limited nuclear wars. In Israel there were hostile demonstrations when he visited, and former Defense Minister Moshe Dayan was anything but friendly on French television when he spoke of Kissinger's departure from government:

> That was a man we had everything to
> fear from, because he ended up exchang-
> ing the security of Israel for the good
> graces of the oil companies. Kissinger is
> going and it's a great relief for the Israeli
> people.

To a malign imagination like Gold's, the specter of oil conjured up a miasma of Rockefeller influence and money that clung to Kissinger like a cloud of corruption and gave to his eyes, cheeks, and lips the glistening look of a *shnorrer* who has been very well lubricated. Gold shivered anew at the sophomoric lunacy and preposterous intellectual claims of that noisy *balaboss*. The gaudy militarism of the portly *trombenik* was more Germanic than Jewish, and at least one newsman had fortuitously spied in Kissinger a puerile compulsion for "Teuton his own horn." There was foul brutality in the flippant remark attributed to him about the Christmas carpet bombing of North Vietnam, an act of warfare unmatched for enormity in modern times which Kissinger, depending on whom the bustling *bonditt* was trying to finagle, both opposed and approved:

> We bombed them into letting us accept
> their terms.

For the very life of him Gold could not recall such rakish and jocular contempt for the victims of massive bombardment as ever coming from a Jew, or from many Christians since Adolf Hitler, Heinrich Himmler, Joseph Goebbels, Hermann Goering, Hjalmar Schacht, and Joachim von Ribbentrop.

So astir was Gold's mind with thoughts of his memoir of Kissinger that from Ralph to home seemed a journey of moments, and he was assidulously engrossed in his files by the glow of the setting sun that same day. Belle brought his dinner on a tray a minute before he was going to yell for it. The pot roast was succulent. The coffee was steaming and strong. Kissinger, that *klutz,* Gold noted in silent triumph while chewing wolfishly, had *boorrrchet* and cried real tears like a *nebbish* in Salzberg when questioned about perjury and had beamed like a clever *shaygetz* in Washington later when the suspicions appeared well founded. Gold was already restless to begin propounding doggedly and positively that his subject, Henry Kissinger, in all but the most confining definitions of cultural anthropology or bigotry, was no more Jewish, let's say, than Nelson Rockefeller, the prismatic apogee in a succession of patrons Kissinger had always managed to secure at pivotal points in his career. The first, a dynamic and eccentric voluntary German exile named Fritz Kraemer, was attracted by an enterprising letter composed by young Kissinger when he was but an infantry private in Louisiana during World War II, a rank and military specialty in which, biographers Marvin and Bernard Kalb record from a family member, "Henry" was "unhappy" and, in his own words, "acutely sorry" for himself. Gold hoped to use this letter in his book as an example of Kissinger's early attainments as a writer. It was not odd to Gold that this ambitious man of the worst reputation who had lied to the world about so much would tell Nelson Rockefeller and others he was Jewish just to make a good impression.

He lied about peace and lied about war; he lied in Paris when he announced "peace was at hand" just before the Presidential elections and he lied again afterward by blaming North Vietnam for bad faith when all his *hondling* went *mechuleh*.

KISSINGER CHARGES UNTRUE, HANOI AIDE IN PARIS SAYS

Hanoi was correct and Kissinger was not.

> Q. What concessions did the United States make to get this agreement?
>
> A. What concessions did the United States make? The United States made the concessions that are described in the agreement. There are no secret side agreements of any kind.

There *were* secret side agreements. (Jews, by reputation, made much better bargains.) The lonesome cowboy was *ba-kokt* again, and it was his allies in South Vietnam who would not accept the *tsedreydt mishmosh* of a truce he had *ungerpotchket*. So, *Moisheh Kapoyer*, the North was bombed to placate the South and salve the hurt feelings of the *mieskeit* and his *umgliks*, and not, as Kissinger falsely indicated, to force new concessions. Authority for this lay again in Anthony Lewis of *The New York Times*, without fail a more honorable source of information about Kissinger than Kissinger:

> The real purpose of the Christmas bombing, we now know, was to persuade South Vietnam to accept the truce. General Alexander Haig, then Mr. Kissinger's assistant, had gone to Saigon and promised to show that the United States was ready, in General Haig's elegant phrase, to "brutalize" the North.

Ai-yi-yi—another *metzieh,* that General Alexander Haig, with
his brain of a *golem's,* a *gantsa k'nocker* under Nixon and Kissinger whose *goyisha kup* divined some "sinister force" behind the
erasure of that eighteen and a half minutes from the incriminating
Watergate tapes. Kissinger was an ingrate to his benefactors
("Kissinger bad mouths practically everybody he knows, Presidents included") and could *funpheh* like a *gonif* when pressed for
the truth:

> Thus, while the White House regarded
> him as a wholehearted supporter of the
> Christmas bombing of North Vietnam,
> he led reporters and legislators—by nods
> and grimaces, by innuendo against
> Nixon, and by stressing the human ca-
> tastrophe of the decision—to believe
> that he was opposed to it.

Twisting and turning like a worm or a snake, the *vontz* was *nisht
aheyn, nisht aher* on issues igniting the fiercest controversy. The
chuchem hut gezugt:

> I have always considered the U.S. in-
> volvement in Indochina to have been a
> disaster.

And *er hut gezugt:*

> No, I have never been against the war in
> Vietnam.

When confronted head-on by biographers Kalb about discreet
hints, spread, as was his wont, by himself, that he disagreed with
Nixon's bombing policy, he confessed:

> I was in favor of attacking the North. It
> was an agony for me. . . .

Oh, that *shlemiel.* To *him* it was an agony, that *Chaim Yankel.*
He was never altogether comfortable with Congress and was said

to prefer a dictatorship without any parliamentary body to restrain him:

> "What I've been trying to tell him," said Rep. John Brademas, the deputy majority whip, "is that foreign policy must conform to the law, but I don't think I've been getting through."

No Jew Gold could think of suffered this same handicap of comprehension. Gold saw the strangest contrasts preserved between the ridiculous aura of success and knowledge that surrounded the self-satisfied *behayma* and the legacy of diplomatic wreckage and *tsuris* he had left in his wake. For Gold, his vaunted intelligence and brilliance remained as apocryphal and elusive as Nixon's grasp of fundamentals and Spiro Agnew's high IQ: no distinctive sign of any existed. A *farzayenisht* to his detractors, he was a ceaseless *mechaieh* to a biographer like Gold. Every *Montik* and *Donershtik* the scampering lummox was in the papers again with some new *mishegoss* like a *shmegegge* from Chelm. On Monday in the New York *Post* was a photograph of Kissinger looking like a simpering *shlemazel* in the sash and star-shaped medal of the Grand Cross First Class of the Order of Merit, one of "West Germany's highest decorations." On Tuesday Gold found this:

> #### NAZI SCANDAL IN BONN ARMY
>
> German army lieutenants staged a symbolic "burning of Jews" at the West German Armed Forces University in Munich. Nazi "Sieg Heil" salutes were exchanged as the young officers set fire to pieces of paper scribbled with the word "Juden" [Jews] and burned them in wastebaskets. Said a spokesman from the Defense Ministry, "The participants did not have a basically anti-Semitic point of view."

Gold wasn't all that sure. A fair man, he understood that even to juxtapose such items in print in this most coincidental relationship was a reprehensible action to be perpetrated only by someone like Gold lacking all decency and compassion for shallow, socialite warmongers like Kissinger. But surely, the dope was at least in part responsible for the close sequence by pushing in front of every camera that bright and thirsting *punim* that only a gentile *machetaynesta* could love. And Gold had the headlines to prove that Kissinger had been willing sycophant to anti-Semites in the past:

<u>WOODWARD & BERNSTEIN:</u>
KISSINGER'S VIEW OF NIXON
Anti-Semitic, Second Rate
And a Nuclear Warmonger

Gold had many more items of derogatory information but desired to avoid giving to his text even the faintest hue of any personal animus. If his thesis were sustained, he would become the country's first Jewish Secretary of State—if he became Secretary of State. He would even include the one or two complimentary things he'd found. In the Kalb biography, for example, there was praise for Kissinger as a Harvard student by a contemporary who described him as "extraordinarily able":

> But what a son of a bitch! A prima donna, self-serving, self-centered. You were either Elliott's protege or Carl Friedrich's. Kissinger managed to be on excellent terms with both.

In Professor William Yandell Elliott, another *chuchem* at Harvard, Kissinger found, he says, not merely an academic patron but a friend and an inspiration:

> On many Sundays we took long walks. He spoke of the power of love, and said that the only truly unforgivable sin is to use people as if they were objects.

Kissinger urged sending B-52's against Cambodia, supported dictatorships in Chile, Greece, and the Philippines, was dedicated to the perpetuation of racist minority rule in Africa, and contributed to the reelection of Richard Nixon. He had been kissed on the face by an Arab who detested Jews and handed a flower by the Chancellor of West Germany. Gold had a title he liked. He would call his book *The Little Prussian*.

HE DID not think that Kissinger would mind. As a gentleman with indisputable cravings for money and prominence he could scarcely advocate the suppression of these aspirations in others. And he was known to enjoy a good joke, for he was always trying to make one:

> Kissinger, who enjoyed a reputation as a swinger, was asked to explain his often-quoted remark that "power is the ultimate aphrodisiac."
> "Well, that was a joke," he said.

Probably, he was closer to the bull's-eye of humor when asked by reporters how he preferred to be addressed:

> "I don't stand on protocol," he answered. "If you will just call me 'Excellency' it will be okay."

There was laughter all around.

> "Your Excellency," wrote General Mustafa Barzani, the Kurdish rebel leader, in a final, pathetic message to Henry Kissinger after all aid abruptly was ended for an insurrection against Iraqui rule fomented and financed by the U.S. Government. "Our movement and people are being destroyed in an unbelievable way with silence from everyone. Our hearts bleed to see the destruction of our defenseless people in an unprecedented manner. We feel, your Excellency, that the United States has a moral and political responsibility towards our people who have committed themselves to your country's policy. Mr. Secretary,

> we are anxiously awaiting your quick re-
> sponse."

The only response to this betrayal of an ethnic group was a profound silence, although his Excellency, a fellow of sensitive nature who showed he could *kvetch* and *krechtz* like a *kronkeh bubbeh* when his tender feelings were hurt, defended himself more loquaciously in London later against accusations of something squalid and obscene in the usurious passion with which he appeared to be exploiting his former government positions for money:

> In his view, said Henry A. Kissinger, it's
> okay for him to make millions. "I think
> one has to consider that I was deeply in
> debt when I left office as a result of my
> public service."

Oy-oy-oy, crooned Gold to himself disapprovingly, for the words did not smell kosher. From such a *meshiach* the public needed service like a *luch in kup.* He very much doubted the *koorveh* had lived better as a Harvard professor than since. Yet, Gold now found himself in mysterious sympathy with the mercenary longings of the *chozzer.*

"Make money!" his father had exhorted maniacally throughout his lifetime. "That's the only good thing I ever learned from the Christians!"

Kissinger already had such *saychel,* as did, according to this paragraph in *Newsweek,* several of his confederates and *nuch-shleppers:*

> A number of his top aides also will be
> leaving. Several, including Deputy Sec-
> retary Charles Robinson, Under Secre-
> tary William D. Rogers, and Director of
> Policy Planning Winston Lord are
> wealthy men. Other aides, like Deputy
> Undersecretary of State Lawrence Ea-
> gleburger, are looking for a chance to
> make some money in private industry.

Gold identified with them all, deeply relieved by proof that his was not the only heart in the land roused to a stronger beat by the lovely nearness of money or his the only ears to whom the word itself was as blithesome a sound as could be heard in the language. Gold had good reason for his favorable inclination toward Deputy-Under Eagleburger (Gold could have been a Deputy-Under also had he been willing to settle for so little):

> It is reported that Lawrence Eagleburger, one of Kissinger's close associates, has the ability to say, "Henry, you're full of shit."

And Gold was indebted to reporters Robert Woodward and Carl Bernstein for acquainting him with William Watts, a Kissinger assistant who quit in protest over the invasion of Cambodia:

> Watts then had a show-down talk with General Alexander Haig. "You've just had an order from your Commander in Chief," Haig said. "You can't resign." "Fuck you, Al," Watts said. "I just did."

Gold was entranced.

"Fuck you, Al"?

"Henry, you're full of shit"?

Azoy zugt men to such *machers* as a General and a Secretary? The boys from Brooklyn could have handled that. With mother's milk they'd imbibed the good sense to think so realistically of such *momzehrem* in government from Tsar Nikolai in St. Petersburg to the *chozzerem* in City Hall and the *scutzem* in the social establishment in Washington, D.C. Gold wondered where in his book to put the letter from young Henry to that impressive German exile Fritz Kraemer, who arrived at the military base in Louisiana in a dazzling blaze of exotic authority to talk to the troops of the need for fighting fascism. The prose in the letter was spare:

> I heard you speak yesterday. This is how it should be done. Can I help you somehow? Pvt. Kissinger.

It was Kraemer who helped; and the fleet-footed *momzer* was elevated from infantryman to German-speaking interpreter for the commanding general. When the division moved overseas in the closing months of the war, he took quite naturally to the many alluring privileges and responsibilities of military government and was promoted to run the district of Bergstrasse in the state of Hess. His powers were extensive—including the power to arrest without questions.

> "When it came to Nazis," Kraemer recalls, "Kissinger showed human understanding."

There is good in the worst of us. Outside of government he continued "Teuton his own horn." Reminded of charges of "duplicity" and "immorality" and even that he was a "war criminal" in Vietnam, he defended himself lamely, and *er hut boorrrchet:*

> "I got the troops and prisoners home."

A *nechtiger tog!* More credit for that belonged even to Gold, who had at least gone on one peace march. Nor was Henry quick to grab blame for the 20,492 dead Americans or hundreds of thousands of Vietnamese who were killed in the years he was fucking around merrily with his diplomatic hijinks and vulgar arriviste playboy partying. He admits to a weakness!

> **KISSINGER ADMITS TO A WEAKNESS**
> "It was in the field of international economics that I had my greatest weakness," Kissinger told a reporter who dined with him in Acapulco recently. "The worst errors the U.S. committed against its North Atlantic allies and against the undeveloped nations were in this field."

Moisheh Pupik was as good as Gold when it came to finance and economics. But *azoy:*

KISSINGER IS JOINING
COMMITTEE AT CHASE

Henry A. Kissinger will join the Chase
Manhattan Bank first as vice chairman of
its international advisory committee and
later as the panel's chairman. The
spokesman for Chase declined to say
how much he will be paid. David Rockefeller, chairman of Chase, expressed delight that a person of Mr. Kissinger's
stature and achievements had agreed to
lend his considerable expertise to Chase.

Gold was astounded that a person of Kissinger's low stature and
despicable achievements would be allowed into a respectable
house, even the White House, but into a *house of finance?* It was
time to put money in mattresses and in Italian banks. Such a *gesh-
rei* should go up if he ever went near the *pishkeh*. But *nuch a mul:*

GOLDMAN, SACHS HIRES KISSINGER
AS INTERNATIONAL AFFAIRS ADVISER

Goldman, Sachs & Company, a leading
investment banking and brokerage firm,
announced that it has retained Henry A.
Kissinger as a part-time adviser and consultant. The amount of compensation to
be paid Dr. Kissinger was not disclosed.

Und nuch mer:

In the first contract of its kind a former
Secretary of State has agreed to serve as
adviser and consultant to a television
network for five years at a reported price
of $1 million.

Und vus nuch? In mit'n d'rinnen the slippery prick was *shoyn* a
Trustee for the Metropolitan Museum of Art because of "his
known commitment to the value of cultural exchange." Here Gold
had a good joke:

In 1974 when Henry Kissinger visited
Mr. Carter in the Georgia governor's office, the then Secretary of State gazed
admiringly on a Butler Brown oil painting and said, "I didn't know you collected Andrew Wyeths."

Zayer klieg, that *grubba naar*, but he was probably making more
in undisclosed compensations than Gold earned in salary, even
without any under-the-counter *shtupping* he might still be getting
from the Rockefellers. People knew what Kissinger had received
from the Rockefellers: cash, sponsorship, jobs, wedding parties,
the use of apartments and private planes, of the main swimming
pool at the Rockefeller estate for a flop-eared hound named Tyler,
and of private vaults in which to conceal government papers from
bona fide historians and other competing writers.

KISSINGER'S PHONE TRANSCRIPTS
MOVED FROM ROCKEFELLER ESTATE

The State Department said today that
Henry A. Kissinger had stored the transcripts of his telephone conversations at
the private New York estate of Vice
President Rockefeller. After a reporters'
group said it would sue to gain access to
the transcripts, Mr. Kissinger changed
his mind and included them in the grant
to the Library of Congress of his papers
and official documents.

According to a State Department press
officer, the transcripts were "kept in
government-approved storage areas in
Pocantico Hills, N.Y." Under question-
ing by reporters, he acknowledged he
meant the Rockefeller estate. Mr. Kissinger and Mr. Rockefeller have close
ties.

REMEMBER THE NEEDIEST!

But what did the Rockefellers get from Kissinger? Harvard
professors could be purchased more easily, but a loser like

Nelson might not know that. He stoops for coins in paid advertisements!

> Henry Kissinger
> creates a unique history
> of American leadership,
> *in precious metal* . . .
>
> PORTRAITS OF GREATNESS

There was a photo of Kissinger in vest and shirtsleeves cap-
tioned:

> After selection of the subjects by Dr.
> Kissinger (top), the portraits are meticu-
> lously sculptured (left), and the metals
> are then minted, one by one, in special
> hand-fed coining presses.

And a coupon stating:

> Please enter my subscription for *Por-
> traits of Greatness*, consisting of fifty
> finely sculptured portrait medals honor-
> ing the great Americans who have guided
> our nation in its rise to world leader-
> ship—as personally chosen by Dr.
> Henry Kissinger.
> No payment is required at this time.

Even Belle thought this contemptible. A society in which such a
blithering hypocrite was lionized as a celebrity instead of shunned
and despised was a society not worth its salt, and Gold promised
he would say so when he outlined to Pomoroy his plans for *The
Little Prussian.* He swore he could not understand why anyone but
a book reviewer would want to read the laundered memoirs of a
man whose actions of moment were already on the record in glaring condemnation, or why anyone but an obsequious clod would
spend a dime to own a copy; while if every tenth person with a
distaste for Kissinger bought a copy of Gold's book, he would
outsell his rival by millions.

Pomoroy was undecided about the commercial expectations in Gold's presentation but agreed to accept a book on Kissinger in place of one on the Jewish experience in America, since the research was practically complete. When Gold had trouble reconciling himself to the incredible situation of hustling a book while awaiting a call to high office, he remembered that Kissinger was doing exactly the same. In a novel no one would believe it.

"Kissinger will die when he reads it," Pomoroy said, looking no gloomier than ever.

Gold thought that might hurt sales. What pissed Gold off most now about the sly *schmuck*, apart from his coveted fame, was the plentitude of jobs from which he apparently could feed as hoggishly as he wanted, while Gold, on tenterhooks, still starved for only one.

"Why don't you get Pugh Biddle Conover to use his influence?" Ralph had suggested. "It would make things easier."

"Why can't you get your father to use his influence?" Gold complained to Andrea when he returned to Washington to fuck her again and act on Ralph's advice. "I bet that would make things easier."

Andrea responded keenly. "We'll go see him tomorrow. They must owe him something."

They owed Pugh Biddle Conover, as Gold learned by eventide of the ensuing day, a great deal, for the esteemed career diplomat had lied under oath seventeen times under five consecutive administrations and was venerated by all political factions in Washington for such evenhanded altruism.

"**C**OME in, my lad, come in, come in," Pugh Biddle Conover sang out with phenomenal gusto from his souped-up wheelchair when his eyes fell on Gold. "I'm so sorry to see you. I have been praying almost daily that one or the other of us would be dead before it was necessary to meet again. You are touched by my sentiments. I can tell by your tears."

Sickening presentiments of the mortification that impended clouded Gold's hopes. He looked toward Andrea for inspiration.

"You must be much nicer, Daddy," she said, cupping her father's trim, courtly face in her hands from behind for a moment.

"I'm feeling poorly, my pet," Conover answered with a devilish smile, fairly bursting with vigor and health. "I was feeling fine until he walked in."

"That's the kind of joke, Daddy," said Andrea, "he may not understand."

"Enjoy your ride, my darling, and put your fears to rest. I promise we'll be as sportive as butterflies together while you're gone. By Jupiter, I swear I'll drink his fortune to the lees a hundred times if he fills my medicine cup to the brim and takes a spot himself." Conover dismissed her with a friendly wave.

Gold was glad to see her go. Appearing a foot or two taller with her riding crop, high boots, jodhpurs, scarlet dress coat, and black velvet hard hat, she seemed to embody a curious kind of emasculating sexuality that had set his teeth on edge. He thought of taking a riding crop to her buttocks that very night if her father did not suddenly prove more accommodating. Pouring whiskey from a decanter, Gold allowed his glance to roam past the panes of the French doors to the luxurious space outside and his thoughts to dwell upon himself as master soon of the gardens, driveways, stables, meadows, and woods through an orderly process of dynastic succession. His kids might benefit from the civilizing influence such short visits as he would allow them might have on their character. How the fuck would he meet the taxes and pay so many salaries?

"Enough?" he inquired with a secret smile when the large glass he was holding was filled practically to the top.

"A millimeter or two more and I'll be greatly in your debt," Conover replied politely with an astute look of amusement. "Don't mind if you spill a lot. I have money for more. Your health, you pig!" he shouted when Gold had brought him the glass of straight whiskey. He smacked his lips appreciatively after taking three or four tremendous swallows that had Gold watching as though stunned. "You've saved my life, you skunk. Once more you've given me cause for rejoicing, Goldstein—"

"Gold, sir."

"A thousand pardons for that unintentional slip, my friend. I would not offend you for the world. Today, dear Dr. Gold, it is my sincerest wish to see you thoroughly contented." Conover's trenchant look would have kindled mistrust in someone far more gullible than Gold with far less cause for suspecting the presence of evil intentions. "There is something you want from me today, isn't there?"

"I would not have intruded on you otherwise," said Gold in a manner both entreating and refined.

"Then speak freely, my friend. What is it you wish me to do for you, Sammy?"

Gold sighed heavily as another unavoidable debacle appeared in the making. "Samuel Adams," he said. "Samuel Clemens, Samuel Morse, Uncle Sam, Samuel Johnson."

"But the earliest known appearance," countered Conover with laughter that was mellifluous and foxy, "is in the Book of Samuel in the Old Testament. And that Samuel was anything but a Johnson, wasn't he?" Conover was seized with a mild fit of coughing.

Gold refilled his empty glass. "You've taken a number of our very best names from us," said Conover, "but Sammy is not among them. Sidney, Irving, Harold, Morris, Seymour, Milton, Stanley, Norman—all of them noble, all no longer ours."

"Abraham Lincoln," said Gold in spirited rebuttal. "Aaron Burr, Joseph Conrad, and Daniel Boone. Isaac Newton, Benjamin Harrison, Jonathan Swift, and Jesse James."

"Henry," returned Conover, "was the name of English kings. William was a conqueror and Harold the king he vanquished at Hastings. Now every Ikey, Abe, and Sammy goes around called Henry, Bill, and Bernard. We had a saint named Bernard. Now it's a name for dogs. I worked a while with your Henry Morgenthau and your Bernard Baruch. Your Bernie Baruch was an adviser to Presidents, but none of them listened. I've met many like that from all walks of life over a long period, and I've found that not one was as good a person as I was, or thought so either. If I were you, Goldilocks, instead of trying to ape me I would make it a point always to present myself as Jewish since you'll never get by as anything else."

Gold felt the blood rush to his face. "I don't have to take this from you, you know," he said with quiet rage, drawing himself up ostentatiously.

"Yes, yes, you do," said Pugh Biddle Conover, "if you want to get anything from me today, even food for lunch. I may even take the Porsche away from Andrea and make you walk back. I often wonder, Neiman Marcus, why anyone with brains and self-respect wants to be as shallow and unproductive as someone like me. Why should it trouble you for a second if I find you detestable? But I am boring you. I can see it in your eyes."

"Not at all," Gold answered very weakly. "It bothers me only," he lied, "because I'm going to marry your daughter. And because you have the influence, perhaps, to be of service to us with my career in government."

His host nodded affably, his shrewd eyes sparkling. "The first makes no difference to me. I am beyond prejudice, as you've surely noticed. You will never be invited here, and I hope I may always feel free never to come to your house. The help I would give you anyway, just to minimize the blot on my family tradition once you become part of it. It's not merely because you're Jewish that I don't like you, Kaminsky. I don't like you because you're human. Mankind stinks, Hymie, and Western mankind stinks no less foully than all the rest. You are not among the individuals, it pains me to note, whom I would judge among the exceptions. I can think of a number of gifted Jews I've admired, but I've never met any of them, which is all to their credit. It's the people who come seeking me out I can't stand, because I know they want something. Although I must confess, my dear Manishevitz, that I've never met anyone I've liked but a rich Protestant."

"Harris Rosenblatt?" suggested Gold with confidence.

"That Jew?"

Gold was pushed off stride. "He thinks he's a German."

"What's the difference?"

"It made a huge and very tragic difference not too many years ago," said Gold with sincerity.

"It makes none to me now," answered Conover. "Harris Rosenblatt is a stuffy fool." With a pleased smile playing about his face, Conover lowered his pink lids a moment and chuckled in a way that rankled, as though nourishing his spirit on a ruthless and invigorating recollection. "He's bringing his daughter up to be a Protestant, giving her riding lessons and other things like that, which he mistakenly believes will elevate her in class and add to her physical attractiveness. He's thinking of changing her name. To Blatt." He paused again, seized with a fit of choking laughter, and held his glass out for more. Conover drank deeply until his hilarity had subsided and his voice was restored. "I told him—I told him I'd be honored if he changed her name to mine, and he promised he would. That idiot. Does he really think I'd be honored if he named that little Jewgirl after me? But I pray you—don't misunderstand. I wish him luck. I wish him joy. I wish he fathers a baby boy."

Gold started as though stuck. His tone was icy. "I am pleased to see, sir, that your memory and taste for juvenile doggerel and inscription have not grown smaller since our last meeting."

Conover looked up at Gold from his wheelchair with complete surprise. "What are you talking about, young man?"

"You were speaking in rhymed verse."

"When?"

"Just now." There began to creep over Gold the feeling that he was an unwilling participant in an ominous hallucination.

Conover obviously was no longer entertained. "Have you gone mad?"

Gold floundered defensively. "A minute ago," he sputtered. "You do it all the time. Don't you realize?"

"I do no such thing, sir," Conover informed him. "I was discussing our acquaintance in common, Harris Rosenblatt, and expressing the hope that he fathers a boy. And when his boy has grown some curls, I hope he has a pair of girls. He shot a dog of mine last week, you know," Conover recalled with a flush of pleasure.

"He shot a dog?" Gold inquired numbly.

"Yes, he did." Conover was quaking again with a wheezing laughter, almost doubling over. "One of my favorite hounds, a gorgeous animal. I told him it was the custom after a good hunt to pick out the dog who had performed best and kill it. As an act of humility. And then I gave him his choice."

Gold gazed at him in fascinated horror. There had been times in the past when he'd found himself considering human beings he believed he could, in clearest conscience, put to death on the spot with his bare hands—the first ten fashion designers, for example, whose names appeared in the newspapers, or the next six interior decorators—but never in memory had he found himself within arm's reach of someone toward whom that temptation for homicide had been restrained by so frail a doubt.

"And he shot it?"

Conover nodded merrily. "In the head. Blew it to pieces with his shotgun. That fatuous fool. He can look thirty years ahead with his municipal bonds but not six inches in front of his face when it comes to caste. It will take at least three generations and much genetic good fortune for any of his descendants to pass. What does his wife look like?" Conover cocked his head with a cruel light filtering into his face. "Anything like a Hebress?"

"There's no such fucking word," Gold responded quietly, deciding there was nothing to forfeit by reacting with anything less than true emotion to the persistent goading of his skilled tormentor. "She does look Jewish, if that's what you mean."

"Then it will take at least four. You know, Dr. Gold—may I call you Doctor? Your co-religionist Henry Kissinger didn't seem to mind, but he was a German too, wasn't he?—but I digress. I was brought up to consider myself superior to most people, and nothing in life I've experienced has caused me to question that premise. So tell me, Lehman Brothers, why should I have to pretend I enjoy someone like you when I don't?"

Gold saw they were quite alone. "To save your life," he answered, putting both hands around the old man's neck and squeezing.

"That's the only good reason I've ever been given," said Pugh Biddle Conover in a much huskier voice after Gold had released him, gently rubbing his flesh where he had been hurt. "Tell me, my good friend, do you like niggers? I have three or four hundred working for me here and I don't care to learn the name of a single one. How many blackamoors do you number among your closest friends?"

The answer was none. "But that doesn't mean I feel they should be discriminated against."

"Nor do I feel that I should be discriminated against," said Conover. "If you want the right to avoid the close association of Negroes, why should I not have the right to keep myself distantly removed from people like you, if I choose to find you just as inferior and distasteful as you find them? And I do choose, Goldman, Sachs, Bache, Halsey, Stuart, and all the rest. The fact is that I want nothing to do with any Jews but my doctor, lawyer, dentist, accountant, bookkeeper, secretary, broker, butcher, travel agent, tailor, business partner, realtor, banker, financial manager, best friend, and spiritual adviser. One thing I like about all you Jews but Kissinger is that you've kept out of foreign policy because we wouldn't let you in. Did he really get down on his knees and pray with that Nixon? What a ludicrous picture. Kissinger on his knees with his head bowed and his hands pressed together devotionally. We laughed here for months. Do Jews always kneel when they pray? I thought they merely whimpered."

"I wouldn't know," Gold said tersely. "I don't pray."

"You're praying today, though, aren't you?" Conover retorted in mockery. "What position in government are you praying for?"

"Secretary of State," said Gold.

"Oh, I could get that one for you easily," Conover laughed softly. "But I'm not sure I will. Let's think about it seriously during lunch. Lunch should be stimulating. I always eat alone."

Gold ate by himself in a stupor. This time the pickings were slim: a pastrami and lettuce sandwich on white bread with mayonnaise and salt butter and a container of milk served with a straw. There was not a grain of doubt in Gold's mind that it was a diabolic intelligence of infinite capabilities that was toying with him.

The infamous repast concluded, Gold hid with his face in his hands in a corner of the garden until Andrea had returned from her ride and, after showering, was again attired in the dress and shoes in which she was once more feminine, familiar, gorgeous, and dull. She little suspected that her riding days were numbered. Gold was determined to put a stop to that recreational activity the day they married and did not question his ability to crush her spirit if need be and have her driveling in psychotherapy in a matter of months. Andrea often moved gracelessly, bumping into the corners of furniture with her unthinking lurches, and her knees were usually black and blue.

"I'm a Sagittarius," she explained.

Gold's response to this information had been saintly: he pretended he was deaf as a post. She had a habit of leaving things behind forgetfully that was no longer nourishing to his sense of virility and maturity and soon might grow maddening.

She could tell in a glance that his mood was embittered.

"He doesn't like me, Andrea. He just won't approve of me because I'm Jewish."

"How did he find out?"

"Someone must have spilled the beans," said Gold in a voice that had never been drier.

"We'll tackle him together," said Andrea. "He'll be like an angel if he's had lots of wine."

If color of flesh were proof, Conover had steeped himself in casks, for his face and forehead were ruddier than ever when, with deafening blares from his Klaxon, he came careening around through the doorway of the drawing room in his motorized wheelchair and braked to a halt in a squealing stop that left rubber skid marks on the parquet floor. His manner was jaunty and his eyes fairly bubbled with excellent and insane spirits. Gold noted enviously that the accomplished epicure had changed from fitted tweed to a brown velvet blazer and had doffed his knotted neckerchief for a blue silk foulard that absolutely gleamed. Gold could not conceal from himself the dream that someday he might look and dress exactly that way.

"Ahoy, my children, halloo, halloo, halloo," he was hailing heartily even before he zoomed into view, balancing an emptied brandy snifter in one palm precariously. "How I long for the sight of my dear ones. Zounds and by thunder, what a pity they're not here. Andrea sweet, you must never, never again leave me alone with this sweating mute. I believe he comprehends. I can tell by his sagging jaw. I swear, it's a day's work to extract a syllable from him. And he wouldn't give me any medicine." Here Conover's tone of buoyant admonition gave way to one of feeble complaint, and Gold could see he was in for another difficult time.

Andrea was not taking him seriously. "I'll get some."

"Let Schwartz do it. He wants to make a good impression. Tell me again what brings you here and what you want me to do."

"We're waiting for a government appointment," said Andrea, twisting flirtatiously a strand of her father's hair. "And Bruce thought—"

"Bruce," laughed Conover.

"Bruce thought," Andrea pushed on gamely, "you might know people with influence who could speed things up."

"It was clever of you to sense that, Mr. Wise," said Conover as Gold approached.

"The name is Gold, sir. Bruce Gold. Whether you approve of that or not. And I'd be oh so grateful if you would make some effort to keep that in mind. After all, at least a minimum of civility is prescribed even between people who dislike each other."

Conover rested his gaze upon Gold for a minute as though seriously considering the application of those words and said:

"There are gold ships and there are silver ships, but the best ship is friendship. Your health, you frog. Let us both thank God we'll never sail together. Ah, now my mean spirits are banished. Ask anything, my lad, and I could not find it in my bountiful heart to refuse. Please continue, honest Abe."

Gold was suddenly too stubbornly proud to say a word.

"We thought there must be many, many people in government for whom you've done things, Daddy," Andrea cajoled seductively, fondling her father's hand and brushing her cheek across his neck. "Aren't there people who owe you something?"

Mere mention of that supposition mellowed Conover like a charm. They owed him, as he recounted, a great deal.

"Ah, yes indeed, at least seventeen times that I can remember I lied in public under oath," he repeated languidly, shaping the vowels in his honeyed accents and rolling the words around on his tongue like a connoisseur tasting a fine cigar. "And that's not just an old man's boasting. I'll take my oath on it. I can show you the evidence—scrolls, plaques, certificates, wreaths, sashes, and medals, all commending me for public service and my valorous, unselfish attitude. I lied to the public to protect the President and I lied to the President to protect myself and my colleagues, and I lied to the Congress four times a year just to keep from growing rusty, and do you know something? I never lost even a modicum of respect among my peers for doing so or a single friend. The difference between crime and public service, my good Goodgold, is often mainly more a matter of station than substance. Yes, they do owe me much. Four cabinet positions, in two different administrations, of course. Ambassadorships? One European ambassadorship, four Latin American, sixteen Asian, and four hundred and thirty-three African. They owe me six judicial appointments to lower courts anywhere in the South or Chicago, and the right to six trial balloons each for any eight people I choose as serious candidates for the Vice Presidential nomination, but in four successive elections. I suppose I'll be long gone before I've time to use them all, and I've forgotten whether or not I'm allowed to pass them on with my estate. I'll have to check with my Jew law firm—my Christian ones are not much good at law. You can look into it for me, Abie, if you want to, but spare my Irish Rose, hey, hey. 'Black bottom, the niggers got 'em.' They don't write songs like that any more, do they? Frankly, I don't much care about these appointments or even what happens to the country, as long as my capital is safe. I've been able to sell off two of the serious-Vice Presidential-candidacy-considerations recently, one of them, I believe, to a wide receiver for the Houston Oilers, whatever that is. Would you like to have yourself mentioned six times as a prospect for the Vice Presidential nomination in the next Presidential election campaign. Rappaport, as a going-away present, if only you'll go away? As God is my witness, I pray you will not let being a little sheeny inhibit you, you kike. I hear they're giving mentions now to coons, Greeks, dagos, spics, and women. Would you go in public like a beggar with your hat in your hand merely to appear to be under consideration for the Vice Presidential nomination with a long line of other humble mendicants, or for a Cabinet job you'll be leaving in disgrace or disgust in two years? I refused. I don't lower myself to people I feel superior to. I liked your Abe Ribicoff for that, but not for anything else. Would you like to be mentioned for Vice President next time? I'll let you have it free. If nothing else, it will bring you invitations to homes in which your attendance will be cause for greater rejoicing than your presence is here. Be a good fellow, Felix Mendelssohn, and fill up my medicine cup one more time. God, how sick I am by now of all those Guggenheims and Annenbergs and Salomon brothers. When you've met one Schlesinger you've met them all. Faster, can't you? Jump, dammit. I've got darkies from the delta that move faster than you do. 'Oh, darling, how my heart grows weary.' Aaaah, thank you, my savior. They say that Jesus was a Jew, but frankly I have my doubts. May your life follow an everlasting circle of success, and be like driven snow. Be careful how you tread it, for every mark will show. Your health, Brendan.''

''My name,'' said Gold, ''is Bruce.''

''An old Gaelic name, if I am not mistaken.''

''You are mistaken,'' Gold corrected. ''But there are people who argue that the Gaels are one of the lost tribes of Israel.''

''But not very convincingly,'' scored the venomous old man

neatly. "I won't come to your wedding, you know, although I suppose some prenuptial amenities are in order. I will want the members of your family to dine here first, including your wife, of course. She'd be most welcome. And I, in turn, I suppose, will have to journey for a dinner with your family somewhere in Brooklyn, I fear. I've never in my whole life been in Brooklyn. One time I could have been the candidate for Vice President, but it was understood I would have to go into Brooklyn with Nelson Rockefeller during the campaign to some place called Coney Island and eat a hot dog while news photographers took pictures. I wouldn't go anywhere to eat with Nelson Rockefeller. He made loans to people who never paid him back. If his brother David did that I wouldn't keep any money in his bank. He gave fifty thousand dollars secretly to Henry Kissinger. Imagine—for fifty thousand dollars then you might have bought a small Klee or Bonnard or a large Jackson Pollock, and all he got for his money was a medium-sized Kissinger. You know the type? Of course you do—look who I ask. A noisy, babbling fellow who was always trying too hard to be entertaining and made war like a Nazi."

Here even Gold's sense of fair play was affronted. "Sir!" he could not forbear from objecting. "A number of his relatives, I believe, were destroyed by the Nazis."

"But he wasn't, was he?" Conover answered serenely with acid in his voice. "And neither were you. How far do you think he would have gone in the world as a history student in Germany if Hitler had allowed him to remain? You wish to champion him, Silver? For shame!"

"Gold, sir, and for God sakes—please don't put me in the position of defending the one person on earth I disapprove of most."

"What do you suppose Rockefeller saw in him, Brass?" Conover asked in a musing way. "We know about Nixon and that chimpanzee Ford. But I thought Nelson had some brains at one time. He went to Brown, didn't he?"

"Dartmouth."

"Oh. I wasn't given that Vice Presidential nomination, by the way, and neither was Nelson Rockefeller. It went, if I recall, to Henry Cabot Lodge, who did travel to Coney Island to eat a hot

dog but lost anyway. Henry Cabot Lodge was never very successful at anything, and neither were the Ellsworth Bunkers in Vietnam, or the Graham Martins. If you want good advice, my lad,
you'll stay out of the diplomatic corps and the foreign service
community. It's an undergraduate society for backward students
who crave honors. If you ever call me Dad or Father even once,
Golddust, I warn you now—I'll put a ball between your eyes."

"You're babbling, Daddy," Andrea said.

"I'm sick, darling. It's not every day I have to put up with
someone like him. My boy, if ever you are lost at sea, drop right in
and think of me."

"We're going to be married, Daddy," Andrea told him with a
seriousness of purpose that filled Gold with admiration, "whether
you like the idea or not."

"And change your name to Gold? I'll drain my glass to that, my
lad, and give you what expert advice I can. You must never call
me Dad, Father, Governor, Squire, or m'Lord. And learn this
again, my boy, before you grow old, that learning is better than
silver and goldsmith. By thunder, *that* was her name—Gussie
Goldsmith! My first love." The most extraordinary change came
over Conover's face with this exclamation of surprise, and he continued as though in the loveliest of reveries. "Fill my cup, my son.
My heart wells with emotion. My eyes brim with tears. I am
flooded with sweet memories. A Jewish girl she was, a rather
pretty Jewish girl from an old Southern family in Richmond, Virginia, with strong family connections in Charleston, South Carolina. Ah, Gussie Goldsmith. A little odd as a person, I realized
even then, but I was smitten. We were both so very young. She
loved to knit and sew."

Gold could hardly believe his ears when he heard the conversation going off on such a tangent. "That would hardly apply to
Andrea and me, sir," he said. "I think it safe to say that both of us
are mature enough to know what we are doing."

"I cannot say she cared for me at all," said Conover. "But I
was so deeply infatuated, more deeply in love than I've ever been
with any woman since, including your mother, my dear. I was
ready to give up all, despite her constant knitting and sewing and

an unusually morbid fascination she took in funerals and burial plots. How I dreaded the day that I would have to face my family with the news that the girl I had resolved to marry was Jewish. I did not know if I had mettle enough to handle it."

"It must have been an exceedingly severe test for you," said Gold.

Pugh Biddle Conover chuckled regretfully. "I never had to face it. Her family thought themselves too good for *me*. I wept when we parted, I shed tears. And you see, I haven't forgotten her. Ah, crazy, sweet Gussie Goldsmith. With her wool and her knitting needles. At our last meeting I begged her to write something tender for me that I promised to cherish always, and I remember those last words from her as clearly as if they were written yesterday. 'There is a word in every language, in every heart so dear. In English it's forget me not, in French *la souvenir*.' I see her knitting still. I wonder what became of her."

Gold was irritated in the awkward lull that followed the revelation of these tedious sentimental recollections and counted on Andrea to return the conversation to its original purpose.

"Bruce—" Andrea began after a fitting interval of decorum.

"Bruce," Conover snorted.

"—is getting a government appointment," Andrea persevered. "Perhaps in the State Department. We want you to expedite it if you can and make sure it's a good one so that we can marry in good fashion and be treated well afterward. I know you want me to be happy."

"I will comply with dispatch," Conover assented agreeably, "if it will take him out of my life. But you must promise me one thing in return. You must promise that if you ever have children and they look anything like him, they will not be brought up in the Christian faith. Elope and I'll add ten million to your wedding present. Wait, I have a better idea. Don't elope. Gold, my son, you must send me the names and addresses of all in your family so that I can contact them by mail." He laughed with huge delight. "I can just imagine what some of those names will turn out to be." Had Gold a bread knife at hand he might have plunged it into the chest of the gloating old villain. Instead, Conover slipped another stiletto into his. "I think I'll have Sambo here call out their names as, arm in arm, they approach my staircase."

So graphically did this depicted scene burn itself upon Gold's imagination—"Mr. and Mrs. Julius Gold." "Dr. and Mrs. Irving Sugarman." "Mrs. Emanuel Moscowitz." "Mr. and Mrs. Victor Vogel"—that he knew immediately it could never be enacted. He paid almost no attention to the rest of Pugh Biddle Conover's words.

"Stay for dinner, Andrea, and let him drive back alone. We can geld some colts for breakfast tomorrow. I've got some beauties. Let him take the Volkswagen. Or maybe he'd prefer a camel."

Gold chose the Volkswagen over the camel and headed toward Washington in a dazed state of moral collapse. How much lower would he crawl to rise to the top? he asked himself with wretched self-reproach. Much, much lower, he answered in improving spirit, and felt purged of hypocrisy by the time he was ready for dinner.

He sallied forth into the Hotel Madison after showering and dressing, saw the price of the snails *forestier*, and felt as small as one. He was out of place and understood with potent prescience that he always would be. Amidst all the people filling the crowded, bustling dining room he was "solitary as an oyster," in that unique simile of Charles Dickens, a long winded novelist, in Gold's estimation, whose ponderous works were always too long and always flawed by a procession of eccentric, one-sided characters too large in number to keep track of, and an excessive abundance of extravagant coincidences and other unlikely events. Gold had still not recovered fully from the strain to which he had been subjected, and took but spiritless notice when perhaps the longest shadow in the universe crept across his table almost a full minute and a half before the figure casting it arrived and halted. For a second, Gold had the impression that Harris Rosenblatt had grown into the tallest, straightest, strictest human being walking the face of the earth. His complexion now was Saxon white. The expression bearing down on Gold in silent greeting was permanently mapped by hard and rigid lines, and the voice that spoke was edged with flint.

"I have time for only a quick drink," Harris Rosenblatt sternly said with an efficiency of manner that left Gold feeling he was the one who had intruded, and then, frowning attentively before he seated himself, scoured the room darkly with the look of someone incessantly watchful who knows in his bones that fearful things are abroad. "People were saying very good things about you in the Treasury Department today, Bruce, very good things about your report on the work of the Presidential Commission."

"They like my report?"

"I like it too, though I haven't read it. You're to be congratulated. Everyone speaks well of it."

"Harris, I never wrote a report," said Gold.

"That's the kind of report I like best," said Harris Rosenblatt. "No waste."

"Even though I said nothing?"

"As a result, nobody's criticizing you. If you said nothing, you said it well, and that speaks well of you."

"Harris, I've just got back from Pugh Biddle Conover's. Did you really shoot a dog last weekend?"

"Indeed I did." Harris Rosenblatt grinned proudly as he made the admission. "It is an old custom among us horsemen and hunters to shoot your favorite dog after a successful outing. It's a discipline against pride and trains us to attach less importance to our material possessions."

"How does it do that?" inquired Gold.

Harris Rosenblatt gave thoughtful consideration to the question before replying. "I don't know."

"Harris, know any ways I can make a lot of money quickly without doing any work for it?"

"It would be unethical for me to say."

"Unethical to tell me or unethical to say you know any? Which is it?"

Harris Rosenblatt said, "I don't know. But I have inside news that you can use for your personal profit if you want to. The government will have to try to balance the budget or it will rue the day."

Gold was adrift. "How can I use that for my personal advantage?"

"I don't know."

"Harris, you're in bonds. We had a Secretary of the Treasury not long ago, William E. Simon, who earned somewhere between two and three million dollars a year working in municipal bonds before he came into government. What in the world can a person do in municipal bonds that makes him worth two or three million a year?"

"I really don't know."

"What do you make?"

"Two or three million a year." Harris Rosenblatt stood up. "I must go now. How is Lieberman these days?"

"Still a *grubba*, still a *zshlub*."

"I don't understand Yiddish," Harris Rosenblatt told Gold at once, "and any words I may have known as a child I have forgotten. Although," Harris Rosenblatt continued in a softer tone with a kind of confiding geniality, "I used to be Jewish, you know."

"I used to be a hunchback."

"Isn't it amazing," exclaimed Harris Rosenblatt in a glad cry, "how we've both been able to change!"

GOLD was feeling solitary as an oyster again at the family dinner he swore would be the last he was ever going to attend, even before Sid entangled him in Isaac Newton with a simple restatement of the innocuous proposition:

"A force exerted in one direction produces a reaction of equal force in the opposite direction."

"Says who?"

"Sir Isaac Newton," Sid answered blandly.

"Sure," said Victor.

"It's one of his laws of motion," said Ida.

"His third," said Belle.

"Even I know that," said Muriel.

Gold's thoughts had been concentrated on the looming dissolution of his marriage and he was quite unaware until he found himself in the middle of this circle of derision that his was the voice that had taken Sid's gambit.

"Wait a minute." Gold was mildly flustered. "What was it you said, Sid? Now don't change it. Just repeat it."

"A force exerted in one direction produces a reaction of equal force in the opposite direction. My, oh my, Harriet—is this chopped liver good. It's the best you ever made."

"I went back to the old butcher."

Gold evaluated Sid's words carefully and was profoundly dejected. "Is that what you said before? Sid, you didn't change anything?"

"Why should I change Sir Isaac Newton?" Sid's was a look of unspotted honesty as he mopped his dish with a piece of bread. "It's as clear as E equals MC square."

Gold gave up inelegantly. "I'd rather not hear any more about Sir Isaac Newton."

"That was Albert Einstein." Sid could not keep from laughing.

"Sure," said Victor.

Gold was thankful his father was not yet there. He was in a quandary about Belle: he had not the knack for facing her with his decision, and decided to have his lawyer break the news he was going after he'd gone. Next came his mission with Milt, who wanted Esther to marry him. Gold, drawing Milt aside, plumbed his mind in a minute or two and sent back assurances through Harriet by way of Ida that Milt was pure of salacious expectations and owned a modesty of person as great as her own.

"I'll soon be seventy, Bruce," Milt said, stammering. "And I've always been a bachelor. I just don't want to live alone any more. I don't think Esther wants to be alone, either."

Then his father arrived with Gussie and loaded the atmosphere like a charge of electricity. He was still in the week-old depression about which Gold had heard. His fuming sulk had been provoked by Gold, the egocentric old battler quickly disclosed—"It's him, what then?" his father snarled curtly when asked how he felt—and exacerbated by the boredom and spreading physical pains that were arriving with the coldness of encroaching winter. Twice already on successive days he had groused to Sid in the waning bad temper of defeat about the lack of a suitable home for him in Florida. In a way, Gold was sorry to see the lunging old bull coming to an end. Gold cracked his knuckles in suspense as he waited for whatever tempestuous grievances were steaming in the old man's emotions to come bursting forth.

For one thing, Julius Gold, like Pugh Biddle Conover, did not take kindly to the notion of Jews in public office. "Why should it be a Jew that's blamed when they're caught or make their mistakes?" For another, he was irate with the knowledge of Gold's visit to Conover's estate. "A fascist he was, and anti-Israel, always. Name one." Clambering to his feet in anger, Gold's father

warmed rapidly to the attack and was as fiery as a burning coal.
"Go ahead, Mr. Smart Guy. I dare you."

"One what?" pleaded Gold.

"One millionaire who ever amounted to anything. You tell me
when."

"When what?"

"Don't what me—I'll give you what, you dummy. You tell me
when the name Rockefeller even became respectable. Or Morgan
even, that J. P. Morgan with the purple nose on his lap was a
midget. I remember when people would spit and turn away at such
names. Even Senators from the West. And now you go riding on
horses with someone like Conover. Hey, Jew—where do you
come to horses? Since when does a Jew ride a horse? When did
you learn how to ride with a horse?"

"I didn't ride."

"Who got you there?"

"I was invited," said Gold in a contrite tone, his own resentful
wrath failing him disastrously each time it was his turn to reply.
"By someone who knows him. He can be of help to me."

"With what?" cried Julius Gold, his cheeks blowing and con-
tracting. "Just remember, sonny boy. You lie down with dogs, you
get up with fleas."

"If you ever forget you're a Jew," said Gussie Gold in a tone of
stately rebuke, "you can rest assured that a gentile like Conover
will remind you."

"They know it, for God sakes," Gold replied to her, "and they
accept me there for what I am."

"Yeah?" said his father. "And what are you? You going into
government with them? As what?"

"As Secretary," said Gold, in a voice falling lower with embarrassment, "of State."

The old man wound his face up into an expression of disgust and
asked, "What kind of job is that for a Jewish boy? Sid here worked
with the horses at the laundry when he had to, but he stopped
when he could. He didn't ride them. You tell me what business a
Jew has in government here. You name me one Jew who ever went
into government who was any good."

Gold's memory went into a state of temporary paralysis when challenged by this difficult question. "Brandeis and Cardozo," were the best he could produce. "And Felix Frankfurter."

"They were forty years ago," his father jeered. "And those were judges. I mean in government."

"Herbert Lehman?"

"A hundred years ago. And he was first a Governor and then a Senator, dumbbell, and he was not so hot either. You name me one Jew who ever worked for a President who wasn't a disgrace to the government and a disgrace to the Jews." None came to mind right then. "And all those Christians ain't so hot either, you know. Even that bastard Roosevelt. Ten thousand Jewish babies he wouldn't let into the country, they went to the fires instead. A cripple he was. With a limp he walked and didn't want we should know, that liar." An unexpected smile flickered anomalously beneath the old man's expression when he rested for breath, and he uttered a single croupy chuckle. "A cripple," he observed, with a more human note stealing into his voice, "is always good for a laugh."

Gold could be confident that his were not the only sensibilities upon which these words fell with revolting effect. His own natural propensity for evil was not unknown to him, but he realized now that there were heights and depths of cruelty in thought that stretched outside even his most vengeful fantasies.

"Oh, Pop, that was awful," he said, shaking his head in grief and bewilderment. "That was really an ugly thing to say."

"And he was so beautiful Roosevelt with those crooked legs?" his father retorted with a renewal of rancor Gold found quite alarming. "It was pretty what he did to those Jews on that boat he wouldn't even let stop in this country, they had to go back to Germany? File and forget, he wrote on the letter, and he wouldn't even let them bomb the railroad tracks taking the people to the death camps. I know all this from my friends in Florida, and I believe them before you. And now you go showing off with a man like Conover? A Nazi, an anti-*Semitt*. Like Lindbergh, he was," Julius Gold went on. "Maybe worse than Henry Ford."

"Well, he's not that way now," Gold lied without a moment of indecision. "Things have changed. I've got an important friend in Washington who tells me there's no more anti-Semitism left. I think we're being accepted now, without any prejudice, and we're being assimilated."

"Yeah?" scoffed his father. "Who's doing the accepting and who's doing the assimilating? Not me. *A goy bleibt a goy,* the way I see it, and without Israel we got no one to protect us, because we don't know how to fight any more and they do. *You* assimilate. I tell you one thing—you ever bring any of your Conovers here and it's goodbye, Charlie. I'm going back to Florida for good."

"Give him a call," said Harriet to Gold. Her words, so blunt in import, were deafening in result.

"Find me a place, Sid," the old man said sorrowfully in a hoarse whisper after a long, loathing glance at Harriet, and hobbled with an effort to a chair. "Get me a condominium if you think I should have one." There was a terrible finality in the way he was drawing to his close. "And find me some different topic to talk. I'm tired of his twisted brain."

"I think," said Gold's stepmother, "that another screw has come loose."

The sight of his stepmother with her knitting needles awoke in Gold's mind a vague perplexity of association that glimmered elusively for an instant just a hairsbreadth away from recognition and then disappeared for all time when Sid said:

"I see by the papers today that they've discovered some language ability in the right side of the brain."

"The brain has two sides?" asked one of the sisters.

"Of course," said Sid with a superior benevolence that rubbed Gold the wrong way. "There are two sides to every question."

"The brain is not a question," Gold pointed out moodily without looking up.

"It's an answer?" said his father.

"There are two sides to everything," Sid explained directly to Gold, talking down.

"To everything?" Gold, with a delicious quiver of exultation, knew he finally had him. "This orange?"

"Of course," said Sid.

"Where are the two sides to this orange?"

"A top and a bottom," said Sid. "There are two sides to everything."

"A triangle?"

"An inside and an outside."

Gold announced then that he was leaving Sid's house and that he was never in his life attending another family dinner. Like Joannie, he would see them one at a time—maybe.

Politely he congratulated Esther and Milt again on their approaching nuptials.

He decided without a wrench to leave Belle the next day. Andrea would make good the loss. He had no doubt he would be disowned by his father, brother, and sisters and rejected by his children. The future looked bright.

IN THE morning he conferred with his lawyer.

"How much of your money do you want her to have?"

"None."

"I'm in favor of that."

"On the other hand, I want her and the children to have everything they're accustomed to and never have to worry."

"I may have to look for a loophole."

In the afternoon he went for his medical examination. Mursh Weinrock, smoking cigarettes like a smoldering mattress and waxing fatter and rounder even as the witnessing eye beheld him, consigned him to the inspection of the assistant now sharing his practice, a very serious, humorless young man who maintained the gravest silence for the longest time, riveting Gold in terror with implications of tragedy by the incomprehensible sobriety of his manner. The dire presentiments of fatal diagnosis spreading through Gold's mind began to assume a hundred different forms.

"When was the last time," the long-faced young physician inquired just when Gold felt he could endure the portentous atmosphere not one instant longer, "you had a bath?"

Gold rose from the undignified position he had been instructed to assume on his hands and knees, pulled up his underpants, dismounted from the examining table, slid into his trousers, and strode without knocking into the capacious, dark private office of Dr. Murray Weinrock.

"Did you tell him to ask me that?"

"What?"

"When was the last time I had a bath."

"That was pretty good." Weinrock laughed without noise, as though husbanding energy for more constructive employment elsewhere. "I knew he was a bright one."

"For Christ sakes, Murshie," Gold pleaded. "When the fuck do you find time to rig up these practical jokes? Can't we get on with it?"

Weinrock sent him next to Lucille for tests. The handsome black woman seemed out of temper.

"You been chasing around after the doctor's wife again, ain't you?" she muttered with a murderous scowl.

Before Gold could utter a denial, a young girl popped her head in to announce, "The sugar in his urine is very high."

As Gold stared over her shoulder, Lucille wrote: *Sugar. Low normal.* "The lab says you got high cholesterol in your blood." On her clipboard she wrote: *Cholesterol. Low normal.* She rose chuckling with a sidelong glance of deadly malevolence. "Well," she said, "I think I just killed me another one."

"Another what?"

"Another Jew. Get over there for the cardiogram. Take off that shirt before I cut it off. Get up on the table and lie down before I put you up there and knock you down. I mean, lay down."

"You meant lie down, Lucille. You talk better English than I do."

"Don't sass me. You been fucking the doctor's wife again, ain't you?" She was fastening the electrical connections as she spoke. "I knows you has, so don't lie."

"Oh, come on, Lucille, stop it. You're an educated woman, not a mugger."

"White motherfucker, don't shit me. I seen your urine filled up with all those dirty hormones. Lie still and relax or I'll put a knife in your chest. Uh-oh. There it goes. Ever had a heart attack?"

"No," said Gold, with a start.

"Bullshit. You had a heart attack and went to another doctor, didn't you?"

"I did not."

"You sure?"

"Why?"

"Lie back, bastard. Lie back and be calm, or I'll cut your throat. Ever had a stroke? You've had a stroke, then, haven't you? And went to another doctor, didn't you?"

"What the hell are you talking about?" shouted Gold.

"Look at those goddamned lines," Dr. Weinrock's nurse shouted back in a voice just as tumultuous. "You mean to tell me you never had a heart attack? Or a stroke?"

Murshie Weinrock looked in, alarmed. "What's going on?"

"He won't lie back. He keeps jumping up to look at the lines. He's worried about having a heart attack or a stroke."

Weinrock's bedside manner was a blend of petulance and cajolery. "Come on, Brucie, stop acting like a child. Let's finish the examination and see what's wrong. Now that you're becoming such an important man, I want to make sure you're healthy."

"What were you doing all those years before I became an important man?" Gold took him to task when he was fully dressed and back in the private office. "Weren't you making sure?"

"I really don't have time. You see how busy I am."

"Suppose I was really sick?"

"I wouldn't take you, Bruce," Dr. Weinrock answered with frankness. "Oh, I would never take on a patient who really needed help. I don't enjoy being around sick people. Now, let's see." He fell silent while intently perusing the data on Gold. "Much as I hate to admit it, I have to agree with the medical opinion of my lazy kid brother. Spotty says you're a prick."

"He tells me that about you."

"With me he's referring only to my narrow-minded, reactionary politics."

"Will I be able to—"

"You will be able to endure the anguish of power and the agony of power and to shoulder handily the burdens of office. Your cholesterol and uric acid are up, but not dangerously. Your blood nitrogen is high, but I don't worry about that, mainly because it's your blood nitrogen and not mine. The growth on your lung still doesn't show up in the X-ray. Your prostate is slightly enlarged, but so is mine. And, I see by the electrocardiogram—" he glanced up reprovingly—"that you're still fucking my wife."

"I can't keep away from her, Doctor."

"In short, you're falling apart rapidly at a healthy, normal rate. How are things at home?"

"Fine." Gold was relieved. "Belle's okay and I'm getting along pretty well with my kid Noah now and—"

"Noah?" Mursh Weinrock asked in a startled way.

"Yes. He's my oldest, and—"

"That's a terrible name to give a kid, Bruce."

"What?" Gold, pricking up his ears, could not believe he had heard him accurately.

"Really terrible."

Gold looked steadily at the large, owlish head of his physician a long time before replying. "We don't think so. He was named after my wife's father."

"It's not even Jewish."

"It's not?"

"Of course not. Noah came before Abraham, and Abraham was the first. Noah was a drunkard. Why'd you ever name your kid after a gentile drunk?"

"He doesn't mind," Gold said tartly. "Why don't you mind your own business?"

"Yes, he does."

"How do you know?"

"How do *you* know?"

"Mursh," Gold entreated urgently, on the spur of the moment, "maybe you can help me on this. Is there something about me, something in my makeup perhaps, that causes people to want to make fun of me? Is there something that inspires humor in others, am I of a type that encourages sport?"

Weinrock, leaning back with interlaced fingers on his belly, lowered his eyelids and looked wise. "Yes, Bruce, I'm afraid there is."

"What?"

"I don't know."

The moment for parting had come. Belle turned ashen for an instant when he reentered the apartment with the dazed air of a man who had lately experienced some indescribable tragedy.

"I'm okay," he reassured her faintly. "I just have to be very careful about what I eat. What's for dinner?"

"Calf's liver and bacon, with mushrooms, mashed potatoes, and sautéed onions."

"That sounds fine," said Gold. "No, not calf's liver. I have to watch my cholesterol."

"Is there cholesterol in bacon?"

"There's fat. I have to watch my weight too. And I don't think I can have mushrooms. I have to watch my uric acid."

"Are you sick?" Belle studied him with veiled concern.

"No, I'm in perfect health. I have to watch my blood pressure too."

"How do you do that?"

"He didn't say. Cut down on my salt, I guess."

"It seems to me," said Belle, "that you'd be better off if you were sick. You wouldn't have so much watching to do."

Gold did not like the sound of that but put back the bankbooks anyway and decided to live with her a little while longer.

GOLD found himself with an immense unwillingness to admit that the closer he drew to marrying Andrea and serving as Secretary of State, the deeper he fell into doubt that he wanted to do either. Andrea never helped with the dishes. She was not proving as malleable to his influence as he had formerly hoped, and there were salients of character that were going to prove resistant to even his most apostolic attempts at modification. He could tell from watching her with her father that she was a person who never did anything she didn't want to and always succeeded in doing everything she did. Thus far she was ever agreeable and obliging, albeit with an impassive emotional restraint that frequently evoked a stultifying spirit of futility and tedium. Sex with Belle for him by now had become largely a matter of routine. Sex with Andrea was also now a matter of routine, although the spectrum of experimentation was infinitely wider. In that area Andrea spoke with an experience and natural candor that were often quite shocking to Gold, and assented to proposals suggested by him in a bantering vein which he had not the weakest wish to carry through.

"You and your father," he said to her, "certainly seem to do a lot of touching, don't you?"

"Me more than him," she answered with no uneasiness. "I discovered when I was still a little girl that if I sat on men's laps and squirmed a lot, I would always get more attention. So I've been doing it ever since."

"You've been doing it ever since?"

"Yes, like this." She was already sitting on his lap, and Gold marveled at her lack of emotion as she demonstrated. "Ever since I was a child, I guess, I've always loved just about anyone with a prick, because I could see that's where all the power and action was. So I was always trying to hang around boys, and squirming and touching was a way they would let me."

Somehow Gold was able to rise and drift away from her without showing the extent to which he was once again affected by ideas that could not strike him as anything but warped and peculiar. "Andrea, you must not say things like that to people," he cautioned with overcompensating kindliness that disguised only thinly the disapproval she had evoked.

"Not even to you?"

"Well, maybe," he relented, not unmindful that he might be discarding a refreshing source of titillation, "just to me."

"I don't know things like that," she confessed gratefully. "I'm a Sarah Lawrence girl, even though I didn't finish there, and they always told me to speak the truth as I saw it. At Bennington, you know, we had this professor of art we used to keep score with. Three hundred and twenty-four of us fucked him in the two years he was there. I guess you fuck a lot of your students, don't you?"

"No," Gold contradicted her emphatically. "I do not."

"Never?"

"Graduate or undergraduate?"

"Either."

"Sometimes," he admitted. "Not for a long time. Hardly ever."

"At Smith," she added calmly, "we used to go after our fathers."

Gold had to swallow first. "Your fathers?"

"And that was much more fun."

Gold began wondering again to what kind of girl he was planning to be married. "I'm not sure I heard you correctly, dear. Your fathers?"

"Yes."

"Oh, my God," he said and put a hand to his head. "Who started that?"

"I was one of the first," she answered. "I almost got the senior achievement award for thinking it up."

"And your father?"

"He was one of the first. And always one of the best." Andrea read his mind suddenly with a gleeful cry. "Not our own fathers, stupid," she chided boisterously with a high-pitched laugh that was another one of the traits he no longer found as endurable as formerly. "That would be just awful."

"I was feeling something like that," Gold said wryly.

"We did it with each other's," she explained with condescending gaiety. "We played switch, Brucie. My father was always one of the easiest and always had the most fun. All I had to do was bring a friend home for the night and whisper to him that she thought he was sexy. After that he was a pushover. They all agreed he was an A fuck. I bet he still is. Don't your daughter's friends try to get down with you?"

"No," cried Gold.

"Oh, come on. I bet they do and you don't even know it."

"My daughter's friends, Andrea," he informed her with asperity, "are twelve and a half years old. There are certain areas, my dear, in which a minimum amount of reticence is normally desirable, and I think you are pouring your secrets out recklessly in one of them now."

"I disagree, Bruce," she told him easily with that inexorable strength of purpose he was coming to recognize and fear. "I know we're both going to do a lot of screwing around after we're married—"

"We are?" His astonishment clearly denoted he did not like that idea at all.

"What kind of marriage will it be if we don't?" she inquired.

"What kind of marriage will it be if we do?"

"An open, truthful marriage," she replied with a rapt earnestness, as though picturing for him the rosiest and most fulfilling of relationships. "And we'll have such interesting, funny stories to tell each other."

The mere idea of such an open, truthful marriage filled with daily conversations about what did you do to whom today was revolting to him, but he replied with what he felt was exemplary tact. "We'll have more to say about that before the wedding, darling."

"No secrets, Bruce, and nothing held back. I will tell you everything and I want you to tell me everything."

"I will tell you everything," he replied, taking her into his arms. "And if you want me to be honest, I will tell you now that I don't want to be told everything."

But it was the kitchen, rather than the bedroom, in which the forerunners of ineluctable incompatibility seemed most prolific. Gold could forgive a frigid woman, almost as readily as he could forgive a passionate one, but how long could he suffer with an excellent grace a woman who in the kitchen was essentially oblivious? In time there would be cooks and maids, but who would oversee them? With each passing week the dreadful thought was gathering in his head like a low-hanging cloud that she was not perhaps merely slothful and uninterested in certain areas of domestic responsibility but also stupid. Three times he'd been forced to expound on slab bacon for her enchanted edification—once when frying thick slices for eggs, once for French toast, and once while dicing pieces with shrimp and scallions for inclusion in the Chinese fried rice he served with the clams in black bean sauce he succeeded in cooking for her to absolute perfection—and she was absorbed hypnotically in each repetition as though he had not dilated on the subject of slab bacon to her before. By the third time he was irascible, not tickled, at the oddity in circumstance that found him, a Jew, dissertating to her on the esoteric virtues of slab bacon. She did not help clear the dishes after that meal either, and he did not deign to ask.

But it was the episode of the Estonian black bread that nearly took all the heart out of him.

"Darling, where's that big Estonian black bread I brought down last time? I've searched everywhere."

"I threw it out," she told him in innocence.

Into Gold's eyes there crept a look of alarm. "You threw it out?"

"It was getting hard."

"It was getting hard?" He listened in a sort of trance and gave a hollow laugh. "Darling it's supposed to get hard. That was just the outside slice that got hard."

"The crust was hard too."

"Darling, the crust is always hard."

"I didn't know that, darling."

"They bake such large loaves with a thick crust so they'll stay fresh for weeks, darling. Did you think we would eat a five-pound Estonian black bread in a day?"

"I'm sorry, darling." Andrea truly was penitent. "You know how weak I am on Eastern European home economics."

Stoically deciding to make the best of things, Gold reached for a packaged white bread and then unwittingly posed the question that gave the death blow to all blissful hopes for the future and transformed the character of their approaching marriage from one of love into one of convenience.

"Darling, have you any Tiptree Little Scarlet Strawberry Preserves?"

All Andrea could offer was a jar of jam with a supermarket label. Gold was aghast. I bring her Black Forest ham with Pommery mustard and the juiciest baked salmon, and she gives me shit. What the fuck was the matter with these people? Didn't they care about anything but riding horses and owning money? They ate California oranges when they could get Florida and did not seem to know that Comice pears were better than Seckels and Anjous. Hopelessness enveloped him like an enervating fog at the mere idea of trying to convince her that the difference between an ordinary supermarket jam and Tiptree Little Scarlet Strawberry Preserves lay at the essence of their chances for a happy union.

This was something Belle understood. "He's a gourmet and doesn't know it," Belle said with laughter many months back when they were still able to joke with each other. "He thinks he's just particular. I'd like to see one of these young girls please him for more than a week. It would take her ten years just to learn how. I'd like to see him even get one to try. When he asks for two-minute eggs he means three minutes. He wants his underwear ironed and thinks he doesn't. When we go out he takes longer to dress than I do. I'd like to see one of his college students figure out when he asks for rye bread with seeds whether he means caraway seeds or black seeds. When he asks for fish for dinner he usually wants liver and when he asks for liver he wants to eat out. God help you if you ever give him a California grapefruit. I feel sorry for any young girl who steals him away.''

Gold remembered Belle's speech with a smile. The only flaw he could find in her summation of him was her ingenuous belief that he was most likely to be captivated by the artifices of someone young. His friend in the suburbs, like Belle, was approximately his own age. Andrea, already asleep beside him, was past thirty-five, and he doubted he could ever be intrigued again by anyone younger. Belle had a faint mustache now, he recalled, and he smiled at this too.

Gold lay awake for an hour bemoaning his plight. His blessings were one with his tribulations: he was about to effectuate a painful divorce from Belle; he was about to enter into a painful marriage with Andrea, a woman at once submissive and weirdly independent, who both frightened and bored him; and he was about to embark on a vulnerable new career in government and politics whose fate, at least initially, would be largely dependent on the patronage and goodwill of an inhumanely selfish and malicious father-in-law who disliked him intensely and sadistically. And as though his life with all that were not sufficiently complicated, he tumbled head over heels into love the very next day with another woman almost his own age who was separated from a mountainous husband with a brutal temper and had four children: the eldest old and tall enough to beat Gold to a bloody pulp with his fists should that notion possess him, the next in age a girl worldly and pretty enough to seduce him should she choose to, and the youngest pair, twins of different sex, still tender enough in years for the tantrums, fevers, and digestive upsets and messes of early childhood that turn parenthood into an uncivilized nightmare.

The first in the series of events transporting him to this pass was a phone call from New York from Belle, who ought at least to have tried to cope with the crisis herself. Gold was stunned when he awoke in Andrea's bed and learned in routinely calling his hotel that there was an urgent message from Belle. His daughter Dina had been expelled from her school. The vixen had bitten him deep in the fleshy part of his leg, and at a most inopportune time.

GOLD was in a rage when he stormed into the office of the principal with newspaper clippings attesting to his probable emergence as a person of vast political influence. He pulled no punches because the reigning official was both a woman and a black.

"Your words," he began with a sputter and picked up velocity as he went along. "You'll have to change them. Don't you read the newspapers? I can't have a daughter of mine in trouble in school at this time. Either take her out of trouble or redefine your words so she's not in trouble, and that's it. *Fartig!* I'll ruin you. I'll cut off financial aid. I'll let the whole world know you're running a segregated, selective private school while pretending to be integrated and impartial."

The poor woman was shaken by his vehemence. "But, Dr. Gold, that isn't true. We're *known* as segregated and selective, although we secretly are integrated."

"Then I'll let the parents know you're integrated and drive all the whites away. You're after headlines, aren't you? That's the reason you're doing this, isn't it?"

"She's refusing to do homework. We can't very well lower our standards, can we?"

"That's progressive education," countered Gold. "And you can so lower your standards without harming or helping a single student. Read my piece called 'Education and Truth *or* Truth in Education.'"

"Dr. Gold," the woman tried futilely to explain, "if we keep her in and fail her, she'll be held back and you'll waste a full year's tuition. If she leaves there'll be nothing derogatory on her record and you'll receive a refund."

"How large a refund?"

"A fraction of the total."

"Keep her in."

"Dr. Gold, I'm sure you wouldn't want us to overlook our rules just to make an exception of your child."

"Why not?"

The woman could hardly have looked more surprised. "You would?"

"Yes. She is exceptional, isn't she?"

"In a recalcitrant, unproductive way."

"Good," said Gold. "Make an exception of her for that and treat it as experimental education. I'll do the homework for her if you attach that much importance to it."

They came to terms on that. In the anteroom outside the open door there awaited him with parted lips a pretty woman with ash-blond fluffed-up hair who hurried after him breathlessly and caught at his arm when he had gained the corridor.

"Dr. Gold, please," she said after bringing him to a stop. "I think it's so unfair. Your daughter is not an exception. And I think it's unjust for you and the administration to label her an exception."

"Who the fuck are you?" asked Gold.

"Linda Book," said the woman. "I'm one of Dina's teachers."

"You the one who's complaining?"

"Oh, no, Dr. Gold. I'm her favorite. We're very close friends and it hurts me to see her stigmatized as an exception. She's really so exceptional."

Gold looked into her sensitive gray eyes with the knowing interest of someone watching a new fish swim into his ken. He gave the softest gasp of appreciation when he realized that hers was probably the most beautiful face of a woman of his own approximate generation that he had ever seen. Her blouse and skirt were a bit on the shiny bright side, which was all to his taste, and she had good-sized breasts in a soft brassiere. A second later he knew he was on the very verge of falling in love with her, and he glanced at his watch to see if he had time.

"Ride downtown to my studio with me," he requested. "I want to talk longer with you."

"I have a class in five minutes."

"Cut it."

She appeared a bit flustered by his air of command. "At least," she said, "let me freshen up."

He waited downstairs in a cab for her and they fell immediately into an orgy of lubricious kissing that soared in ardor and noise until they arrived at his building. He was almost certain afterward that for a period of about a minute during the ride she had one foot on his shoulder. They were as formal and correct as rigid, weaving drunks in the lobby and elevator. As soon as his key turned in the lock she came at him again with the same famished voracity, and they resumed as passionately and calisthenically as before, with a lustful grinding of bellies and pelvic bones and a bruising banging of thighs and knees. He held her ass. She pulled his hair. He remembered to shut the door.

"I can't ball you today," she told him the moment they were inside, "but I give good head."

Actually, her head was only so-so, but Gold did not criticize and Gold did not care. Before the sun set that same day he learned that Linda Book was the easiest person to give his heart to that he'd ever met. Gold had this penchant for falling in love. Whenever he was at leisure he fell in love. Sometimes he fell in love for as long as four months; most often, though, for six or eight weeks. Once or twice he had fallen in love for a minute. Confident that this new attachment had no better chance of surviving than the others, he yielded himself to it completely. In the throes of romantic discovery, he told her all about Andrea, and much about Belle. In the freshness and exhilarating sweep of adventurous new feeling, he asked her to come with him secretly to Acapulco on his trip with Andrea, scheduled during her Christmas vacation, and she quickly agreed.

"I may have to bring two children."

"That's out of the question."

"I'll leave them with my husband."

"We may be followed," he thought it prudent to advise her, thinking of Greenspan.

"My husband wouldn't go that far," said Linda Book, "although he's desperate for a reconciliation. He hates being separated from me."

"Smart fellow," said Gold. "He'd be a fool to give you up."

Linda blossomed like a rose. "You know how to make a woman happy. But I must warn you now. I'll never want to marry you."

Gold could not find the right words for a moment. "The mold!" he cried at last. "They broke it! They broke the mold when they created you!"

IN THE cold light of morning he lingered over breakfast with his head in both hands, wondering what the fuck he had done.

SID gave Gold a check for thirty-five hundred dollars. Gold put the check in his pocket.

"I'll also need some advice, Sid, about Acapulco. I'm not really going for the government, and there'll be two of us."

Sid pursed his lips in consternation. "I'm not sure the places I mentioned are right for Belle."

"Not Belle, Sid. Belle and I are finished. We're not really together any more."

If Sid was distraught he hid it well. "How come I haven't heard?" he asked with only mild surprise. "The girls still talk to her, don't they?"

"I'm not sure she knows." This was growing to be an awkward confession to have to keep making. "I'm sort of hoping she'll catch on. There's this girl in Washington I'm engaged to secretly and want to marry."

"You're really in love, huh, kid?"

"Yeah, Sid, I am. But that's with a different one."

"You mean there are three?" Now Sid sat straight up and a look of keenest joy brightened his face.

Gold nodded sheepishly. "And there's also a Jewish FBI man named Greenspan who might still be checking me out for good character."

"Tell me something," Sid said after asking the waiter for another round of drinks. "Why aren't you marrying the one you're in love with?"

"Her husband wouldn't let me," said Gold. "He doesn't even like the idea of being separated. He's a big violent man with a savage temper and I mustn't let him find out."

"That's funny."

"She's got four kids."

"That's funnier." Sid was chuckling heartily. "Is she having her teeth capped?"

Gold answered with amazement. "How did you know?"

Sid merely smiled in a paternal way. Then he explained, "Every time I fell for a girl she decided she had to have her teeth capped."

"Linda's having just a couple. I offered to pay."

"Don't commit yourself for more."

Gold was again embarrassed. "Two of her kids need orthodontia," he confessed, "and I told Linda I'd help there too."

"Why are you marrying the one in Washington?"

"She's a lovely girl, Sid," Gold answered with persuasive feeling, "really nice, and her father can help me with his influence. There's money there and that might make it easier for me to help Linda with those dental bills."

"How's her teeth?"

"Good, Sid, good."

"Is she tall?"

"Very. With long legs and very strong bones. Healthy, and really quite a beauty."

"Then take her to Acapulco," Sid urged genially. "It sounds like you might have some fun."

"I'm going to, Sid," said Gold, "but there's the problem. I don't like to be away from Linda and I want to sneak her along too."

"What's the problem?" Sid asked.

"Is it possible?" asked Gold. "Can I really do something like that without getting caught?"

"Sure, it's possible," Sid assured him with zest and called for two more drinks. "I've got this friend in Houston I do business with who goes with this Mexican television actress who goes with this airline pilot who's married to this woman with the Mexican Tourist Bureau who can help with travel and hotel reservations."

"She may have to bring two of her kids."

"The more the merrier," Sid chortled, "if you can afford it. And a maid or baby sitter to take care of them so she's free nights."

"I hadn't thought of that. Sid, how can I hide so many people? Two hotels? Three?"

"One," answered Sid concisely.

"One?"

"Sure, one. It accounts for your being wherever you're seen and you don't waste time shooting back and forth. Please don't take offense, Bruce, but I think that maybe for the first time in my life I'm finally proud of my kid brother."

"And all this while," reminded Gold, thrilling a moment with the compliment, "there's this FBI man who might find out and ruin everything. By the way, what's she like?"

"Who?"

"That Mexican television actress," said Gold.

"Not bad, I hear, if you like them short, dark, shapely, and passionate. She goes off like a string of firecrackers, I'm told. And I always thought you were kind of stuffy. I never thought you had nerve for something like this."

"Sid, I don't," Gold decided, wilting. "I'm going to call it off."

"Over my dead body," Sid told him in an affronted voice that commanded the attention of others in the small restaurant. "I haven't had this much fun in fifteen years. What could go wrong? Boy, oh, boy—I wish I could go along, but I don't think my heart or Harriet would stand it. Listen—we'll book you into the Villa Vera in two private cottages back to back. You'll have your own kitchen and private swimming pool with each and can avoid the public areas. I'll work out the right room numbers. The way I see it you won't even have to worry about this Greenspan or the FBI."

"Forgive me for intruding," said Greenspan of the FBI, "but I'd like to make a suggestion. He'll need a third room for himself to make and receive private phone calls from each of the ladies. He can use secret business with Washington as a justification. I recommend three connecting suites, with his own in the middle."

"You seem to know an awful lot about this," Sid said appreciatively after Gold introduced them.

"I've worked for Presidents," was Greenspan's understated

reply. "Your place—it's a pigsty," he said of Gold's studio when they entered. "I say that more in sorrow than anger. I've been meaning to tell you for weeks."

"Greenspan, don't butt in," said Gold with a look plainly indicating he was both worried and irked. "I don't want Belle to know anything about this."

"She knows, she knows," said Greenspan in a soughing litany. "Everything but the names. Since when has Belle ever been guilty of stupidity?"

"Then why hasn't she said anything?"

"What can she say?" answered Greenspan with an expression of absolute grief stealing over him. "If you only knew how my heart bleeds for her every time I hear her talking to her mother or trying to pretend that nothing's wrong when she speaks to your sisters. What a woman she is, what a wonderful wife and mother she—"

"Greenspan, stop, for Christ sakes."

"Why should she be the one to say something and make it easier for you?" asked Greenspan. "If you won't complain, why should she do it for you? Sure, she'll give you a divorce, but first ask. Why should she be the one to say you want a divorce, if you won't do it? Oh, Gold, Gold—I must know something, for my own information. It's off the record, I swear. This schoolteacher, this Linda Book."

"What about her?"

"You sure come a lot with her, don't you?"

"What's it your business?" Gold answered icily.

"You hardly ever come at all with the one you're going to marry."

"So?"

With a saddened, meaningful look, Greenspan replaced his hat. "You're a *shonda* to your race."

"And you, Greenspan, are a credit to yours. Will you be in Acapulco? What should I do if I get in trouble?"

"You can talk to the wall."

Gold fell into a mood of melancholy introspection the moment he was alone. For a prudent man he was reckless. For a sane one he was mad. Gold needed no inner voice to tell him he was courting trouble. All his life he had hated trouble. All his life he had been afraid of failing. Now, it seemed, he was distressed he might succeed.

WHAT could go wrong? asked Sid. Gold could easily foretell as he left the elevator at the gym and turned toward the locker room. To begin with, there was that electrifying flash of lecherous attraction between him and the Mexican television actress that erupted on first sight on the tarmac of the airfield in Mexico City when they were waiting with Andrea for the connecting flight bearing Linda from Houston, and which burned in plain view like phosphorous with a fragrant, steaming brilliant heat that everybody nearby could scent and feel. The raw, magnetic force of their reciprocated animal desire could not be withstood and barely brooked delay. With a native quickness for which he could never be sufficiently grateful, she agreed in a throaty murmur to steal away to Acapulco the following day for a clandestine tryst with him in the empty chamber between the others, while the swarthy pilot who was her lover surveyed him evilly with baleful yellow eyes and muttered something sinister that Gold heard as though in a coma and politely requested he repeat.

"The Angel of Death is in the gym today," said Karp the chiropodist a second time from his oracle's perch on his low wooden stool in the aisle of lockers into which Gold had turned.

Gold came to a stop, blinking. "What are you talking about?"

"There's a man having a heart attack in the main gym upstairs. They're waiting for the ambulance now."

Grimly Gold continued to his locker, determining, as usual, to breast the cryptic tides of destiny and confront the morbid omens.

Statistically, he solaced himself, the odds against two men dropping dead of heart attacks in the same gym on the same day were
weighted heavily in his favor. Empirically, the harsh truth dawned,
the chances were no different than ever if one of the men already
had, and the transportation arrangements were filled with compli-
cations that neither Sid nor he could have foreseen. Because Linda
did have to bring the two younger children, she traveled directly to
Acapulco from New York and arrived at the hotel four hours before Gold and Andrea, who departed from Washington with stops
at Houston and Mexico City. Or, because she did not have to bring
the children, she insisted capriciously that she go on the same
plane, and Gold found himself in transit with her too. That neither
was impelled to recognize the other did little to ease the strain. Or,
having cemented arrangements for traveling by herself on that
same flight, she then arrived, as a consequence of a late-hour
stance of perverse noncooperation by her bellicose husband, accompanied by the two children, who fell into a disagreeable funk
immediately their eyes, with shattering disappointment, alighted
on Gold. In seconds he was unmanned by the degrading need for
treating the encounter as circumstantial, their previous acquain-
tanceship as slight and entirely professional, and the independent
selection by both vacationing parties of the same plane for the
same distant hotel as indeed a most extraordinary occurrence.
With failing courage he watched Andrea's incisive doubt grow
more manifest with every word exchanged. Another grueling test
awaited him at the registration desk in Mexico, where all rooms,
through some staff oversight, he shakily surmised, were reserved
in his name, and just as this delicate contretemps was almost suc-
cessfully untangled, Spotty Weinrock, of all people in the world,
was standing there before him in a luminous golden cotton sweat-
suit, irreversibly intent on going jogging with him on the small oval
track two floors above.

"We can have a nice long talk while I'm learning how."

"I come at this hour to be alone." Gold should have remembered he had no chance ever of staring this otiose, imperturbable
childhood friend out of countenance. "You shouldn't jog, not without a doctor's examination and a stress test. It's dangerous. Okay

then, but don't try to keep up with me or run as long. You're overweight and out of condition and I'm not. I mean it—you wouldn't be the first one to drop dead."

"There's a guy with a heart attack upstairs in the gym now."

"I don't care about him!"

"Is this what you call fun?" asked Spotty Weinrock with a hateful smile, pulling alongside Gold and running with him easily midway through the second lap.

"Slow down, you fuck, or you'll soon have to stop," Gold warned. "I don't want to talk. You're not allowed to run side by side. Just fall back behind me and take your time."

"Is this how slow you always go?" asked Spotty from in back.

The effect upon Gold was excruciating. "I don't want to talk!" he yelped in a squeezed-out scream through a neck in which every vein and muscle was stretched in fury. His heart was beating with a louder noise than his pounding feet were making against the track. The grotesque ordeal was afflicting him rapidly with an enervating anemia of the will, and he sat down to rest in a cushioning armchair as soon as he was alone in the center suite after each of the women had been installed in rooms on either side without further conflict. Both thought he was transacting confidential official business with Washington. Linda's children were no longer there. His composure restored, he was able to have a banana daiquiri from room service with Linda, a banana daiquiri alone, and a banana daiquiri with Andrea when he'd completed another lap and again was with her. He fucked Andrea first to get that out of the way and was unable to perform with Linda when she rang him for that purpose on the telephone in the middle room.

"Fag!" cried Spotty Weinrock cheerily and went flitting ahead of Gold like a sunbeam in his golden track suit, as though Gold were standing still.

Gold was flabbergasted by this blinding display of speed but held morosely to his own dogged pace with something scarcely human in his contorted visage. The pain that always rose in his chest at the beginning was intensifying, rather than subsiding, and he lost count of the number of laps he had run and was forced to start all over just when, with a violent start of tremendous surprise, he heard the phone in his room again.

"It's the White House," he lied with a leap out of bed.

It was Andrea, with whom he then had a light lunch in the patio dining room. Then he had a heavy second lunch with Linda in the bedroom, which he consumed without appetite. The waistband of his walking shorts was turning sharp as an iron file. In less than two hours he had nurtured a cumbersome paunch that bounced when he moved and made jogging this afternoon an arduous chore instead of the strenuous and salutary regimen he normally found it. His breathing was more labored than usual and his pulse rate felt swifter than he knew was good for him.

"Fag!" sang out Spotty Weinrock playfully and sailed by him again.

Gold kept his eyes down and pretended not to notice that Linda was restless and growing insurgently fractious at being kept under wraps. Andrea too was tired of being kept under wraps and already was phoning about the area to people she knew with vacation homes. Linda wanted to carouse at the pool and Andrea wanted a drive into town. In a backward glance as the car pulled away, Gold took a mental snapshot of Linda at poolside in close conversation with a slender, tall, lithe, insultingly good-looking Mexican youth with gleaming teeth, and he experienced, to his chagrin, that jealous debilitating pang that is recognized universally as heartache.

"Fag!" denounced Weinrock and passed him again, as airily and blithely as a spirit with feet skimming on air.

Gold's own legs felt leaden, and he forced his gaze further downward into a dejected mode of inflexible concentration as Spotty ran from view while he had dinner with Linda and dropped her at a discotheque and had a second dinner with Andrea before driving with her to a party at a home near Kissinger's owned by friends of her father. Both women were complaining at the amount of time he was spending on the telephone with Washington.

"Fag!" called Weinrock and flew by him again.

"You'll drop!" Gold yelled reluctantly, but was too late to be heeded, so he stole unhappily from the party to look in on Linda at the discotheque. Linda was encircled now by four handsome dancing young men, all courting her rhythmically with the seductive, possessive allure that is the exclusive property of the self-assured scions of very rich Latin American millionaires. It was not necessary, all let him know, to trouble himself with the problem of getting her back to the hotel.

"Fag!"

And when Gold drove at breakneck speed to return to the party, he was dismayed to find Andrea surrounded by several loud and drunken burly men from the Southwest who were trying to solicit her participation in a group-sex supper dance together with a number of stunning models with whom they'd arrived while Gold was absent.

"I'm here with my fiancé," Andrea was trying civilly to refuse as Gold came up vengefully behind her, "and I'm not sure he'd approve."

"Oh, don't worry about him," said the largest and most muscular, sliding his arm around Andrea's shoulders with the lewd self-assurance of the impervious extrovert. "We'll take care of him."

"How?" said Gold curtly with his hands bunching into fists. "How will you take care of me?"

"Any way we want to, little man," said another of the group in a husky outburst of laughter.

"You think you can stop us?"

"That's an awful lot of woman there for a little fella like you."

A brawl would be futile and he took Andrea's arm and backed away.

"Fag!" cried Spotty, and it was just about midnight when Linda Book returned to her room and sent Manolito away without even a peck on the cheek when she saw Gold stewing there in a raw humor. They made love then with results that were mutually sublime. Spotty slid through the bedrooms sideways with another provoking reiteration of that homosexual epithet as Gold trudged back to bed with Andrea. As he dreaded most, Andrea now was baking at a sensual temperature. A soft groan broke from his lips at her advances. He was not lying when he spoke briefly of a splitting headache and nausea and of an overall fatigue. At three in the morning he was awakened in agony from a troubled sleep by the telephone ringing again in the middle room.

"It's the goddamned White House again."

Still grumbling, he limped through the rooms to explain to Linda in a haggard voice that he had to spend every night with Andrea because they were engaged to be married.

"Fag!" called out Spotty Weinrock and this time skipped by in the springy, floating gait of the male ballet dancer in black leotards who was also on the track. A mustached fuck was running backwards, infuriating Gold; every eccentric distraction on the track always infuriated him. The basketball players on the courts below were screaming at each other in brutal argument again.

Gold held adamantly to a determination to ignore them all the next morning when he sank down to rest in darkest spirits in his own room after breakfasting twice. His ankles were hurting terribly and he was sweating profusely. His future had never looked worse. Then the passionate Mexican television actress arrived, as did shortly afterward her hot-blooded Mexican airline pilot, who prowled the grounds for Gold to avenge his honor in the most primitive and unspeakable ways imaginable. Just as the Mexican television actress was ready to go off like a string of firecrackers, the jealous lover learned Gold's room number and came charging up the stairs. When Gold rushed to the window to jump to escape, he was horrified by the curious sight of a taxi arriving with Belle, who'd journeyed all the way after him with the thought they might still patch things up if they were off together. The crazed lover was banging both fists on the door. Notoriety would be disastrous to him. He berated himself mercilessly for his indefensible folly. What was he going to do?

"What am I going to do?" he helplessly wailed to the four walls.

"Go to the temple and say prayers," directed Greenspan coolly, materializing from one of the side rooms attired in Acapulco sports clothes.

"I'll do no such thing."

"Then go past the temple to the airfield," continued Greenspan, "and take the first plane out for anywhere. Get back to Washington however you can. I will tell them about your urgent business one at a time and send them out without meeting each other. Oh, Gold, Gold, you're such a *shonda*."

"And you, Greenspan, are such a credit." Gold clasped him gratefully to this breast in the Russian manner and hugged him about the shoulders with strong feeling.

"Fag!" chirped Spotty and breezed by him once more.

That fuck! cried Gold inwardly with the fiercest scowl as commonsense reality exposed itself to him suddenly with the force and flashing illumination almost of a bolt of lightning. Spotty had been doing two laps to his one, sometimes three, sometimes four. Oh, that base cocksucker—no human on earth could run that fast!

Gritting his teeth and breathing wrathfully through his nose as he maintained his even pace, he watched stealthily with murder growing in his heart. There were four landings in each corner of the room where the track curved, and on each landing was exercise equipment or a stairwell. Spotty ran off the track to a landing and hid until Gold went by, then came down in back to pass him again. The maleficent motherfucker had been hiding, resting, and waiting on the landings all along in the cruelest, most insensitive prank Gold could conceive of.

"Fag!"

Gold mistimed the lunge he made for Spotty Weinrock's throat with his left hand, broke stride, and stumbled. Anguish exploded in his chest then with an immense, cramping, darkening pain. The room began spinning, the lights dimmed. The ground rose to meet him with sways and undulations as he felt his legs wobble and give way, and, like a wounded warrior plucky to the last, he ran almost fifteen more yards on his knees before toppling to the track and lying still as a stone with his eyes staring, as though he had been brought to his doom by a mortal fright.

"Are you all right?" someone said.

His hearing was unimpaired.

"Give him mouth-to-mouth resuscitation," suggested the ballet dancer.

"I will not. That's disgusting."

"Boy, are you lucky," Spotty said in his golden uniform. "The ambulance just came for that other guy."

His vision remained also.

"Doctor, can he be moved now?" a strange voice complained. "The rest of us want to jog."

"Put him in a private room," said Spotty Weinrock. "He's a very important person."

Gold felt his heartbeat falter critically again. "I'm not! Spotty, tell not a soul."

He could speak too, and he screamed blue murder the next morning in Roosevelt Hospital when he saw he was still not in an oxygen tent.

"Doctors say you don't need one," explained the phlegmatic black male orderly who brought him his breakfast.

Gold was appalled by what he saw on the tray: scrambled eggs that glistened, bacon that dripped, four pats of butter—enough cholesterol to lay waste a generation of marines. "It's a mistake, I tell you. I'm not going to eat it."

The orderly smacked his lips when he'd finished it all. When a woman came for information Gold would not give even his name. He was wary with the doctors and requested permission to call his own physician. The pay phone was in the hall.

"Can I get out of bed by myself and walk there?"

"It's up to you."

He needed a dime. They gave him a dollar. Mursh Weinrock was there at noon and conferred with the medical men in undertones while preparations were made for Gold's transfer to a private room.

"What do you want an oxygen tent for?" said Weinrock when they were alone. "It's cheaper this way. Did you trip and fall or did you collapse? What'd you feel?"

"I felt like murdering him, Mursh, with my bare hands. I kept getting madder until I couldn't stand it and then this thing went off in my head and my chest. I was scared. Then I got weak suddenly and everything went black. I didn't trip. It was your fucking brother Spotty. I'm going to kill that bastard someday."

Weinrock was nodding. "He breaks my mother's heart a thousand times a week. There's no sign of cardiac damage. It sounds more like anxiety, but we can't be sure. I've had many a patient drop dead right after showing a perfect electrocardiogram. It's a reason I don't like to take on sick people." He recommended a ten-day stay for observation. Few visitors, few phone calls. "No one will know you're here unless you tell them."

No visitors, no telephone calls, no letters, no flowers, no greeting cards, no bananas in baskets of fruit—the ten days that followed were the most forlorn of Gold's life. How many people wondered where he was? He pondered also, with bewildering compunction, the moral mystery originating in his final words to Spotty Weinrock at the gym: "Tell not a soul." A heartbeat away from death and his dominant concern was not life, but that corrupting illusion of triumph, public success.

And so it was still.

Gold contacted nobody until about to be discharged in health that was certifiably excellent. He called Belle first.

"What hospital?"

"I've been sick, Belle. I'm getting out tomorrow."

"With what?"

"Nothing. Where did you think I was? I've been away for almost two weeks."

"You told me you had to go off somewhere to straighten yourself out," said Belle. "So I thought you were probably straightening yourself out."

"I'm okay," he quickly assured Andrea. "The doctors are positive it was nothing."

"What doctors? Where are you?"

"In the hospital, darling. In New York. Didn't you even miss me?"

"With what?"

"With nothing, darling. I just told you. It was just a checkup."

"Why didn't you tell me, darling?"

"I wasn't allowed any calls or visitors."

"With nothing?"

"Where did you think I was, Andrea? It's been ten days. Didn't you notice I was gone?"

"I knew you had to go back to your wife one more time to work out the divorce," said Andrea. "I thought you were working out the divorce."

His call to Ralph was crucial. "Something personal came up and I had to go away for a while. I'm sorry I haven't been able to be in touch with you."

"About what?" asked Ralph.

"About everything. You told me things were starting to happen."

"And they are, Bruce," said Ralph. "Conover is pushing strongly in your behalf. The President asked to meet you."

"I can come tomorrow."

"I think he's busy tomorrow. The Embassy Ball would be a good place to meet."

"The Embassy Ball?"

"I hope you'll come if you're invited. I told the President that you were writing some important position papers. So try to draw up a few."

"On what?"

"On any positions you choose. I don't think anyone's going to want to read them. Where are you now?"

"At my studio," lied Gold. "Ralph, didn't you miss me? Didn't you notice we were out of touch?"

"I missed your hotel room," said Ralph. "I can tell you that. Sleeping with just my wife and Misty, Candy, Christie, and Tandy for almost two weeks hasn't been easy. You ought to try it some time and see. You and I have to get together very soon to talk about the Embassy Ball and what you should say to him there if you're invited."

"Tomorrow?" asked Gold.

"I'm busy too," said Ralph.

"How can I get invited to that Embassy Ball?"

"It's practically impossible."

"Fuck him," said Gold for the first time as he crossly dialed another number. Neglect, moped Gold, abounding everywhere, closing me in like a poisonous tide, drowning me, closing over my head, filling my nose with fetid—

"Spot Modes," greeted the girl on the telephone brightly. "May I help you?"

"Mr. Weinrock, please. Bruce Gold calling."

"Mr. Weinrock is in the market."

"What the fuck does that mean?"

The girl hung up. Gold reached him at the gym.

"Spotty, you bastard, nobody knows I'm even in the hospital. I told you not to tell anyone, so you didn't, huh? Not my wife, not a single soul, did you?''

"I can keep a secret," said Spotty Weinrock.

"Not a person in this whole world knows what I went through. Was there anything in the newspapers?"

"I don't read the newspapers."

"It shows how people care. I could drop dead tomorrow and no one would even notice."

"I can follow instructions when I have to."

"Did you have to, you prick? And you didn't even come to visit, did you? Suppose I died, you son of a bitch? Would you have told anyone then? My wallet was still at the gym with all my clothes and they wouldn't even know who I was. You can keep a secret, all right. How in heaven's name can you keep such a secret?"

"To tell you the truth," said Spotty Weinrock, "I forgot."

"You forgot?" The painful words were still sinking in.

"I got kind of busy, Bruce, and I forgot you even had a heart attack."

"It was not a heart attack!"

"I was pretty scared, anyway," said Spotty Weinrock. "I couldn't stop worrying about you."

"Till when?" scoffed Gold with a bitter laugh.

"Till I forgot."

Gold thrust his face toward the telephone as though it were the enraging incarnation of the person he was addressing. "You forgot?" he repeated through tightened jaws in a voice quivering with a black storming anger that sifted through his entire system and caused every muscle to tremble. "Money, Weinrock, money, you cocksucker. How much do you owe me now?"

"About two thousand."

"Pay up, you lousy bastard."

"Okay."

"This minute, you fuck. Or I'll put you in prison. I'll get liens. I'll serve papers. Spotty, Spotty," said Gold with a catch in his throat as his voice cracked and he tried without succeeding to fight back the tears rolling from his eyes, "how could you be so insen-

sitive? Why didn't you at least come to visit, just to see for yourself
I was alive?"

"I tried, Bruce. Three times I was going to visit and made up my
mind that nothing was going to keep me away."

"And what happened?"

"I forgot."

"Do you know what it feels like?" said Gold with a sob. "Do
you know what it feels like to have to lie in a hospital day after day
without visitors or phone calls, with what might have been a fatal
heart attack, and have nobody care? It feels like shit. Suppose I
died?"

"I cared," said Spotty.

"You forgot."

"Somebody would have reminded me."

"Nobody else knew," Gold reproached him further. "I would
have been buried in a pauper's grave. Even I would have been
more thoughtful than that."

"I have to go jogging now. I belong to this group."

Gold washed and dried his face before telephoning next the one
person he thought of who might have missed him most.

"I called you at your studio only yesterday," she said. "I left a
message on your machine."

"Only yesterday? Where'd you think I was until then? It's been
ten days."

"I thought you were busy with your wife and with your
fiancée."

"Is Dina back in school?"

"And doing beautifully," said Linda Book. "I've been doing her
homework for her. Tell me what hospital you're in. I have this
dental bill I want to mail you."

"I'll be getting out tomorrow," said Gold. "I want to see you
first."

In a fevered ecstasy of abandonment and slavish indiscretion, he
could now easily picture all his carefully laid plans flying asunder
into a bohemian muddle of debauchery and irresponsible disgrace,
and he did not care. He wanted her in his arms, wanted her body
beneath him, covered by his own. What would Conover say when

he found out? How many people who ever read about him would truly believe that a thinking adult like him would endanger his marriage—nay, two marriages—and a brilliant budding political career for a lascivious fling with a married woman with four children with whom, as was also true of Andrea, he could never become in any other way intimate? That didn't seem to matter.

"I love you very, very deeply, darling, and I wish so much that I didn't." Gold could safely afford the luxury of such lavish words and sentiments because he knew that the emotion in which they had their birth was not going to last. He did not dream, however, that the demise of this tender feeling lay as near as the dental bill she handed him. He calmly mixed a gin and tonic for each. By then his agitation had lessened. "How come your husband isn't paying for any of these? I thought he was such a good provider."

"He isn't going to pay for anything any more since he found out we're together."

Several questions rose simultaneously in Gold's mind and broke into pieces against each other in the burbling struggle to get out. "Together? Found out? How? How together? Are? What do you mean found out? What do you mean together? How are we together?"

"Like this. He knows all about us."

"Knows all about us? How did he find out?"

"From the children."

"From the children? How do the children know?"

"I told them."

Gold looked at her steadily with a troubled eye. "You told them? You told your children? What did you tell your children?"

"That we're lovers."

"Lovers?"

"You keep repeating everything I say."

419

Gold was lacking the necessary equilibrium for timely repartee. "Is that what we are, lovers?" he asked credulously.

"Of course, darling," answered Linda with a smile. "I'm your lover and you're mine. What did you think we were?"

Gold did not hesitate long to give the answer that first sprang to mind. "Fuckers."

"Lover is so much sweeter," said Linda Book with the ethereal sensitivity of a poetess, "so much richer in meaning and value, don't you think?"

"Don't you have to be very seriously in love to be a lover?" asked Gold.

"Oh, no," she corrected him. "All you have to be is a fucker."

Gold had never looked at himself as a lover before and was not altogether convinced he liked the idea now. "So that's what I am, huh? A lover."

"Of course you are, you fucker," said Linda Book. "And a darling too. I rate you an A minus." Gold was stung only superficially by this backhanded tribute, for there was the impact of catastrophe in the words that followed. "And I'm so proud that someone as intelligent as you finds me sexy and attractive. Even my husband is impressed."

"Good God!" Gold hurtled to his feet. "He knows my name?"

"Gold is a very nice name," she said. "And I wouldn't be ashamed to have it as my own."

"Jesus Christ, Linda, that's not the point." Gold lifted a pillow from the bed for the sole purpose of having something in both hands he could slam down. "Where the hell are your brains? I'm a very distinguished man. Next week I may even be invited to the Embassy Ball. Why the fuck did you have to tell anybody about me at all?"

"Because I believe in the truth."

"Why?" he insisted on knowing.

"Why?"

"Why in this case couldn't you believe in a lie? Why in the world did you have to tell your children anything?"

"Because in our family," retorted Linda Book without any trace of concession, "we don't believe in keeping things from each other."

"Do they understand what being lovers means?" Gold demanded scornfully. "I didn't."

"Oh, yes. The older two did."

"What did they say?"

"My son said he would kill you," she said. "My daughter wanted to know if you were any good. I told her you were an A minus who would probably graduate to an A if you could last. The younger two were more accepting."

"Oh, were they?" said Gold with a rather wild shake of his head. "I'd like to know how you explained to them what lovers are."

Linda Book met the challenge with unconcern. "Oh, we have this illustrated German sex book for children. It shows a little boy with his penis erect and a little girl with her vagina exposed and it explains in simple language any child can understand that he shoves it in."

"Shoves it in?" Gold's voice nearly failed him.

"Yes. And I explained to them that you and I do the same thing with our penee and that's why we're lovers."

"They understood?"

"Immediately. They said we were fucking."

Gold stared at her with bulging eyes for a moment and then went plunging about the room in shocked silence for several seconds. "Linda, you're a schoolteacher?" he addressed her with his jaws knotted and with his mouth drawn back as far as a human mouth could go, and all at once he looked as though he were congenitally snaggletoothed. "You went to college, got your degrees? You completed education courses? You got your license, a nice shiny diploma?"

"Oh, yes," said Linda with the same collected smile. "I communicate very well with children. Your daughter will vouch for that."

"My daughter!" Gold's voice was a hysterical cry. "Holy shit! She's friends with your kids. She sleeps at your house. Dina. Do you think they told her too?"

"I should hope they did," said Linda. "Our children are all very open with each other about sex."

Gold moaned and shivered in terror. "I didn't want her to know!"

"It will bring you closer together."

"It will put us at sword's point at each other's throat. Goddammit, she'll tell my wife."

"It will bring you and her closer together too."

"I'm leaving my wife to marry Andrea. Is there no way you can get word to her as well? Listen, Linda, marriage for us is out of the question, definitely out."

"Oh, we agreed on that," said Linda without taking offense. "I could never afford to give up my support or my alimony."

"Which you are now not getting," said Gold with an uncordial gleam of triumph, pacing. "Because you believe so much in the truth. What is this horrifying obsession with the truth that all you women seem to be in the grip of these days? Where does it come from? Goddammit—I may be Secretary of State soon. Do you think it's helpful for a thirteen-year-old child to know that the Secretary of State is fucking her schoolteacher? Can't you imagine what will happen to my home life and divorce if my wife does find out?"

"It will clear the air," said Linda. "When my husband found out it certainly cleared a lot of air."

"And he stopped giving you money. How do you think my wife is going to feel about all these dentist's bills when she finds out they're for you and your kids?"

At last the seriousness of the matter impressed itself upon her. "Do you think we shouldn't have told him?"

"What did your husband say when you told him?" asked Gold.

"He said he was going to kill you."

"You shouldn't have told him. Greenspan, you fuck," he shouted in violent anxiety as soon as he found himself alone with a wall he could talk to. "Where the hell are you?"

"I know, I know," said Greenspan when Gold began relating his troubles. "It's why I say you're a *shonda*."

"Her husband wants to kill me."

"It's a federal offense to kill a public official, but you're not a public official yet."

"Tell him I'm about to become one," Gold begged. "Go see him for me. Bring a gun."

"He says you're fucking his wife," Greenspan reported back.

"Tell him I'll stop if he promises not to assassinate me."

"He wants you to marry her and take full financial responsibility for her and all four children," Greenspan reported back.

"He's out of his fucking head," said Gold. "I thought he was madly in love with her and would never let her go."

"He'll let her go, he'll let her go," said Greenspan.

"It's out of the question," said Gold. "I'm already married to one woman and about to marry another, and we Jews don't take our marriages lightly."

"I told him that."

"Tell him I'll go for the dental work for all of them until it's completed, but that's all."

"He says it's a deal," Greenspan reported back. "I had to threaten to shoot him." He declined without words the drink Gold offered in celebration. "Now, Dr. Gold, what about you? Do you really think you have the right character to be Secretary of State or any other high government official?"

Gold considered the matter. "What do you think?"

"Are you really going to stop fucking his wife?"

"No."

Greenspan surveyed him with a look holding generations of disappointment. "You're no worse than the rest," he decided, "but certainly no better. He doesn't think you will, either."

"Greenspan, we can drive a better bargain. Tell him I'll really stop if he picks up all the dental bills."

"Now, it's a deal," Greenspan reported back. "Just a little wine, please. *L'chaim.*"

"*L'chaim,*" Gold toasted him in return.

"But what I said still goes," Greenspan stressed at the door.

"What's that?"

"I forget. Let me think. Oh, yes. You're a *shonda.*"

"You're a credit."

The way was clear now, Gold saw, for his triumphant return to Washington.

"WITH Conover promising to champion you after you marry Andrea," said Ralph, dressed in another monogrammed shirt that caught Gold's discriminating eye, "there is nothing in the world that can block your appointment, unless something gets in the way. I say that with as much assurance as I've ever been able to give you in the past."

"And Andrea won't marry me until I already have the appointment," grumbled Gold. "The two of them are playing games with each other. Can't I meet the President now? I'm sure I can convince him if I had just one meeting with him."

Ralph had been shaking his head even before the request was concluded. "At the Embassy Ball, if you can get invited. I think he's still busy with Russia. The President worries a lot about Russia. He wants to meet you at the Embassy Ball, in front of photographers. Try to come if you're invited."

"If the President wants to meet me there," said Gold, "it seems to me I'm important enough to be invited."

"If you aren't important enough to be invited," countered Ralph, "he won't want to meet you there."

"What's so special about that Embassy Ball?" Gold argued. "Ain't I as good as some of the other people who'll be going?"

"Better," said Ralph. "But this is the social world, Bruce, where competence doesn't count. You aren't wealthy and you don't yet hold the right position. Try to remember who you are. Let's face it, Bruce—Jews don't really make it in America. They never did. I hope you're not offended by my frankness."

"True honesty never necessitates an apology," said Gold, recovering by feeble degrees from the downturn in spirit he had suffered. "Is what you say true, Ralph?"

"I think so, Bruce. Not unless you're very, very rich and remain a European. Jews can't really go far in this country socially, and none have. Christians find it difficult enough, but for Jews it's just about impossible. I can think of no exception."

Gold was drawn into a deeper exploration of the subject with a kind of unaccountable fascination. "Kissinger?"

"Oh, no," snickered Ralph. "He goes to sporting events and accepts too many invitations to parties with entertainers. He's just another writer now scrounging about for royalties and publicity. I hope that doesn't sound snobbish, Bruce."

"Not at all, Ralph," said Gold. "Walter Annenberg and Lillian Farkas? They were ambassadors."

"Under Nixon?" Ralph's sniggering headshake made additional refutation superfluous. "Annenberg was succeeded as ambassador to England by Elliot Richardson. And *there's* a man of low character I can't stand and would not trust for a moment. He was willing to ride with Nixon but unwilling to do the dirty work. What did he think they needed him for—his special abilities and his fine New England background?" Ralph was still smiling with his jeering expression as he hitched up his trousers at the knee before carefully crossing his legs. "He wanted credit for virtue for refusing to fire the Watergate prosecutor. Can you imagine how much longer he would have lasted in public life if he *had* fired him? Elliot Richardson will be at the Embassy Ball, Bruce, but you won't. It's unjust, but it would be hypocrisy for me to say I really care."

"Will you be at the Embassy Ball?"

"I'm always invited to the Embassy Ball."

"What about the Guggenheims?" Gold pursued. Ralph was indicating the negative. "The Warburgs, the Schiffs, the Belmonts, the Kahns?"

"No, Bruce. I can't think of a single one who was ever accepted into good society," said Ralph, "except for some daughters, perhaps, who married upward into a better class and were absorbed without telltale clues. And certainly not the ones with genius or talent. Those are anathema regardless of birth, although we don't produce many. American democracy is the most rigid aristocracy on earth, Bruce, and every social climber needs at least one unscrupulous marriage to succeed."

"What about Eisenhower and Nixon, Lyndon Johnson, and Gerald Ford?"

"Presidents?" Ralph sniffed. "Presidents never make it into good society. They're helpful but gauche. And when they're no longer helpful they're merely gauche. Just look who their closest companions are while in office and after."

"Kennedy?" asked Gold.

"Oh, no," said Ralph in gentle admonition. "The Kennedys were always déclassé. That was part of their charm and much of their pleasure. No Irish Catholic male can ever do it on his own, Bruce. Not here. The Irish can't make it and neither can native-born Italians, although wealthy Arabs may if they mind their manners, so you see, it's not just Jews who are ostracized and excluded. As I believe I've told you, Bruce, there is no anti-Semitism any more. I'm glad I can speak so freely, because I believe you know exactly how I feel."

"I'm not sure I know exactly how you feel, Ralph," Gold replied with a bit of tension, deciding to relieve himself at last of a somber distrust that had been preying recurrently upon his mind. "I notice you never have me to your house."

The response to this was mild. "You never have me to yours, Bruce."

"You don't come to New York, Ralph. But I'm in Washington often."

"I come to New York a lot, Bruce."

"You didn't tell me that."

"You haven't asked me, Bruce." Ralph laughed amicably. Gold was at a loss to reply. "We shouldn't quibble over this, should we? Bruce, would you really want me to visit you in your apartment on Manhattan's West Side? It's not as though you own a suite at the Pierre or the Ritz Towers, is it?"

Gold could not gainsay even to himself that he would not want Ralph to visit him at his apartment on Manhattan's West Side. "I suppose you're right, Ralph. The important thing is not our social worlds but our friendship. There's a definition of a friend I once heard expressed by my Swedish publisher. He's Jewish, Ralph, and he lived in Germany under Hitler as a child until his family escaped. He has only one test of a friend now, he told me. 'Would he hide me?' is the question he asks. It's pretty much my test of a friend too, when I come down to it. Ralph, if Hitler returns, would you hide me?''

The question threw Ralph into a flurry and he clambered to his feet, his fair skin turning pink. "Oh, gosh, Bruce," he exclaimed hastily, "we're not friends. I thought you knew that."

Gold was equally confused. "We're not?"

"Oh, no, Bruce," stressed Ralph in embarrassed apology. "And I'd feel just awful if I thought I've ever said or done anything to give you the impression we are."

Gold felt this more than he wished to show. "You used my work at school, Ralph. We were pretty close then."

"That was college, Bruce," said Ralph, "and it was important that I get my degree. But this is only government. People in government don't have friends, Bruce, just interests and ambitions. Don't look so dismayed. Would you hide me and take any risk?" Gold's impassive silence denoted he would not. "If you did, Lieberman would inform on both of us and call himself a patriot."

"Ralph," said Gold, "I think by now Lieberman really believes all that repressive, elitist, racist, neoconservative bullshit and is not just sucking around you people for money and invitations."

"That's just the thing I dislike about him most," said Ralph. "He has no right to our beliefs. He hasn't even made much money. Let him at least go out and make a fortune before he begins pretending he's one of us."

"Ralph, there's one thing I simply must know," said Gold. "In college I worked harder than you and was a better student and more intelligent. Yet, you got higher grades and even had my paper on *Tristram Shandy* published. How were you able to do that?"

"I was smarter, Bruce."

"You were smarter?"

"You were doing my work for me, weren't you?"

Ralph delivered these answers with unassuming candor, and Gold, after shifting them around awhile, found himself haunted again by the mysteries of Ralph's head and Ralph's pants. Ralph still never needed a haircut or showed signs of ever having one. His trousers always were sharply creased and meticulously bare of wrinkles, and Gold wondered if he wore each suit only once.

"Less than once," Ralph obliged him with a frank reply. He flung open the bifold doors of a closet containing dozens of suits fastidiously hung. "I change for every appointment. I've been getting by on pressed pants when my college degrees and inherited riches weren't enough."

"How can you wear a suit less than once?" asked Gold.

"What a concise and profound intelligence you have!" cried Ralph. "And they thought Kissinger was brilliant! Little do they know. Oh, Bruce, if only you'd come up with a cure for inflation and unemployment. Nobody else even tries."

"You'd steal it," said Gold.

"I wouldn't have to any more," said Ralph. "It's enough you're my protégé. Or devise a plan for decreasing this eternal conflict with Russia. You ought to be able to do that. You were probably a Communist once, weren't you?"

"I was never a Communist," Gold averred forcefully.

"But can't you think of something anyway?"

Gold was not inclined to try. "The curious thing about Russia," he joked lightly, putting, in imitation of Ralph, both shoes up on the polished, unscarred coffee table between the facing leather chairs, "is that it's a good place for people who are poor and a terrible one for those who are well off, while this country is just the reverse. Why don't we simply exchange?"

The effect of this upon Ralph was stupendous. First the coffee cup fell from his hand and he gaped at Gold as though thunderstruck. Next a lamp went over with another shattering crash as he bolted to his long legs with a look of amazement as stark as any that had ever alighted on human face before.

"It's yours!" he cried suddenly in an outburst of devotion that caused Gold to shrink back instinctively with alarm. "The credit! It will all go to you! I swear it!" Dashing to the glistening red phone on his desk and hammering on a buzzer there furiously, Ralph continued ranting disconnectedly in a delirious expulsion of emotion Gold had never seen spout from him. "You'll be rich, rich! The Nobel Prize—it's tax free! The President, the President!" he bellowed into the phone. "It cannot wait! Oh, why, oh, why couldn't I think of that—or anyone else? Oh, shit! He's locked himself in his study again. I'll run this over to him myself. This is too hot for the hot line." Ralph bounded back across the office to his closet for a fresh change of trousers. "I promise you— I will not trust this to anyone else. My God, what a plan, what a brilliant idea! They can ship us all their professionals, profiteers, and high-level bureaucrats and we can send them all our poor and homeless and wretched and miserable. Let *them* be the land of the free for a while. We'll be Monaco, St. Moritz, and Palm Beach. It's a perfect solution for both countries and there can never be strife between us again." Ralph donned a matching jacket and studied himself in a full-length mirror. "You're in, Bruce, I guarantee it. You won't even need Conover or anyone else from now on. I'll be so proud to have you as a friend someday."

Gold was roused by these final words to a kind of frenzy of his own. "Are you saying that I don't have to marry Andrea?"

"Not even for a month," said Ralph. "If you don't want to marry Andrea, don't. You want to stay married to Belle? Stay married to her."

"I didn't say that."

"Although Conover," cautioned Ralph, "would be an implacable foe if you disappointed him. There'd be stormy confirmation hearings, ugly rumors, waves of anti-Semitism. But you'll ride it through. This will be bigger than Kissinger's détente and Monroe's Doctrine. Keep near a telephone. Now you'll certainly be invited to the Embassy Ball. I'll stake my life on that."

BY THE time Ralph telephoned to inform him sadly that it was impossible to obtain an invitation for him to the Embassy Ball, Gold already had secured one through a lucky, and forbidding, encounter in the lobby of his hotel with the former governor of Texas with whom he had served on the Presidential Commission not long before. There are men who place their hand on the shoulder of another in friendly greeting. There are others who do so to assert possession over whoever or whatever comes within their grasp. On instant of contact Gold recognized the unmistakable intent of one of the latter, and he turned with a tremor to discover who was claiming him captive. The Governor, handsome, large, and dominating as earlier with silver hair, piercing blue eyes, and clefted, strong jaw, gazed down at Gold possessively with a smile of cold command.

"What you planning for lunch, Gold?"

"I was thinking of having something light later with my fiancée."

"You're eating with us now at the Hay-Adams. You'll have steak and eggs with home-fried potatoes. The steak will be cooked to a crisp. Pass that damned chili sauce, Homer. Give some to him too. I liked your report, Gold. I recommended it highly."

"I never wrote it."

"It's what I liked most about it. Doing anything new?"

"I'm thinking of writing a book about Henry Kissinger."

"Why waste time? Nobody's interested any more. Do one on me. Gold, I like you. You remind me a lot of this famous country singer from Texas I'm crazy about, a fellow calls himself Kinky Friedman, the Original Texas Jewboy. Kinky's smarter, but I like you more. I feared for you a while back there that you might be inclined to say something personal in your determination to fart around with the inevitable."

"I've resisted the determination ever since, sir," said Gold in dutiful homage. "I followed your advice, Governor, and I never force anything mechanical or kick anything inanimate."

The Governor pressed his napkin to his lips and sat back. "What are you doing in Washington, Goldy? Anybody who comes here more than once is after something."

Gold was asking for help when he replied. "I've been promised a Cabinet appointment, Governor. But I've not been able to meet the President."

"Shoot," said the Governor, "you can meet him tonight at the Embassy Ball."

"I can't get an invitation."

"Homer, give Gold an invitation to the Embassy Ball," said the Governor. "And call the committee and tell them he's coming." Homer had bunches of invitations to the Embassy Ball stuffed in most of his pockets. Gold felt the massive hand of the Governor taking hold of his shoulder again. "Gold, every Jew should have a big gentile for a friend, and every successful American should own a Jew. I'm big, Gold, and I'm willing to be your friend."

"I will support you, Governor," said Gold "in any cause to which you choose to commit yourself."

"That's fine," said the Governor. "You people learn fast. I had a run-in some time ago with that other member of your faith."

"I have no faith," said Gold.

"That Henry Kissinger," the Governor went on, unmindful of Gold's defensive protestation. "Funny-looking fellow with that nose of his and bumblebee mouth. Had hair like Kinky's, but Kinky is smarter. Had a reputation for backbiting and slanderous remarks about others." The Governor interrupted himself for a deep, ruminating chuckle before drawling on, "He's the one who got down on his knees with Nixon to pray to God on that rug. Laughed my head off when I heard about that and gave a barbecue on my ranch for seventeen thousand people to celebrate. Make war, said Nixon, and he made war. Pray to God, said Nixon, and he prayed to God. Seems to me his God was Nixon. Gold, do Jews always—?"

"No, sir. They do not."

"Didn't think so," said the Governor. "Only Jew I ever saw kneeling was a girl giving blow jobs in our fraternity house because that's the only way we'd let her in. Then he complained about those two nice young men who wrote about it. Homer, what was it he said?"

"Said they were lacking in decency and compassion, Governor," said Homer.

"Complained those nice young men Woodward and Bernstein were lacking in decency and compassion, after he was the likely one to spread the story. Had my showdown with him when he made the mistake of telling the press he sometimes thought of himself as a lonely cowboy riding into town to set things in order.

Well, as you can imagine, the cowboys in my state did not take kindly to that. Half my constituents wanted to go up after him with a lariat. I called him on that at a National Security Council meeting. I was Secretary of something or other then, and I said to him, 'Gold—' "

"I'm Gold, sir," pointed out Gold.

"It don't make that much difference—you fellows all look pretty much alike to me. I told him he didn't know sparrow's shit about cowboys if he ever imagined he felt like one. Cowboys ain't short, ain't chubby, and don't talk with no Jewish accent, I told him. And he said, 'It isn't Chewish, sir. It's Cherman.' "

Gold tried desperately to control his excitement. "He said that, Governor? He said it wasn't Jewish?"

"And I told him that if he ever came riding into my state as a cowboy he'd be very lonely indeed, because there'd be plenty of real ones who'd be happy to teach him the difference. And he said, 'I'm terribly sorry, Governor, and I promise never, never to do it again.' " The Governor laughed once more, savoring the recollection. "I told him if, however, he ever wanted to present himself in Texas as a real horse's ass, none of us would dispute him. We were eyeball to eyeball, and he blinked. And from that time on I knew I had his pecker in my pocket."

Gold was silent only for the instant needed to draw breath. "Was it circumcised?" he asked with a beating heart.

"I don't know," said the Governor. "All peckers look the same once they're in my pocket. Come to the Ball tonight, Gold. When the President arrives, right after they finish 'Hail to the Chief' and that damn 'Ruffles and Flourishes,' you push right on up to him and state your request. Anyone tries to interfere, you just tell him you're mine and I said it's okay."

"The President won't object?"

"He's in my pocket." The Governor's lake-blue eyes were glinting. "You rent your clothes tonight from this place. Homer, give him our business card. We get kickbacks."

Gold looked pretty good in his white tie, top hat and tails: lean, penetrating, dynamic, and sensual. Gold felt he looked pretty good until he arrived at the Ball in the only taxicab amid a gathering swarm of chauffeured maroon, black, and silver limousines. Ralph was nervously on the lookout for him inside the entrance, wearing an expression that was vividly disturbed. There was a long-distance call for Gold he could take in a private waiting room.

"It's Sid," said Ida, weeping. "He's had a heart attack."

"It looks pretty serious, Bruce," stuttered Max, taking the phone. "I think he's very sick."

"He's dead," said Belle.

"Oh, shit," said Gold with stinging tears spurting into his eyes. He does this to me every time. He'll ruin my whole day, my whole weekend.

"Anything wrong?" asked Ralph.

"It's my brother. He's dead."

"I'm sorry," said Ralph. "You'll want to leave immediately, won't you?"

That thought had not entered Gold's head until Ralph put it there, and he could think of no way of expelling it without risking the opinion that he was not worth his salt or as good as gold.

"It's terrible," he said, "terrible."

"I know just how you feel," said Ralph. "I'll get you a limousine."

In seconds secret servicemen were bearing him outside to a waiting automobile. As Gold pulled away he saw the President's car arriving. Everything, he lamented, happens to me. And he learned once again what he'd known all along and intended to write about soon, that every change was for the worse.

THERE was as much bitterness at Sid's funeral as there had been at his wedding. Mourners connected most closely by blood to one of the two contending families divided themselves into separate camps. Gold was a reluctant link between. Harriet was devastated, at first by a grief that was pure only briefly, and then contaminated by a vengeful rebellion against the general knowledge that Sid's affections for her had dwindled over the years into a bored and complying acceptance. Her senses were in shambles, with the meanest among them foremost. Much of her frightened awareness of loneliness and loss seemed to pour itself into a fanatic concern with possessions and almost all of the energies of grief were converted into safeguarding them with a savage vigilance against the pilferage and impending rapacious onslaughts she imagined. More and more openly she sniped with sharper nastiness at the other Golds for the amounts of money Sid had dissipated among them. None had volition to reply.

The burdens of responsibility for the numerous roles to be filled fell increasingly upon Gold and, surprisingly, old Milt, who embraced eagerly the opportunity to render competent service. Harriet's two sons were officious and proud, and of hardly any use with the practical arrangements of the funeral and the ceremonial ones of ritual and courtesy. One son-in-law had separated from her daughter and did not come at all. The other appeared bored and drifted up and down the carpeted floor at the mortuary as though interviewing for a boon companion with whom to trade disrespectful wisecracks in a corner of the chapel.

Sheiky from Neptune Avenue paid a condolence call at the chapel the evening before the burial services, red-cheeked and bald in a plain dark suit with baggy pants. He kept his hands in his pockets until the occasion for extending one in greeting had passed. Then he gave Gold an envelope containing three checks for five thousand dollars each.

"We won't need money, Sheiky."

"Keep them and see. Tear them up if you don't. Or give it to Israel. I don't mind seeing my money go to Israel."

"Sheiky, how'd you make your money?" asked Gold in that familiar state of perplexity that arose whenever he remembered Sheiky and his fortune. "From peddling ice cream and costume jewelry to getting rich in computers, real estate, shopping centers, and reinsurance—when did you learn those things?"

Sheiky from Neptune Avenue studied Gold steadily with his old look of impudence a long time before granting a reply. "I never thought of it as computers or real estate," he answered with the same flippant look of childhood that asserted itself also in the rude independence of his younger brother, Fishy. "Angles and loopholes—that's about the only business I've ever been in, like everyone else who makes it big. And I could always move pretty fast. That your father over there? Will he remember me?"

"Pa, this is Sid's friend, Sheiky from Neptune Avenue. The one with the millions."

Julius Gold was sitting upright in a small upholstered chair as though he could neither rise nor sag. Recognition dawned slowly in bleary eyes so blank as to appear almost sightless, and he was sluggish in finding the thought he wished to express.

"Sid always told me you were smarter. I wouldn't believe him. You smarter?"

Sheiky from Neptune Avenue answered with a sympathetic smile. "Yeah, Mr. Gold. I think I was."

Julius Gold nodded a second. "No, you're not," he retorted listlessly. "He was smarter. What did he know, that dummy?"

Someone in back of Gold was weeping. Harriet had sent word that she did not want Gussie at the funeral or in her home. Harriet sent word now that she wanted just Gold to walk with her to the farthest wall of the room for another look at Sid in his coffin. Harriet had ordered the open coffin. She held Gold's arm with both her hands. Gold averted his gaze from the lifeless face in the coffin with a feeling of nauseated pain. Harriet moaned quietly.

"Why did he have to do this to me? He knew how I hated to be alone. That's why he stopped taking those trips."

Gold felt her nails through the sleeve of his suit and realized he'd never fully understood till then how thoroughly he detested her. Then he broke and screamed:

"Sid, you fuck—why did you have to die? Who will take care of us now?"

But no one heard. His words were smothered in sobs.

THEY SAT *shivah* in Harriet's house, a location greatly inconvenient for those living in Brooklyn. There were vacant bedrooms but none were offered. By evening prayer of the first day, the day of the funeral, they knew they would need the money from Sheiky to pay for an apartment and furniture and living expenses in Florida for the old man and Gussie. All he owned was the spending money from his annuity and Social Security. Sid had been paying for just about everything else. And Sid left everything to Harriet. Even the annuity had come from Sid: the consolidation and sale of the old man's leather business was a fiction contrived to surround the old man with the illusion he was a person of sufficient means to retire prosperously. Now Gold's father was a burden to be shared only by those willing to assume it.

The worried creases in Irv's forehead darkened as Ida instructed Gold to establish beyond doubt that Julius Gold would not be able to continue living so well in the future. Esther and Rose, with Max consenting, offered everything but did not have much. The two sisters had been weeping copiously—at times neither could walk without assistance—and desisted now and then as if only to avoid the appearance of attempting to overshadow Harriet and her mother. Victor stole to Gold's side to volunteer monthly payments if Muriel were never informed. Muriel wanted Joannie to pay for everything.

"She's got the most money now, hasn't she? And she couldn't even tear herself away for the funeral, could she?"

Only Gold knew that Joannie's marriage was ending in a way that might leave her without money and that it would have been practically impossible for her to fly in from California any sooner than the following evening. When the time came to unfold the news of his financial plight to Julius Gold on the second day, he was not much surprised.

"I raised him from a baby," said Julius Gold distantly, as though Gold, Milt, and Belle were strangers. Milt was in the room with Gold to supply financial explanations. Belle was a steadying influence. "My son Sid. And now he's dead. He was like a father to me. You don't know."

"I know," said Gold.

"He took care of me better than anyone. Always he let me be what I wanted."

"I know," said Gold. "Sid was a wonderful person."

"You don't know," said the old man. "Not like you."

"Pop, why do you pick on me?" His father shook off with revulsion the hand Gold reached out to touch him. "Just because I had to wear eyeglasses and got good marks in school?"

"Sure," said Julius Gold. "That's why."

"Didn't you ever like me?"

"Sure—when you were small I liked you. But that's all." In the melancholy silence that followed, the old man's swollen eyes were further filled with tears. "I don't like it she tells me Gussie can't come here and can't go there." He looked fully at Gold suddenly with a remarkable kind of curiosity. "You got children?"

Gold sank down until his face was level with his father's and peered at him closely. A chill spread through his veins. "Sure, Pop. Three. Don't you remember? Dina, your favorite grandchild. She's our daughter. Don't you remember?"

Paying no attention to the question, the old man began talking as though Gold had not spoken. "You got children, don't let them send you to Florida. The old shouldn't be with just the old. The old should be with the young, but they don't want us no more. My wife was sick in my house, I never put her out till she went to the hospital and died there. My mother died in my brother Meyer's house, and I stayed with her and talked, even when she couldn't hear. You can ask Sid, but Sid ain't here no more and that's it, *fartig*. It's warm there and it's for old people.''

"Pop." Gold paused in a tremulous hush, chastened beyond measure by the fearful proximity in which he found himself to the very frangible boundaries of amnesia and senile rambling of mind. "You're old."

"When you were young," said his father without physical flourishes and barely any modulations of emotion, "I remember I never hit you. I didn't have to. All I had to do was look and yell, and you turned into a scared child. I made you behave. Once I made Sid run away for the whole summer just by looking and yelling. Now I'm the child. You talk to me like I don't understand. Don't talk like I'm a baby. If I get cranky it's because I can't always sleep when I'm tired and my hip hurts. Not because I'm dumb. Now she tells me through my grandchild she don't want me to smoke cigars in her house. It's Sid's house, not hers. He's my son, not hers. I know what I'm saying."

"Not all the time, Pa," said Gold tenderly with the apprehensive feeling he was communing with a mind that might not be altogether whole.

"Then that's the time to baby me," said the old man almost without spirit in a cranky and pathetic whine. "Not now, when I make sense. Tell me something. A riddle. Tell me, how is it that a father can take care of seven children, and seven children, now six, can't take care of one father?"

Gold, with patience wearing thin, did not enumerate for him that the wise Yiddish folk proverb traditionally made reference to a mother rather than a father, that the posturing, melodramatic old fuck had never been able to provide for anything close to seven children at one time, and that his children *had* been supporting him. "Pop, we are going to take care of you," he said in a voice kept low. "That's why we're talking."

"Don't make me go back to Florida."

"Not until you want to, I promise. Gussie wants to go now."

"I don't care about Gussie."

"You can stay in New York."

"I want to be with my friends," he complained.

"How can you be in both places? You can fly down to Florida to your friends whenever you miss them."

"Where can I stay here?"

"Wherever you want."

"I want to live with my children."

"You can live with your children," Gold assured him from the bottom of his heart. "You can even move right in with us if you want."

"No, he can't," Belle told him decisively when they left the room. "He can't live with us."

"I know he can't," said Gold, grumbling. "I'm glad to see you're not perfect."

"What will you do if he says he wants to?"

"I'll tell him he can't," said Gold "That's the time to let him know he has to do what we want." Gold sat down tiredly. "Unregenerate." Marveling, Gold fetched a long breath of inexpressible weariness and went pale with incredulity. "And without any redeeming social value. Once long ago he bought me a toy. Now I'll have to help carry him."

"I wouldn't mind that," said Belle. "You've always been good with me about my mother."

Then there came the first of Ralph's phone calls. Ralph began with radiant messages of sympathy from Alma, Amy, Honey, Misty, Christy, and the President. With Belle watching, Gold listened a minute more and said he could not consider a government appointment then and might not want to in the future. Ralph responded with a kind of immune, fatherly indulgence that terrified Gold very much.

"You have to, Bruce. You can't say no to the President."

"Why not?"

"Because nobody does. You have to say yes when your President asks."

"Who does?"

"Everybody, Bruce. You can't say no when your President asks."

"Ralph, I feel shitty tonight. My brother's dead and my father's old."

"I understand," Ralph said with solicitude. "I'll call you back after you've had time to recover."

Gold was fidgeting when he faced Belle. "I'm not really comfortable with rich people," he explained. "I never have been."

Belle's nod was noncommittal. "We'll have to do something about Harriet. We'll never be able to last here a whole week."

Mursh Weinrock arrived as one of the visitors, without jokes, his teeth stained with nicotine, with fingertips and complexion to match. Gold realized there'd be distant relatives and old family acquaintances of whose existence he had not thought in decades and a goodly number of whom he would have traveled seven leagues out of his way to escape meeting.

It was problematic which had the stronger title to bereavement, his father or Harriet, but all the tactical advantages in weaponry resided with the latter. Her paranoid distrust and vindictiveness were contagious and bred a palpable atmosphere of one-sided hostility which neither she nor her children, mother, and sister took pains to conceal.

"Help me up," Gold's father at length said to him. "I want to go home. She don't want us here and I don't want to stay." Clinging heavily to Gold's arm, he moved from the house without even a perfunctory farewell to anyone in his dead son's family. "I never wanted to bury a child," he murmured mournfully as they crossed the sidewalk to the car. "Not even you."

After a moment of astonishment, Gold allowed those words to find their place amidst the various other corrosive recollections of recent origin that were seething in his brain with such depressing and infuriating effect: Ralph would not hide him, Conover would taunt him, the ex-Governor of Texas owned him. Who would teach him to defend himself? When Ralph phoned an hour later, he decided that he did not want the government appointment.

His season in the White House was over.

BY the morning of the third day Gold had organized his family to complete sitting *shivah* for Sid in Esther's house, with Rose and Ida helping with the cooking and refreshments and neighboring families in the apartment building furnishing the male adults needed to comprise the *minyan* of ten for the prayers at morning and sundown. The men assembled after breakfast before leaving for work and returned in the early evening before darkness had fallen. Gold spoke to the secretary at the college about reconvening his classes for regular meetings the week following. As he was leaving Esther's that third day for a trip back into the city the downstairs bell rang with someone wishing to speak to him. Gold could not for the life of him guess who it was.

"It's Greenspan, Dr. Gold," rasped the voice on the intercom. "Lionel."

"Bulldog, what do you want?" asked Gold impatiently. "We're all through."

"The White House wants you to change your mind."

"I'm not going to call them."

"They'll call you. What's your sister's phone number? Will you open the door and let me up?"

"No," said Gold. "The number's in the phone book, goddamn it. And please stop bothering me."

"Under what name?" entreated Greenspan.

Gold gave the grilled aperture into which he was speaking a pitying look. "Bulldog, what is the name on the bell you just pressed?"

Greenspan took nearly half a minute to reply. "Moscowitz."

"That's her name, Lionel. How do you think you reached me just now?" The phone rang even as Gold was turning the doorknob.

"I'm sorry to bother you again," said Ralph. "But I think we're ready to offer you an appointment in the State Department right up near the top."

"Ralph, I don't want it," said Gold.

"Sure you do, Bruce," said Ralph, sounding entirely convinced. "Your President needs you. He often says you're the only person in the country with whom he feels completely comfortable. Is it because you feel you aren't good enough?"

This nettled Gold. "I'm good enough."

"Because you're Jewish?"

"Not because I'm Jewish."

"It's because I said I wouldn't hide you, isn't it?" guessed Ralph with surprising astuteness. "I'll say I'll hide you, if you want me to."

"Goodbye, Ralph," said Gold and was nearly knocked over when he collided with Harris Rosenblatt striding out of the Harvard Club onto West 44th Street in the city. "Harris, what were you doing in there?"

Perhaps Harris Rosenblatt only looked a hand or two taller and a tone or two whiter because he had grown a stone or two leaner. "I belong," he announced with exalted self-confidence, rubbing his perfectly straight sides as though congratulating himself on lacking a paunch. "I'm a member."

"How can you be a member of the Harvard Club," asked Gold in frank naiveté, "when you went to Columbia with me and dropped out of graduate school because you knew you were going to fail?"

"I'm a millionaire, Bruce," Harris Rosenblatt enlightened him, "and every millionaire is a Harvard man. Although not every Harvard man, of course, is a millionaire. There's really only one outstanding university in the country, Bruce, and I'll never regret that I went to the Harvard Club for lunch today." They paused at the corner before parting. "We must have dinner soon with you and Belle when you've taken your position on the President's staff."

"I'm turning it down," said Gold, looking rather shamefaced.

"Then we must not have dinner," Harris Rosenblatt gruffly decided. "What will you do instead?"

"Something of very great importance," said Gold. "I'm writing a biography of Henry Kissinger."

"Of who?" asked Harris Rosenblatt.

"Henry Kissinger."

"Who?"

"Henry Kissinger. He used to be Secretary of State. He's the one who wanted to go down in history like Metternich and Castlereagh."

"Like who?"

Gold abandoned the project and ascertained at the apartment that Dina was safe and could manage on her own till evening when he drove back with Belle. With Kissinger gone, he was stuck only with the book on the Jewish experience in America he owed Pomoroy and Lieberman.

ON THE fourth day he succeeded in alleviating one of Joannie's problems by reassuring her that a messy divorce would not compromise his career in the least. Joannie returned from a condolence call to Harriet with news that Harriet would like to see Esther and Rose again soon to talk about old times with Sid. Muriel's crude rejection of every attempt at conciliation with Joannie rankled Gold until Greenspan rang up again from the downstairs vestibule to report that the White House was trying to reach him by phone and getting a busy signal.

"Bruce, he wants me to ask you again," said Ralph. "This time he may actually be offering you the position of Secretary of State."

"Ralph, I don't want it," said Gold.

"Was it anything we did at the U.N.? Is it something we're going to do to Israel?"

"No."

"Bruce, the President is going to be very disappointed. He's counting on you to help with his punctuation."

"Nothing doing."

"What about that piece you gave him? 'We Are Not a Society *or* We Are Not Worth Our Salt.' "

"He can keep it," said Gold.

"Reprint rights too? Can we publish it under his own name?"

"If you'll leave me alone," Gold pleaded with fatigue. "Ralph, please stop bothering me. And call off that Greenspan."

"I'll try," said Ralph. "But it's like talking to the wall."

"Greenspan, go away," Gold shouted across the street on the fifth day at the surreptitious, unshaven figure in back of the telephone pole as he left for the messages and fucking student papers accumulating for him at the college. When he returned at twilight, Greenspan was upstairs in Esther's apartment wearing a prayer shawl and a *yarmulka*.

"We needed one more for the *minyan*," said Victor, "and I found him downstairs in a car."

Rose had another swelling in her breast and this time would go into a hospital for a biopsy. There was a waiting period of twelve days for a room.

"*Yiskadal v'yiskadish*," Gold began the prayer for the dead, reading the Hebrew words phonetically from an English text after Greenspan had started the evening prayers.

Greenspan was the only one there who could read the language in the original. Greenspan still had not shaved. Gold was embarrassed that all the men in the family had, in violation of the ban against shaving during the seven-day period of mourning. Greenspan was invited to stay for dinner and encouraged to invite his wife.

"Greenspan, please leave," Gold whispered.

"And will you need us tomorrow night too?" Greenspan hinted. "My wife bakes beautifully."

"Shame, shame, Greenspan. You're a *shonda*."

"Am I supposed to spend my whole life in coffee shops and cafeterias?" Greenspan wanted to know. "How often do you think I get a chance to eat like this in my line of work?"

"But you're taping all this, aren't you?" Gold accused.

"My bug is sealed."

"Why is he holding his hands on his belly?" Julius Gold demanded with a scowl, raising his voice in interest and irritation for the first time in almost a week.

"He's got a bug in his *pupik*," said Gold to his father. "Keep it covered, Greenspan. Here comes my stepmother with some words of wisdom you must never forget."

"Cackle, cackle," said Gussie Gold.

The number of visitors was diminishing nightly. Muriel turned civil to Joannie finally with a curiosity almost baldly salacious and she and Ida began bickering with each other as of old. Joannie was leaving early that evening, to prepare for her flight back to California the next morning. She said to Gold, at the elevator, "How are things with you and Belle now?"

"As good as ever."

"Does she know that?"

Gold kissed her goodbye with genuine feeling and decided to patch things up firmly with Belle if he could.

"Belle," he began in a roundabout way on the sixth day, almost faltering at the start. "How is your mother? Does she know we're together again?"

Belle nodded before speaking. "She knows."

"She knows?" said Gold. "How did you tell her?"

"I didn't tell her."

Gold spoke with puzzlement. "How does your mother know we're together again if you didn't tell her?"

"I never told her you were leaving," Belle said with a smile. Then she requested a favor for the children. "I had calls from the boys. They'd like to come home for the weekend."

"Aaaaah, let them," said Gold as Belle turned to answer another phone call from Ralph.

"I don't want to talk to him."

"What should I say?" asked Belle.

"Tell him to kiss my ass."

"I'll tell him no such thing."

"Ralph," Gold began.

"I have to, Bruce," Ralph said in apology. "When the President tells me to try, I have to at least make the call, don't I? It's not about Secretary of State this time."

"What is it then?"

"He's written a screenplay."

"So have I."

"So have I," said Ralph.

"I have no connections for screenplays,"[4] said Gold. "Tell him to get a good agent and try to close a deal for an option."

"He likes to keep his options open," said Ralph. "Was that Belle on the phone before? If it was, please give her my love."

"And you give mine to Alma."

"Alma who?" said Ralph.

Gold gave a grimace of annoyance. "Alma your wife and Alma your fiancée. Isn't Alma the name of the girl you're married to and the girl you're engaged to?"

"Oh, gosh, Bruce, they're both over," said Ralph with surpassing affability. "I'm certainly glad you haven't found out about Andrea yet. And I hope you won't be angry when you do."

"Andrea?" Gold was glued in place with a speechless expression for a moment. He had forgotten entirely that he was still engaged to Andrea. "Found out what?"

"That we're together," said Ralph. "She and I."

"Together?" said Gold. "How together? What do you mean together? In what way are you together?"

"As lovers."

"You mean you're fucking?"

"Oh, we've been doing that for years," said Ralph.

"Even while she and I were engaged?"

"But we were never friendly," Ralph put in quickly. "Then we found ourselves together one evening and really got close. She paid us a compliment, Bruce, you and me, I think, although I'm not sure which one, or even if it really is a compliment. She said I was as good as gold."

GOLD FELT like a big *schmuck* when he finally found his mother's grave after the final prayers on the last day and saw that every character on the headstone was in Hebrew. He recognized not a one. The earth had no message for him. He put his arm around the weatherbeaten stone monument for a moment in a strange kind of hug and that felt a little bit closer and warmer. He left a pebble on her grave.

Returning for Belle by way of Coney Island Avenue, he came upon a softball game in a schoolyard played by boys wearing *yarmulkas*, and he left the car to watch. Athletes in skullcaps? The school was a religious one, a *yeshiva*. Some of the teen-agers had sidelocks, and some of the sidelocks were blond. Gold smiled. God was right—a stiff-necked, contrary people. *Moisheh Kapoyer*, here it was winter and they were playing baseball, while everyone else played football and basketball.

And a stubborn dispute was in progress. The boy at first base had his back to the others, in a pose of limp exasperation. The pitcher was sulking and refused to throw the ball. The batter was waiting in a squat with his elbows on his knees, his head resting with disinterest on one hand. As Gold watched, the catcher, a muscular, redheaded youth with freckles and sidelocks and a face as Irish or Scottish or Polish as any Gold had ever laid eyes upon, moved wrathfully toward the pitcher with words Gold for a minute had trouble believing.

"*Varf!*" shouted the catcher. "*Varf* it, already! *Varf* the fucking ball!"

Gold continued to Esther's for Belle and drove home. He owed Pomoroy a book. Where could he begin?

JOSEPH HELLER

When you want your masterpieces bone-tickling funny. Or simply gut-wrenching.

___**GOD KNOWS** • The wonderfully funny/sad story of David (*Old Testament* David), a cocky, erstwhile crony of God. He's growing up, growing older, and, God knows, growing wiser. Quintessential Heller—and brilliant to boot!

13185-5-27 **$4.50**

___**CATCH-22** • The World War II classic recounts the amazing adventures of the 256th bomber squadron and its lead bombadier, Capt. Yossarian.

11120-X-94 **$4.95**

___**GOOD AS GOLD** • Bruce Gold has problems. He's a professor bored with teaching, a writer who hates reading. And as a husband and father, don't ask...Funny, touching, and hauntingly original.

13186-3-18 **$4.95**

___**SOMETHING HAPPENED** • A corporate executive is beset by drives and fears which are obscure in their origins. One of the finest explorations of modern American life.

18133-X-29 **$4.95**

At your local bookstore or use this handy coupon for ordering:

 Dell

DELL READERS SERVICE—DEPT. BR804A
P.O. BOX 1000. PINE BROOK. N.J. 07058

Please send me the above title(s). I am enclosing $_____ (please add 75¢ per copy to cover postage and handling). Send check or money order—no cash or COUs. Please allow 3-4 weeks for shipment. CANADIAN ORDERS: please submit in U.S. dollars

Ms Mrs Mr. _____

Address _____

City State _____ Zip _____